Tell No Tales

Also by Eva Dolan

Long Way Home

EVA DOLAN

Tell No Tales

Harvill *Secker*

LONDON

Published by Harvill Secker 2015

10 9 8 7 6 5 4 3 2 1

First published in Great Britain in 2015 by
HARVILL SECKER
20 Vauxhall Bridge Road
London SW1V 2SA

A Penguin Random House company

global.penguinrandomhouse.com

A CIP catalogue record for this book is available from the British Library

ISBN 9781846557781 (hardback)
ISBN 9781448163298 (ebook)

The Penguin Random House Group Limited supports the Forest Stewardship
Council® (FSC®), the leading international forest-certification organisation.
Our books carrying the FSC® label are printed on FSC®-certified paper. FSC®
is the only forest-certification scheme endorsed by the leading environmental
organisations, including Greenpeace. Our paper procurement policy
can be found at www.randomhouse.co.uk/environment

Typeset in Charter ITC Std by Palimpsest Book Production Limited
Falkirk, Stirlingshire

Printed and bound in Great Britain by Clays Ltd, St Ives plc

DAY ONE

I

At 5 a.m. it was easy to tell which houses were still occupied by the English. No signs of life. No thoughts of getting up for a couple of hours at least.

Sofia stood at the window, the bedroom in darkness behind her, watching one light after another come on, skylights glowing in the converted attics. She remembered sleeping on an air bed under low eaves, three other girls squeezed in with her, fifty pounds a week, and at night she could see stars through the gaps in the slate roof. There was no skylight in that house, only a hatch which opened from below to let them out when the van arrived to take them into the endless black fields of the Lincolnshire fens.

It was a long time ago now.

She switched on the lamp and dressed quickly, leggings under her jeans, a vest and a long-sleeved T-shirt and one of Tomas's thick grey sweatshirts over the top. It was minus five last night and the pack house would be freezing. It was better than being out in the fields, she reminded herself, tramping up and down the rows with fingers so numb from cold that you could cut yourself and not realise until you felt a sudden, wet warmth.

She dragged her long brown hair into a hasty plait and tucked it into her collar, looking at Tomas's dirty washing sitting in the corner of the bedroom, mud crusted on the hems of his trousers and another man's blood on the thigh.

The image flashed quickly before her eyes, the Kurd's severed hand on the pack-house floor, Tomas holding him upright, raising his wrist above his head to slow the bleeding as the old man screamed.

She snatched up the khaki combats, the jumper and the T-shirt which were spotted with blood even though she was sure Tomas wasn't wearing them that day. They shouldn't be in the house.

Someone else's blood – it attracted bad luck to you.

Sofia shoved them into a carrier bag which wasn't quite big enough, punched them down with her small, bony fist. The stains would come out if she soaked them in vodka but Tomas wouldn't wear them again.

In the bedroom across the hall Jelena's mobile was ringing. A different ringtone this week and Sofia was tired of telling her not to waste her money on them.

She heard Jelena moving around, the loose floorboard near her dressing table clacking.

'Ignore him,' Sofia shouted.

Jelena came out onto the landing, her pyjama top hanging loose over the waistband of her jeans, thick white socks on her feet.

'Ja sam neznalica njemu.'

'English,' Sofia said wearily. 'You will not get better if you do not speak.'

The phone kept ringing in Jelena's hand, the screen flashing in time to the music. 'I text him last night, tell him no.'

'You should say nothing. No text. Nothing.'

'I make him understand,' Jelena said.

'You encourage him like this,' Sofia told her. 'You must give him nothing.'

Jelena ran her fingertips through her ponytail, a nervous gesture she had brought with her from childhood. 'He will not stop if I do not speak to him.'

'I will speak to him.'

Sofia held out her hand but Jelena turned away, pressing the phone to her shoulder.

'No. He will stop.'

He did. At that very moment. As if he could hear them.

'We will change your number.' Sofia rubbed Jelena's arm, forced herself to smile. 'Tonight, I will deal with this. Do not worry.'

She went down into the small white kitchen at the back of the house, put on the lights and the television and ran the tap until the water came through properly cold, trying to act like everything was normal. Like last night's conversation had never happened. Hours later she had been sure she could hear Jelena's muffled voice coming across the hall as she lay in the centre of the bed, trying to sleep, wishing Tomas was there next to her.

She lit a cigarette from the gas and waited for the kettle to boil.

Anthony was a small, timid man, but he was persistent and she knew at some point she would need to act. Her eyes strayed to the knife block on the black melamine counter – five sturdy wooden handles and five nicely weighted blades.

It would not come to that, she reassured herself.

The kettle rattled to the boil and Sofia called up to Jelena as she poured water into the cafetière, brewing the coffee strong, telling her they were going to be late if she didn't hurry. She refilled the kettle to make up the flasks and took the bag of ruined clothes out to the bin.

There was frost in the air, spiked with chemicals from the industrial estate nearby, and her breath blossomed in front of her when she exhaled, the cold pricking her nose. Underfoot the grass crinkled softly. It needed cutting but that was Tomas's job and neither of them knew how to work the temperamental lawnmower he'd bought from the car boot sale at the football ground. He said it was like a woman, required a strong hand, and Sofia told him Slovak women were not like lawnmowers, they only needed one blade to get the job done. He laughed and kissed her, promised he would show her how it worked when he had a day off.

She dropped the bag into the bin and closed the lid slowly, aware of a rustling sound coming from the shadows behind the shed. A cat sprang out and ran across the garden, a white blur gone in an instant.

Jelena was taking their packed lunches out of the fridge when Sofia went back inside, beans and pasta in tomato sauce Sofia had cooked at the weekend and bagged up in individual portions for speed. Sofia had learned how to live on very little and even though they were earning well now the habit stayed with her. The more they saved the sooner they could stop working like this, always for other people's benefit and so many pairs of hands skimming off the top.

Jelena placed the Tupperware containers in her rucksack and tucked in their flasks, took one out again to double-check the lid.

She was concentrating too hard, her bottom lip between her teeth.

'You have spoken to him,' Sofia said.

Jelena zipped the bag slowly. 'I say I will not see him.'

'What did he say?'

Her eyes were shining, huge and blue. She swallowed but didn't reply.

Sofia knew what he said. Always the same threat but he didn't have the balls to see it through. He would have done it by now if he was going to. An act like that, you did it in the heat of anger and the heat was gone from him now, whether he understood that himself or not. He would get bored, move on to someone else. Another poor foreign girl who would be charmed by his English accent and his big German car.

'We have to go,' Sofia said. 'We will be late for work.'

She took Jelena's arm as they left the house and dragged her through the gate, joining the other people coming out with their Thermos flasks and packed lunches, everyone moving in the same direction, down towards the main road.

Half past five and the rest of the city was still sleeping, but Lincoln Road was bustling already. The terraced houses lit up and disgorging their occupants onto the street, the road running steady with delivery lorries and white vans heading into the centre of Peterborough, transporters full of workers coming home from shifts cleaning offices, twelve hours packaging produce on the Eastern Industrial Estate. One lot out and a quick turn-around to collect the day workers.

A van pulled up across the road, outside the Polish grocer's where Sofia and Jelena no longer shopped. They sold counterfeit cigarettes and vodka which was illegally stilled on the fens by a Bulgarian family, rough, raw stuff that was only fit for cleaning your sink with. Out front a few men, just off shift, sat at the cafe tables drinking bottled beer, shattered but not ready for bed yet.

They stood at their usual spot outside the bus shelter, the only two workers for the Boxwood Farm van. The first stop on the driver's route. There was another man waiting this morning though, hunched and tired-looking, vaguely familiar. Someone Tomas knew. When he muttered a 'good morning' she managed to reply, but her attention was focused on Jelena, reaching into her pocket for her mobile. That ringtone blaring.

Sofia shot her a look as she checked the display.

'Who is that?'

'Marta,' she said, angling her body away to shield the screen, taking a couple of small steps closer to the kerb.

The man said something else and Sofia answered him shortly, watching Jelena bite her lip as she listened to the voice on the other end which was definitely not Marta.

In the distance car horns blared above the traffic noise and an engine revved, a deep, throaty rattle as a white Volvo shot across lights and accelerated up Lincoln Road, swerving erratically around a cyclist. Sofia froze as its headlights washed the pavement, silhou-etting Jelena's figure, her back to the car, phone to her ear. Sofia opened her mouth to scream but no sound came out. Then she heard a bang and something slammed into her and the world turned black as her head hit the ground.

2

By six fifteen they had shut down a hundred-yard stretch of Lincoln Road. Both lanes blocked off, signs diverting the traffic along the narrow side streets, which would be snarled up with delivery lorries trying to get into the shopping centre and vans making for the covered market behind Peterborough Cathedral.

BBC Cambridgeshire was already reporting a hit-and-run. They were sketchy on the details, but DI Dushan Zigic knew there was one dead at the scene, two more, unlikely to make it, on the way to Edith Cavell's A&E department.

The initial newsflash had reported the dead and injured as migrant workers. Fifteen minutes later the hourly bulletin made no mention of ethnicity, only a group of people waiting at a bus stop. The press officer must have called them from her bed to shut them up that fast, Zigic guessed.

She was fighting the tide though. Before he left the station the desk sergeant showed him footage of the accident on YouTube, filmed by a steady hand as people from the cafe opposite ran across the road to help, shouting in languages Zigic didn't understand.

The desk sergeant told him to be grateful – they had an image of their driver from it. Not that it showed much, medium build, dark clothes, the man's face a pale smudge as he sprinted off towards the rat runs of bedsit land, escaping along the same side street that Zigic turned down now.

Ahead of him a car was executing a three-point turn, finding the access onto Lincoln Road blocked off by the police cordon. Zigic flashed to let them pass then pulled onto the kerb outside a new development of three-storey houses.

As he got out of the car he checked for CCTV along the narrow lane, spotted a single camera mounted under the sagging gutters of the building on the corner, trained, bizarrely, on one of the upstairs windows.

Zigic ducked under the perimeter tape and entered the crime scene.

Everything looked washed out and insubstantial under the early-morning light and he realised he'd never seen Lincoln Road at a standstill before. Cars were backed up from either end of the crash site but nobody was honking or shouting and the hush which had descended only added to the sense of unreality.

The car was real though. A bulky, old model Volvo with a replacement driver's side door badly resprayed in a slightly off shade of white. It had ploughed through the group waiting around the bus shelter and only finally lost momentum when it slammed through the front wall of the terraced house behind it.

He saw the interior of the living room, stripped back to bare plaster and shrouded in dust which hadn't yet settled, a light fitting hanging from the ceiling, no bulb in it. A new bathroom suite still swaddled in plastic was shoved into a corner, waiting to be shifted upstairs. That was something, he thought. No fatalities there.

But it felt like a small mercy when he looked at the shattered carcass of the bus shelter, its Perspex walls snapped and blood-stained, its red plastic seats tangled under the Volvo's rear wheels. Nearby sat a rucksack, split open, spilling two Tupperware lunch boxes and a flask.

A blue-suited scenes-of-crime officer shouted at him.

'Ziggy – shift or smile.'

He saw the photographer at distance and got out of his sight line, stood in the middle of the road, watching the man move in closer, panning slowly across the body of the Volvo, then moving closer, up to the open driver's door and the airbag which was still inflated and spotted with blood. The photographer focused on the shattered windscreen and the buckled bonnet, then a shallow dent on the roof of the car where a body had landed, blood still tacky on the paintwork. The wipers had kicked in on the rear windscreen and dragged the blood across the glass.

At the north end of the crime scene a small crowd was gathering, corralled by a couple of community support officers in high-visibility jackets. The onlookers were too far away to see anything, but Zigic noticed at least half of them had their phones held out, recording the action for whatever fleeting posterity it would find online.

'We've got two survivors,' DS Ferreira said, coming across the street to him.

She had been the first on the scene just after dawn and from the way she was dressed he imagined she hadn't been home long at that point, a creased black top under a short leather jacket and jeans tucked into knee-high boots; last night's clothes still on.

She lived a couple of minutes further along Lincoln Road, too close to escape being involved.

'Witnesses?' Zigic asked.

'Dozens, yeah, and they're all saying the same thing. He accelerated up here from the south, jumped the lights and swerved across the traffic to hit them.' She frowned. 'The driver made it out. Took off up the road there on foot.'

Two more vehicles sat smashed in the middle of the road, their front bumpers locked together, bonnets crumpled, a red Seat and a courier's van. They were lucky it hadn't caused a major pile-up.

'There's no way this was an accident,' Ferreira said.

'Let's not jump to conclusions, Mel.'

'Riggott's given us it, he obviously thinks it's deliberate. And racially motivated.'

'He's got a heavy caseload.'

'Like we haven't.'

The photographer gave the all-clear and moved away to pack up his equipment. Within seconds three more interchangeable, androgynous figures descended on the car and Zigic watched them work with a vague feeling of envy. It was a standardised procedure for them, the same at every crime scene: photograph, document, collect, collate. And once that was done the messy process of extracting guilt from the information became someone else's problem.

'Have we got IDs on the victims yet?' he asked.

'Two of them, yeah. The paramedics had the other one away before I arrived. I sent them back to the office a few minutes ago. Hold on, I'll give you them now.' Ferreira took out her mobile, swiped the screen. Zigic's phone beeped as they hit his inbox. 'I talked to the driver who was coming to collect them – he's pretty shook up.'

'As you'd expect.'

'He was running late, so he's blaming himself now. You know the deal, if he'd been on time they wouldn't have been standing out here to get run down.' Ferreira shrugged and it was more like a shiver. 'He's gone to Edith Cavell with one of the women.'

'How bad is she?'

'The paramedics think she'll make it but her sister took the full force. She was standing at the kerb.'

A trailer with a hefty orange crane on its cab pulled up to the perimeter tape and Ferreira hollered at the uniforms to let it in. They needed to get the street running again as soon as possible. Almost seven now and the rest of Peterborough was stirring towards work, waking to the news of this horrific event. The speculation would build quickly and DCS Riggott had made it abundantly clear that a swift resolution was needed.

'Nobody wants this to get politicised,' he'd said.

But it would. Once the press, and the public, caught on to the fact that it was being investigated by the Hate Crimes Department the racial element would become the focus. Zigic wondered why Riggott didn't handle it in CID if he wanted to keep a lid on it, and realised he was probably covering his arse already – you didn't make it to his rank without knowing how to delegate blame.

'Alright, we need to talk to the families, see if any of the victims pissed someone off recently.'

'So you do think it was deliberate.'

'We need to cover all the angles.'

Ferreira planted her fists on her hips, looked away at the car. One of the forensics officers was squatting down by the passenger-side footwell, another had the boot open, going through the contents, bagging an empty water bottle and a travel rug.

The chief scenes-of-crime officer, Kate Jenkins, walked over to them, tucking her springy red hair under the hood of her bodysuit.

'Don't know about you two, but I can think of better ways to start the day.'

'How long do you think you need here?' Zigic asked.

'Straight to business. Fair enough.'

'Sorry, Kate.'

'I understand.' She nodded towards the ever lengthening line of cars stretching north. 'Can't have a few deaths holding people's day up. We'll take some preliminary samples to be on the safe side but we can do the serious work back at the garage.'

'Have you got anything?'

'The blood on the airbag's fresh, almost definitely from the driver judging by the placement,' she said. 'Some hairs, fingerprints. He wasn't careful. Although it looks like he had his seat belt on, so that message got through.'

'Will it have left a mark?' Zigic asked.

'The airbag definitely.' Jenkins' mouth twisted. 'The seat belt? Maybe. Depends on how fast he was going.'

'The witnesses we have said he was accelerating,' Ferreira told her.

'It's fairly likely then.'

A horn blared across the road, a white van running into the edge of the cordon on Taverners Road, and quickly the note was taken up by more cars. The spell was broken and suddenly the waiting traffic became like a single angry entity, shouting, swearing and gesturing out of open windows.

Jenkins scowled at the van. 'Guess I should crack on then.'

12

'This is going to start getting nasty,' Ferreira said. 'Maybe we should draft in some more uniforms just in case.'

'Call in and see who you can get down here.' Zigic's mobile rang. 'What is it, Bobby?'

'The Volvo's registered to a Paul Devlin, lives over in Stanground.'

'Has he got form?' Zigic asked.

'Couple of speeding tickets, nothing major.'

'Until now.'

3

Paul Devlin lived on a nice quiet development of semi-detached houses with large bay windows and well-maintained front gardens, carports to the side, most of them still occupied at this time of morning. It was an area dominated by retirees now; Zigic's grandparents lived a few minutes away on the same estate, surrounded by people just like them who had bought from new and never moved on.

His grandparents were among the first foreigners to move into Stanground and back in the 1960s they weren't made welcome. Their neighbours fancied themselves as professionals, engineers from the long-defunct Perkins plant, people who worked in banks and offices. They didn't appreciate the sudden influx of Slavs and Italians who brought big, boisterous families with them and filled the classrooms of the local primary with kids who had English as a second language, didn't like the idea of overpaid brickyard workers dragging the area down.

They wouldn't like the new township being built beyond the estate either, Zigic guessed. Seventy per cent social housing and all the problems which went along with it. Maybe that was why there were so many For Sale boards in the neat front gardens, despite the downturn in the property market.

He turned onto Alma Road and parked behind the patrol car sitting twenty yards away from Paul Devlin's house. Two uniforms got out, big men ready for action, and they fell in step behind him as they approached the place, boots dull against the pavement, radios squawking into the peaceful morning air, clashing with the birdsong.

The curtains were drawn at Devlin's front windows, no lights on, but there was a car in the driveway, a brand-new Corsa waxed to a high shine.

Zigic signalled for one of the men to go round the back and heard him bang through the metal gate as he rang the doorbell, a wonky two-tone chime sounding.

He waited, aware of the neighbours stirring. Saw an elderly woman appear in the window to his right, half hidden by thick net curtains bleached a brilliant white. Behind him a door opened and a reedy voice called across the road.

'He's at home. He doesn't work.'

The man was in his dressing gown, bowed legs sticking out, a small black dog between his feet, yapping excitedly.

'Thank you, sir,' Zigic said. 'Please, go back inside.'

He rang the doorbell again and squatted down to peer through the letter box. The hallway was spartan, laminate floor and white walls, coir matting on the staircase. There was a black padded jacket on the post, similar to the one worn by the man he'd seen on YouTube running away from the crime scene.

'Shall I get the ram, sir?' PC Blake asked.

Feet appeared at the top of the stairs, began to trudge down slowly in backless slippers.

'No need.'

Paul Devlin opened the front door in his boxers and a Coldplay T-shirt, one eye half closed and his blond hair sleep-mussed. He looked about the right build for their man, five ten, solid but not fat. He yawned into their faces as he asked what they wanted.

Zigic flashed his warrant card. 'I'd like you to come with us please, Mr Devlin.'

'What?' He made a perfectly confused face, blinked, wrinkled his chin. 'Why?'

'Your car was involved in a hit-and-run this morning.'

Devlin took a step back, eyes widening, and Zigic crossed the threshold.

'One person's dead, two more might not make it.'

Devlin swayed where he stood, eyes on the open door and Blake's meaty form blocking it, and Zigic got ready to grab him if he decided to make a run for it.

'But my car's outside,' Devlin said.

'Your other car,' Zigic told him, impatience clipping his words. 'It'll be better for you if you come quietly now.'

'Other car? My old Volvo?' Zigic nodded. 'I sold it a couple of weeks ago.'

'It's still in your name,' Zigic said.

'I gave him all the paperwork, he told me he'd sort it out.'

Behind Zigic the PC sighed, like he'd heard this kind of nonsense a thousand times before and he was in no mood to listen to it again.

Did Devlin look like a man who had run away from a fatal crash within the last couple of hours, though? The skin of the left side of his face was reddened, maybe from the airbag deploying, or maybe from a crease in his pillow. Zigic stepped closer to him, saw gunge in the corners of his bloodshot eyes, a smear of crusted drool on his chin.

'Would you lift your T-shirt please, sir?'

Devlin clutched at the hem. 'What? Is this some kind of joke?'

'Just do it.'

He complied reluctantly, someone who was used to being pushed around, Zigic thought.

'All the way, please.'

Devlin's exposed chest was milk white and almost hairless, but there was no sign of bruising from the seat belt, not even a hint of abrasion. Zigic told him to cover up again.

'Who did you sell the car to?'

'Some guy on eBay. Him and a mate came to the house, paid me cash, and took it away.'

'I need a name.'

'He was foreign,' Devlin said.

'That isn't an answer.'

Devlin shoved his fingers back through his hair, stared at the floor for a few long seconds, eyes wide, before he shook his head.

16

'I can't remember. He said he was local, if that's any help.'

'You must have a phone number for him,' Zigic said. 'How did he arrange when to come?'

'I'll check.'

He headed back upstairs and Zigic told Blake to go and speak to the neighbours, see if any of them noticed Devlin go out earlier this morning, or if they remembered two men calling at the house to take the car away. He'd bet someone saw something, the neighbourhood watch was Stasi-like around here.

A moment later Devlin came back down the stairs, phone in hand, shaking his head.

'Sorry, I deleted it.' He shrugged. 'There was no point keeping it once he'd paid.'

Zigic crossed his arms. 'So, basically, I might as well arrest you right now.'

Devlin put his hands up. 'Look, I can show you the auction details on eBay. It'll have his buyer ID on there – can't you get his name and address and everything from that? You can do that, right? They'll tell you if you ask.'

He started swiping at his phone's screen.

'I can't believe this is happening.'

Zigic looked back out through the open door, saw PC Blake pointing towards the house, a small, blonde woman with a baby on her hip nodding, talking in a fast, animated fashion, her free hand gesturing wildly. Devlin wasn't their man. Zigic was 90 per cent sure of that. The eBay auction could be an elaborate ruse but he doubted it.

'Here.' Devlin handed his mobile over and Zigic checked the completed listing, a small photograph of the white Volvo sitting on his driveway, a sold price of four hundred pounds. 'Bogdan879 – that's his user ID.'

Zigic nodded. 'That's very helpful, Mr Devlin, thank you. If wouldn't mind coming down to the station, I need you to make a statement.'

'Now?'

'Yes, now. Get dressed.'

PC Blake crossed the road as Zigic went out onto the drive.

'Lady over the road remembers two ugly-looking blokes turning up the other week,' Blake said. 'Arrived in a burgundy Mitsubishi 4x4 with blacked-out windows. Big lads, she reckons, six foot, dark-haired, built like the proverbials. They were here about fifteen minutes, giving the car a good going-over.'

'And they definitely took it?'

'Yes, sir.'

'OK, that's something.' Zigic nodded, more to himself than Blake, feeling the momentum building, a definite line of inquiry emerging. 'Take Devlin to the station and park him for a bit.'

'Yes, sir.'

Zigic climbed back into the car and rang Wahlia as he pulled off the kerb, gave him the eBay user details, told him to work his charms.

'Any news?'

'Mel just called, they've taken the car away and the road's reopened.'

'That's the council off our backs anyway.'

'Riggott's sent up a couple of helpers too,' Wahlia said. 'I've got them going through the witness statements and the CCTV, thought that's what you'd want.'

'Great, thanks, Bobby.'

'And the press officer's looking for you.'

Zigic's hands tightened around the wheel. 'Of course she is.'

4

Ferreira watched the low loader pull away from the kerb, the Volvo firmly secured to its flatbed, on its way to the garage for the next round of forensics examinations. The perimeter of the locus was quickly dismantled, the police tape stripped away, releasing the vehicles built up beyond it, and within a few seconds the traffic on Lincoln Road was moving freely again. Like nothing had happened.

She cast a last glance at the patch of pavement around the broken remains of the bus shelter, where a council crew were preparing to clean away the final traces of the accident, then walked away in the opposite direction, heading home to change out of the night before's rank clubbing gear.

Her parents' pub, The Angel, sat at the quieter end of the New England suburb. It was a sprawling white-painted brick building surrounded by terraced houses carved up into rent-a-room flops, Polish nail bars and Lithuanian hairdressers', convenience stores specialising in Eastern European produce and counterfeit tobacco, cafes and off-licences with tables out front, the kind of places which were buzzing at 7 a.m. as the night-shift workers came home. She passed a tattoo parlour with a man standing smoking a joint in the open doorway and a second-hand furniture store where the owner was beginning to bring his wares out for the day, pine chairs and old fridges, a sagging sofa already on the pavement.

She rolled a cigarette as she walked, trying not to think about the black-haired man she'd seen impaled on a metal pole from the bus shelter, still alive she was sure as she ran towards him.

The pub's front doors were thrown open onto the street, a blackboard outside announcing that they were serving a full English breakfast. They pulled in a lot of natives at this time of morning, builders and van drivers en route to the retail parks nearby, the kind of men who wanted to drink a beer with their breakfast without being judged.

Ferreira slipped down the side of the building and into the car park, where a delivery van was ticking over, no sign of the driver but the cellar doors were open. He was probably down there listening to her father cracking jokes. He'd decided early on that the famous British sense of humour was the best way to assimilate and he'd taken to it so enthusiastically that around other men his entire conversation was set-up, punchline.

She ran up the metal fire escape, ignoring how it swayed under her, and let herself into their living quarters. Four bedrooms, a sitting room and two bathrooms for five people. The pub opened at 6 a.m and closed when the last customer left and the only way to manage those hours was in shifts. Her brothers did lates, her parents days, and if she wasn't careful they'd have her down there now clearing tables and loading the dishwasher. *Just twenty minutes, Melinda – do you think the whole city will descend into chaos if you aren't at your little desk?*

She showered quickly, finding the water tepid as usual and nothing but a hand towel to dry off with, dressed in fresh black jeans and a grey jumper, stamped her feet into her boots as she brushed her hair with one hand and packed her bag with the other.

Her bedroom door opened as she reached for the handle and her mother poked her head in. She looked tired, despite her heavily applied make-up, as if the only thing keeping her eyes open was how tightly she'd drawn back her greying hair. Always in the same neat bun, ever since Ferreira could remember.

'Mum, I haven't got time for this.'

'For what? I only want to know if you are staying for breakfast.'

She grabbed her keys. 'I've got to go.'

'They are saying on the radio that there was an accident.'

'We're not sure it was yet.'

Her mother crossed herself. 'Such people there are to do this.'

Ferreira kissed her on the head and made for the door.

'Be careful, Melinda.'

'Always am.'

She hit the rush-hour traffic in the city centre and for the thousandth time cursed the distance between her home and Thorpe Wood Station, then she cursed the driver in front of her for stopping at an amber light when the pedestrian crossing was obviously clear, then the roadworks on the Crescent Bridge which held her up for five minutes even though there wasn't a workman in sight.

Wahlia called as she pulled into the station car park, asked if she was planning on coming in today, and she looked up to see him staring out of the office window, gestured for him to get her a coffee and received a two-fingered salute in return.

She ran up the steps, ducked through reception where a reporter from the *Evening Telegraph* was gossiping with the desk sergeant, after information he wouldn't be allowed to print. She went upstairs through the bustle and hum of CID, heard DCS Riggott's sharp Belfast accent rattling across the office and saw that the press officer was on the receiving end, standing with her arms folded and an expression of amused contempt on her face.

Wahlia met Ferreira at the door with a mug of black coffee.

'Thanks, Bobby.'

'Don't get too used to it.'

He went back around to his side of the desk, where his phone was playing amplified hold music, interrupted every so often by a voice reassuring him that his call was important and would be dealt with soon.

'Where's Zigic?'

'In his office.'

The door was closed but through the venetian blinds she could see him moving, the room too small for a man of his height to pace properly. There were two extra detective constables, drafted in from

21

CID, working quietly at the usually unoccupied desks across the room, one hunched over, chewing on a pen lid as she watched CCTV footage, another just as focused on the screen of his computer, tapping his fingers against the keyboard.

Ferreira went to the whiteboard where the investigation was plotted out, their victims listed on the left. Jelena Krasic, deceased; Sofia Krasic – the sister she presumed – at A&E; a man, seriously injured, currently nameless.

It looked worse, she thought, all of that carnage. It looked like a massacre.

There was a single name in the suspects column.

'What's happening with this Devlin guy?' she asked.

'He's giving a statement right now. Don't think he's our man,' Wahlia said. 'He sold the car on eBay, I'm trying to track down the buyer. If they ever fucking answer.'

He had the feedback profile open on his computer – Bogdan879 and a list of positive reviews from people he'd bought cars from. Ferreira reached over and scrolled down the page. Dozens of cars going back across the last four months.

'He's a dealer then,' she said.

'Looks like it.'

'So pretty unlikely he was driving.' She went back to the top. 'I thought they told you where the person was based on here. It just says UK.'

'Devlin reckons he's local,' Wahlia said.

'Did he give a description?'

'Two blokes, dark-haired, well built.'

'Driving a burgundy 4x4, right?' she asked, heading for Zigic's office.

'Yeah.'

She knocked on the door and went in, found him standing behind his desk with his arms crossed, an expression of muted fury on his face as he stared at the flat-screen monitor.

'The BBC have picked it up,' he said. 'Look at this.'

The footage was on a loop, filmed on a camera phone from the middle of the road, focused on the Volvo. She saw the driver sprint away from the car, figures running after him, followed until they disappeared round a corner, then it reset and the moment the Volvo ran into the bus shelter came so swiftly that she gasped.

'They can't show that.'

'There it is,' he said, dropping into his chair heavily.

A cool voice spoke across the muffled screams.

'Although details remain sketchy at this point it is believed that the victims are all migrant workers local to the area. Within the last few minutes Cambridgeshire Constabulary have confirmed that they are not ruling out a racial motive.'

The voice went on, detailing the immigration figures for Peterborough and hinting at unrest among the natives, housing shortages, overstretched local services, peripheral issues which had no bearing on the situation.

Zigic closed the page, let out an uncharacteristic string of expletives.

Ferreira waited for the outburst to pass, then said, 'If you're done, I think I know who Bogdan879 is.'

5

'We've missed it,' Ferreira said, twisting to look back between the seats. 'Yeah, I'm pretty sure it was where all the signs were. You need to double-back.'

Zigic drove on into the Eastern Industrial Estate, passing self-storage places and builders' merchants, low-rise retail developments arranged around concrete standings.

There were a few houses built close to the busy road and they all had the same forlorn look about them, patches of neglected front garden and exhaust-stained facades, overgrown trees blocking out the light and cracking the pavements. Even inside the car he could smell the sickly sweet chemical scent coming from some hidden factory and hear the constant drone of the power station which loomed ahead of them against the grey spring sky.

He swung the car around in the entrance of a glass manufacturer's and followed Ferreira's directions back the way they'd come, turned down First Drove, going slowly along the patched and uneven single-track road.

Dozens of small businesses were crammed cheek by jowl in badly maintained buildings, with cheap signage and spiked metal gates, some of them no bigger than a double garage, a bike shop next to a wood yard ringed with a high barbed-wire fence, companies selling solvents and ceramics, an alien landscape of obscure specialities.

There was a sense of hustle around the place though, a lot of cars and vans with their side doors thrown back, men milling between them, and he wondered how a city as deprived as Peterborough kept all of these companies running.

'He's right down the end,' Ferreira said. 'Past the greyhound track.'

Ahead of them Zigic saw the blue-roofed stadium curving away, all red brick and dark glass, and the broad oval of grass at the centre of the track, two men in high-visibility vests standing talking as they watched their muzzled dogs chasing each other in tight circles.

He pulled up outside Hossa Motors.

It was the last lot on the road, nothing but a Portakabin on a scrap of tarmac surrounded by a low brick wall topped by a high fence, its vicious spurs snagged with ripped carrier bags and plastic wrapping which rustled in the breeze. Beyond that was a stretch of wasteland running down to the River Nene, a line of electricity pylons marching alongside it, following its course all the way out to the Wash.

'How do you know this bloke?' Zigic asked, as they walked through the gate.

'My brother bought a car off him last year. Total wreck.'

There were eight vehicles parked in two rows with little space between them, mostly hatchbacks, nothing over three thousand pounds, and they looked decent from a distance. But as they got closer Zigic noticed patches of filler around wheel arches, grazes on bumpers and mismatched tyres.

The door of the Portakabin banged open and a mountainous figure in a black leather jacket came down the steps, shaking the building on its blocks. He was lightly tanned with dark hair cut close to his scalp, a square face wearing an expression of hungry affability, tinged sinister by a chipped front tooth and gold incisor which winked out of a broad smile.

'Good morning, my friends.' He spread his hands wide, looked between them and finally settled on Zigic. 'A little car for the little lady?'

Zigic showed his warrant card. 'Bogdan Hossa?'

The smile froze for a split second then evaporated. He nodded. 'I run a respectable business, officer. All very clean.'

25

'I'm sure you do, sir. We're here about a car you bought a couple of weeks ago. A white Volvo, registration . . .'

Ferreira rattled it off.

'You bought it through eBay.'

'All legal, yes,' Hossa said. 'The man ask for cash. I pay cash. Is his lookout to be clean with taxman.'

'Have you sold the car yet?'

Hossa nodded slowly. 'There is problem?'

'We need to know who you sold it to.'

'I want no trouble,' Hossa said.

'We just need to know who bought the car,' Zigic said. 'You keep records I presume.'

'I will find for you.'

They followed him into the Portakabin, where two desks sat at right angles, one under a mess of paperwork and car magazines, the other, which Hossa went to, clear except for a laptop which probably cost more than any of the vehicles out on the lot. Music was coming out of it, all bass and badass posturing, and Hossa switched it off before he sat down.

'Who else works here?' Ferreira asked, perching on the desk.

'Ivan. My cousin.'

'And where's he?'

'He go buy breakfast. Van near Wickes – he has girl there.'

Hossa started tapping away at his laptop and Zigic saw Ferreira sifting through the paperwork on the other desk. Hossa was watching her out of the corner of his eye but he said nothing.

'Where are you from, Mr Hossa? Originally.'

'Slovakia.' He frowned. 'I make business there when I am young. Sell cars. Do well. Then men come, say, "Nice business, Bogdan, we will take this." And they take. Then I come to England. This does not happen in England.'

Not very often, anyway, Zigic thought. And not a business like this.

'I sell this car on Tuesday.' Hossa leaned back in his chair and knitted his fingers across his chest. 'To John Smith.'

'What's the address?' Ferreira asked.

'No address.'

'But you took a copy of his driver's licence?'

Hossa's face darkened. 'Ivan sells this car. He is not careful.'

'He got the money at least?' Ferreira asked, an edge coming into her voice.

'This he is careful with.'

'Then we need to speak to Ivan,' Zigic said.

Hossa glanced at his watch, a gaudy rose gold thing with a huge bezel studded with diamonds. 'He will be back. You wait, yes?'

'Yes, Mr Hossa, we wait.'

They settled into silence, Hossa staring pensively at his shoes, emitting an occasional soft snort. Ferreira started to roll a cigarette and asked Hossa if he minded before she lit up.

'Please, no.' He gestured at his chest. 'Asthma.'

She went outside and Zigic saw her wandering around the cars as she smoked, checking tax discs and the numbers etched on the windows, looking for something they could use for leverage against Hossa and his cousin if they decided not to cooperate suddenly. Zigic doubted it would come to that. If what Hossa said was true he wouldn't risk losing another hard-built business by antagonising them.

He thought of the name the buyer had given – John Smith.

It could be real but his gut instinct said it wasn't. He was sure that only an English person would use it as an alias though. It was too culturally specific.

Outside, a burgundy 4x4 with blacked-out windows pulled onto the lot, stopping with its bumper a few feet away from the Portakabin and the man who got out made Bogdan Hossa look svelte. Three hundred pounds of soft fat in grey joggers and a brown suede jacket. He carried a striped plastic takeaway bag in one hand and a tray of hot drinks in the other, banged the car door shut with his backside.

Hossa stood up as he came in, said something to him in Slovakian, his tone sharp.

Ivan looked at Zigic. 'White Volvo, yes?'

'That's the one.'

'I sell this car.'

Hossa let off another volley of machine-gun Slovakian at him and it looked like the words hit hard.

Ivan skulked around behind his own desk and put his breakfast down.

'You did not ask this man address,' Hossa said.

'He says he has no house.'

'Was he English?' Zigic asked.

Ivan shrugged, bored-looking.

'It is very important that we find this man.'

'English maybe, yes.'

'You must have spoken to him. Did he have an English accent?'

Ivan lifted a white styrofoam carton out of the bag, opened it to reveal a fat burger and chips.

'He is slow,' Hossa whispered.

Zigic massaged his temple with his fingertips, watching Ivan take a massive bite out of his burger, ketchup dripping onto the paperwork across his desk. He certainly looked slow, but his English seemed fairly good. If his build wasn't completely wrong Zigic would have suspected he was driving the Volvo that morning.

'What did the man look like, Ivan?'

'Normal man. He wear hat.' Another big bite of the burger and when he spoke again it was around a mouthful of meat and soggy bap. 'Red hat.'

The door of the Portakabin banged opened and Ferreira nodded for him to join her.

Outside a fine rain had begun to fall, the wind rising. She brushed her hair away from her face and it whipped straight back.

'The hospital just called,' she said. 'Sofia Krasic has come round. She wants to talk to someone.'

'Is she coherent?'

'She said she knows who was driving the car.'

28

6

There was a figure standing at the foot of the bed when Sofia opened her eyes, a small, dark man in a white coat stabbing his mobile phone, his tie bright red like a knife wound. She thought of a man she had seen lying dead in the street, his chest cut open, a wiry ginger dog lifting its muzzle from the wound, fur stained with blood and flecks of black gore.

That was not now. She had been almost the same size as the dog then.

This was a hospital bed. She could smell disinfectant, vomit. There was no noise though. She was in a private room. This was strange. The private room and the man who must be a doctor watching over her.

A foggy feeling came down over her and she drifted for a while, aware of a woman's voice at a distance, a man's answering, low and rumbling. Hands moved quickly across her body and she wanted to protest but she was too weak.

The pain was no more than a smudge at the edge of her consciousness, an unpleasant grey, like a looming storm cloud. Sofia ignored it, listened to the rhythmic sound of the machinery.

The man was speaking again and through her lashes Sofia saw him, standing close to her bed, holding a clipboard, heard words coming out of her mouth but couldn't control them. He smiled, patted her shoulder and at some point, without her noticing, he must have left because she was alone.

Gradually she became more aware of the pain gnawing at her, a dull ache in her legs and her arms, a sharper pain every time she inhaled.

She tried to remember when that had happened but the memory was jumbled and elusive. Jelena's pale face, her bright blue eyes, a scream.

She gasped.

Jelena standing on the roof of the tractor shed, ten feet above the ground and the ladder gone. Their mother shouting and the wind rising, thunder or gunfire in the distance. She told Jelena to jump. She'd catch her. And Jelena did, without hesitation.

Sofia felt the tears running down her cheeks and was sure that she would choke on them, knowing that if she did it wouldn't matter.

She saw Jelena turn away from the road, lower her gaze and frown. She saw the car aiming for her. She saw her own hand shoot out stupidly as Jelena flew into the air, screaming until her head hit the windscreen.

Sofia tried to roll over, away from the memory, but the pain in her ribs flared so sharply that she passed out again for a minute or an hour.

In her delirious state the same few seconds kept replaying, disjointed and unreal, the car sometimes a tank, sometimes a bullock, Jelena dressed in her confirmation dress and work boots, eleven years old and dead, twenty-four and alive.

She saw Tomas dressed in black, his gloved hands and his face covered. But she knew it was him in there. Hiding from her.

She didn't want to see what happened next. Knew there was blood coming. Lots of blood.

She turned away from the memory, resurfaced in the room, starting at the sensation of someone gently patting her cheeks dry with a tissue, standing over her, blocking out the light from the car's headlights.

No. That was not here or now.

This was not him.

Did she know this man from home? His flat, high cheekbones and hooded green eyes looked so familiar. When he spoke she didn't know what she was hearing and what she was remembering, the words coming out disconnected from the movements of his lips.

She closed her eyes and when she opened them again he was sitting very close to her. She tried to focus but he was hazy around the edges.

'I'm Detective Inspector Zigic. Dushan. Can you hear me, Sofia?'

It was like being underwater, everything muffled and blurred, and she tried to fight her way to the surface.

'Please – Jelena?'

'I'm very sorry, they did everything they could.'

She crashed back down, feeling a terrible pressure across her chest, the man's face rushing away out of focus, heard him speak, just a low murmur, and then wailing which only a small part of her brain knew was coming from her own raw throat and bruised lungs.

She saw the blood on his hands.

He would not get away with it.

She said his name.

'What? Sofia, I can't hear you.' The man leaned closer. 'Did you see who hit you?'

'Anthony Gilbert.'

'Who's he?'

'Jelena's boyfriend. Her ex. He did this.'

7

'He's got form,' Ferreira said, relaying the conversation she was having with Wahlia as Zigic drove, catching sight of the patrol car dispatched from Thorpe Wood Station a hundred yards back, shooting off the Serpentine Green roundabout, cutting up a Royal Mail van to gain a few more seconds, lights and siren blaring.

'For murder?' Zigic asked, hands tight on the wheel.

'No, stalking. First offence back in 2004,' Ferreira said. 'An ex-girlfriend. He trashed her car, broke into her house – there was a dead cat. She got a restraining order and that was the end of it.'

'They don't usually stop so easily,' Zigic said.

'No. Sounds like he moved on to someone else though. '06 he's done for criminal damage, same thing, slashed the car tyres. Harassment, threatening behaviour. This one was a barmaid at his local, no prior intimacy.'

'Did he back off?'

'Eventually,' Ferreira said. 'Nothing for a couple of years then there's an assault charge, brought and dropped. That was another ex . . . What, Bobby?' She swore, listened and when Zigic glanced away from the road he saw her eyes widen. 'He went for the boyfriend too, tried to run him over in his works car park. This is it. This is the fucker we want.'

Zigic accelerated past a line of vaguely Scandinavian-looking houses on Hampton Ridge, the estate proper sprawling away behind them, hundreds of acres of carefully planned closes dominated by heavily ornamented cod-Georgian town houses, screening the cheaper, densely built social housing, along with the methadone clinic and the drop-in centres and the halfway homes. Man-made lakes peeped out here and there, the water dull under the gloomy sky, patches of grassland left to give the impression of clean, countrified living on this reclaimed rubbish dump which was slowly but surely sinking into the sludge below.

He turned into the main entrance as Ferreira wrapped up the call.

'Piece of shit,' she said. 'This road, right here. Then next left.'

'We don't know it's him yet.'

'Stalkers will go through anyone to get at their victim. You know that as well as I do. Most people, they want revenge or whatever, they wait until you're on your own then they strike.' Her hand knifed the air. 'Stalkers are a whole different ball game. That obsession *has* to be satisfied no matter what.'

Zigic murmured agreement, counting down the house numbers. It was a pretty street, red brick and slate roofs, lead canopies over the doors, a lot of window boxes and topiary. Anthony Gilbert would look like a good catch initially and he obviously had no problem getting girlfriends, just behaving like a decent enough human being to keep them.

There was no car on his driveway and Zigic felt a cold twist in his gut at the possibility of a drawn-out manhunt.

Ferreira jumped out of the car before he'd fully stopped and charged up to the front door, banged hard with the side of her fist. Zigic sent the uniforms down the back, heard their boots crunching on the gravel as Ferreira knocked again.

The curtains in the living-room window were closed but there was a two-inch-wide gap between them and through it he saw a lamp burning on a side table, the glow from the television spilling across the floor. A tufted cream rug, the edge of the sofa.

'The key's still in the door,' Ferreira said. 'He's there.'

PC Blake came back onto the driveway at a jog.

'He's in the kitchen, sir. Looks like he's had an accident.'

Zigic followed him along the narrow path between the houses. Next door, children were playing in the garden, screaming and laughing, the sound of a ball hitting brickwork over and again and then a wobbly thud as it struck a window and their mother yelled at them.

'There,' Blake said.

Through the panel in the back door Zigic saw Anthony Gilbert curled up on the kitchen's white-tiled floor, still in his pyjamas, a pool of vomit near his face.

'Call an ambulance right now.'

'Yes, sir.'

'And get the ram.'

'Sir.'

A minute later Blake returned and Zigic stood back to let him work. Blake set his body and took aim, measured once, twice, and threw the ram at the wooden door frame just above the lock. It flew open, banging against the internal wall so hard that the glass panel shattered.

Zigic went in, broken glass crunching under foot, and squatted down next to Gilbert. He pressed his fingers into the man's neck. His skin was cold but there was a pulse, weak and erratic. He moved him into the recovery position and told Blake to go and look for something to cover him up with.

On the black granite counter a tumbler sat next to a half-empty bottle of vodka and four spent blister packs of ibuprofen. Forty-eight pills gone. More than a gesture.

'Guilt-induced overdose?' Ferreira asked, coming up behind him.

'Maybe.' Zigic picked up Gilbert's mobile from the floor. 'He's in his pyjamas though. Why would he get changed to kill himself?'

'I'd want to be comfortable, wouldn't you?' She stood over him, her toe a couple of inches away from his head. 'Do you think he can hear us?'

'Probably.' Zigic swiped his thumb across the phone's screen and it lit up, showing a photograph of Anthony Gilbert and a young blonde woman with heavily made-up eyes, their cheeks pressed close together, both smiling, faces shining drunkenly.

'That's Jelena Krasic,' Ferreira said.

'Are you sure?'

'Yeah. She was still at the scene when I got there. They were just moving her body.' Ferreira's eyes drifted down to Anthony Gilbert's prone form; she drew her foot back as if considering kicking him, but then wandered away to a noticeboard hung over the breakfast bar. 'Be handy if he left us a signed confession.'

'Go and have a poke about, Mel.'

Zigic scrolled through Gilbert's call logs, saw he'd rung Jelena Krasic several times before six o'clock that morning, knowing she would be up already, getting dressed for work. He'd called the previous evening too, almost hourly, short calls which she evidently hadn't answered. Zigic went back further, saw the pattern repeated day after day, upwards of twenty phone calls, most of them ignored, but Jelena answered occasionally and those conversations lasted no more than a few minutes. Zigic imagined Gilbert wheedling and begging, promising her it would be different this time, that whatever he'd done to scare her away would never happen again.

Or he was threatening her. That was more in keeping with what they knew of his character.

The call logs showed Jelena had phoned him just after five this morning, spoke to him for twenty-five seconds before she rang off.

Was that it? Zigic wondered. A final, unequivocal no which provoked him to act?

The car had been bought two days ago though. This was premeditated murder and Gilbert wouldn't be able to blame it on a moment of madness.

Blake came back into the kitchen as Ferreira left, a fake-fur throw bundled against his chest. He laid it over Anthony Gilbert, folded it back from his face, which was drained of all colour, his lips very pale, beginning to take on a bluish hue.

A siren was wailing at distance and within a couple of minutes the ambulance pulled up outside the house, drawing a few neighbours out onto their doorsteps. Zigic sent Blake and Jones to speak to them as the paramedics attended to Gilbert, working quickly and precisely, speaking in two voices, bright and optimistic to Gilbert, serious undertones to each other.

Zigic got out of their way. He went into the living room and found the BBC News Channel playing on the flat-screen television mounted above the fireplace. He looked over the bookshelves – a few dozen paperbacks and stacks of men's magazines, DVD box sets arranged alphabetically, the usual stuff.

There were framed photographs of Gilbert with Jelena and Sofia Krasic, a blond man in a couple of them, his arm around Sofia, but mostly it was Jelena and Gilbert, photos taken in a procession of bars and restaurants, in this living room, Jelena curled up on the leather sofa with a glass of wine in her hand, sitting on the rug in front of the fire, dressed in nothing but a man's shirt too large for her frame. It had the look of a shrine.

One of the paramedics went out and returned with a stretcher.

Maybe Gilbert didn't expect it to go this far and only realised what he'd done when the adrenalin wore off. Or maybe Jelena was different to the others, so special that he believed he couldn't live without her and this was always going to be a murder–suicide.

'No sign of a note,' Ferreira said, coming up behind him. 'Let's hope the bastard pulls through, hey.'

8

DCS Riggott was in Hate Crimes when they got back, standing in front of the board where the hit-and-run was plotted out, immaculately dressed as usual in a black wool suit and crisp white shirt. Zigic always felt dishevelled next to the man, but Riggott wasn't a copper really, never ventured into the field these days. Although he had a formidable reputation among the older officers, who could remember him kicking in doors and bashing heads, the ones who shared his vicious temperament but not the politicking skills which ensured he rose through the ranks while they hit their pensions exactly where they started out.

He clapped his hands together as they walked over.

'Ziggy, a result already. I always said you were a sharp one.'

'We haven't made an arrest yet,' Zigic said, shrugging off his parka. 'But it looks promising.'

'Your man tried topping himself, I hear.'

'The paramedics think they got to him in time.'

'Grand.' Riggott nodded, eyes on Anthony Gilbert's most recent mugshot, a lean, unremarkable face, brown hair and designer sideburns. 'This sort of thing demands a trial. People want to see proper punishment meted out. We're a biblical lot when it comes to multiple murder.'

'We're not there yet.'

'He'll confess. Sure, if he's guilty enough to kill himself it won't take much pressure to crack him, you mark my words.'

'Do you want us to stay on this?' Zigic asked. 'It doesn't look like a hate crime and we've got other cases.'

'You want to be happy you've got a success story on your books.'

Riggott glanced towards the whiteboards lined up along the opposite wall, too much blank space on them for comfort and no immediate prospect of a breakthrough. 'What's the progress in that direction?'

'We're working on it.'

Riggott moved across to the boards.

Two murders three weeks apart, the victims both men of foreign origin. If they were women, or English, people would already be hinting darkly at a serial killer, but these were closing-time kickings dished out on rough side streets where violence was routine and those on the receiving end rarely reported it. Unglamorous and commonplace and so far they'd been able to keep the link between the crimes out of the public domain.

Each had warranted a single front-page splash, a clutch of mentions on the local news which petered out inside a week, replaced by more teatime-friendly horrors.

'We need more coverage,' Zigic said. 'Someone saw something – you know what it's like round there at night, the streets are heaving. We just need to get them to come forward.'

Riggott didn't speak for a minute but studied the crime-scene photographs and forensic reports in silence, frowning at the short list of suspects and lines of inquiry which ended abruptly, shut down through lack of witnesses or unbreakable alibis.

'You've got lucky with this hit-and-run,' he said finally. 'Show people a jealous ex-boyfriend and they don't ask questions. But we've got the nationals poking around now and you do not want them catching on to these murders.'

'Maybe it'd be good if they do,' Zigic said. 'A bit more attention might bring a witness out of the woodwork.'

'It might so,' Riggott conceded, stroking his jaw with his fingertips. 'Or it might permanently fuck your career. You see what happened to the fella from Soham? Good copper, one of the best about, but the press had his balls off him. Once you invite them in you can't control them.'

'This isn't that kind of case.'

'No, it's the racially motivated murder of two dead immigrants in a city with a burgeoning far-right movement and a shiteload of discontentment about services and housing and any other thing you care to mention.' He stepped in closer, lowered his voice. 'You know where the Chief Constable is today? Out at Milton golf club playing the big bollocks with a delegation from Tata.'

'What's that got to do with anything?' Zigic asked.

'You're sharper than that. Tata are looking to take over the old Perkins plant on Eastern Industrial, right? Fifteen hundred manufacturing jobs guaranteed for both of our career spans. Now, how do you think the old bastard's going to react if his new friends start asking him about crime in the city? If they raise concerns about the safety of their workforce?'

'I've not come across a boss yet who cares about the safety of their workers.'

'Leverage,' Riggott said. 'Raise concerns, drop the price. Catch yourself on, son.'

Zigic crossed his arms, seeing where this was going.

'This department is a publicity stunt,' Riggott said and put his hand up when Zigic began to argue. 'No offence, you're doing important work and you're doing a fine job. But we both know the Hate Crimes caseload could be handled within CID. Now would not be a good time to go drawing attention to yourself.'

'Meaning what?'

'Meaning, a certain someone with shiny buttons on his epaulettes will be starting work on next year's budget very soon and he won't take kindly to you putting a spotlight on his city's myriad, unsolvable social problems.'

Zigic turned away, looked at the photos of the dead men.

A Somali boy, seventeen or eighteen years old, they hadn't been able to establish his age exactly. The friends he was sharing a flat with in Bretton knew him only as Didi, couldn't tell them how long he'd been here, or how he'd got to England, couldn't even tell them if he had any family they needed to break the bad news to. They provided a photo, Didi smiling behind a can of Coke, his eyes almost closed. When his body was found his head was completely ruined, kicked and stamped on so many times that every bone in his face was broken, and they only identified him from his medical records at the local health centre.

The second man, Ali Manouf, was just as comprehensively beaten, another face caved in under heavy boots, injuries more extensive than Zigic had ever seen before, and he couldn't imagine the kind of hatred which would drive someone to that.

It wasn't just murder, it was obliteration.

Manouf they knew a little more about. An Iranian engineer who'd paid Spanish smugglers to get him into England and provide him with false papers. He'd handed over the money only to find himself dumped on the side of the A1 just north of Peterborough without the promised documents. Police manning a speed check on the road picked him up and turned him over to the Immigration and Borders Agency. His claim for asylum was being processed when he died. The official Zigic spoke to said they would likely have denied him leave to remain.

He had been staying at a halfway house off Lincoln Road, working on the black at a sweatshop nearby, sewing party dresses for a big high-street name, and his boss told them how grateful he'd been for the overtime when offered it. He'd left at 2 a.m. and walked home with the extra cash in his pocket, probably feeling like he'd had a better day than usual, until he'd run into the man who'd murdered him.

Both men were considered decent by the handful of people who knew them, quiet, polite, determined to keep their heads down and avoid trouble. Neither were fighters, which was probably why their killer targeted them.

Three weeks since Didi's murder and four days since Manouf's they were no closer to an arrest. Zigic went to the boards first thing every morning and looked at the dead men's faces, keeping them clear in his mind so he wouldn't forget what was at stake. But what dogged him was the belief that soon the blank whiteboard in the

40

corner would be wheeled out, a third victim filling it, because someone who was capable of this level of violence wouldn't stop until they were caught.

'So you want me to hush this up?' he asked.

Riggott put a hand on his shoulder. 'I'm advising you to spend the next few days concentrating on building a strong case against Anthony Gilbert. Once he's charged the pressure goes away, you follow?'

He knew Riggott was right but he resented having his actions dictated by the demands of the press and the machinations of the city council. Riggott hadn't wandered up here of his own accord, this wasn't friendly, off-the-cuff advice, it was an order couched in camaraderie.

'Fine.'

'Good man. Press conference at five,' Riggott said, heading for the door. He stopped to click his fingers at Ferreira. 'Mel, make sure he's wearing a suit.'

She watched him leave, eyebrows drawn together in a scowl. 'What, I'm the fucking wardrobe mistress now?'

Zigic dragged himself away from the boards and poured a coffee, finding the extra officers he'd been given had taken a toll on supplies. Someone had bought pastries though. Small victories, he thought, as he bit into an apricot Danish.

'Have we got anything back from forensics yet?'

'Blood on the airbag is a type match for Gilbert,' Wahlia said. 'Jenkins is still working up trajectories, shit like that, I didn't understand half of what she said to be honest.'

'We don't need all that,' Ferreira said, hunched over her desk rolling a cigarette. 'We just need the bastard to wake up and talk.'

'And if he denies it?' Zigic asked.

Ferreira sealed her cigarette. 'Then we ask harder.'

'And what if he doesn't wake up at all?' Zigic said, dipping the end of his Danish into his coffee. 'Then we've got nothing for the CPS. Go back over to Hossa Motors and see if you can get a positive ID from Ivan.'

Ferreira grabbed her jacket and left the office.

'Have you got hold of his bank records yet, Bobby?'

'Still waiting on them.'

'What about the CCTV?'

Wahlia shook his head. 'Bad news on that front. We've got nothing before the car appears on Lincoln Road just before the incident.'

'And afterwards?'

'Grieves is on it.'

Zigic went over to the woman's desk and she quickly brushed away a few pastry flakes from her lunch. She'd been made up from uniform eighteen months ago and still didn't seem entirely comfortable with her new rank, softly spoken and painfully timid when it came time to talk up; Zigic wondered how she'd survived as a PC. She was diligent though and had a good eye for detail, something her more bombastic colleagues didn't share.

'He was chased down Green Lane,' Zigic said. 'Is that right?'

'Yes, sir. Four men gave pursuit.' She showed him the CCTV footage from the crash site, the driver jumping out of the car, catching his foot on the seat belt, half tripping but managing to keep on his feet. Then he was running, fast, a small gang following, twenty or thirty yards behind him.

'We lose them for a minute,' Grieves said and switched to another view. 'Then here on Dogsthorpe Road one of the cameras picks him up again. A couple of the men have fallen back.'

She switched to a different view. A street of Edwardian villas, cars parked on the road, bins out on the pavement, everything shadowy and ill-defined, the street lamps only throwing out dim light, with long stretches between them.

'Then at the end of All Saints Road he's gone.'

'Have we got any more?' Zigic asked.

Grieves shook her head, sending her bobbed red hair swinging around her face. 'Our last sighting is at 06.08, sir.'

'Plenty of time to get back home to Hampton and swallow the medicine cabinet,' Wahlia said. 'It's a hike though.'

'OK, Deb, why don't you stay on this for a bit, see if you can find out where he emerges? If we're lucky we might get his face on camera.'

'Yes, sir.'

Wahlia moved away to answer his phone and Zigic topped up his coffee, took it with him into his office. He closed the door and dropped into his chair, the leather sighing under his weight.

For a moment he did nothing, only looked at the photographs of Anna and the boys on his desk, smiled back at them automatically then felt stupid for doing it. Anna was taking Milan to the dentist today and he didn't envy her it – last time he refused to open his mouth no matter how gently they all coaxed him, and then it was apologies and awkward laughter while Milan watched them all from under a furrowed brow, as if scenting a conspiracy against him. He was older now though. Maybe he could be reasoned with. Or bribed.

Zigic straightened with a deep breath and dragged the keyboard towards him. He dug into the files until he found what he wanted. It was a short video clip, ten seconds long and four days old, retrieved from a security camera outside a halal butcher's, a few feet away from the alley where Ali Manouf was kicked to death.

His killer entered the shot from the right, his body made shorter and wider by the angle. He wore a black padded jacket, dark jeans and heavy boots which Zigic knew were spattered with blood and bone and flecks of grey matter even though he couldn't see them. Enough gore to leave a trail of footprints. The man's face was obscured by a balaclava with a fine gauze across the eyes; he was careful, wouldn't even give them that thin strip for identification.

He turned to the camera, drew himself up to his full height and raised his gloved hand in a stiff-armed Nazi salute.

9

'We need a strategy for this,' Marshall said, standing with his arms folded in front of the monitor, as footage from the hit-and-run on Lincoln Road played on a loop. 'Just in case it's one of ours.'

'They are not *ours*,' Richard Shotton snarled. 'Not even in this office, between us. We create distance and we maintain it. I will not tolerate any insinuation of links to those bloody jackbooted, tattooed oiks.'

Marshall's eyes dropped to the polished concrete floor. 'No, sir, of course.'

Shotton strode over to the office's long glazed wall and stood looking out across the gravel driveway at the facade of the main house. His wife was coming down the front steps, her coat over her arm, slipping on her sunglasses as she popped the remote locks on her car. She waved to his driver as she climbed in and the man gave her a salute – their little joke. He clearly fancied her but Shotton couldn't blame him. Forty-five years old and she was still a glorious-looking creature.

She sprayed the side of the Range Rover with gravel as she pulled off, a few more dings for the battle-scarred beast. In the last few weeks it had taken heavy damage, kicked and slammed by protesters, the rear window shattered by a placard bearing some misspelt anti-fascist slogan. His security could have dealt with them but it would have been terrible press coming after his triumphant performance at the Cambridge Union.

And right now press was what mattered.

Four months ago a snap by-election, prompted by some shady expense accounting on the part of his Conservative predecessor, saw

Shotton elected for the constituency of Cambridgeshire North, but he knew better than to rest on his laurels. He'd won with a narrow majority on a low turnout and any first-year PPE student could tell you how often the electorate used these mid-session changeovers as protest votes against the current government.

The general election in May might not be such an easy ride.

He needed to consolidate his position and up until this morning he felt confident of doing that.

The party already held four seats on Peterborough Council, another three in Fenland, and the polls he'd commissioned showed a strong backing in the area for their core policies, suggesting his win was more than just the locals sending a message to Westminster.

Not that he needed the polls.

He'd been pounding the streets, getting out there, talking to ordinary folk, going to their village fetes and community open days, testing the waters, and he knew that they were ready to cast their votes his way come the election. He was giving them what they'd wanted for years and now they were finally prepared to admit it in the polling booth.

Across the country they'd identified twenty-four constituencies with similar demographics; slim majorities, rising unrest, council seats already won, paving the way for the English Patriot Party to become serious parliamentary players.

They wouldn't win them all of course but six or seven this time round would improve their standing nationally, force the Westminster elite and the left-wing media class to admit their growing relevance.

As long as he could manage this situation.

He went back to his chrome-and-glass desk where Marshall was standing with his iPad on his forearm, fingertips moving nimbly over the screen.

'Alright, plan of action.' Shotton spread his hands wide. 'The line is – "This hit-and-run is clearly a terrible accident and our sympathies go out to the friends and families of those involved."'

'There's already speculation online that an English Nationalist League member might be responsible.'

'We won't dignify that with a response.'

'I think we need to be prepared,' Marshall said. 'This woman from *The Times* is quite likely to ask the question and it's best to have a response.'

'Don't worry about her.' Shotton settled into his chair, looking out through the floor-to-ceiling windows again, sunlight glinting off the Range Rover's bodywork as his driver washed it down. He pressed a button on his phone. 'Send Christian in here, please.'

'I'm not sure how he's going to help,' Marshall said.

His iPad chimed. 'And . . . it's starting. The HuffPo are running a piece on the presence of high-ranking English Nationalist League members in Peterborough.' He scanned for a moment. 'They've got a photograph of you and Ken Poulter.'

Shotton groaned internally. He hadn't spoken to Poulter in public for over a year, aware of the negative impact on PR, but there was always some dedicated muckraker out there who'd put the hours in to smear him.

'Anything in there I need to worry about?'

'Apart from the photo of you hugging a man with barbed wire tattooed around his neck?' Marshall didn't look up from the screen. He rarely did. The thing might be surgically attached to him for all the time he spent away from it. 'They're insinuating a causal link between the hit-and-run and the atmosphere of racial tension in the city. You're being singled out as an agitator.'

Shotton rocked back in his chair, looked up at the vaulted ceiling, white between the sturdy pine rafters. An agitator. When had that become a bad thing? he wondered.

Somebody had to ask the questions the rest of the world were too scared to raise.

Churchill, Thatcher, Benn. They were all agitators and it hadn't done them any harm.

'They keep banging the same old drum.'

Marshall sighed. 'We need to offset some of this damage.'

'No, we do nothing. Not until we have a better idea of what's going on.' Shotton knitted his fingers together over his chest. 'A good general appreciates the value of stillness.'

Christian's hulking blond figure appeared on the other side of the glass door, the main office behind him, only one of the four desks manned, Elizabeth, his secretary working her charms on his social diary. The rest were in mothballs until the end of the month when the real work would start.

Then it would be a electrifying chaos of ringing phones and churning printers, press releases and mission statements, placards and bumper stickers and the stale-skin smell of working through the night. Everybody pulling together, fighting hard to get ticks in boxes, making the long push towards 7 May.

The mere thought of it made him rise from behind his desk, energy shooting through his body like the old days, waiting for the call to scramble.

'Come in, Christian.'

'You wanted to see me, sir?'

He stood with his hands tucked in the small of his back, big feet planted wide and his gut sucked in. Still every inch the copper even though he'd been out of the force for a couple of years now, an injury sustained on the rugby pitch removing him from the front line and sending him straight to an agency he was far too good for. Deferential when he needed to be but sharp. Shotton liked that. Liked that the man had an instinct for ensuing ruckus. You couldn't put too high a price on that in a bodyguard.

When his contract was finished they would take him on full-time. After all, loyalty didn't come on a short-term basis.

'This hit-and-run in Peterborough – have you heard anything about it from your former colleagues?'

'What hit-and-run?'

'Don't you watch the news?' Marshall asked.

'My kids have cartoons on in the morning.'

He looked faintly embarrassed by the admission.

'This morning,' Shotton said. 'A car took out a group of migrant workers on Lincoln Road – that'll be a Thorpe Wood job, won't it?'

'Yes, sir. I'd think so, sir.'

'Right. Well, make some calls, would you? See what the thinking is for us.'

Christian nodded. 'Of course.'

'Subtly, please,' Marshall said. 'I don't want to be having a conversation about this with their press officer later.'

Christian ignored him, kept his attention fixed on Shotton. He was used to a sight more bad attitude than Marshall could muster.

'Is there anything else, sir?'

'Not right now, thank you, Christian.'

He left with a nod, returning to the main office where Elizabeth's expensively educated voice rang out across the quiet. A personal call by the sounds of things, but Shotton would forgive her.

'Do you think that was wise?' Marshall asked. 'The Chief Constable could keep you better informed with less chance of a leak.'

'Weir's an overambitious shit. The less he knows about this situation the better. If he thinks we're concerned he'll start digging around for a way to hold it over my head. Christian just wants to keep this job. He'll achieve the same thing for a lower price.'

Shotton returned to his desk and sipped the cooling tea Elizabeth had brought him twenty minutes earlier, thinking ahead to the afternoon's interview. Some young woman from *The Times*. They'd headhunted her from the *New Statesman* and she was an influential political blogger in her own right, with extremely good contacts and killer instincts, far more powerful than her years suggested. It was a changing world and he knew he'd better get used to it. Political clout was still held in the hands of men like him, but when it came to the media he couldn't rely on the boys' club.

She'd take the route they always did, he imagined, pressed to hit her deadline, and the usual answers would satisfy her. How he'd moved up to Peterborough because he had happy memories of his time at Uppingham nearby and the long stint at RAF Cottesmore during the nineties. That would give her an excuse to precis his service record and use the photograph of him climbing into a Tornado GR4 with a cigar between his teeth. They all used it. Then how he met his wife at a charity fund-raiser and her human rights work. The women always wanted to talk about Gabriela and he was happy to oblige, knew any politician was only as good as their other half in the eyes of the electorate.

Marshall let out a murmur of annoyance.

Shotton ignored him, looking at the photo of Gabriela on his desk. She hated being away from London and he couldn't blame her, Peterborough was the worst sort of backwater, unaware of its own shortcomings, but they would be off again as soon as possible. Back to the little flat in Kensington for as many nights a week as they could get away with.

Marshall swore and this time he didn't wait to be prompted.

'Our Twitter feed is going crazy.'

'Fabulous.'

'No,' Marshall said slowly. 'Not fabulous. We're getting bombarded with tweets from those jackbooted oiks you want to distance yourself from and they are vomiting filth at us. *Supportive* filth.'

'Damage limitation then.'

Marshall moved over to the window. 'It has to start at home.'

Shotton followed his gesturing hand to the Range Rover. 'I'm not downsizing to a Prius if that's what you're suggesting.'

'You know full well what I'm suggesting,' Marshall said.

He did. Marshall had been banging on about Selby for months.

'He's got to go. Right now. Before someone makes the link back to the English Nationalist League.'

'Selby's not going anywhere.'

'The man is a convicted criminal –'

'That fight wasn't his fault,' Shotton said.

'Do you think the press will bother with the context?' Marshall shoved his glasses back up his nose with an angry stab of his middle finger. The subconscious gesture lost on neither of them. 'You are employing a murderer. That's the headline.'

Oblivious to their argument Selby continued washing the Range Rover, down on his knees in the gravel, soaping the hubcaps with a pink sponge. If you didn't know what he'd done, what he was capable of, you'd never guess from looking at him. He was just like any other forty-year-old bloke with thinning hair and a thickening middle. He looked more like a copper than Christian did.

'Look, I like the man, I really do.' Marshall's voice was low and reasonable, ever the cold-hearted professional. 'But he has long-standing links with some very unsavoury people. I mean, there isn't a far-right group he hasn't been a member of at one time or another.'

Selby got to his feet, moving with more snap than was decent in a man his age, and went round the other side of the vehicle, ducking behind the bonnet.

'Youthful indiscretions,' Shotton said.

'And if they were only going to reflect on *him* I wouldn't argue.'

Oh-so-logical, so fucking bloodless. He'd turn his grandmother over to white slavers if the numbers supported it.

'But as your driver he represents you and you are giving tacit approval to every group he's been involved with by continuing to employ him.'

'By employing you I'm backing the bloody Trots then,' Shotton said. 'Maybe you should both go.'

Marshall swallowed his reply, eyes straying towards the iPad. Again.

Shotton moved in on him.

'I am not sacking Selby.' He stepped closer, into Marshall's personal space. 'He is my staff and what I choose to do about him is none of your damn business.'

Marshall forced himself to look up from the infernal device.

'There are plenty more number-crunchers in the think tanks, Nicholas. You'd do well to remember that.'

Marshall nodded, stepped back like a retreating courtier, and Shotton waved him out of the office.

He dropped into one of the black leather armchairs arranged face-to-face next to the windows, and watched Selby walking back to the triple-bay garage to refill his bucket. He was a liability, no question about it. All that dirty history. All of those dangerous friends.

But he'd be damned if he was going to let Marshall order him around.

He had no convictions, that was the problem. He'd spotted the way the wind was blowing and followed it. Ten years ago he would have joined the Tories. Twenty he'd have been singing 'The Red Flag' and sitting at Tony Blair's feet. He was just another weak-willed careerist looking to bask in the glow of a better man's glory.

The movement had seen hundreds of them come and go across the years and nobody had made much progress, not the wannabe mandarins or the jumped-up football hooligans who considered themselves soldiers. They were still around though, as persistent as nuclear waste and twice as toxic, and they all had to be managed successfully before you could grasp power.

Shotton took out his mobile phone and brought up a number, waited out four rings before the man answered, radio noise cutting off abruptly at the other end, but he didn't give him a chance to speak.

'I think you've got something to tell me, haven't you, Mr Poulter?'

IO

Bogdan Hossa was bouncing up and down on the bonnet of a bright blue Seat when Ferreira entered the lot, showing a young man how good the suspension was, but she noticed he wasn't using his full weight, his thighs taking most of the strain as the car creaked. The young man didn't look impressed. He was backing away, shaking his head, and finally Hossa conceded defeat, letting him go with a wave and a promise that the car would be full price tomorrow.

'You come back, madam.'

'I need Ivan to take a look at something for me,' Ferreira said, casting her eye around the yard, remembering what she was going to ask him earlier before the call from the hospital derailed her. 'Why don't you have any security cameras, Mr Hossa?'

'We have camera,' he said, sounding wounded. 'Must have for insure cars.'

She looked around the lot again, didn't see any.

'Where are they?'

He smiled, gestured for her to turn round and pointed to the roof of the Portakabin which was littered with rubbish, a sheet of discarded blue plastic tossed up there and forgotten.

'Here. See.' He walked towards it and she followed, finally catching sight of a small black lens winking out from under the sheet. 'Clever, yes?'

'Very clever,' Ferreira admitted. 'How many weeks of footage have you got?'

'I –' He stopped. 'Only one week.'

Hossa met her eye eventually and she saw a combination of defiance and unease.

I'm not interested in your business dealings, Mr Hossa,' she said gently. 'Whatever you have to do to keep selling cars, that's up to you. But this man is a murderer. I'm sure you understand how important it is that we catch him.'

'I want to help police.'

'That's just good business, Mr Hossa.' She smiled, showing him she was amenable. 'Having a friend in the police is useful. Even in England, yes?'

They went into the Portakabin where Ivan was dozing behind his desk, feet up, a napkin tucked into the front of his jumper. A pizza box sat within grabbing distance and the smell of toasted bread and tomato sauce made Ferreira's stomach growl. She almost flipped the lid to see if there was any left.

Bogdan shouted at Ivan and he came round with a snort.

'Lazy shit.'

Ferreira took out Anthony Gilbert's mugshot and showed it to Ivan.

'The white Volvo – you remember?' she asked. 'Is this the man you sold it to?'

He leaned across his desk, his weight making it crack, and studied the photograph for a couple of seconds.

'He has hat,' Ivan said. He covered his own forehead with his hands. 'This. Not see face.'

Ferreira tucked the photograph back into her pocket and returned her attention to Bogdan Hossa, seeing the worried expression on his coarse features as his fingers hovered over the keyboard.

'You will leave laptop here please?'

'I'm going to need to take it,' Ferreira said. 'I'll give you a receipt and I promise I'll get it back to you as soon as possible.'

He was still hesitant.

'I can get a court order if I need to.'

He bristled at that. 'I cannot run business with no laptop. Please, I have family. Four children, wife, mother, sister. Ivan. I need business open.'

Ferreira heard the fear in his voice, thought it was genuine. What had he been through back home to make him so wary of the police? They were corrupt enough in Portugal but she knew the forces in Eastern Europe were often worse, just another street gang taking what they wanted, backed up by a legal system rotten to the core. Maybe his last business had been lost with a conversation which started like this.

'Look, let me take it now and I'll bring it back to you by the end of the day.' She held out her hand. 'You have my word, Mr Hossa.'

His head dropped, revealing a walnut-sized bald spot cut by an old scar. 'What can I do?'

Ferreira wrote him out a receipt and tucked the machine into her bag, left him staring at the empty desk like some vital part of him had just been amputated.

She went slow up First Drove, trying to avoid the potholes, thinking about where she could get some lunch. She stopped at the first fast-food van she came to and ordered a Coke and a bacon butty, ate it sitting on the bonnet, watching the traffic go by.

As she pitched the empty can into the bin her mobile rang.

'Sergeant Ferreira?' A man's voice with the marked drawl she associated with television costume dramas. 'Dr Harrow. I'm afraid the gentleman from your accident has passed away.'

'What happened?'

'His injuries were more serious than we first assumed.'

He had a metal pole through his chest, Ferreira thought, how did they assume that was anything but serious?

'OK, thanks for letting me know.'

'We have some of his things if you'd like to send one of your chaps over.'

'I'll take care of it. Thank you.'

She picked up the parkway and headed for the City Hospital in Bretton, catching glimpses of the low-rise housing development between the screen planting which crept up the banks either side of the road. In a few weeks the trees would be in leaf and the rows of terraces would be completely obscured. She thought of the murdered Somali man who'd lived in a flat on the estate, sharing two rooms with four other men. He owned little more than the clothes he'd died in, still didn't have a proper name, just Didi.

Some outlandish theories had done the rounds at the station, the uniforms in the canteen suggesting a ritualistic killing linked to African witch doctors or revenge for some war crime committed back home when Didi was a child soldier. Zigic came down on the gossip hard, knowing that a misplaced word in the pub could lead to hysteria.

It was human nature to search for elaborate reasons behind mundane events, she guessed, and maybe they would have pursued those lines if it wasn't for the CCTV footage they'd found.

She toed the accelerator thinking of the black-clad figure standing over the young man's body, raising a salute to the camera as Didi's fingers twitched, his brain already dead. She'd forced herself to watch the whole attack, flinching at every silent boot strike, feeling the bile rise up in her throat as Didi's head was stamped to pulp, but it was the salute which stuck with her, the significance of it lost on no one who saw it.

And that was a small group. Outside Hate Crimes only Riggott and the council CCTV operator knew about it, a state of affairs Ferreira wasn't sure she was happy about.

It felt like they were colluding in the violence by concealing the motive.

She knew that some things had to be kept from the public, held back to eliminate the crackpot fantasists who scoured the news for crimes to falsely confess to, but how long were they going to continue pretending these were ordinary, entirely random murders?

Riggott wanted it hushed up. He was getting pressure from above and so he was leaning on Zigic, who would lean on her and Wahlia in his gentle, perfectly reasonable way, making it clear he was power-less to disobey the DCS.

At some point they would have to start calling this what it was though, a serial killing.

Ferreira pulled into the car park at City Hospital, found a space near the door and headed down to the mortuary, feeling an appreciable chill in the stairwell as the glass wall gave way to painted concrete, taking her below ground level. The air was thicker here, she was sure, recirculated countless times and heavy with the breaths of the diseased and dying. She tried to lighten her step but her heels clicked insistently, echoing between the bare walls. There were no posters down here, no artwork, just the black line at hip height which led inexorably to a pair of stainless-steel swing doors with reinforced portholes.

A disembodied voice floated across the mortuary as she walked in, a dull monotone the same pitch as the freezer hum. She followed it to the adjoining office, an overlit cupboard lined with files jigsawed on metal shelves, saw a bald guy in blue scrubs and an Aran cardigan sitting with his head in his hand, talking on his mobile.

'Yeah, well, I told them that but they won't do anything about it. He's been here longer than me, they trust him . . . I'm talking to my rep tomorrow . . . I don't know, it's my word against his. He's been doing it for years I should think.'

Ferreira coughed lightly and the man glanced over his shoulder, told the person on the other end of the phone that he would call them back.

'The public aren't allowed down here, miss.'

She showed him her warrant card. 'You're new, aren't you?'

'My second week.'

'Dr Harrow just called me. I'm here to pick up some personal effects.'

He nodded. 'OK. What's the name please?'

'We haven't ID'd him yet,' Ferreira said. 'It's from the hit-and-run this morning. He had a pole through his chest if that's any help.'

'It's unbelievable someone would do that deliberately,' he said, unlocking the door to the property storage room. 'They're saying online that it was racially motivated – is that right?'

'No. Ex-boyfriend.'

He went into an even smaller cupboard with more metal shelves containing dozens of white plastic sacks stamped with the hospital logo, stickers on them bearing names and times of death. They smelled of stale fluids and dried blood.

'I don't know if that's better or worse,' he said, checking the labels.

Neither did Ferreira so she let the statement hang, thinking of all the women Anthony Gilbert had attacked over the years with little or no punishment. It was inevitable that eventually he would kill one of them and yet nobody took the threat seriously. Now two people were dead, and even if he pulled through, the overdose would provide a potential defence for his barrister, maybe earn him a short stay in a psychiatric unit rather than the long category-A stretch he deserved.

'OK. This is you.'

The man re-emerged from the cupboard, holding out a bag to Ferreira. It was almost empty. His clothes would have been cut off in A&E and tossed aside she guessed, and she remembered seeing the grubby white sole of his left sock as he was loaded into the back of the ambulance, his shoe lost somewhere at the scene.

Ferreira thanked him and headed back up through the chilled corridor and the stairwell, hearing someone crying several flights above her. She strode out through reception where a small child was throwing an elaborate tantrum, snarling and kicking as his mother looked on bored, waiting for the boy to tire.

In the car she opened the bag and went through the man's meagre belongings. A set of house keys on a worn leatherette fob, a mobile phone with a cracked screen and a handful of loose change. No wallet. It was possible he didn't have one but highly unlikely, and she swore under her breath, wondering what kind of bastard would rob a man lying dying on the side of the road.

She resealed the bag and went back down to the mortuary, found the bald-headed man on the phone again, his conversation picked up as if he hadn't been disturbed. This time when he saw her an expression of mild annoyance crossed his face.

'I need to see the corpse,' Ferreira said.

He pushed away from his desk and she followed him across the white-tiled floor to the bank of stainless-steel refrigerators droning lazily into the hush, noticing a moth hole on the back of his chunky cream cardigan.

The drawer stuck as he tried to open it and he smiled.

'This one's tricky.'

He hauled on it two-handed and there was a sound like shearing metal then a bump and it slid out the rest of the way.

The right side of the dead man's face was badly grazed, spots of grit from the pavement embedded in his pale, pockmarked skin, and dried blood at the corner of his mouth which nobody had thought to clean away. Her eyes strayed to his chest, a thatch of thick black hair fanned out across his shoulders and his narrow ribcage, which had been cracked for the surgery that failed to save his life and pushed back together once the surgeons finally stepped away. It was difficult to tell now what was injury and what was intervention but looking at the churned mess above his heart Ferreira was surprised he lived long enough for the ambulance to arrive.

She took a couple of photographs of his face with her mobile phone and thanked the man as she left, hearing the terrible shearing sound once again as he fought the drawer home.

II

Zigic stood at the office window, looking down at the car park while he waited for a fresh pot of coffee to brew. Three floors below he saw a maintenance man sweeping the ugly brown steps outside the main doors, dispatched by the press officer to make sure everything looked good for the cameras which would be arriving within the next hour.

The coffee machine spluttered out the last few drops and he poured himself a cup, trying not to think about how many he'd had already today, enough to give him mild palpitations, but there was nothing else to do now but wait and hope that Anthony Gilbert woke up soon in a confessional state of mind.

Hate Crimes was enveloped in the usual mid-afternoon lull which, on casual inspection, could pass for an industrious hush. Grieves was going through Anthony Gilbert's bank records, trying to track down cash withdrawals to tally with the four hundred pounds he'd paid Hossa Motors for the Volvo. Nothing so far but it was such a small amount of money that with careful planning he might have scraped it together with odd tenners and twenties, covering his tracks in that regard just as assiduously as he had elsewhere.

Parr was scanning the information line messages sent through from control, a mix of badly directed sympathy, armchair hypotheses and racist glee. He looked shattered, slumped in his seat, eyes drifting, but Zigic guessed some of that was due to the new baby at home.

He didn't know if he could face that again. Sleep broken every two hours for feeds, regardless of which of them actually got out of bed to do it, being woken by crying in between, or, even worse, the sudden awareness that there was no crying then the clutching panic that something must be wrong.

Anna had made her decision though. Later this year when Stefan started school. That would be the best time to get pregnant.

Across the office Wahlia blew out a fast hard breath and rocked back in his chair. Anthony Gilbert's laptop was open on his desk, delivered fully cracked by a techie about twenty minutes ago.

'Think we got a problem here.'

'What've you found?' Zigic asked, feeling an unpleasant pricking sensation.

Wahlia stood up to let him get a better look at Gilbert's Facebook page. He was in the private message section, the sidebar clouded out, the inbox on the other side showing a selection of faces, a conversation with Jelena open, dated two days ago, and it didn't read like a stalker and his victim.

Jelena signed off her last one with two kisses and an 'I love you'.

'Are we sure this is definitely her account?'

Wahlia reached for a packet of gum. 'The messages go back for about six months. I've checked out her page and that was registered in '09, she didn't use it much but it looks legit. Lot of photos of her and Sofia. There's a bloke who might be Sofia's boyfriend, Tomas.'

'Blond guy? Kind of Hitler Youth looking?'

'That's the one.' Wahlia folded a stick of gum into his mouth, pointed at the screen. 'Gilbert was sending her links to hotels, picking out clothes for her.'

'Typical control freak.'

'Suppose some women think that's gentlemanly,' Wahlia said. 'She seemed flattered by it.'

Zigic scrolled back up through the messages, seeing discussions about recent dates, Jelena gushing, saying what a great time she'd had, how lucky she was to go to such nice places. Gilbert's dialogue was all about her, seemed disconnected from what she was saying.

'*I love walking into places with you,*' Zigic read. 'What does that mean?'

'That he gets off on other guys being jealous? She was totally out of his league, wasn't she?'

'She was a few years younger.'

Wahlia pulled another chair over. 'She's like an eight – if you're going to be a wanker about women – and he's, shit, a five on his best day. A two if you factor in his personality.'

'Jelena was poor though. He probably looked like an escape route.'

Wahlia nodded, took off his heavy-framed black glasses and polished them on the hem of his shirt. Said, 'Maybe that's why Sofia didn't like him. He was taking her little sister away.'

Zigic went further back into the messages, past long strings of elaborate, late-night sex talk which made him blush, not the content so much as the knowledge that neither of them ever meant for it to be seen. Murders exposed every hidden corner of people's lives though, and as he kept going he became more convinced that this relationship was not what Sofia had led them to believe.

Her name cropped up occasionally, always as an excuse to break a date, and at the beginning Gilbert tried to encourage Jelena to ignore her sister's opinion of him.

When he returned to the most recent messages he saw how little progress Gilbert had made; all of that wheedling, the chipping away at Jelena's resolve, but still Sofia had to be assuaged.

Sofia would not like this. It is best Sofia does not know. She will calm down. Be patient, darling. I will explain to her.

'How does this line up against what we've got from her mobile?' Zigic asked.

'Still waiting on it.'

'Call them and tell them to drop whatever else they're doing,' Zigic said. 'Christ, how hard can it be to shove the SIM card into a new phone?'

'I'll chase them up.'

Zigic thought of Sofia Krasic at the hospital this morning, demanding to speak to a policeman through the fog of pain and medication. Every word she had uttered looked like a torture but she had been determined to tell him Anthony Gilbert was responsible.

How certain could she be though?

So far they had nothing concrete to tie him to the vehicle only a match to his blood type, one too common to mean much. His neighbours hadn't noticed him leave the house or return, and it was a small close, the houses built tight together, the kind of place where you got to know the familiar rumble of a specific engine or the way the people opposite's door rattled.

All they had to go on was Sofia's word and Gilbert's overdose and very soon Zigic was going to stand in front of the assembled press and declare the case as good as solved, based on those things alone.

Ferreira came into the office carrying a white plastic sack, dumped it on her desk and shrugged out of her jacket.

'You two look serious.'

'Sofia Krasic was spinning us a line about Gilbert,' Wahlia said. 'Jelena was still seeing him.'

'Why would she lie about it?' Ferreira asked, taking a sleek, silver laptop out of her bag. 'Hossa Motors CCTV footage.'

She called Grieves over and told her to take it up to the technical department and get them to run a copy off onto a hard disk straight away.

'Tell them they do not want me up there.'

Grieves hurried out, clutching the laptop to her chest.

Ferreira sat down, gave them both an expectant look.

'So, what do we think?'

'That Sofia's going to have some explaining to do,' Zigic said.

'He tried to kill himself. He's guilty.' Ferreira took a small tin out of her handbag and started to shred tobacco into a liquorice paper. 'Course, the television was on when we got there, he might have seen the footage on the news and been overwhelmed with grief.'

'That still doesn't explain why she'd lie about him stalking Jelena.'

'How would she know he's got form?' Wahlia asked.

'She couldn't have known that,' Zigic said. 'Unless he was stupid enough to mention it. Which is unlikely.'

Ferreira stuck her unlit cigarette in her mouth and went over

62

to the murder board, picked up a black marker pen from the shelf underneath.

'While we're sharing shitty news.' She rubbed out 'unknown one' which was written in red and added it to the deceased list. 'He didn't have any ID on him. I've got his stuff but it looks like someone pinched his wallet from the scene or he forgot it when he left the house.'

'Did you get a photo?' Zigic asked, going round to her side of the desk.

'On my phone.'

'Sofia might know who he is.'

'Yeah, and she'll probably lie about that too,' Ferreira said. She went and opened one of the long bank of windows on the opposite side of the office, perched on the narrow sill and lit her cigarette. 'Aren't you supposed to have a suit on?'

Zigic shot her a mock-stern look and she grinned.

'Black, do you think?' he asked, emptying the property bag onto her desk. 'Or charcoal grey? Since you're our resident fashionista.'

'Navy blue,' she said. 'It's professional but it doesn't look like you're trying too hard. White shirt, black tie.'

He picked up the key. 'Half Windsor knot?'

'What else?'

Zigic dropped the key again. It wasn't going to tell him anything. He thumbed the power button on the man's mobile but the screen stayed black. Another job for the techies.

He glanced at his watch. 'I'd better shift.'

An Anglia News van was turning into the station car park as he pulled out. They were an hour early but they obviously expected a scramble and wanted to grab a prime spot. The press officer promised it would just be a brief statement but he knew already exactly how trapped he was going to feel, the lights in his eyes and the cameras on him, like some old-school interrogation technique they were no longer allowed to use.

Two people were dead. A brief statement wouldn't be enough to satisfy the hacks.

He slipped off the dual carriageway and slowed sharply as he approached the edge of the village, catching up to the back of a horsebox which looked more secure than most armoured vans. It turned into the driveway of a sprawling 1970s mansion on Castor Heights, the kind of house which screamed slum landlord or drug dealer gone legit. Down the hill he passed rows of small stone cottages, cars parked out on the winding road as the last stragglers from the village primary's after-school club bundled their kids home in a flutter of bags and coats and craft projects, which left the pavement scattered with glitter and pasta shapes.

A broad, blonde woman with twin girls waved at Zigic as he went by and he put his hand up, trying to remember her name. Anna had insisted they have the woman and husband over for dinner last year and the evening had been so excruciating that he had drunk too much wine and almost fallen asleep at the table, listening to the husband drone on about his work in the City, while the women talked over each other at double speed, discussing private schools they couldn't afford, ski resorts they wouldn't go to, and how difficult it was to find honest cleaners. Which they didn't have. The one small comfort was that the man was too much of a narcissist to ask Zigic about his job.

He stopped at the village shop and bought an *Evening Telegraph* from the bundle just delivered by the till. The owner had her back to him, concentrating on filling the fridge, so he left the money on the counter and slipped out before she could cross-examine him.

The front page was taken up by a photograph of the scene, shot from such a distance that it was impossible to make out the details. The article was short on those too. Their deadline hit too early for them to use anything from the forthcoming press conference and all they had to go on was the statement released at lunchtime. It was neutral in tone and more tactful that he expected, no mention of a racial motive.

He reversed into the drive ready for a quick getaway and let himself into the kitchen through the back door. Milan was sitting at the long pine table bent over a colouring book, his pencils lined up neatly in front of him, bracketed by a rubber at one end and a sharpener at the other. He was concentrating on a picture of an oak tree, three different greens clutched in his right hand which he kept switching between as he did the leaves.

Zigic kissed the top of his head. 'Let me look at your teeth.'

Milan turned his face up and bared them in a wide grin.

'Was the dentist nice?'

'She gave me a lolly.'

'She didn't give me a lolly when I went.'

Milan considered it for a moment. 'Were you naughty?'

'I hadn't flossed,' Zigic said, taking a bottle of water from the fridge. 'Maybe that's why.'

'You can have mine.' Milan slipped out of his chair. 'I hid it so Stefan can't find it.'

He ran out of the kitchen and Zigic followed, hearing the vacuum cleaner going upstairs in the boys' room, the muffled thump of Stefan jumping up and down on his bed. Anna's voice cut sharply across the drone and the jumping stopped, followed a few seconds later by the vacuum.

Zigic went into the master bedroom and looked at his suits hanging in clear plastic protectors, pushed away and forgotten at the far end of the wardrobe. They stuck to civilian clothes in Hate Crimes, a command decision he'd made early on, aware of the kind of people they would be dealing with and the negative connotations provoked by anything that smacked of uniformed authority. That was the official line anyway. The truth was he just hated wearing one.

He picked out a narrow mid-grey suit, single-breasted, three-button, a white shirt and a dark blue tie. Changed his mind and switched it for a black one.

Anna came in as he was pulling on his trousers. She eyed the outfit on the bed.

'A blue tie would look better with that suit.' She fetched the one

65

he'd just put back and laid it against the jacket. 'It must be something important if you're dressing up.'

'Press conference at five,' he said. 'There was a hit-and-run on Lincoln Road this morning. Bad one. Two dead.'

'I saw the news. Why are you handling it?'

'Where it was, everyone assumed it was going to be racially motivated.' He shoved his feet into a pair of black brogues, squatted to tie them. 'Which it might still be. We're just not sure yet.'

Anna handed him his shirt and when he'd slipped his arms into it she began to button it up.

'And I thought you'd crept out to see me,' she said, a slight smile touching the corners of her mouth as she brought it close to his. 'We could lock the boys in the cupboard under the stairs so we're not disturbed . . .'

'Tempted, but I really haven't got time.'

'This is how it starts, you know? Middle age.' She knotted his tie and folded his collar back down over it, stepped back to admire her handiwork with that glint still in her eye. 'I forget how good you look in a suit. Very authoritative.'

He laughed. 'Seriously, I've got to go.'

'You get a girl started then you run off.'

He grabbed his jacket from the bed, kissed her quickly and bolted for the door before she stepped up her efforts. Milan was waiting for him in the kitchen, holding both hands behind his back, and he glanced around conspiratorially, checking Stefan wasn't watching before he produced an orange lolly in a plastic wrapper which was sticking ominously to the sweet.

'Thank you.'

'I only had a bit of it,' Milan said.

Zigic tucked the lolly into his breast pocket and shouted his goodbyes.

12

Fifteen minutes later he pulled into the station car park, struggled to find a space and eventually tucked in behind Ferreira's red Golf. Another news van had arrived, its side panel open while the crew hauled out their equipment to take upstairs. A couple of local print hacks he recognised were standing smoking on the steps, laughing over their war stories, and he walked in without acknowledging them, feeling the nerves stirring in his stomach.

Upstairs Wahlia was swearing at the vending machine in the hallway, squaring up to it like his gym-toned bulk would do any good. Ferreira shouted at him from the office, 'You want to hear what it said about your mum.'

Zigic tried to block them out, checked on Grieves and Parr, discovered nothing new had happened during his absence. He went to the murder board and looked at the scant progress they had made in the last ten hours, wishing he had something more significant to take to the Media Room with him.

He paced into his office and out again, poured a coffee he didn't drink and watched the comings and goings in the car park, thinking about Sofia Krasic lying to him from her hospital bed and whether she might have cost them the most important hours of the investigation by pushing her own agenda.

If Gilbert wasn't driving the car, if this wasn't about him and Jelena, then the person they were actually looking for could be long gone by now.

Then it was time and he was moving through the doors into a dull blue room full of cameras and lights and the babble of low chatter, rows of chairs lined up facing a long table with the force's logo on the wall behind it, more of the chairs occupied than not, a larger gathering than he'd ever had to face in here. He recognised a few of them, the ones in the front row, but beyond that they were indistinct, blurred by his nerves. Nearby he saw DCS Riggott standing talking to a veteran in a bad suit, the press officer peeling away from them, heading in his direction. Riggott patted the old guy on the back and followed.

The press officer shoved a sheet of paper into Zigic's hand and retreated, replaced at his elbow by Riggott who nudged him in the direction of the table.

The chatter subsided as they took their seats and Riggott cleared his throat noisily to silence them completely, moved the microphone in front of him a touch closer before he spoke, his usually abrasive Belfast accent tempered in deference to the occasion.

'Ladies and gentleman, thank you for coming this afternoon. I'd like to introduce Detective Inspector Dushan Zigic. Dushan is the senior investigating officer in this case. He will be giving a short statement, then we'll take your questions. Dushan?'

'Thank you. The inquiry into this morning's hit-and-run on Lincoln Road is now a murder investigation . . .'

The cameras snapped and he kept reading, hearing his voice coming out stronger than he expected, detailing the vehicle involved and the number of deaths and injuries. The statement was all padding and as he spoke he became aware of how many questions it left to be asked and that in few minutes those questions would be fired at him.

'Somebody out there holds vital information which can help us find the person responsible for this callous act,' Zigic said, lifting his eyes from the statement. 'And I would urge anyone who has any information about this crime to come forward and contact us. Thank you.'

Hands went up then across the room and the questions started.

'Why is this investigation being carried out by the Hate Crimes Department?'

Riggott jumped on that one. 'We do not currently believe this to be a racially motivated crime. DI Zigic's team is handling the investigation because they're familiar with the area and the particular challenges of carrying out an investigation there.'

'Do you believe the nationality of the victims may have motivated the driver?'

Riggott again, his voice hardening. 'There is absolutely no evidence to suggest that this was a racist attack.'

'Can you confirm that Jelena Krasic's boyfriend has been hospitalised with an overdose?'

How did they know that?

Zigic waited a beat, no answer from Riggott so he took it.

'A man we believe to have been involved with Ms Krasic is currently being treated for a suspected overdose, yes.'

'Is he a suspect?'

'At this stage in the investigation, I'm keeping an open mind,' Zigic said.

A young man with horn-rimmed glasses and folk singer's beard put his hand up.

Zigic pointed to him. 'Yes?'

'Alistair Whitman, *Independent*. Are you investigating potential links between today's hit-and-run and the recent murders in the area of Ali Manouf and the young Somali man known as Didi?'

A murmur passed around the room. Apparently the rest of them hadn't done their jobs quite so well as the young man now smirking at Zigic from the second row.

'There is absolutely no evidence to suggest a link between the crimes you've mentioned.'

'Have you made any progress at all with those murders, Detective Inspector Zigic?'

'We are here to discuss this morning's hit-and-run. If you have questions pertaining to any other investigations I suggest you direct them to our press officer, Ms Gilraye, at a more appropriate moment.'

Riggott intervened then, unable to fully smother the anger in his voice as he proceeded with the usual niceties.

'Thank you for coming this afternoon, ladies and gentlemen. If we have any further developments to report you will be informed through the usual channels. Thank you.'

DAY TWO

13

Nicola Gilraye was waiting for him when Zigic got into Hate Crimes, sitting on an empty desk with her feet on a chair, looking at the whiteboards where the murders of Ali Manouf and Didi had spread to their eventual dead ends, witness statements which added nothing, suspects identified and swiftly eliminated through unbreakable alibis or DNA.

There was a copy of the *Independent* on the table next to her. He knew she read the papers online, so it was just a prop brought along for effect.

She was big on effect and Zigic imagined that as a press officer style would always be more important than substance, which was why her suits were always precisely tailored and her make-up so well applied that you could only see the old acne scars along her jawline when you were a few inches away from her. At a distance she was television perfect, petite and blonde and very slightly plastic.

'I take it you've seen the *Independent* this morning.'

'Shame they're not as malleable as the locals.'

'Not quite as easy to get nationals' balls in your palm unfortunately.' A faint smile flitted across her face. 'But I think the best way to counter it for now would be a nice, friendly interview in tonight's *Telegraph* with one of the family members.'

'I don't know.'

'Ziggy, sweetheart, do I come in here telling you how to make some Kosovan cabbie ignore your war criminal surname? I wouldn't dream of it.' She slipped off the desk, heels clicking down onto the floor. 'You need time to work these cases, don't you? You cannot afford for people to start looking for a political angle in this yet. And believe me, when you've got your man I will have the press rain down their approval on you; you will be embarrassed by the love. But today you have a problem which is best solved by my putting a beautiful Slovenian girl on the front page of the evening paper.'

'Sofia Krasic?'

Gilraye nodded.

'She's still in hospital, you know,' Zigic said.

'That isn't necessarily a problem, is it? She got out of it with minor injuries I heard.'

'If she wants to talk to you . . . fine.'

'I thought Paul Naysmith might be the best person to speak to her,' Gilraye said. 'His balls are in my palm after all. It'll be half a page of entirely apolitical suffering. She speaks English, doesn't she?'

'She's been here years.'

'Not all of them do.'

Zigic swallowed his annoyance, knowing she was right, thinking of his grandparents, both here since the early fifties but you would take them for migrants straight off the bus if you spoke to them. A couple of months ago a man in the post office had barracked his grandmother for taking a pension she had no entitlement to, thinking she had only just come over, told her it was her fault his wife couldn't get a hip replacement. She gave him the benefit of her English then, every piece of bad language she'd picked up working in the local brickyard canteen.

'I need to talk to her this morning,' he said. 'I'll let you know when I'm done.'

'Be a sweetie and find me a decent picture of the sister,' Gilraye said, already dialling. 'Teeth are good, legs are better. *Dovidenja*.'

As the stairwell door came to a slow close behind her Zigic felt a sense of discomfort settle between his shoulder blades. It stayed there as he hung up his waxed cotton parka and opened the bank of windows in the east-facing wall, letting some fresh air blow in, clearing the noxious pine scent the cleaners had left behind them.

Last night, lying in bed unable to sleep, he had begun to wonder

74

if the hit-and-run even had a deliberate target. Was the driver just looking for a group of migrant workers to take out and they were simply unlucky enough to be standing at a point on Lincoln Road where he found it easy to accelerate and build up enough speed to do an impressive degree of damage?

It was a spectacle. An act guaranteed to attract attention from the press and prompt the inevitable debate about immigration in the city. If that was what the driver was trying to achieve he had done it. First item on the evening news last night, a brief mention on the BBC News Channel just before midnight, and this morning on page 11 of the *Independent*.

Zigic thought of the CCTV footage from their murders, the masked man dressed all in black, raising a stiff-armed salute to his intended audience, knowing exactly how they would react when they saw it. But they hadn't reacted. Not publicly at least. Five days on from Manouf's murder, four weeks from Didi's, the man was still a nobody, his agenda kept under wraps.

Would that be enough to provoke a change in tactics?

He put the coffee machine on and ate a Mars bar he found at the back of his desk drawer while he waited for it to brew.

Gilraye had left the paper behind her, folded open at the headline.

They'd told less than half the story but it was easy to be judgemental when all you had to do was produce five hundred words a day.

He poured a coffee and retreated to his office. The door had been left closed overnight and the small radiator under the window turned up high so that the room was stifling now and fusty-smelling, as if the heat had peeled all the old layers of sweat and smoke and body odour from the previous occupants off the walls.

There was a reason he rarely used the office but for now he wanted the privacy, even with the rest of the department empty. Soon they would start arriving, Ferreira and Wahlia coming in muffled by their inevitable hangovers, Grieves and Parr sparking from the promotion to a major investigation. Once they were all settled at their desks he would have to go out there and explain how they were going to find a man they had already spent the better part of a month trying to identify with no success.

He opened the case file on Didi's murder and began to reacquaint himself with the finer details, ashamed how much he had forgotten in a matter of four weeks, distracted by court appearances and other cases, less violent ones but solvable. Then Ali Manouf's murder five days ago.

It felt like longer, the first forty-eight hours stretched in his memory as they chased down witnesses from the cafe round the corner from the alley where Manouf was killed. Just after 1 a.m. on Sunday and the street was packed with people promenading between the bars, drinks in hand, hundreds of potential sightings of their killer but nobody saw anything. Too many bodies on the street for one more man to stand out.

He must have walked away calmly, they figured, rolled his balaclava back from his face so he blended in with the crowd.

They spoke to the people Manouf worked with, the other men who lived in the shared house on Taverners Road where he was dossing, waiting for an answer from Immigration about whether he would be deported. They were hoping for an argument, something easy to explain his death and allow them to break the potential link between him and Didi. But Ali Manouf was too placid for that, an educated man who had realised his new situation was best handled with politeness and self-containment.

Then the CCTV footage emerged and there was no more pretending this was an isolated incident.

Didi's murder inquiry was different. A mess of theories and conjecture complicated by the quarter-ounce of marijuana they found tucked away in his orange puffa jacket. If he was dealing around New England there was the turf element to consider, and they pulled in a dozen local dealers who claimed to know nothing about him, assumed the men were lying but couldn't prove it. Then the post-mortem revealed high levels of THC in his blood and hair, pointing to sustained use, a habit verified by his friends and funded, one of them finally admitted, by shoplifting.

The friends were coming into the frame when footage of the murder arrived.

He remembered Ferreira returning to the office with it, her tan skin paled by what she had just seen, a haunted look in her near-black eyes. And she left the room while Wahlia and he watched it, said she couldn't face it again, and he was surprised by her uncharacteristic squeamishness until Didi hit the pavement and the first boot strike crunched into his temple.

They were braced for it when similar footage emerged of Ali Manouf's murder and that experience at least yielded a lead. As the man stood over Manouf's body he lifted his balaclava, just a couple of inches, enough to free his mouth, and spat on him.

Forensics ran the DNA through the system, returned a blank. Ruling out most of the local neo-Nazis who would have headed their suspects list. The main players all had form of some sort and Zigic doubted anyone would be stupid enough to spit on a dead man if they were already to known to the police. That fact sprang up like a brick wall between them and the killer.

If he was part of a group, he was traceable. It would take persistence and ingenuity but they could get him. As a loner, he was far more dangerous.

Ferreira spent two days solid stalking the right-wing forums with a dedication bordering on obsession. She seemed disappointed by how little reaction the murders had provoked, commented that they were getting more careful what they discussed, that the language was changing, the moderators stepping in more often.

They were aiming for respectability, she said.

Zigic thought of the quote from Richard Shotton in today's *Independent*, a carefully weighted statement, no overt racism but it was there between the lines, couched in politicised terms which would appeal to the kind of disaffected, white working-class voters his English Patriot Party had convinced to turn out in great enough numbers to secure him a by-election win last November.

Zigic wondered how his well-oiled propaganda machine would cope when this case finally broke. The jackbooted origins of his party, which he was working so carefully to hide, marching back into the limelight.

A fist rapped on his door and Ferreira came in without waiting for a reply.

'You want a coffee?'

He lifted his mug. It was cold now. 'Actually, yeah. This is rank.'

Wahlia arrived a couple of minutes later, wearing the same black jeans and plaid shirt he'd left the office in last night, his usually immaculately styled hair fluffed up on one side and flat on the other, new blond highlights greasy-looking.

'Didn't this one own a hairbrush?' Ferreira asked. 'Or is that deliberate?'

'I'm working a new look.'

'You'll just do whatever *GQ* says, won't you?'

He slumped in his chair. 'I hate it when you're perky in the morning.'

They bickered on as Ferreira rolled a cigarette and Zigic did the decent thing, poured Wahlia the biggest mug of coffee he could find and put it in his hand, offered him the stash of Pro Plus he kept in his desk for emergencies. Wahlia waved it off, insisted he'd be fine as he booted up his computer.

'Have you seen this?' Ferreira was brandishing the newspaper Gilraye had left behind on her desk. 'Richard Shotton. They're going to Nick Griffin's prettier little sister for quotes now.'

She slapped the paper down and stomped over to the open window, lit her cigarette and took a furious drag which hollowed her cheeks.

'I would love this to be one of his people,' she said.

'I think Shotton's a little bit more careful than that,' Zigic pointed out.

'He's a piece of shit.'

'With a seat in Parliament.'

Parr trudged in with his tie askew and a spot of baby sick on his lapel, damped and scrubbed at but still there, flecked with white from the towel he'd tried to clean it with. He grunted a good morning and went to the desk he'd claimed near the window.

Grieves arrived ten minutes later, the last one in but she looked more alert than the rest of them put together, bright-eyed and smiling, ready for business in a navy-blue skirt suit. Zigic had told both of them civvies was fine but they were still operating under Riggott's rules and would take more deprogramming before they adjusted.

'Alright. So you'll have heard what happened at the press conference yesterday.'

Nods all round.

Zigic moved to stand in front of the whiteboards covering Ali Manouf's and Didi's murders, felt their dead eyes staring at the back of his head.

'And for the benefit of our recent arrivals there is, at present, nothing to suggest that the hit-and-run is connected to these men's deaths,' he said. 'That wasn't just bluster for the hacks, that's the truth. There is almost certainly a link between the murders though and we're working on the assumption that the same man is responsible.'

Grieves put her hand up.

'You don't have to do that, Deb. Go on.'

'Why do we think the same man's responsible?'

'CCTV footage. We can't see his face but the build's the same and his . . . actions after the crime are identical.'

'What actions?'

'He gives a Nazi salute,' Ferreira said.

She was watching Grieves closely when she spoke and Zigic wondered what she was looking for – shock, disgust, approval? Ferreira seemed to believe most English people were prejudiced, a

79

result of her upbringing he supposed, the racial abuse she'd suffered. He knew she'd had a tough time in uniform, where the prevailing attitude was white guys versus the world and a Lisbon-born graduate with a short fuse would have a target on her back.

Was there some lingering enmity between the two women? He was going to have to deal with that before it became a problem.

'Were the victims chosen at random then?' Grieves asked, turning subtly away from Ferreira. 'Wrong place, wrong time?'

'It appears that way,' Zigic said. 'They didn't know each other. We haven't been able to establish any links between them. So, yes, right now we're assuming they were attacked purely because of their ethnicity.'

'Were they asylum seekers?' Parr asked.

'Manouf was, Didi wasn't.'

Ferreira flicked her cigarette out of the window. 'You think it would have made a difference if they were?'

'No, ma'am.'

'They were attacked because they were alone at the time and they were vulnerable,' she said, her voice taking on a strident edge. 'These men have no family over here, no close friends and no support network. You look at them.' She gestured at the board. 'They're both short, thin, not the kind of blokes who can put up much of a fight. Our killer is looking for easy targets.'

Parr straightened in his chair. 'Because he's weak?'

'Because he's a pathetic coward and a bully who wants to inflict maximum damage with minimum risk to his person.'

'He is a highly dangerous individual,' Zigic said, tapping the whiteboard with his knuckles. There was a still from CCTV tacked up in the suspects column, worse than useless for ID purposes but it gave them something to focus on. 'There's footage of the murders if you need to be convinced but they don't make for pleasant viewing.'

Grieves and Parr looked at one another, just a quick glance.

'Our focus for today remains on the hit-and-run but I want to start a full review of the files on Didi's and Manouf's murders,' Zigic said, trying to inject some enthusiasm into his voice as he put his attention on Grieves and Parr. 'You two need to get up to speed this morning, don't do anything else, just absorb those case files. We're going to take the whole thing apart, right from the beginning. Somebody knows who this bastard is.'

14

They were clearing breakfast away on Ward 6 when Zigic went in and he noticed how many of the plates were being loaded back onto the trolley untouched, the plastic covers condensated and the cutlery still wrapped.

In a bay further along somebody was calling for a bedpan in an urgent tone. A nurse told them to go in the bed, they'd clean it up later.

Zigic knocked on the door to Sofia Krasic's room.

There was no reply.

He went in and found the bed empty. The blue waffle sheet was on the floor and the backless gown with it. He picked them up and put them on the chair.

An auxiliary nurse stuck her head round the door. 'She's gone, love.'

'Where? They can't have discharged her yet.'

The woman shrugged. 'Reckon she just left.

How had she walked out unchallenged? A bruised and battered woman with broken ribs and head trauma, the lone survivor of an incident even the overstretched doctors must have realised was suspicious.

Zigic went out through the double doors, along the dark corridors with their posters for cancer and tropical diseases, intermittent bursts of colour from the corporate artwork, prints of kittens and blown-up flowers which were somehow more depressing than the thought of rotting alive.

He swore at himself as he started the car, thinking he should have posted a guard outside her room. He pulled off the kerb and back into the traffic, the tail end of the morning rush hour clogging up the area around Bretton Centre, and with the roadworks on the parkway unmanned but seemingly permanent now, it took him fifteen minutes to get to Sofia's house. There were a couple of builders smoking outside the place opposite, watching a badly corroded skip being unloaded from its flatbed, and they eyed him as he got out of the car.

He knocked on the front door.

There was music playing inside and through the frosted-glass panel he saw the hall light burning, then a blurred figure coming towards the door.

Sofia Krasic looked smaller and more broken in her pyjamas than she had in the controlled surroundings of City Hospital, more like Jelena than he had noticed before. Their faces were almost identical, only the colouring different.

'What are you doing here?' he demanded, ushering her back into the house. 'How did you even get here?'

Sofia gestured vaguely towards the door. 'Work. I call. My boss, she come, bring clothes, take me home.'

'You need to be in hospital,' he said. 'You can't just leave. They need to take care of you.'

'I do not need care.'

She walked away from him, into the living room at the front of the house. On another day the room might have looked inviting, with the sheepskin rug in front of the electric fire and low cream armchairs stuffed with cushions, but the grief was heavy in the room, greying and dulling everything.

Sofia went back to the place on the sofa where she had set up a bank of pillows to keep her ribs at the most comfortable angle. There was a bottle of vodka between the cushions and Zigic got to the pills on the coffee table before Sofia could stop him.

'Co-codamol? You can't take these with alcohol.'

'Is safe. I take before.'

Zigic opened the packet, found six pills missing. A brief image of

Anthony Gilbert unconscious on his kitchen floor flashed in front of his eyes.

'Have you taken all of these?'

Sofia gave him a smile, sad and a little crooked. 'You think I try to kill myself?'

'How many of them have you taken?'

'Only one. They are strong pills.'

'You're still going to have to go back to the hospital.'

'I have to do nothing,' Sofia snapped. 'That place . . . they leave the old to die in their own filth. They would not let a dog be like that. The English, they are crazy, care more for animals than people.'

Zigic sat down in the armchair, elbows on his knees. 'Look, Sofia, your ribs are broken –'

'Only bruised,' she said, dragging a hot-water bottle out from underneath her and placing it on the left side of her torso. 'I have bruised before. Two, three days, I rest.'

'You might have internal bleeding.'

'You are doctor? No, you are not. You are police so do not tell me what I need.'

The phone in the hallway began to ring and Sofia stirred to answer it.

'Stay there, I'll get it.'

Zigic picked up the phone and a woman started speaking instantly, her accent too thick for him to penetrate. He went back to the living room and gave Sofia the handset.

She listened for a couple of seconds, her face darkening, then she pressed the phone to her shoulder and held the hot-water bottle out to Zigic.

'Would you fill please? From kettle. It must boil. Thank you.'

It was still hot but he took the cue and left the living room, went as far as the bottom of the stairs and listened to Sofia calling the woman Mama, faking brightness into her voice from somewhere.

She was speaking quickly, too quickly for Zigic to follow her perfectly, but he heard her say Jelena was well, she was working,

84

yes, she was at the farm also now, Sofia's voice beginning to thicken until she had to clear her throat, excusing it as a cold, nothing important. Her tone changed abruptly then and she said she would send no money. No more. The conversation was over ten seconds later.

'You hear this?' Sofia asked.

Zigic returned to the living room. 'If you don't tell her we will.'

'*You* will?' Sofia snatched the hot-water bottle. There were tears in her eyes and when she spoke he could see how hard she was fighting to maintain her composure. 'It is not your business to do this. You do not know this woman.'

'Your mother. Jelena's mother. She isn't just some woman.'

'Your mother is . . . domestic goddess, yes? Cook and clean and make beautiful home for her family?'

Zigic couldn't deny it.

'That woman . . .' Sofia glared at the phone. 'That woman you tell me is mother tried to sell Jelena for five hundred US dollars to soldiers in Belgrade. Jelena was eleven.'

Her words hung in the air for a few minutes while Zigic tried to think of a suitable reply, knowing there wasn't one.

Outside the skip slammed against the road and one of the men shouted to the driver. There was barracking and laughter, the sound of the cab door slamming. It was all so simple and banal and did nothing to block out the image in Zigic's mind of his own sister at eleven, still a child despite her long limbs and her clever mouth, being bartered over by men with blood on their hands.

'Jelena's papers say she was born in Ljubljana.'

'They are very good papers.'

'And what about you?'

'My papers are also very good.'

Sofia uncapped the bottle to take another long drink and he stopped himself commenting. Wouldn't he be doing the same thing in her position?

'If you're not going to go back to hospital you should have someone here with you. What about your boyfriend?'

'Tomas is in Poznań,' she said.

'There's nobody else?'

She looked at him and he felt immediately it had been a stupid thing to say.

'I am not so pathetic. My boss, she bring food later, check I am still alive.' She frowned at what she'd said, maybe realising afresh how close she'd come to death, and the fight bled out of her in front of his eyes, leaving her a small, hunched figure. 'Have you found the man who hit us?'

'You told us it was Anthony Gilbert. Jelena's ex.'

Sofia's frown deepened and for a moment she struggled to focus on him, blinked as if trying to clear her vision. 'Why would I say that?'

'You were very certain, Sofia. You said he was stalking Jelena.' Zigic watched her carefully for some small sign of recognition. 'We came to talk to you. Don't you remember?'

'No.' Her voice was little more than a whisper and she dropped her eyes to her bandaged wrist. 'It could not be Anthony. He loves Jelena.'

'That isn't what you said before.'

'Then I did not know what I was saying.' She gestured vaguely with her good hand. 'The medication . . .'

He thought of her straining in her hospital bed to make herself understood and even in the dimly lit room he had seen the effort it cost her, the words coming through gritted teeth, a film of sweat on her forehead.

They must have been the first words she spoke when she came round, telling a nurse to call them.

'We went to Anthony's house yesterday after I spoke to you and when we arrived we found him unconscious. He'd taken a massive overdose of painkillers.'

Her hand closed around the neck of the vodka bottle, twisting nervously.

'Is he dead?'

'He's in hospital. They have him in a medically induced coma right now, they're waiting to see how much damage the pills have done.'

She dropped her chin, but he still saw the relief on her face and the hint of pleasure the news had provoked.

'Why did you claim he was stalking Jelena?'

'I don't know. I don't remember.'

'So they were still together?'

She didn't answer, only tightened her grip on the bottle.

'This is very important, Sofia,' he said, trying and failing to catch her eye. 'Anthony attempted to kill himself and we need to know why he did that. If it's guilt-induced or if he was simply grieving over Jelena's death.'

Still no answer and and Zigic began to wonder how much she really knew about Jelena and Gilbert's relationship. Living in the same house, working together too, it would have been difficult for Jelena to speak privately to him on the phone – was that why they were using Facebook? Maintaining a dialogue Sofia couldn't eavesdrop on?

Maybe she genuinely believed Gilbert was stalking her sister. Wouldn't it have looked like that to her? All of those snatched, three-second phone calls, just long enough to say 'I love you'?

Then he thought of all the messages between them which mentioned her, painting Sofia like some overbearing mother who had to be appeased, slowly and patiently won round.

Was that why she accused him? Just hatred, deeply buried, burning through the pain. The medication jumbling her thoughts and loosening her tongue, releasing a subconscious fear she'd been harbouring for months, that Gilbert would hurt Jelena eventually, mixing that up with what had happened.

'Why don't you like Anthony?'

She shot him an angry look which pinched the skin around her dark green eyes. 'I know men like him. Big car, big mouth. I tell Jelena, you want some man to buy you? Use you until he is bored and throw you into the gutter?'

'But you just said he loved her.'

Sofia snorted. 'He loves to have a pretty young girl who does not see what he is.'

'And what is he?'

'He was not good enough for her,' Sofia said, with a certainty more maternal than sisterly, born of hard experience and edged with desperation. 'Look what he has done.'

'We don't know who was driving the car yet,' Zigic reminded her.

'He has killed himself, of course it was him. Why else would he do that?'

'He's still alive, Sofia.'

'No. He will die. He is a weak man.' Almost chanting it, like she could stop his heart with the sheer scale of her grief. 'He will not survive. He does not deserve to live.'

She got up and walked across the room, over to the mantelpiece with its half-burnt candles and gilded ikons.

'Did you know they were still in contact?'

'She told me they were not.' Sofia ran her fingertips across a hinged triptych. 'She was secretive. Always she hides things from me.'

'Did she know how much you hated him?'

'I only wanted what was best for her.'

She was replying but not actually answering his questions and he could see her swaying slightly, steadying herself against the mantelpiece, lost in her own thoughts.

'So you encouraged Jelena to break up with him?'

'She would have been happier without him,' Sofia said. 'I knew that. She should have trusted me.'

Zigic went to where she stood, the flat eyes of half a dozen Orthodox saints looking on impassively. 'She didn't break things off with him. They were in love, Sofia. Whether you approved or not. Anthony had absolutely no reason to do this.'

'And you have never hurt someone you love?' she asked, fingers jumping suddenly, knocking over the triptych, the sound echoing the remembered slap in Zigic's head, the sting on his cheek, pink eyes and jasmine perfume and a string of words he'd wanted to take back before he'd finished saying them. 'The people we love are the ones who hurt us most.'

Again he explained it, patiently, slowly, telling her about the conversations between them, the plans they were making for the future, right up until the night before Jelena died. No signs of friction, no motive.

'I understand why you accused him.' Zigic righted the fallen ikon. 'You were confused. You were angry. But it is *highly* unlikely that he's responsible for this.'

'You do not know what kind of man he is,' Sofia said.

He did. Better than her. He wasn't about to reveal Gilbert's long history of obsession and violence towards women though.

If Jelena had listened to Sofia and left him then it would be relevant. Gilbert's crimes were provoked by rejection, the pricking of his overinflated ego which couldn't accept that the women he wanted didn't want him. When that happened he turned on them and anyone else he perceived to be standing in his way.

The reassurance Zigic was preparing died on his lips.

Sofia was standing in his way.

Jelena hadn't dumped him but she was backing away, not seeing him as often, cooling things off to keep her sister happy. It was a softer kind of rejection but to someone like Gilbert it might be enough.

Was Sofia the real target?

Zigic tried to picture the scene, tried to dredge up the preliminary report forensics had sent over; where everyone was standing, the trajectory of the car as it cut across the traffic, speed building.

Early morning. Cold. People dressed in hooded tops and hats. Indistinguishable from one another. Jelena and Sofia who looked so alike . . .

He thought of Gilbert on the kitchen floor, the pills and vodka, too many for a gesture, the man wanted to end it and he'd almost succeeded. Ferreira had said it, half serious, maybe it was grief rather than guilt. He climbs out of the car, stunned by the airbag and the force of the impact, sees Sofia lying on the pavement, still alive.

Sees Jelena on the road, covered in blood, dead.

15

Every time Ferreira went into the centre of Peterborough there seemed to be more empty shops and as she came out of the car park near the city marketplace, heading towards Midgate, she noticed another window opaque with whitewash and found she couldn't remember what had been there.

The buildings were brutal grey monoliths, three and four storeys high, smoked-glass windows and crumbling concrete patched in lines which had never weathered back. She imagined you wouldn't open a business there unless you were on limited capital, maybe not expecting to see out more than two years' trading.

There were pop-up stores selling cheap clothes and pound shops all with the same plastic tat outside them, four different gold-cashing places which would have been based in council flats in Bretton a couple of years ago. Now they were respectable, or near enough, fences with business cards and backstreet accountants, legitimised by austerity.

She turned into the Wheelyard, a few morning drinkers sheltering under the budding cherry blossoms on the corner, then turned along a cobbled alleyway into the cathedral precincts, high stone walls rising above her, spackled with moss and noxious yellow lichen.

A loud woman with a Home Counties accent was leading a group of tourists across the cathedral green, men and women dressed in matching anoraks, almost indistinguishable from one another as they turned their faces up to the building's busy facade, holding cameras or snapping away with their phones. A couple of stragglers detached themselves from the back of the herd and slipped into the small cafe next to Pickman Nye, tempted by the chalkboard out front advertising cream teas, two for a tenner.

They didn't even glance at the dishevelled man standing nearby, clutching a handful of leaflets, holding one out hopefully to them. Ferreira took it from him as she walked passed, thanked him without looking at it, and only realised what it was as she climbed the short flight of stone steps to Pickman Nye's front entrance.

The leaflet was printed on cheap paper, the word 'missing' across the top in English, replicated smaller in another six languages. Underneath it was a photograph of a grey-haired man with coarse skin and a broken nose, badly healed years ago. A name and a phone number at the bottom.

It was so easy to fall off the radar, she thought, as she folded the leaflet and tucked it into her back pocket.

The reception desk was unmanned when she went inside and she rang the bell on the raised counter, heard it echo in the room beyond. They'd redecorated since the last time she was there, laid new brown carpet and added a fresh coat of white paint to the walls, which only reinforced the chilliness of the old stone building. They'd found space for a few more chairs but only two of them were occupied, a man in a tracksuit sitting with his young son, who rustled a bag of sweets and kicked his feet for something to do.

Ferreira remembered that feeling. She was about the same age as the boy the first time she walked into Pickman Nye. Back then this highly respectable employment agency, with its council contracts, was still a grey-area gangmasters squeezed into three small offices above a tanning salon on Cowgate, supplying farm-hands and factory workers at minimum wage, chiselling whatever they could off the top.

Her father dragged her there every day for a week. It was the middle of the summer holidays and the office was stifling, full of recent arrivals who'd been given the number back home and told there was all the work anyone could ask for waiting in Peterborough.

Her father was told the same thing but the job he'd been promised only lasted a month, ended abruptly by a fight with the Polish charge-hand which had cost him two back teeth and a large chunk of pride. She heard her parents arguing about it at night. They left the caravan to do their shouting but they wouldn't stray far with the kids 'asleep' inside, the four of them top and tail in two single beds. The money was running out and her mother's wages weren't enough to keep the roof over their heads and feed them too.

So every morning they took the bus from Spalding, eating into their dwindling reserves, and every morning the hatchet-faced bitch behind the desk said she had nothing for him. Her father was stubborn though, and he waited, made her wait too, watching other men come in and ask the same question only to get a different answer. The woman led them into another office and they came out smiling with directions to their new jobs.

It took Ferreira four days to figure out what was going on. She wandered off to look for the toilet and saw the woman take a carrier bag from one of the men, the hard edges of cigarette cartons showing through the plastic before she dropped them into a filing cabinet. When she explained to her father he ruffled her hair, told her she would be a spy when she grew up.

The next day he spent the last of their cash on one hundred Silk Cut and the woman miraculously found him a six-month contract at a pork processing plant.

She was a philanthropist now, Mrs Pickman, supporting local arts charities and buying incubators for the special care unit at City Hospital, trying to wash the filth off her money.

The little boy said something to his father and the man shushed him gently, drew him into a brief hug then pinched a chocolate button out of his bag and winked as the boy protested. He should have been in school but Ferreira knew a lot of recent arrivals were having trouble placing their kids. The local primaries were overstretched, hadn't been able to adapt quickly enough to the city's changing demographics.

She rang the bell again and as the tone faded a dark-haired man with bleached teeth and a spray tan that clashed badly with his

93

purple shirt came out of the door behind reception, carrying a stack of files he slapped down on the desk. She eyed his name badge – Euan – as she flashed her warrant card.

'We were expecting a call from you yesterday.'

'Something you want to tell me?'

'No, I only meant, well, they were our people.' The files began to slip and he caught them just in time. 'Mrs Pickman is absolutely beside herself. She told me to send flowers. White lilies, very nice.'

Several thousand employees, each pimped out at a margin of two pounds an hour. They could afford to send an ostentatious arrangement, pop a condolence note on headed paper and add it to the shrine at the bus shelter Ferreira had seen this morning on her way in. It was cheap advertising. Showed they cared.

She took her mobile out the back pocket of her jeans.

'I need you to take a look at something for me.' She swiped through menus. 'Just to warn you, it isn't pretty.'

Euan leaned across the reception desk, propped his elbows on the chest-height section of the counter, already trying to get a look at the screen.

'We're having trouble identifying one of the men who died,' Ferreira said. She found the photograph she had taken yesterday afternoon at the mortuary. He looked worse than she remembered, the stark white light and the camera's resolution picking out every pore, every bristle, each small tear in his weathered skin. 'Do you recognise him?'

'Bloody hell.' He took her phone, studied it for a few seconds with an expression that went from shock to repulsion to curiosity. 'No, I don't think he's one of ours.'

'But Sofia and Jelena Krasic were?'

'Yes.'

'He was waiting for collection with the rest of them though,' Ferreira said. 'He must have been going to Boxwood Farm. Could you check the staff lists, please?'

'I'll check,' he said, handing her phone back, 'but I'm positive he wasn't working there.'

'You've got thousands of employees. Don't tell me you remember every face.'

'I don't. But I know everyone who works at Boxwood.' He tapped away at the keyboard, eyes on the screen. 'They're very particular about the kind of staff they want so I deal with them personally. And he definitely wasn't working there. But . . . here we go.'

He turned the computer screen round so she could see it. A long list of names on the left, most in black but two of them were highlighted, Sofia and Jelena Krasic, times on the right, eight-digit codes 'for official use only'.

'This is this morning's shift rota from Boxwood Farm,' Euan said. 'See, they punch in and the system sends the details straight back to us so we can arrange payments. Everyone present and correct apart from – well – you know.'

'Could he have been waiting for a pickup to another job?' Ferreira asked.

'He could have been waiting for a bus.'

The telephone began to ring and he excused himself to answer it, spoke to the person on the other end in halting Polish. She thought it was Polish anyway, picked out a couple of words she recognised. Across the room the little boy had curled up with his head in his father's lap, tucked his trainers under his chair before he put his feet up.

Euan put the phone down. 'Sorry about that.'

'Is there anyone else who might have dealt with this man?'

'Angie, maybe. She's up in Accounting – shall I fetch her?'

'Thanks.'

He disappeared back through the heavy oak-panelled door marked 'Staff Only' and Ferreira dialled Zigic's number, waiting five rings before she got an answer.

'Are you still with Sofia Krasic?'

'Just left.' She heard the remote locks pop on his car. 'She thinks Gilbert was trying to hit *her* now.'

'Risky manoeuvre,' Ferreira said. 'Look, I'm not getting anywhere here. They claim not to recognise our mystery man. Can you ask Sofia? He pushed her out of the way of the car, he must have known her to do that.'

The remote locks shot again. 'Alright.'

Euan returned as she finished the call, trailing a well-built woman with chemically straightened black hair and fibreglass nail tips the colour of dried blood. She launched into the same display of sympathy Euan had spouted and looked like she might throw up when Ferreira showed her the photograph of the dead man. She considered it for a couple of seconds, asked, 'Why do they tape their eyes?' Then said she didn't recognise him either.

Ferreira thanked them for their time and left with the sensation that she'd missed something, heard Euan finally call the waiting man over as the door swung slowly to behind her.

She walked back through the narrow, stone-walled precincts, the cathedral bells ringing out, chiming the half-hour, and as she climbed into her car Zigic called back.

'She didn't know him either. It was the first time she'd seen him at the pickup.'

'Maybe he was waiting for a bus then.'

'With no wallet on him?'

'I'll get on to it,' Ferreira said.

She beat Zigic back to Thorpe Wood Station and went straight up to forensics. She found Kate Jenkins talking to a detective sergeant from CID, both of them standing at one of the long stainless-steel tables which dominated the lab, a set of bloodstained overalls laid out under the searing white lights, the fabric ripped by the telltale marks of shotgun spray.

She hadn't heard anything about a shooting but little of what happened in CID percolated up to Hate Crimes, even though they were under the same command. Hate Crimes was a small, insular department and that was partly why she liked working in it. There was no points scoring, no cliques, and Zigic maintained only the vaguest kind of hierarchy. It was as close to a democracy as you'd find in a police station.

The DS was complaining about Riggott, his face flushed from a recent dressing-down, and Jenkins made sympathetic noises, already moving along the table, their real business finished, Ferreira guessed.

'Mel, I was coming down to you lot in a minute,' Jenkins said.

The DS took the hint and made himself scarce, trudged out of the room with his hands shoved in his pockets, one of his shoes squeaking against the lino all the way to the stairwell door.

'God, that man.' Jenkins rolled her eyes. 'He comes up here, bloody whining about nothing and expects me to listen to it, doesn't even ask how I am.'

Ferreira smiled. 'So, how are you, Kate?'

'Can't complain.'

'What've you got for us?'

'Nothing new, I just wanted to get him to leave.' Jenkins leaned against the counter, glanced at her assistant who was taking swabs from a collection of discarded Coke cans, running a cotton bud along the rim, trying to recover some usable DNA. 'I sent my preliminary report down to Bobby about half an hour ago if that's what you're after.'

'I'm looking for personal effects,' Ferreira said. 'We've got an unidentified victim and all the hospital could give me was a house key and a broken mobile. We're missing his wallet.'

'I might be able to help you there.' She went over to a set of shelves lined with clear plastic storage boxes, pulled one out and brought it back to the counter. 'This was snagged under the car – I haven't got around to looking through it yet. Grab some gloves.'

Ferreira found a box of them and wriggled her fingers into a pair, watching Jenkins slip her own on effortlessly.

She peeled the lid off and removed a red-and-black rucksack with a broken strap, its gauze front panel shredded. The zip was still working though and Jenkins began to empty the contents across the counter; a pair of jeans and a couple of T-shirts, smelling worn but not quite dirty, bundled socks and underwear.

'This doesn't look like he was on his way to work,' Ferreira said.

'Looks like he didn't need to work,' Jenkins said, bringing out a bundle of crumpled notes held together with an elastic band. She flicked through it. 'There's a couple of thousand pounds here.'

'Any sign of a wallet? Paperwork?'

'Bus ticket.'

She handed it over.

'He was heading for Łódź,' Ferreira said. 'Why was he waiting for a bus into the city centre? It would have been quicker to walk to the collection point from there.'

Jenkins ran her hand around the inside of the bag, opened a second, small compartment and found a washbag, nothing unexpected in there.

'That's it.' Jenkins frowned over the man's belongings. 'Why wouldn't he have a wallet?'

'It must have been stolen at the scene,' Ferreira said, thinking of the men who had given chase as the driver bolted along Green Lane, and the ones who didn't, who'd gone to tend to the injured. Any of them could have lifted it in the confusion. 'Fucking jackals.'

'I'll run his samples through the system,' Jenkins said. 'See if he's known.'

'Thanks, Kate.'

In Hate Crimes Grieves and Parr were standing in front of Ali Manouf's board, talking in undertones, their faces drawn into expressions of fixed concentration. Parr had a file open across his forearm and Ferreira could see the lurid red splash of a crime-scene photo on the top.

They wouldn't find any answers there, she thought.

Zigic was under pressure though and this was about being seen to have tried more than making genuine progress.

She found the CCTV footage from the hit-and-run, picked the camera on Lincoln Road opposite the bus stop and saw the group standing waiting for their ride. Sofia Krasic was a few feet away from the unidentified man, who was turned away from her, checking the timetable screwed to the Perspex wall.

She went back, saw him arrive in shot from the north and switched cameras again, kept switching as she caught him passing other groups waiting for other drivers, walking with his shoulders rounded and his head down, always a straight line, never moving for people coming towards him, letting them get out of his way.

Zigic came up behind her and watched what she was doing without commenting. She switched cameras again, lost him, went back, tried another one. Couldn't find him.

'Oxford Road then,' Zigic said, patting her on the shoulder. 'Let's go knock on some doors.'

16

The top end of Oxford Road was dominated by commercial properties, a double-fronted Ladbrokes doing brisk trade, a carpet place
with a cluttered lot, a dingy Internet cafe next to a closed-down
accountant's with a steel roller shutter locked over its front entrance.
The houses were 1930s semis, all with the same terracotta roofs,
and as they started knocking on doors Zigic noticed how many of
them were occupied by small businesses, plaques screwed up on
front walls for gardening services and bespoke wedding cakes and
Chinese medicine practitioners.

More people were home than he expected and they divided up
the street, him on the left, Ferreira on the right, both using the
same careful introduction, a flash of the warrant card followed by
an apology for what the person was about to be shown.

Reactions to the dead man's photograph varied from shock to
prurient glee but most people shook their heads sadly, said how
terrible it was. A few of them had heard the accident, the crash
site was less than two hundred yards away, and several said they
couldn't believe it would happen somewhere like this. It was a
nice area.

Zigic guessed a typical English person wouldn't call it that, but
just off Lincoln Road there weren't many English to complain about
the ethnic mix on the street.

It was decent though and that was part of the problem. If it was
blighted by crime there would be CCTV cameras up and they would
have been able to follow their unidentified dead man back to his
home.

He walked past a semi-derelict garage with metal posts set in its forecourt to deter parking or ramraiders and knocked on the door of the neighbouring bungalow. The paint was flaking on the windows and thick, sun-yellowed net curtains blocked his view of the interior, but he could hear children inside, cartoons playing loud enough that he recognised the voices.

A harried-looking Indian woman opened the door a few inches, holding back a curious little boy with her leg.

'I've got plenty of tea towels,' she said, her accent pure Peterborough. 'I don't want new windows or my trees cutting down or whatever it is you're selling.'

Zigic showed her his warrant card and her brows drew together.

'You're that one off the news.'

'Yes, ma'am.' He smiled at the boy, who was clinging to the woman's leg now, his thumb in his mouth. 'This isn't going to be suitable for little ears.'

She shooed the boy away and her body filled the gap in the door.

'I didn't see anything,' she said. 'Not that time of morning.'

'We're trying to identify the man who was killed,' Zigic told her. 'We believe he lived on this road but he didn't have any ID on him.'

'There's a lot of comings and goings here.' She nodded across the street. 'There's been three different lots in that house since the beginning of the year.'

'You should brace yourself,' Zigic said. 'We only have a post-mortem photograph.'

She took it from him, frowned.

'Poor man.'

'Do you recognise him?'

'I don't know him but I've seen him on the street, coming home from work or what have you. He lives further up that way.' She handed the photograph back. 'Sorry I can't help you more.'

'You've been very helpful. Thank you.'

He turned away as she closed the door and looked along the street. There were only another twenty houses to go but beyond the T-junction was Alexandra Road and if the man used this as a short cut onto Lincoln Road that was a hundred more doors to knock on. He'd have to call into the station for some uniforms.

He wanted to find out where the man was living today, felt they needed to make some progress.

Ferreira was a few houses ahead of him now, talking to a woman in a short, silky robe and the kind of stacked red heels he always associated with strippers. Or maybe it was because the woman was dressed like that in the middle of the day.

There were suburban brothels scattered throughout the city, in semi-detatched houses just like these, no different to their neighbours at first glance, neat and tidy, and the only thing which marked them out was the curtains which stayed closed all day and the men who came and went at regular intervals.

The woman tottered out onto the driveway, pointed across the fence between the houses and Ferreira went up on tiptoes to look.

From the road Zigic could see the place clearly, a single-storey brick building the size of a double garage, tight on the rear boundary of the neighbouring house. It looked newly constructed, probably without planning permission like so many of the recently erected outbuildings in the area, or if it did have planning permission it would have been called a workshop or a studio, anything to explain why it needed running water and electric. But it was living accommodation, no doubt about it.

The woman went back inside and Ferreira was smiling slightly when she met him on the path.

'His name was Pyotr,' she said. 'At least that's what he told her.'

'This was a professional relationship I take it?'

'Couple of times a week for the last six months,' Ferreira said, as they started up the gravel driveway. 'He was Polish, same as her. From Łódź. She said he was going home for a few days to see his family, which explains why he had so much cash on him I guess.'

'But he was coming back?' Zigic asked.

'He told her he was.'

They walked down the side of the house, bins lined up against

102

the wall and a lot of empties in the glass recycling. The back garden was just a square of grass in need of cutting and a small grey-slabbed patio with some ancient plastic furniture on it. A couple of bikes were leaning against the fence, so somebody was home, and as they approached the outbuilding the back door of the house opened.

A rangy young man in a black tracksuit strode over to them, his body set ready for aggression.

'*Kim jesteś?*'

'*Policja,*' Zigic said, showing his identification. 'Do you speak English?'

'Yes, sir.'

'What's your name?'

'Adrian,' the man said, looking from Zigic to Ferreira. 'Adrian Mazur.'

'Do you know the man who lives here?'

'Pyotr, yes. He has gone home.'

Zigic brought out the photograph. 'Is this him?'

Mazur barely flinched. 'Yes, this is Pyotr. How is he dead?'

'He was hit by a car yesterday. On Lincoln Road. Do you know his last name?'

'No. We are not friends. Only neighbours.'

Zigic put the photograph away. 'I need to speak to your landlord, we're trying to find Pyotr's family, to let them know the bad news.'

'I have here.' Mazur took his mobile phone out of his pocket and recited the number. 'He was good neighbour. No trouble.'

Zigic thanked him for his help and he returned to the house. A couple of seconds later his face appeared in the kitchen window, watching them as Ferreira unlocked the narrow door with the key they had recovered from Pyotr's belongings.

Zigic went in first, found the light switch, receiving a small electric shock as he turned it on.

He swore and rubbed the stung tip of his finger.

It was a single room, twelve by fifteen, lit by a lone bulb in a round paper shade. The walls were painted off-white, the floor covered in a cheap, bright blue carpet so thin he could feel the uninsulated concrete beneath it. In one corner was a kind of kitchen area – two double cupboards, a small round sink and a hotplate. In the opposite corner was a shower cubicle and toilet which could be screened with a curtain but wasn't right then. There was a single bed pushed against the rear wall, a stack of newspapers on the floor and a well-worn rug placed to put your feet on when you swung them out first thing in the morning. An ancient portable TV sat on an upturned crate next to the bed, a couple of paperbacks on top of it.

The air in the room was several degrees colder than outside and the smell of damp so strong Zigic was surprised there wasn't mould climbing the walls.

'It's like a cell,' Ferreira said, picking up one of the books. The spine was cracked, the cover bent. She threw it on the bed. 'What are we looking for?'

'Anything with a name on it,' Zigic said.

Ferreira checked under the bed, lifting the mattress and tossing the sheets, while he searched the kitchen cupboards. There were more cleaning products than he expected, and while the tins and jars of food were unbranded Pyotr had bought expensive multi-surface cleaners and extra strong bleach.

The room didn't smell particularly clean though. Not even a hint of the products in the air and when he looked in the kitchen sink he found it was grubby, the toilet too, urine-stained and coated with limescale from the area's hard water. The shower was cleaner but far from sparkling.

'There's nothing here,' Ferreira said. 'The landlord's going to be our best bet.'

They locked up again and Zigic dialled the number he'd been given as they walked back to the car parked at the top of the road. A woman answered. 'Best Lets, how can I help you?'

He gave her the address, didn't go into details but told her it was a matter of urgency. She said she'd call back in a few minutes.

'Have you noticed?' Ferreira asked.

'What?'

She pointed to a rough square of black spray on the wall of a motorbike showroom.

'No, I don't get it,' Zigic said.

'That was EPP graffiti a couple of weeks ago. Now I'm pretty sure the council don't deal with it by sending out a guy with a paint can, so who's done that?'

'The people who own the shop probably.'

'It's not the only one though,' she said, shoving her hands into the pockets of her cropped leather jacket. 'There's another up near the Triangle that's been blacked out, and one outside that halal butcher's round the corner.'

'I didn't realise you were a spotter.'

She shrugged. 'I notice these things. There isn't the new stuff around either.'

Zigic unlocked the car and they climbed in, Ferreira reaching for the heat controls as he started the engine, turning it up full blast in the footwell.

'I think it's them, you know.'

'Them who?'

'The EPP.'

'Why would they do that?' he asked.

'Bad PR maybe, having your name sprayed on walls,' she said, an acidic edge to her voice. 'Especially walls which are within spitting distance of a racially motivated murder.'

'That halal butcher's?'

She nodded. 'It was painted out before Manouf was killed, but still, you have to wonder if there isn't some significance to it.'

'I hate what the EPP stands for just as much as you do, Mel, but they're a political party, not a vigilante group.' He indicated and overtook a wobbling cyclist with a DVD player balanced on his handlebars. 'They wouldn't get involved with something like that with an election coming up.'

'The people in charge might not but what's their membership made up of? Thugs and cranks. When we find this piece of shit he's going to be a member of one of their arsehole offshoots.'

'This is about Ken Poulter, isn't it?'

'That alibi was bullshit and we both know it.'

'DNA ruled him out,' Zigic reminded her.

But he remembered the way Poulter grinned when they showed him the photograph of Didi's obliterated head, how genuinely impressed he looked by the damage, aiming his amusement directly at Ferreira, trying to get a reaction she barely managed to stifle. She left the interview room convinced of his guilt, but even before the DNA tests cleared him Zigic realised he was innocent.

Poulter was a coward, a football hooligan who'd drifted into neo-Nazism when the FA and police started cracking down on him and his ilk, those who needed the weekly violence and sense of belonging which came from standing in a gang of drunken, baying idiots.

Zigic's mobile rang and he asked Ferreira to get it as he negotiated the roundabout in front of Queensgate shopping centre, where an old red double-decker was straddling two lanes, provoking punched horns and hand gestures.

'Can you send over everything you've got for him?' Ferreira asked. A pause as she waited. 'We're trying to contact Mr Dymek's next of kin, but if you want us to come down there with a warrant we can. Maybe we could bring someone from the council with us and see how many of those slums you're renting come up to legal standards too . . . No, that's what I thought.' She turned to Zigic and grinned, gave the woman an email address and thanked her for being so very, very helpful.

'The wonders of shotgun diplomacy,' he said.

'Only kind that gets the job done.'

17

This was the England they were fighting for, Shotton thought, as he walked through the George Hotel's lounge; the stone walls and the mullion windows, a fire crackling in the inglenook. Middle-aged, middle-class couples held muted conversations on the velvet armchairs and leather sofas, all fine, upstanding folk; good jobs worked at assiduously for years, kids gone off to uni and lives of their own. Now all they had to do was come for afternoon tea and flip through the complimentary newspapers, content that they would leave the world no worse than they found it.

They were his people and they had finally started to accept it.

Unfortunately this particular parcel of Middle England lay outside his constituency but the candidate they were fielding would serve them well he was sure. A formidable woman of distinctly Marine Le Pen-ish bearing, educated at the local girls' school, married to a landowner who could trace his roots here right back to Domesday, prime parlimentary material with nary a skeleton in her closet.

An elderly gent in a pair of garish red trousers swerved into Shotton's path, gripping a gin and tonic in his left hand, offering his right to be shook.

'Excellent job you did on Jon Snow.'

Shotton smiled. 'Ah well, he isn't the force of nature he used to be.'

The man was still pumping his hand, grinning. 'He's got too used to those pasty-faced London liberals. Doesn't know how to deal with a real political beast any more.'

'Not sure I could claim to be that,' Shotton said, disengaging from the man's grip. 'I wouldn't have liked to tackle Robin Day at his peak.'

'Are you not in the House today?' the man asked, adopting a wordly tone.

'Constituency matters,' Shotton said. 'That's far more important.'

The man raised his glass a touch and winked. 'Absolutely. We're the ones who put you in power after all.'

Shotton nodded as genially as he could and headed into the back bar, where the person who'd actually put him in power was waiting, suited but shambolic as ever, with his slightly too long hair and his greasy-looking designer stubble.

Walter was a man who could only take power by proxy, too many dodgy deals and expensive bastards in his past to ever stand for office.

Shotton ordered a Scotch from a passing waitress then joined him at a table in the corner, only the most perfunctory of niceties before they got down to business.

'I'm hearing worrying things, Dick. If these murders turn out to be one of your foot soldiers getting out of line you can forget the whole deal.'

'They are not my anything,' Shotton said.

Walter shuffled forward in his seat, lowered his voice but upped the menace. 'I distinctly remember sitting in this very spot twelve months ago, listening to you explain how you were the only man who could keep the peace long enough to get elected.'

'Which I did.'

'By-elections are dry runs,' Walter said. 'We both know that. You got in on a protest vote and if you want to make the position permanent you'd better get your house in order up here.'

Shotton began to protest but stopped as the waitress came over with a tray balanced on her palm, squatted to place his drink on the low table between him and Walter.

He waited for her to retreat, said, 'It's the dead girl's boyfriend.

Nothing for us to worry about. The police are waiting to question him and then this will all go away.'

'Not the fucking hit-and-run,' Walter said. 'Do you think I'm worried about that?'

'I think you worry about everything.'

Walter pulled a newspaper out from the side of his chair, opened and refolded to an inside page. He shoved it at Shotton. 'This is what's going to kill your re-election campaign, Dick.'

Page 11, photographs of two men dominating, some young black lad and an Arab with a sparse grey beard and heavy eyes.

'Third paragraph,' Walter said.

Shotton followed his prompt. *A confidential source within the English Nationalist League revealed that a dozen of their members have been questioned by police and released without charge during the last two weeks, but as yet no arrests have been made.*

'Released without charge,' Shotton said, tossing the paper onto the glass-topped table. 'They're just rounding up the usual suspects so it looks like they're doing something.'

'And what happens when they drag the right one in there?'

'I'm not sure how much clearer I can be on this matter, Walter.' Shotton felt his hand curl into a fist and brought it down slowly on the arm of the wing chair. 'The groups you're concerned with are not going to make waves for us. I have assurances of that. Whatever else you might think about these men they want what we want and they realise that I am their best chance to get it.'

'Rational types, are they?' Walter said, not hiding his disgust. 'You think they're cognisant of the political process at kicking-out time when they're full of lager and some black kid gives them a dirty look?'

Shotton smiled thinly. 'If you were a little better informed you'd realise that that "black kid" was murdered in Little Poland. Not many bovver boys round there at kicking-out time.'

'And yet it's being handled by the Hate Crimes Department,' Walter said. 'Why do you imagine that is?'

'I have it on very good authority that they handle most crimes with an . . . ethnic dimension, shall we say?' Shotton picked up his drink; too much ice in it. 'That bloody Alistair Whitman. Did you read the piece he wrote about me last month?'

'I read everything that's written about my investments, Dick.'

Shotton took a long drink, swallowing the annoyance along with it and the urge to tell Walter to shove his money up his arse.

Noises were being made. As yet little more than insinuations, but he knew there were dozens of potential defectors among the Tory ranks who were sitting back and waiting for a solid result before switching allegiance. Men who could buy and sell Walter out of their petty cash.

There was still the small matter of the election though, and even if he wouldn't admit it, he was becoming increasingly concerned that the murders in Peterborough would turn out to be the work of some splinter group he hadn't negotiated a ceasefire with yet. Or worse, a lone nutter none of them were aware of, seething in his spare bedroom and practising his salutes in the bathroom mirror.

His conversation with Ken Poulter yesterday had done nothing to calm his fears either.

He admitted he'd been pulled in by the police for questioning, let go the next morning having told them nothing. It was natural, Shotton supposed, with him being the ENL's top man, but he didn't like Poulter's cocky tone as he recounted the interview. Like he'd fed them a line and they'd bought it. Meaning there was something still to be found.

Not his own guilt but somebody else's perhaps.

'You need to deal with this,' Walter said, leaning across the table. 'Whatever it takes, you make sure this doesn't impact on us.'

Before Shotton could reply he stood up, conversation over. They shook hands and Walter walked out of the room, leaving the bill unpaid.

Shotton sat for a moment with the subdued conversations murmuring around him, noticed a woman on a nearby table staring like she recognised him but wasn't sure where from.

He took a twenty-pound note out and pinned it under his glass, eyes on the newspaper Walter had left behind as he tucked his wallet away again, thinking of all the money he'd handed over already, the peace promised to him in return. It was a gamble, he knew that as he gave it away, but it looked like a sound one. The ENL and their imitators were never a serious threat and the money was nothing more than a sweetener, designed to stop the marches for six months, keep the graffiti and the posturing to a minimum, make sure nobody gave statements to the press.

'Hold off on the murders for a bit' was not a condition. He thought it went without saying. Especially as they'd done nothing more serious than shout and rage for years.

Shotton walked out through the courtyard, through the deep stone archway, into the car park, where a couple of smokers were exiled.

He knocked on the driver's side window of the Range Rover, startling Selby and Christian, who were bent over something on Christian's mobile phone, both of them laughing, and gestured for Selby to get out. This was not a conversation to be had in front of a former copper with friends in the force.

Selby stepped down and slammed the door.

'Problem, boss?'

'Have you got a light?'

Selby checked his pockets until he came up with a chunky gold Zippo, handed it to Shotton while he dug out his own cigarettes.

They walked away from the vehicle, finding a sheltered spot against the car park's high stone wall, the sound of a train coming into Stamford station, a flock of geese honking as they banked around to land on the meadow twenty yards away.

Shotton took a drag on his cigarette, watching Selby shuffling on the spot, cold in his ill-fitting black suit which was too thin for the weather.

'Marshall wants me to let you go.'

Selby froze with his cigarette halfway to his mouth, thought for a second, then nodded.

'He doesn't like me much. Never hid it.'

'He doesn't have any issue with you,' Shotton said. 'It's your friends he's concerned about.'

'Didn't know he knew them.'

'Your ENL friends.'

Selby stayed silent. He was that type of man, never spoke unless he had something to say. An old-school stoic. It was what Shotton liked about him.

'Have you heard anything about them being pulled in by the police?'

'Over the murders you mean? Few of them, yeah.'

'And what's the situation?'

Selby shrugged, punched his free hand into his trouser pocket. 'Last I heard they were all released. The police have got nothing. Threw their weight around a fair bit, tried to get the lads to turn on each other. The usual.'

'Are they behind it?'

Selby rocked where he stood, flexed his toes inside his spit-shined brogues. 'Not that I know. Hardly the sort of thing you'd brag about down the pub, is it?'

'If you were among friends you might,' Shotton said. 'Have any of the lads spoken to you?'

'I hear things,' Selby said, glancing away towards the Range Rover, sunlight obscuring the interior, but Shotton noticed Christian had lowered his window. 'Some of them aren't too happy about the direction Poulter's taking the group in since he came out of the nick.'

'Gone soft, has he?'

Selby shook his head. 'He's got a sight worse from what I hear. Reckon he was knocked about by the Muzzis inside, he's wanting more direct action now. Fuck the softly-softly approach.'

It was different to what Poulter had said when he'd taken his money but Shotton remembered how his eyes had widened at the stack of crisp twenty-pound notes. Honesty tended to depart quite swiftly in those situations.

112

Maybe Selby was lying though. He had good reason to put the knife into Poulter. He walks out of HMP Littlehey on the Monday and by Friday he's back in charge of the ENL, a hastily arranged poll of the members unceremoniously dumping Selby's brother from the head job.

Poulter was unquestionably a thug. No vision, no strategic capability. He probably didn't even know where he wanted to be in five years' time, let alone what he wanted for the ENL. Beyond the usual drunken rabble-rousing and ethnic-baiting.

'What's Poulter got in mind, then?' Shotton asked. 'Direct action wise.'

Selby shrugged. 'Now that kind of talk doesn't make it outside his inner circle.'

'But the others must be wondering why things have quietened down when Poulter wants to kick off?'

'There's talk,' Selby said. 'The young boys reckon Poulter's behind the murders but they're blood-hungry, they latch onto anything like that.'

'Not an unreasonable assumption, considering his recent stay at Her Majesty's.'

'He wouldn't do it himself,' Selby said, flicking his cigarette away into a puddle, where it landed with the barest fizzle. 'Not at his age and not after he's just done fifteen years. From what I hear he's the first one the police had in. He's an idiot but he's not that stupid.'

'Who would he use?'

'He won't tell me.' Selby looked away, tracking the progress of a middle-aged Indian couple walking out of the George's courtyard to their car, a faint hint of disgust at his mouth. 'It'd have to be someone he trusts though.'

Shotton pitched his own cigarette away, into the same puddle. 'Ask around, discreetly, see who's making a lot of noise. Or not enough.'

Selby stared at him, determined-looking. 'And what if I get a name?'

'You'd like to see the back of Mr Poulter, I assume.' Shotton smiled. 'There really is no place for his kind in the movement any more. Best he's removed from the field, clear the way for someone better suited to the job. Don't you think?'

18

The email from Best Lets was waiting for Zigic when he returned
to his office and he opened up the attachment to find a rental agreement which showed Pyotr Dymek had been living at the unit on
Oxford Road for almost eighteen months, always paid up on time,
had another six months to run on his contract. There were references from the two places he had stayed before, showing that he'd
been in Peterborough for almost four years, and one from the
employment agency he was registered with.

He called them and explained the situation to the man who
answered, got a polite response and a promise to send over Dymek's
file.

'Did you know he was heading back home?' Zigic asked.

'Yes, he informed us last week,' the man said, speaking with the
barest trace of an accent, his words clipped and precise. 'I believe
it is a family matter. We were expecting him to return in a few days.
We have work scheduled for him.'

'Do you have contact details for his family?'

'They will be in his file if we do.'

Zigic rang off and went into the main office.

Grieves and Parr had gone for lunch, leaving their desks cluttered with paperwork. Parr had forgotten his mobile and it flashed
as a message came in. 'Home' on the display.

The board where their hit-and-run was plotted out had filled up
a little during the morning. A photograph lifted from Hossa Motors'
CCTV footage was tacked up near the suspects column, showing a
man of medium build and medium height, who could have been
Anthony Gilbert, standing in front of the white Volvo. He wore a

woollen hat pulled down to his eyebrows and a scarf wound loosely at his throat, hiding a significant portion of his lower face.

'It could be anyone,' Ferreira said.

'Have we found where the money came from?' Zigic asked, turning to Wahlia, who was eating a bagel at his desk.

He nodded, mouth full. 'Four separate withdrawals, a hundred quid a time in the week before it was bought. Different cash machines.'

'He's an idiot if he thinks that's covering,' Ferreira said.

'Blood on the airbag's a type match,' Wahlia said.

'I don't know what else we can do until the DNA comes back then. We've gone as far as we can with this. We need to talk to him.'

Zigic frowned. 'What have we got from Jelena's phone?'

'Same kind of stuff we saw with her Facebook messages,' Wahlia said. 'She was texting him a lot, just the usual small talk but pretty frequent. They were supposed to be meeting up Saturday morning in Carluccio's – she arranged that, not him. She said she wanted to talk about "what happened".'

Zigic wondered how she'd planned to slip away from Sofia. He didn't imagine she'd let Jelena out of her sight easily and it seemed ridiculous that a grown woman could be dominated so completely by her sister. Why was she even lying about seeing Gilbert? Was it just easier to let Sofia feel like she'd won?

'There's one weird thing I noticed,' Wahlia said, pulling a few sheets of paper out from under his keyboard. 'Tomas – Sofia's boyfriend – there are a couple of references to him, but they don't make much sense.'

'Where is he, anyway?' Ferreira asked.

'Poznań,' Zigic said. 'Have we got a number for him, Bobby?'

'It's in Jelena's contacts, I'll find it in a second.' He sifted through the papers, which were heavily marked with pink highlighter. 'So, two weeks ago we've got her saying she tried to talk to Sofia about Tomas.'

'About what?' Zigic asked.

'She doesn't say. Gilbert gets back, tells her to give Sofia space.' Wahlia frowned. 'They don't discuss it any further. Then a couple of days after that Jelena says Sofia is acting strangely, she's being very quiet. She reckons she's missing him.'

'You think he's left her?' Ferreira asked. 'Would explain why he doesn't seem bothered about what's happened. I mean, how far's Poznań when someone's died? You'd get on the first plane out, wouldn't you?'

'She was vague about him,' Zigic said, thinking of how defensive she was when he asked if there was anyone who could stay with her. 'What's his number?'

Wahlia found it and Zigic dialled as he read it out, standing looking at the trajectory of the car tacked up on the murder board, small red dots marking where everyone was standing, small black ones for the positions of their corpses.

It rang straight through to the message service, a man's gruff voice speaking Polish. He waited for the tone, answered in kind.

'This is Detective Inspector Zigic. I'm sorry to inform you that your girlfriend Sofia has been involved in an accident. She's fine, but we need to talk to you.' He left his numbers and ended the call, stood with his mobile pressed to his mouth, looking at the small dots which represented Jelena Krasic. The space between them was so minimal that they overlapped like a Venn diagram; one second she had been standing on the kerb and the next she was on the roof of the Volvo. No time to react even if she wasn't distracted by her mobile phone.

Pyotr Dymek must have had lightning reflexes and Zigic thought it spoke well of the man that he pushed Sofia, a complete stranger, out of the way, rather than saving himself. It wouldn't make the inevitable call to his family any easier but he hoped they would take some comfort from knowing he died a hero.

In his office the computer pinged as a new email arrived.

The agency had sent over Dymek's complete employment history, tax number and bank account, a photocopy of his passport, but all Zigic needed was the next of kin.

Andrea Dymek – wife.

He stared at the words for a couple of seconds. It wouldn't get any easier if he left it.

He looked at the photograph of Anna on his desk, imagining a woman just like her, going about her usual daily routine with no idea what had happened to her husband.

Or did she know already, deep in her bones, that something was wrong? Dymek was due to catch a bus yesterday morning; by now he should be home. Had she waited at the depot in Łódź for him, dressed up carefully, wanting him to see her at her best after months away? Did she have their children with her, bribed with sweets to behave for Daddy? Had she searched for him in the sea of tired faces, expectation making her smile, until the coach was empty and there was nothing else to do but ring him and ask where he was?

Zigic dialled the number slowly, cleared his throat as it rang, lifting his eyes from Anna's photo.

A woman answered after three rings, the sound of children squabbling in the background, a television playing.

'Yes? Who is this?' she asked in brisk Polish.

'Andrea Dymek?'

'Yes.'

'I'm sorry but I have bad news.'

'Pyotr?'

'Yes. Do you speak English?'

'No.'

Zigic continued in Polish, stumbling around the words as he explained that there had been an accident. He'd learned the language in the fields, working with men like her husband during a rebellious summer spent out on the fens during his teens, and the vocabulary he'd picked up wasn't fit for this job, too colloquial, too basic. He wanted to soften the blow somehow but the words weren't there, and as she cried he kept apologising.

'He saved a woman. He was a hero.'

'He should have saved himself,' Mrs Dymek wailed. 'Who was this woman? Was he fucking her?'

Zigic knew that word.

'No, Mrs Dymek. No, she was a stranger to him.'

'Then why did he do that?'

'He was a good man,' Zigic said.

She let out a wail which hit him like a gut punch. 'He was not a good man. Never.'

The phone went dead in his hand.

19

Sofia sat on the edge of Jelena's bed, the duvet cover thrown back and rumpled just as she'd left it, clutching a pillow to her chest, inhaling the smell of her sister's hair, the faint trace of perfume. Her face was damp but her tears had dried up.

She'd been there for hours, ever since Zigic left, had dragged her battered body up the stairs and lain down in the space on the right side of the bed where Jelena always slept. She wanted to sleep but she couldn't, despite the fatigue which made her limbs feel like lead and the hollow ache in her chest. She wanted some respite, just an hour of oblivion, but it wouldn't come.

Even the pills weren't helping.

Her mind kept ticking away. Her thoughts looping, how she should have protected Jelena and what would happen now she was gone. Gilbert was dying and that was good, but what if he survived?

There was too much left unfinished between them.

Jelena had lied to her, stayed in contact with Gilbert, made plans with him even though she'd said she'd ended it.

That was what Zigic believed and as she sat on Jelena's bed she realised it was true. All of those conversations she'd overheard late at night, whispered in here behind a locked door, the ones Jelena had denied the next morning. She should have seen what was going on.

She pressed her nose into the cushion and looked at the dress hanging on the back of the bedroom door, a short tight thing in purple leopard print.

Jelena had bought it a week ago, had squealed when she'd found it on the sale rail in Warehouse and held it up to herself for Sofia's opinion. She'd thought it looked cheap but she didn't say, only followed her into the changing rooms and waited for her to try it on. She'd come out from behind the curtain beaming, standing on tiptoes in the dress and a pair of striped knee socks, saying she would need to borrow Sofia's best black shoes to wear with it.

The tags were still on the dress and Sofia felt fresh tears pricking her eyes as she realised Jelena would never wear it. Those tags would stay there and the night out they'd planned – putting Tomas and Gilbert behind them – would never happen. No more nights like that ever again.

She went over to Jelena's dressing table, saw the purple nail varnish she'd chosen to go with her new dress, one more bottle added to her collection.

Sofia's eyes drifted to the mirror, ringed with ticket stubs from the cinema and notes from bouquets Gilbert had sent her in the early days, photographs of them together taken in booths, one she remembered Gilbert buying from a photographer in a bar – him and Jelena, her and Tomas. She snatched at it and tore it into pieces, took the next one and the next and ripped them up, the stubs and the notes, dropped them into the bin.

Immediately she regretted it.

She sank to her knees and retrieved a scrap lying on the floor, half of Jelena's smiling face, one brilliant-blue eye staring out at her, and she wept again, every sob tearing afresh at the slowly healing tissue around her ribs.

One more pill. Just to take the edge off.

When she was halfway down the stairs somebody rapped on the front door and Sofia froze. They would go away. Her suffering was not so important it would keep them from whatever they wanted to watch on television.

The letter box snapped open and her neighbour Mrs O'Brien looked in.

'Sofia, poppet, I've brought you some soup.'

'I do not –' She choked on the words.

'Now, you don't have to eat it this minute, we can put it in the fridge and you can heat it up later if you're feeling peckish.' The old woman had a soft, musical voice which Sofia had always liked. It was the kind of voice you never heard at home. 'Would you let me in, lovey?'

Sofia unlocked the front door and Mrs O'Brien bustled in, a blur of motion in a long green cardigan. 'I'll just pop this in the kitchen for you.'

Sofia followed her in there and began to clear the debris of yesterday's breakfast from the small pine table. Mrs O'Brien took hold of her hands.

'No you don't. You just sit down there and I'll have a quick tidy for you. You don't want to look at all this mess, do you?'

The plate with the remnants of Jelena's last breakfast was gone in an instant, a slice of toast with one mouthful taken scraped into the bin, the plate put in the sink, and Sofia felt a gnawing in her chest. If she had made her finish it – if they had left the house five minutes later – would she still be alive?

Mrs O'Brien was talking to her but Sofia didn't listen to the words, only the rise and fall of her voice as she stacked the clean plates on the draining board.

She was a kind woman, one of those small round dumpling women who existed for nothing else in life but to care for other people. Sofia remembered just before Christmas when Jelena had caught flu and been too sick to go into work. She was delirious, burning with fever, saying nonsensical things in her sleep, and Mrs O'Brien had stayed with her during the day while Sofia was at the farm. She was the sort of woman their mother should have been.

'Is this from the people at your work?' Mrs O'Brien asked, looking at the box of vegetables on the counter. 'Stupid lot they are sending you that. Why don't you go in the front? I'll bring you through some tea.'

Sofia returned to the sofa, pressed another pill out of its foil and dry-swallowed it, then sank down into her nest of pillows. She closed her eyes and when she opened them again Mrs O'Brien was sitting in the armchair watching her.

'Have you told Tomas?' she asked. 'He was very fond of Jelena, wasn't he?'

Sofia nodded. 'I should tell him, yes.'

Mrs O'Brien fetched the telephone from the hallway and Sofia dialled his mobile number, thinking of what best to say, feeling fresh tears creeping up on her. It went to the answer service and the sound of his voice made her chest hurt.

'It is switched off.'

'The silly boy will have forgot to charge it,' Mrs O'Brien said. 'You know what they're like when you're not around to tell them what to do.'

Sofia ended the call without leaving a message. 'I will try later.'

Car doors slammed outside and through the slatted wooden blinds Sofia saw a man and woman walking through the front gate. A few seconds later the doorbell rang and Mrs O'Brien rose from the armchair, her bones creaking.

'Please, tell them to go away,' Sofia said. 'Whoever they are, I do not want to see them.'

Mrs O'Brien drew her cardigan around herself and marched out of the room. Sofia stared at the wall trying to ignore the voices in the hallway which were getting louder, coming closer as the front door closed.

A woman came into the living room, smiling broadly, showing very white teeth. She was small and blonde, with bad skin under too much make-up.

'Hello there, Sofia,' she said, holding out her hand for Sofia to shake it. 'My name's Nicola, I work with Detective Inspector Zigic. Dushan. You remember him?'

'Why are you here?'

Nicola pulled one of the armchairs – Jelena's chair – closer to the sofa.

'Dushan told me a little about you and Jelena – I am terribly sorry.'

Sofia glared at her through stinging pink eyes. 'What do you want?'

'There's a gentleman from the *Evening Telegraph* who'd like to talk with you about Jelena. Both of you, your lives in Peterborough. Well, I'm sure you understand.'

Of course she understood. The police wanted witnesses and the newspaper wanted to sell copies.

'I will see him.'

The man came into the room then, Mrs O'Brien at his heels. He smiled at her too but there was a more genuine warmth in it and Sofia thought he looked kind.

'Hi, Sofia, I'm Paul.'

She shook his hand.

'Would I make everyone a cup of tea?' Mrs O'Brien asked.

'That would be lovely,' Nicola said, and hustled her out of the living room, complimenting her cardigan and asking where exactly in Ireland she was from.

The man sat down. He asked if she minded him recording the conversation and he placed his phone on the arm of the sofa when she told him it was fine.

'So, how long have you and Jelena been in Peterborough?'

'Six years nearly.'

'She was a very pretty girl,' he said.

'She was beautiful.'

'You look very alike.'

'No,' Sofia said. 'Jelena was always the beautiful one.'

The reporter began to ask the questions he'd come here for, ones the paper and the police would be happy to print. He asked about their childhood home and what had brought them to Peterborough, their work at the farm and did they enjoy it, about what Jelena liked to do, what her hopes for the future were. Bringing her to life so she could die all over again on the front page.

And then there were no more questions and he was putting away his things, thanking her for talking to him. They left in a bluster of condolences, the woman insisting that she should rest now. 'Jelena wouldn't want you to make yourself ill.'

Sofia crumpled as the front door slammed, hugging her arms around her battered body. The tears running fast down her face and she couldn't believe she had any left in her.

The phone began to ring and she ignored it.

She might as well be dead. If she was going to feel like this, if it was never going to go away – and it wouldn't, she knew that.

The phone kept ringing.

'That'll be your Tomas,' Mrs O'Brien shouted.

A fresh sob rocked Sofia's body but she reached for the phone, knowing it wasn't him.

'Hello?'

'Sofia, it's DI Zigic.'

'What do you want?'

'Just checking how you're doing. Have you taken any more pills?'

She looked at the packet, half empty now. 'No.'

'Has Tomas called?'

'He is coming home.'

'Good,' Zigic said. 'You need him with you.'

Sofia closed her eyes, pushing away his concern and her own lie. There was only one thing she wanted from Zigic and she steeled herself before she asked the question which had been plaguing her all afternoon.

'Is Anthony dead?'

Zigic sighed lightly. 'No, he's still unconscious but the doctors are confident he'll make a full recovery now. We'll be able to question him in the next day or two.'

She lowered the phone without responding and pressed the button to end the call.

'Was that himself?' Mrs O'Brien called.

'No. It was no one important.'

Sofia let her head drop back onto the pillows, too heavy to lift now, full of grief and memories and the lies she had told. She thought of Anthony Gilbert unconscious in a hospital bed and Dushan Zigic sitting in his office waiting for him to wake up.

Gilbert would lie too. Or he would tell the truth. Neither would bring Jelena back.

Better that he died and said nothing at all.

20

'He's giving you the eye,' Wahlia said, grinning around the bottle of Beck's he held a couple of inches from his mouth. 'Short guy, plaid shirt.'

Ferreira glanced towards the bar, saw a sea of short guys in plaid shirts, nothing she liked the look of. Not yet anyway, but it was early still. There were a dozen more of them dotted around the Draper's Arms, shooting pool at the battle-scarred table down the back, one pumping the quiz machine next to the dark wood booth they'd got lucky nabbing, and as she scoped out the blue velvet sofas near the front door another one walked in.

'When did this happen?' She reached across the table, flicked the pocket of Wahlia's own red-and-charcoal-check shirt. 'When did plaid become you guys' off-duty default?'

'Hey, I was wearing them years before they were fashionable.'

She grinned. 'Fucking hipster.'

'I'm not a hipster.'

'Yeah, you are. Black geek glasses, big-ass turn-ups, ironic digital watch. You're a hipster, Bobby.' She sipped her dark rum, ice cubes stinging her lips. 'How many pairs of vintage Adidas trainers do you own now?'

'They're an investment.'

'Against what? A global old-skool shortage?'

'It could happen.' He shook his empty beer bottle at her. 'We got time?'

Ferreira checked her watch – the band they were going to see wouldn't get started until ten. It was a five-minute walk through the centre of town. 'Yeah, quick one.'

'Double?'

'Do they come another way?'

Wahlia slid out of the booth and she watched him ease through the crowd to the long mahogany bar, noticing how people moved aside for him. He was short but powerfully built, broad through the shoulders, thick at the arms, hours of gym time giving him the air of a man you did not want to fuck with.

If they knew what a pussycat he was the reactions would be different, she guessed. Hundreds of nights they'd been out together and she'd rarely seen him lose it, even when he was provoked, and that happened often enough, a consequence of his skin colour and the habit he had of sidling up to women who obviously weren't alone.

He was wasted in the office, she thought. Five years older than her, better educated; he should have progressed further than Detective Constable by now and they all knew it.

Laughter erupted from the booth behind her and a fist pummelled against the wooden partition. It was getting loud already, four hours of post-work drinks loosening ties and tongues, everyone pretending Monday wasn't coming, seeing the weekend as an endless stretch of glittering possibilities.

Ferreira drained her glass, crunched an ice cube between her back teeth, thinking of Anthony Gilbert lying in his hospital bed, awake now, with the consequences of his actions filling his overdose-addled brain. He had a long night ahead of him to practise his excuses, find somebody else to blame, and she guessed it would be Sofia Krasic when they finally got him in the interview room. Because it couldn't be his fault, could it?

Wahlia returned with a drink in each hand, a bag of peanuts between his teeth which he spat onto the table.

'I was wrong – short plaid guy was giving me the eye.'

'I hope you let him down gently.'

'Told him my hag was having boyfriend trouble.'

She snatched the peanuts up and threw them at his head. 'Hag?'

'I didn't want to hurt his feelings.' He opened the bag and offered it to her. 'Meant to ask, did you go and look at that place on Thorpe Road?'

'Yeah, it was perfect.' Ferreira took a handful of nuts, the closest thing she'd get to proper food for a few hours. 'Or it would be perfect if I could afford it.'

'Why'd you go and view somewhere you couldn't afford?'

'Thought I could knock them down.'

'How much did you offer?'

'Two hundred a month less. The agent looked at me like I'd just pissed on the floor,' she said. 'You should have seen it, two bedrooms, balcony off the living room, the shower was big enough for three people.' He gave her a goatish leer. 'There's a gym right in the building.'

'You could take in a lodger. Eighty quid a week, you'll cover the rent easy.'

'I don't want to share.' She turned her glass around on the table. 'Christ, the whole point of moving out from Mum and Dad's is having my own space for once.'

Wahlia took a long drink, wiped his mouth on the back of his hand. 'Have you told them yet?'

'What do you think?'

'They'll probably be glad to see the back of you, coming in at all hours . . . my parents redecorated my room a week after I moved out.'

'It's different,' Ferreira said, staring into her drink. 'We're not – I can't – look, we all came over here as a unit, right? To have a better life. But this isn't their home and it never will be. You shouldn't abandon your family in a foreign country.'

He frowned at her, a dash cutting between his thick black brows. 'That makes absolutely no sense.'

'You don't get it.'

'Mel, come on, I totally get what you're thinking, but you're wrong. It isn't disloyal to want your own space. You're not moving

129

to the other end of the country. You'll be ten minutes away.'

She lifted her glass to her mouth but didn't drink, held the rim against her bottom lip. 'Have you noticed, almost every crime we deal with, nearly every dead immigrant, they're with their family? You have to stick together.'

'What, forever?' Wahlia asked. 'How is that having a better life? You might as well have stayed in Portugal and rented fucking deckchairs to tourists.'

'I'm from Lisbon, Bobby, there's not much call for deckchairs.'

'You know what I mean.'

'Yeah.' She took a mouthful of rum. It was spiced, not want she wanted and not what Bobby would have ordered; he knew her better than that.

He tapped the table. 'I'm going for a slash.'

The crowd in the next booth slammed down their shot glasses in unison then cheered the achievement, one voice dominating, as it always did, and Ferreira took another sip of her drink, knowing Bobby was right. It wouldn't help when she broke the news though. There was going to be weeping and shouting and guilt-inducing accusations which would go on for days. She remembered the screaming row when her brother left to move in with his girlfriend last year, their mother calling the girl a witch for stealing her baby boy away, their father trying to be the peacemaker, saying he was too young to get tied down, he should try out a few more women before settling for this one. They'd reached a grudging accommodation but the words couldn't be taken back.

She took her tobacco tin out of her jacket pocket and started to roll a cigarette, aware of a suited man at a nearby table watching her as he listened to his friend talking about work in a bludgeoning monotone. He looked half familiar and as she ran the tip of her tongue along the paper she realised she'd slept with him a few months ago; not a bad experience but not one she felt like repeating.

He was starting up from his stool as Wahlia returned, drying his hands on the back pockets of his jeans. 'Get that drunk, if we're going.'

Ferreira threw down the rum and followed him out through the crush of bodies all smelling of air-conditioned sweat and last-minute deodorant applied from a can in the desk drawer, ducking an arm which flew out of nowhere.

Outside the wind surged up the road, stirring the scattered litter, and Ferreira lingered a moment in the recessed doorway to light up, before they headed towards Cathedral Square, passing the shuttered fronts of cafes and sandwich places, one estate agent's after another. A couple were standing peering at the particulars filling the window of Bairstow Eaves and Ferreira wondered how drunk they were to be doing that in the dark, then the man wandered away from his girlfriend and relieved himself in the alleyway next to it.

'Classy guy,' Wahlia said.

'It's true what they say – all the good ones are taken.'

A cab stopped in the middle of the road and a gaggle of women in high heels and short dresses tumbled out, holding onto one another as they scrambled to find cash for the driver, too drunk or happy to notice the expression of contempt on his face.

'What do you think to Grieves?' Wahlia asked.

'You can do better.'

'No.' He smiled. 'Thanks though. I mean what do you think to her as a copper?'

Ferreira took a deep hit on her cigarette, blinked against the rising smoke. 'We were in uniform the same time.'

'And?'

'She should still be there.'

'You just don't like having another woman in the office.' There was a teasing note in his voice but the subject felt forced and abrupt and she wondered if this was Zigic's doing. He'd pick up on the tension, he was that kind of person, fine-tuned to hidden conflict, and she guessed he'd get Bobby to do his dirty work, knowing she'd be more likely to confide in him.

131

He was right.

'Do you remember that kid who died down in the cells about five years ago? He was sixteen, King's student.'

'Drug dealer?'

'He had an eighth on him when he was brought in,' Ferreira said. 'We're not talking Scarface.'

'He had a fit. Epilepsy or something.'

A moped buzzed past them, weaving ominously on the narrow road, the driver's helmet hanging from the handlebars.

'Yeah, he had a fit,' Ferreira said. 'And that's technically what killed him, but one of the uniforms got him in a choke hold and slammed his head into the wall. *Then* he fitted.'

Wahlia stopped dead on the pavement. 'Grieves did that? You're fucking kidding me. She can't weigh nine stone.'

'Of course she didn't do it, but she was there and she lied about it to get her mate off.'

Wahlia looked down at his feet, dropped the butt of his cigarette and stepped on it very deliberately. 'So, how do you know about it?'

'She told me,' Ferreira said, starting off up the street again, eyes on the cathedral's serrated spires poking up into the night sky, stone lit the colour of rose gold. 'She asked me what she should do and I told her to report it. The guy was a thug, total piece of shit, this wasn't a momentary lapse of judgement, it was his style. And she covered for him.'

They turned onto Long Causeway, more people about now as they drew closer to the clubs, gangs of young men dressed up in their second-best shirts, girls in two and threes, walking briskly with their arms linked, a dozen women on a hen night laughing and yelping as they skipped across the cobbles, angel wings shaking, the lights on their halos flashing.

'Does Zigic know about this?'

'I doubt it.'

'Are you going to tell him?'

132

'What's the point?' Ferreira said. 'It was all hushed up. It's my word against hers.'

'I think your word carries a fair bit of weight,' Wahlia said, as they crossed the road. 'He won't want someone like that on the team.'

Ferreira shrugged. 'They'll be gone in a few days when this case is cleared up.'

They passed a cluster of smokers shivering outside Yates's, a couple of muscular blokes with buzz-cut hair among them, louder than the rest, flexing as they talked. Squaddies, Ferreira thought, bussed in from the base near Stamford for the night, looking to fight or fuck whoever wouldn't put up too much resistance.

'This case isn't going to get cleared up in a few days and you know it,' Wahlia said. 'The hit-and-run maybe, the other thing . . . I don't see where we're heading with it.'

Ferreira's mobile vibrated and she unzipped her jacket pocket to answer it. Frowned when she saw Zigic's name on the display.

'This isn't going to be anything good.'

21

Sofia Krasic was pale under the strip light in Interview Room 2, a bluish cast to her skin, except for the livid patch on her right cheek where her face had struck the floor. She looked scared, sitting with her arms wrapped around her middle, her chin down, and in the silence Zigic could hear her breaths coming fast and shallow, almost but not quite hyperventilating.

Maybe it was pain tightening her hard features. The doctor had checked her out, said she was fit to be questioned, but Zigic wasn't so sure. She should never have been allowed to walk out of the hospital this morning, shouldn't have been mixing painkillers and vodka, and from PC Walsh's version of events she'd taken a blow to her already damaged ribs, a much heavier one than he would admit to throwing probably.

Would anything she said in here stand up in court?

She'd refused a solicitor and that could complicate matters too, create space for charges of bullying or coercion. They would have to tread carefully with her.

So far she'd said very little, only asked if she could smoke, and when she was told no said she needed something to drink.

He left the tapes running while Ferreira went to fetch her a bottle of water, sipped his vending-machine coffee, trying to drown the wine he'd drunk with dinner.

The door opened and Ferreira came in with a bottle of mineral water and a bar of chocolate.

'Ten thirty-eight. Sergeant Ferreira entering the interview room.'

Sofia ignored the chocolate, spent a couple of seconds fighting the bottle's lid, then took a long drink, putting it down again half empty.

'Why did you go to see Anthony Gilbert?' Zigic asked.

'To talk to him.'

Zigic placed his palms flat on the table. 'Let me explain something to you, Sofia. PC Walsh has written up a full report of what happened and he makes it very clear that you were standing over Gilbert, with your hands on his throat.'

'I was only trying to wake him,' Sofia said firmly.

'By strangling him?'

'I was not strangling him. I was shaking him.' She gripped her own shoulders, close to her neck. 'Like this, see. You cannot kill someone like this.'

'But you slapped him?'

She gave Zigic a dead-eyed look. 'You cannot kill someone like that either.'

'What did you really want with Gilbert?'

'I tell you already. I went to talk to him.' She shook her head. 'I thought if I could look him in the eye I would know whether he killed her.'

'What did he say?' Zigic asked.

'Nothing. I could not wake him.'

'And what if he'd told you he did it?'

She looked away. 'You cannot arrest me for something I did not do.'

She'd come close though.

Walsh's report described how he'd stepped away to go to the bathroom and found her with Gilbert when he returned, alerted by her shouting, then the sound of her palm striking Gilbert's face, trying to slap him back to consciousness. Her hands were on him when Walsh burst into the room and she only let go when he dragged her away, fingertips clawing the air above Gilbert's face. She didn't stop shouting though, but turned on Walsh instead, kicking out at him until he wrestled her to the ground.

'You've assaulted a police officer, Sofia. It's a very serious charge.'

'Your police officer attacked me.'

'PC Walsh used an approved method of restraint.'

'He punched me,' she said.

'If you wish to make a formal complaint you're welcome to do so.'

She threw her chin up and Zigic saw an old scar lightly puckering the skin under her jaw, long and thin, a shallow cut intended to threaten more than damage, and for a moment he imagined a blade running slowly across her neck, but he pushed it away. Whatever violence she'd once suffered wasn't the issue here.

'You are all corrupt,' she said. 'You lie to protect each other.'

Next to him Ferreira shifted in her seat, feet scuffing the floor under the table.

It had been a long and frustrating day and Zigic imagined she was as irritated as he was at being dragged away from her evening. An hour ago he'd been on the sofa with Anna dozing against his chest, finishing the bottle of Shiraz they'd opened with dinner, watching a film he'd already guessed the ending to. Just drunk and dozy enough to forget about work for a while.

Sofia's impatience and arrogance had snatched him back here and watching her across the table, seeing the self-righteous indignation on her face, he momentarily forgot her suffering and wanted to punish her for ruining the rare few hours' peace he'd been enjoying.

His shoulders squared as he leaned forward.

'Why did you lie about Tomas?'

She blinked. 'What is this to do with him?'

'You told me he was coming home,' Zigic said. 'And that wasn't true. So why did you say it?'

Sofia started to run her thumbnail along the bottle's paper wrapper, attention fixed on it. 'It is none of your business.'

'Why did he leave you?'

She looked up at that, her dull green eyes darting between them. 'Who says he left me?'

'Hasn't he?'

'Yes.' Through gritted teeth, glaring at him. 'Are you happy? I am alone. There is nobody who cares what happens now. I have nobody who will help me so you can arrest me and put me in prison and nobody will stop you.'

The interview-room door opened and a PC stuck his head in, pink-eyed and sniffling with a cold. Zigic sent Ferreira to deal with him and turned back to Sofia, who was staring at the tabletop while the fingers of her left hand opened and closed nervously, the only sign he'd seen yet that she understood how serious her situation was.

'You wouldn't have got away with it,' he said. 'You took a taxi to the hospital, for God's sake. You asked for Gilbert at reception. And even if you hadn't you'd be the first person we went to when Gilbert died.'

She pressed her fist hard against her mouth, every muscle in her face tensing.

'What were you thinking?'

'I told you, I only wanted to talk to him. You do not know him like I do. Even if he lied to me I would see the truth.'

Zigic saw the tears shining in her eyes and regretted being so hard with her. No matter what she'd done tonight, what she would have done if she'd got the chance, she was still raw with grief.

'You have to stay away from him, Sofia. Do you understand?'

She gave the barest nod.

'If he's responsible we won't let him get away with it,' Zigic said.

Sofia swiped a tear away as it ran down her cheek.

'What will happen to me now?'

Just then Ferreira came back into the room, the PC hovering in the open door as she walked over to the table and bent down to whisper a few words in Zigic's ear.

He was up before she finished. 'Interview terminated at ten fifty-five.'

He turned to the PC, who stood wiping his nose on the cuff of his jumper.

'Take Ms Krasic down, please.'

Then she was standing. 'No, you cannot do this.'

But he was already gone.

22

People were hurrying up Westgate as they approached the crime scene, clubbers clutching bottles and cans, mobile phones in their hands, ready to film whatever they could see. Zigic prayed that the uniforms had done their job properly, sealed off the short stretch of Cromwell Road to stop them getting in.

He realised they hadn't had time when he spotted a couple of high-visibility vests and a single patrol car. Nothing more. Friday night, every spare body they had would be attending drunken punch-ups or post-pub domestics, scattered across the city.

The line of painted terraced houses sat isolated and vulnerable-looking, lying in the shadow of a hulking office block four storeys high, opposite the dark, open terrain of a car park, beyond that a patch of wasteland, screened by security fencing which was buckled and toppled over. The ghouls would find a vantage point if they were prepared to ruin their good shoes scrambling for it, and as Zigic pulled onto the pavement near the buff-brick and smoked-glass bulk of Queensgate shopping centre he saw that a dozen of them had gathered on the scrub, directly opposite the spot where the patrol car was parked with its headlights on full beam, throwing low, hard illumination along the sparsely lit street.

None of them had made it any closer though.

A group of Asian men had formed a cordon across the mouth of Cromwell Road, some with baseball bats, others empty-handed but no less formidable-looking. Sprays of broken glass littered the pavement in front of them.

'Where the hell is everyone?' Ferreira said, climbing out of the car. 'There's supposed to be a van on the way.'

'Let's stay calm, alright, Mel?'

'This is a fucking joke.' She slammed the door and strode across Westgate, putting her hand out to stop an oncoming car, its stereo booming, bass pounding in shock waves.

The air was crackling, tension rising off the men at the end of the street, excitement fizzing around the onlookers, more of them appearing all the time, alerted by text messages, pulled out of the nearby pubs and nightclub queues, wanting to be able to say they were there when the news broke, post photos on their Facebook pages. Zigic knew this could get ugly very fast, the white audience wanting a show from their Asian neighbours. He told Ferreira to call in and check on the backup.

'Everyone they can get, right now.'

Just then a shout went up.

A thickset bald guy bellied up to the cordon, beer in one hand, takeaway bag in the other.

'Shift it, Osama.'

The men held their position, hands tightened around bats, bracing for trouble.

One man spoke up, not the largest but clearly the leader, and told him to go home.

'Fuck are you, telling me where to go?' The bald guy took a step forward, into the man's face, spread his arms wide. 'Get out the way.'

'You are not coming through here.'

Zigic shoved his arm between them. The bald man smelled of whiskey and cigarettes, had a Bluetooth stuck in one ear, a woman's voice bleeding through it, high and insistent, not stopping for breath.

'This is a crime scene, sir. Please find another route.'

'Coppers are they?' he asked, shuffling back but only a few inches. 'Fucking crime scene, my balls.'

Zigic grabbed the front of his shirt and shoved him away. 'Leave or I'll arrest you.'

The man smirked. 'You want to think about who pays your wages, mate.'

He lobbed the bottle he was holding over the men's heads, liquid arcing out before it smashed in the middle of the road, eliciting whoops from the onlookers. Then he turned and walked away, laughing to himself as he headed back into the centre of town.

'You were more polite than I'd have been,' Ferreira said, pocketing her phone. 'Van's on the way. Five minutes. I've told them to hustle up forensics too.'

Zigic nodded, still watching the figure receding along Westgate.

Ferreira nudged him as the cordon parted for an elderly man with a wispy, hennaed beard, dressed in a white djellaba which billowed and snapped in the wind, a black astrakhan hat perched on his head. He looked frail, leaning heavily on a walking stick, but Zigic knew he ruled the half-dozen streets around his mosque with an iron fist, settling neighbour disputes and matrimonial problems. Keeping a hundred small crimes a year from their proper place on the police system.

'Inspector.' He held his hand out and Zigic shook it. 'Such are the things which bring us from our beds at night.'

'Mr Shahzad, I take it we have you to thank for the security.'

He put his hand to his chest, bowed lightly. 'When I hear of what has happened I realise we must protect the area. Your people arrived very punctually but they are only two and the road is busy this time of evening.'

'It's greatly appreciated,' Zigic said. 'Could you show us the body please?'

They walked past houses with their windows lit up, people visible behind the curtains, a few standing in their open front doors, a man in striped pyjamas, a woman holding a grizzly child on her hip. Zigic was aware of the loose throngs of onlookers in the car park, indistinct in the gloom.

Shahzad led them to a house at the centre of the row. The two uniformed officers were standing nearby, both pale and shaken-looking, one sucking furiously on a cigarette he hid behind his back as they approached.

A body lay half on the pavement, half in the road, hidden by a white sheet. Blood had soaked through it, creating a large dark stain which hinted at what they would find underneath.

'We have covered the young man,' Shahzad said. He gestured away. 'For his dignity.'

It created complications but now wasn't the time to worry about that.

Ferreira squatted down and gingerly took hold of the corner of the sheet, the material sticking and sucking as she peeled it back from the man's head. Shahzad turned away, muttering what sounded like a prayer.

What remained was completely unidentifiable, a gruesome pulp of blood and bone and grey matter, the man's face caved in, his skull cracked and sickly misshapen, glints of very white teeth through his ripped cheek, a small spot of gold in a flap of skin which had been his ear.

Ferreira replaced the sheet and exhaled slowly as she straightened up, a queasy expression on her face. She pushed her fingers back through her hair, her eyes fixed on the blooming stain.

They were both thinking the same thing. The ferocity of the attack, the ethnicity of the victim. Zigic glanced along the road, looking for CCTV cameras, knowing their man would want to salute them once again. The nearest was fifty yards away, pointing at the entrance of a house which had been converted into office space.

A siren wailed at a distance, cutting through the murmur of voices and the dim sounds of music wafting across the car park from the pub. Zigic started planning how to deploy the approaching uniforms, knowing he needed them to take control of the locus but that he might not have enough to do that and start the door-to-door. He wanted to speak to the neighbours straight away, while their memories were still fresh and unpolluted by speculation or sleep.

He didn't want to give them time to think better of coming forward.

Blue lights appeared at the top end of Westgate, three vehicles in convoy, the sirens blaring closer.

'Will you take him now your people are here?' Shahzad asked.

'We have to wait for forensics,' Ferreira explained. 'They need to take photographs, make a preliminary examination with the body in situ.'

'No, you misunderstand,' Shahzad said. 'The man who did this terrible thing, you will take him away?'

Zigic's attention snapped back. 'What? You know where he is?'

'We have kept him for you.'

'How did you get him?' Ferreira asked.

'The people in the house heard screaming.' Shahzad nodded towards the front door and Zigic saw a smear of blood on the flaked white gloss paint. 'They came outside to see what was happening. They are holding him for you.'

Zigic glanced at Ferreira, saw the triumph lighting her eyes, a grim smile tightening her face, and felt the same dark pleasure. They had him. None of their own doing but what did that matter? They had their man.

'They were brave to tackle him.'

'We must keep our streets safe,' Shahzad said, a hint of accusation in the comment.

He rapped on the front door with the head of his cane and a thin young man with a bushy beard reaching to his chest opened up, looked between them quickly and stepped back to let Shahzad inside.

Zigic and Ferreira followed him into the living room. It was small and neat, a riot of heavy patterns, paisley carpet and papered walls, a burgundy three-piece suite too large for the room, a flat screen hanging over the old gas fire, the same scene you'd find in a thousand terraced houses in the city.

Except for the man sitting on the floor with his wrists bound. He wore black head to toe, combat trousers and a shirt with military styling, leather gloves and highly shined boots smeared with blood and brain matter which he had tracked across the carpet and wiped on the rug. Someone had pulled off his balaclava and thrown it down nearby, leaving his dirty blond hair standing at angles from his square head. He had a bruise under one eye but it was days old and Zigic marvelled at the restraint they had shown.

Three men stood around him, two armed with large kitchen knives, the third held an iron bar, and curled up on the sofa a little boy, no older than four, watched them with his thumb stuck in his mouth, bored but still interested as only children that age can be.

'What's your name?' Zigic asked.

The man stared back at him, blue eyes steady, flat and cold and without expression. Maybe it was shock at being caught but Zigic didn't think so. There was a hardness to the man's creased and lined features, a firm set to his thin-lipped mouth which suggested defiance even in this situation.

He looked like a captured soldier.

'Get up.'

The man didn't move.

Ferreira started towards him and Zigic grabbed her elbow, held her back. He could be armed for all they knew, and given the violence he was capable of without a weapon he didn't want to risk anyone else getting damaged.

Shahzad spoke a few low words and the guards quickly descended on the man, dragging him to his feet. He threw his chin up, stared down his nose at them, baring smoke-stained teeth in a hungry grin.

Zigic opened the front door and called the uniforms in. One took a set of handcuffs off his belt and snapped them around the man's wrists, over the twine which had been used to bind them. They found the firmest holds they could and walked him out to the car, flanked by the men from the house who were ready in case he decided to make a break for it.

He went passively though, walked past the shrouded corpse like it was nothing to do with him, didn't even glance towards it.

144

As the group reached the patrol car a chant started from the end of the street.

'E – E – ENL.'

Ferreira smirked. 'I fucking knew it.'

Half a dozen ragged voices, each man shouting, fists pumping the air.

'E – E – ENL.'

Ferreira snapped at the reinforcements jumping down out of the recently arrived van, divided them up quickly and set them in a second cordon, twenty-five feet away from the body.

As they formed into position a couple of people in the car park took up the call, then the rest followed, maybe not even knowing what they were shouting for, and suddenly they were surrounded by it, bombarded.

'E – E – ENL.'

Zigic banged on the top of the patrol car. 'Get him out of here.'

Ferreira was on her phone again. 'I don't care what you have to do, just get some more fucking bodies down here . . . Yeah, listen?' She held her phone up for a couple of seconds, catching the chanting. 'That's what two minutes before a riot sounds like, so just do it.'

The cordon of men at the top end of the road parted for the patrol car to get through.

More people were arriving, laughter and excited screams cutting through the chanting which was increasing in volume and fervour, threatening to become a pounding war cry. Zigic realised it was only a matter of time before they tried to break through Shahzad's men.

'We need to do something,' Ferreira said, stepping up close to him. 'If – fuck – *when* this gets nasty we're going to have to explain why we let a group of armed civilians close off our crime scene.'

'I know that, Mel.'

He counted the uniforms they had. Eleven bodies, not enough to secure the scene and hold off twenty or thirty drunks.

'Never mind how we're going to get around them detaining our suspect at knifepoint.'

Zigic shoved his fingers through his hair. 'Let's deal with this cock-up first, shall we? Any suggestions?'

'You could try reasoning with them.'

'This is exactly the time to be funny.'

'If it kicks off it would look better for us if we can say we at least tried to calm things down. I'm not expecting them to listen.'

She had a point. He hated thinking like it but in the cold light of day, in Riggott's office, he was going to have to explain this mess.

He went to fetch a loudhailer from the van, smelled spilled coffee and diesel and testosterone-spiked sweat inside, strong enough to provoke a wave of adrenalin which sent his blood pumping. All those Friday and Saturday nights in uniform, piling out not knowing if you were going to get stabbed or bottled trying to keep the closing-time crowd from killing each other.

And now here he was again.

Clutching the loudhailer he moved through the cordon of widely spaced uniforms, Ferreira at his heels, following him into the stretch of nowhere land behind Shahzad's men. They stiffened as the crowd they were holding back began surge and jostle, voices rising.

'E – E – ENL.'

He saw faces twisted with anger and drink, raised fists gripping bottles. A gang of twenty men now, spilling off the pavement into the road, forcing the cars to go around them.

'E – E – ENL.'

He saw the lengths of wood and the iron bars in the hands of Shahzad's men as they held firm, shoulder to shoulder, with puffed-out chests thrown at them.

'Ladies and gentleman,' Zigic's voice cut across the chanting, 'please clear the area. This is a crime scene and your continued presence will result in arrest.'

A bottle smashed a few inches to his left, provoking laughter and jeers. He fought the urge to move away.

'We need you to clear the area right now.'

Something struck his head and he stumbled, blinking as his vision swam, the crowd smearing into one pulsing mass as they surged through the cordon. He dropped the loudhailer.

Ferreira was shouting as she pulled him away and he heard heavy boots running, men yelling and swearing. His feet didn't want to cooperate and he half fell a few steps, only Ferreira's hand under his arm keeping him upright until she dumped him against the wall of a house, blood in his eyes. He grabbed for her but she was already gone.

A high, animal scream cut through the air then the chanting started again, amplified through the loudhailer.

'E – E – ENL.'

Then there were other hands on him, dragging him across the pavement as bottles rained down around them, one landing close enough to send splinters flying into his ankle. He kept blinking, wiping at his face, but his vision wouldn't clear.

He heard the distorted whoop of approaching sirens and someone talking to him.

He dropped back against nothing and sprawled flat on the ground, looking up past popping spots at the night sky. Closed his eyes and when he opened them again Ferreira was standing over him, a telescopic baton in her hand, wild-faced and shouting.

'Move that van – over there.'

He turned his head and saw the Westgate end of the road blocked off with two patrol cars parked bumper to bumper. A man in a plaid shirt tried to scramble over but was forced back by the uniforms positioned behind them, receiving a swift crack on the wrist from a baton which made him howl.

When Zigic turned the other way he saw the white-sheeted corpse a few feet away from him, the fingertips of one hand poking out as if the man was about to throw the sheet aside and get up. Shahzad stood nearby, looking across the scene with a stony expression, talking on his mobile in an urgent voice.

147

Finally the chanting stopped and the scuffle sounds began to die down.

Zigic struggled up, head spinning, and Ferreira pushed him back against the wall.

'Take a minute,' she said. 'I've got it under control.'

As she spoke another man climbed onto the bonnet of a patrol car, stood for a second with his hand raised in a Nazi salute before the uniforms dragged him down, slamming him hard into the pavement.

'It looks under control,' Zigic said.

'We've got most of them. Just a couple of heroes left.'

The crowd on the car park were still filming but they'd fallen silent, no more than onlookers now, and as he scanned the area beyond the patrol cars he saw a dozen men sitting on the pavement with their hands cuffed behind their backs, blood on their faces, clothes torn. One by one they were loaded into the back of a waiting van, the drunken bravado bled out of them.

'You OK now?' Ferreira asked. 'How many fingers am I holding up?'

He glanced at her hand. 'Enough to call it insubordination.'

'Yeah, you're fine.' She took out her tobacco and started to roll a cigarette. 'Don't know about you but that all felt pretty organised to me.'

'It's Friday night,' Zigic said, dabbing at the cut on his forehead. 'One of them was probably passing, called the others.'

'Not in those numbers.' She stuck the cigarette in her mouth and began to fight her lighter for a flame which didn't want to come. 'We're hardly in the heart of clubland here. What have you got? Maloney's over the road, not exactly hospitable to ENL types, and a couple of restaurants I'm guessing they wouldn't have been in since they don't serve pie and chips.'

'We've got him, Mel. It doesn't matter why they were here.'

The lighter finally caught and she took a deep hit. 'It does if he's one of them.'

23

Zigic washed his face in the Gents, nothing but cold water coming out of the taps but it shocked some of the tiredness out of him. He snatched a handful of paper towels from the dispenser and scrubbed at the dried blood which had run down his cheek and neck, soaking into the collar of his jumper. It would stain but the jumper was black so he guessed it didn't matter.

Gingerly he lifted his hair away from the cut on his scalp, saw that it had clotted finally. The doctor suggested stitches but it would have meant shaving a patch away to do the necessary and he didn't fancy walking around with an odd bald spot at the front of his head for the next few weeks.

He dumped the towels in the bin and returned to the office.

Wahlia was back at his desk before they left the crime scene, chasing up forensics and contacting the main operator for CCTV footage of the area, now he was collating the first round of witness statements which had come in, everyone happy to cooperate for once.

Grieves and Parr arrived half an hour later, pulled away from their Friday nights, neither too sharp-looking initially but they got their game faces on quickly. Parr was finishing up with the witnesses, two men left but neither spoke English and they'd had to call in a DC from London Road Station to translate. At her desk, fortified with strong black tea and biscuits, Grieves was scanning the lists of previously questioned suspects and their known associates, trying to put a name to the man who was currently sitting stoic in an interview room, waiting for whichever duty solicitor was unfortunate enough to be on call on a Friday night.

He had no identification on him, nothing in his pockets, not even a phone. He had allowed himself to be swabbed and fingerprinted, but so far he hadn't spoken a word and mutely refused to sign the forms put in front of him.

If he thought that kind of passive protest would save him he was mistaken.

The number of witnesses they had, the forensic evidence, it would be enough for the CPS even if he never said a word between now and his trial.

Zigic walked over to Ali Manouf's board, pausing to look at the image of his murderer that they had lifted from the CCTV camera, that balaclavaed face no longer a mystery. A third whiteboard stood next to it now, the victim and the killer unnamed still but the suspects column was headed with a photograph sent up from the custody suite.

He was around forty, Zigic thought, square-faced and hard-boned, with a pronounced brow which shadowed his small blue eyes, and dark blond hair thinning at the temples and streaked with grey. An Aryan *Übermensch* long past his prime.

Some people couldn't meet the camera when they were photographed, shame or fear or guilt would drop their eyes, or they picked a spot away to one side, trying to hide what was going on in their heads, but this man stared straight down the lens, showing the same defiance he'd shown as he sat on the floor with his hands bound and blood on his boots, not a speck of weakness on display.

It was a zealot's stare and Zigic hoped he considered himself a crusader, a one-man ethnic-cleansing exercise, because if he did at some point he would talk. He'd have to – what was the point of going on a politically motivated killing spree unless you broadcast your twisted ideology to the world?

Ferreira came into the office popping a can of Coke and dropped heavily into her chair.

'You get something from our rioters?' Zigic asked.

'A lot of fascist grandstanding, some questions about whether

I'm legal to work here, and three of them want to press charges for police brutality,' she said. 'I've left uniform to deal with them – public order, isn't it, really?'

Zigic perched on the corner of her desk. 'Any of them pressing charges against you?'

'I know my job better than that. I went in from behind, can't be ID'd that way.' She smiled, on and off in a heartbeat. 'Your head OK now?'

'It was just a scratch.'

'I picked up a Zippo,' she said. 'Sent it for fingerprinting, I'm pretty sure that's what hit you if you want to make something out of it.'

'It's not worth the hassle.'

'But it's nice to know who did it, right. Add them to your shitlist.'

It sounded like a joke but he'd bet she had one, dozens of names, hundreds probably, tucked away somewhere on her phone.

'Do we know if it was an organised protest?' he asked.

'They're saying not. But a dozen ENL blokes in the area by chance?' She sneered. 'Their membership doesn't hit three figures in Peterborough and a quarter of them just happen to be out and about tonight.'

'No match on his prints,' Wahlia said. 'So if he is ENL he's kept his head down.'

'Yeah, no messing about for him, goes straight to multiple murder.' Ferreira swallowed another mouthful of Coke. 'He's old to be clean, don't you think? Man with that kind of temper.'

'People can snap for all kinds of reasons,' Zigic said, thinking of all the murderers who went to the dock with spotless lives behind them, the ones who their friends and family and co-workers couldn't believe were guilty, because everyone thought they could spot a 'wrong 'un' and how could they possibly have missed it?

The phone on Wahlia's desk rang and he snatched it up quickly, listened to the voice on the other end for a few seconds, thanked them and hung up.

'Solicitor's here.'

'Have we got photos yet?' Zigic asked.

'In the printer.'

He collected a dozen sheets of still warm, glossy paper from the tray, lurid, hi-res images of the dead man. It had been a sickening sight at the badly lit crime scene but the stark illumination from the arc lights brought out every detail, the close-ups revealing the true ferocity of the attack, tread marks on the man's tan skin, a ripped eyelid, a burst of grey matter, the nauseating jut of his broken spinal column pressing against the side of his neck.

Ferreira handed him a cardboard file.

'You won't guilt him into confession with them.'

'I don't want one,' Zigic told her, going into his office to collect a few more photos from the pile on his desk.

They headed down to the interview room, the corridor chilled, ghosted by the smell of sweat and vanilla perfume. A burly uniform was stationed outside the door to Interview Room 2, and inside a second, larger man stood guard with his hands tucked into the small of his back, posture ramrod-straight.

The duty solicitor was in the corner, fiddling with her mobile, keeping one eye on her client, who sat at the table in a white plastic coverall, his clothes taken by forensics for testing along with the heavy black boots which had done so much damage.

He didn't look at them as they entered the room, only stared straight ahead, blinking occasionally, his face blank, hands placed flat on the scarred tabletop.

'Are you ready?' Zigic asked. 'Or do you need some more time with your client?'

The solicitor slipped her mobile away, smoothed her skirt over her hips, nervous-looking as she approached him. 'No, I don't think that will help.'

They took their seats around the table and Ferreira started the recording equipment, running down the time and who was present, reminded him of his rights. The man sat in the chair opposite Zigic, looked through him like he didn't exist, and when Ferreira prompted him to state his name he remained silent.

'Refusing to tell us who you are won't make this go away,' Zigic said.

No reaction. Not even a flicker of eye movement or a slight twitch of his fingers, which were splayed on the table, short, thick fingers with broad nails, neatly cut. They weren't a worker's hands, Zigic thought, no nicks or scars, his skin soft.

'Has he told you who he is?'

The solicitor shook her head. 'He hasn't spoken to me. I think you should consider the possibility that he requires medical attention. He may be in shock.'

'The doctor's seen him. He's not in shock,' Zigic said. 'Are you?'

His plastic bodysuit crinkled softly as he breathed, but he didn't reply, only maintained the thousand-yard stare, utterly impervious.

'Let me explain something to you – silence is not a defence. We have witnesses who saw you murder this man, we have blood on your clothes which will shortly be confirmed as his. These things are not open to interpretation. They are facts. And your silence doesn't change anything. Maybe you think that we can't charge someone without knowing their name.' Zigic spread his hands wide, waiting for a reaction which didn't come. 'But you're wrong. We can and will charge you and without any explanation or cooperation on your part you will serve the longest sentence possible. You are making the situation worse for yourself. That's all.'

Not a flicker, not a single glimmer of awareness in his cool blue eyes.

Zigic wondered what could possibly be going through the man's mind right now. Did he believe he could simply sit out the next twenty-four or forty-eight hours, play dumb, show them nothing, then get released? Was he that naive?

'Maybe he's deaf,' Ferreira said.

His solicitor twisted in her seat, glanced at him. 'Or he doesn't speak English.'

Zigic frowned, tried to catch his eye. '*Jaka jest twoja nazwa?*'

Nothing. He tried a few words of Serbo-Croat, switched to Latvian, then Lithuanian, knowing his pronunciation was bad and his vocabulary severely limited, but all he wanted was a reaction, some small sign that they were getting through. Ferreira asked him the same simple question in Portuguese then French then German. He didn't even look at her.

It seemed impossible he wouldn't recognise any of the languages. They dealt with plenty of migrants and most had at least a smattering of English. Even the ones who didn't attempted to make themselves understood, with mangled words or hand gestures, knowing they had rights and wanting to exercise them.

Regardless of his nationality, he had decided not to cooperate.

Zigic opened the slim cardboard file and brought out the crime-scene photographs, laid them out in a grid in front of the man. His eyes dropped and widened and the merest hint of a smile lifted the corners of his mouth.

Then Zigic took out the older photographs, Didi's and Ali Manouf's wrecked heads replacing that of their most recent victim, and as he spread them out he realised how the attacks had rendered the dead men indistinguishable from one another.

The smile was gone now but the man was still looking at the photographs, his fingers curling away from them.

'You didn't think we'd make the link?' Zigic asked. 'You were unlucky tonight, but you were stupid with Ali Manouf – that's the man's name – spitting on him. It's almost like you wanted to get caught.'

His bodysuit rustled as he brought his hands together, folding one over the other.

Zigic removed the final photograph from the file; this one lifted from the CCTV camera on Castle Road, a black-clad figure giving a Nazi salute.

'You wanted us to see this,' he said, leaning across the table, the

154

man meeting his eyes finally. 'You've obviously got something you want to say. Now's your chance.'

The silence stretched, five seconds, ten, with nothing but the sound of the clock ticking and the slight creak of boot leather as the guard at the door eased his weight from one foot to the other. The man pressed his lips together, blinked slowly, and Zigic could see the thoughts scudding behind his eyes now, unreadable but something was stirring in there, confession or denial he didn't care, he just wanted to get the man talking.

A minute ticked past, then another, and Zigic felt the long evening weighing heavy on him, the beginning of a hangover conspiring with exhaustion and frustration, making his head throb. He bunched his fists and rested his chin on them, watching the man make his calculations, trying to decide if there was more to be gained by talking than remaining silent.

Abruptly the look in his eyes changed, like a switch being flipped, and they were blank again. He'd made his decision.

'Anything?' Zigic asked.

Nothing.

'Maybe you just need a bit more time to think about it.' He gestured to the guard. 'Take him down to the cells.'

The PC called in his mate from the corridor and the two of them escorted the man out of the interview room, one on either side, hands around his upper arms. His solicitor followed them out and Zigic got up to stretch his legs, paced around the table while Ferreira gathered the photos into the file.

'He can't keep it up forever,' she said. 'You don't do something like this unless you want attention.'

'I was expecting a rant.'

'He's shocked he's been caught, that's all. Tomorrow morning, when it's sunk in, then he'll talk.'

Zigic hooked his hands around the back of his neck. 'We don't need him to.'

'But you want him to.'

'Don't you?'

'I just want to charge him,' she said. 'He talks or he doesn't, what's the difference? We know why he did it already.'

The interview-room door opened and Parr came in, excitement lighting up his face.

'We've got something, sir.'

Zigic stopped pacing. 'What?'

'Two of the witnesses, the blokes from the house, the ones who tackled him.' Parr was almost vibrating. 'They saw someone else with him. He ran off when they came out.'

DAY THR

24

'You need to get him talking,' Riggott said, sitting in Zigic's chair, leaning forward, fingers steepled, deep shadows under his eyes from the strip light. He'd shown up in his civvies, ten minutes before morning briefing, and gestured towards the office without a word.

'What do you suggest?' Zigic asked. 'Take a phone book to his ribs?'

'You can waterboard the piece of shite for all I care. We need him to give up his partner.'

'He won't even tell us own his name. He's not going to come across.'

'Persuade him.'

'Persuasion requires a desired outcome,' Zigic said. 'And I don't think we've got anything he wants. You talk to him, the man's a rock. He's not scared, he's not interested in pushing his agenda.'

Riggott snorted. 'Fucking agenda.'

'Three murdered migrants,' Zigic reminded him. 'He's politically motivated.'

Riggott swivelled in the enveloping leather chair, eyes roaming around the office, taking in the empty corkboards and stretches of beige wall pricked all over from old drawing pins, the greasy smears of long-removed Blu-tack which had seeped through the paint job. The only decoration Zigic had brought to the room were a few of Milan's and Stefan's drawings, stuck to the side of a filing cabinet with small black magnets, and a pair of framed photos on the desk.

'It's not very homely in here.'

'It's not meant to be,' Zigic said.

He glanced through the window onto the main office, saw Ferreira arrive with a tray of takeout coffees and a handful of brown paper bags from McDonald's, watched the rest of them cluster around her, everyone shattered-looking after only a few hours off. He'd sent them home at two, told them to be back by seven thirty. He'd snatched a couple of hours' sleep on the sofa, woke up with Stefan poking his cheek, more tired than he was when he crashed out, fully clothed, too exhausted to even kick off his shoes. He hauled himself up, poured two double espressos on top of his hangover and showered in cold water to shake some energy loose.

Today should have been a relief. They had their murderer, the case should have been as good as over, nothing to do but organise the ample evidence against him and prepare the paperwork to send over to the CPS, but the presence of a second attacker changed everything.

'We've got the culprit,' Zigic said. 'We'll be able to charge him today.'

'Aye, and that'll buy you some breathing space,' Riggott told him. 'But you've two witnesses who know there was a second man at the scene and they won't keep quiet about it. Not in a community like that.'

As if he didn't know the stakes already.

'We'll get him,' Zigic said, sounding more confident than he felt.

Riggott stood up, came round the desk, his body all sharp angles, mantis-like. 'You wouldn't have caught this one without the neighbours stepping in.'

'We got lucky, I'd be the first person to admit that –'

'And you won't get lucky again.' Riggott gave him a pointed look, grey eyes bloodshot, his own heavy Friday night stamped all over his face. 'Best prepare yourself for a firestorm over this riot. Don't need to tell you who the ACC's going to send out as a baffle, do I?'

'We contained it,' Zigic said. 'Under very difficult circumstances. Christ, it took almost half an hour to get reinforcements out. In the middle of town. We were given nothing, no support. It's a miracle there were no serious injuries.'

Riggott stepped up closer. 'That talk does not leave the office, you hear me, son?'

'We weren't the only people there. The ENL are going to use it for their own ends. There's too much political capital in it for them to ignore.'

'Let Nicola worry about killing their press,' Riggott said, softening slightly, placing a hand on his shoulder; paternal, placating. 'I've put word out this case is top priority – anything you need now, you've got it.'

Riggott strode out through Hate Crimes, pausing for the briefest words of encouragement before heading home to the rest of his weekend, the Saturday papers and a lazy brunch, a round of golf perhaps, a few pints down his local at lunchtime.

Zigic went over to the boards, the latest one holding more information than the other two put together, and it gave him a lift, knowing that as tough a task as they were facing, they were finally making progress.

He saw the same feeling on the rest of the team; beyond the tiredness and the dishevelled clothes, there was a sense of optimism. Grieves and Parr were laughing at some private joke, sharing a chocolate muffin broken into pieces on a flattened-out bag, while Wahlia and Ferreira stood close together near the window. That conversation didn't look quite so light-hearted, Zigic realised, as Wahlia tapped her on the knuckles with a spoon, his thick brows drawing together as he frowned.

There was something going on but now wasn't the time.

'Alright, everyone, let's get started.'

They returned to their desks, where last night's abandoned tasks were waiting to be picked up again. Grieves had brought a couple of photographs in this morning he noticed, one of her boyfriend and one of her dog, stuck them to the front of her computer, making the space her own. If Riggott wanted to transfer her over permanently he wouldn't argue; he'd been promised replacements for the two officers who had left almost three years ago, but budget restraints kept the desks empty.

Some good might come out of this mess at least.

'OK, so in light of what we found out last night our main priority today is identifying the second man at the scene. He might have taken part in the assault, he might just have been observing, but if our witness statements are valid we have to assume he was involved.'

'What about the earlier crimes?' Grieves asked. 'Do we think he might have been at them too?'

She didn't put her hand up this time. She was getting settled.

'That's what I want you to look at, Deb. There's no sign of him on the CCTV footage from those attacks but the coverage in New England is patchy at best and there's a chance we might have missed him, especially as we were concentrating on tracking a lone figure. Go back through them, see if we've got two men around the area at the time.'

She nodded. 'Yes, sir.'

'First thing though, I want you to concentrate on the footage from last night.'

'But there aren't any cameras on Cromwell Road,' she said.

'Try the footage online,' Ferreira said, not looking up as she shredded a clump of tobacco between her fingertips. 'There's plenty of it already. Chances are he stuck around to see what happened to his mate, bask in the rage.'

'There's an office a few doors up,' Zigic said, turning his attention back to Grieves. 'They've got a camera on their entrance, you'll need to get in touch with them. Mel, I want you to work on the amateur footage.'

She sealed her cigarette. 'OK.'

'Like you say, he probably stuck around and you know the local players better than Deb. Anyone who stands out, anyone sober probably, just see what looks wrong to you. They're going to be all over the riot, so hit the forums when you're done, see if anyone's mouthing off.' She pulled her keyboard towards her immediately, straightened in her seat. 'Especially anyone who was actually at the scene.'

'On it.'

Zigic pointed at Parr. 'Witness statements, right? Pull everything from Didi's and Ali Manouf's murders, find the people who were closest and talk to them again. Take our man's photo, see if anyone recognises him, or saw two men hanging around.' Parr nodded. 'And have both areas recanvassed. He probably reconnoitred before the attacks, maybe not alone.'

'Yes, sir.'

Zigic turned to the map of the city centre, the murders plotted with red dots, close together. All three taking place within a quarter-mile radius.

'There's a chance he's local to New England, so speak to the shopkeepers, do the pubs, the cafes. See if anyone knows anything about him. We've got clearance for all the uniforms we need. Make the most of them.'

'Yes, sir.'

'OK. Quicker we do this the better chance we all have of getting some kind of weekend in.' There were soft snorts of derision and Zigic smiled. 'Didn't think you'd fall for that.'

His mobile vibrated and he wrapped up the briefing as he brought it out of his pocket. Nicola Gilraye.

'Ziggy, are you near a screen?'

'Why?'

'You've made the BBC again.'

He went into his office and opened up iPlayer, Gilraye still talking in his ear. 'They've got your riot at number two in the running order. We need to get a statement out now.'

'That's your job, Nicola – what do you want me to do?'

'Tell me something I can use.'

He watched the headlines play through, leading on Syria, a massacre in a village which had left dozens dead, shaky footage of bloodstains in the road and shot-marked buildings in the background. Then another segment filmed on a mobile phone – citizen journalism in action – Cromwell Road at the height of the violence.

'Are you seeing this?'

'I'm looking at it,' he said, watching a bald man in a leather bomber jacket rush the cordon, head down, determined, until a baton struck his ribs and felled him. The camera panned left and caught a second man climbing onto the bonnet of a patrol car, the white-sheeted corpse visible at the edge of the shot. 'We knew this was going to happen. Why aren't you prepared already?'

Gilraye ignored his question. 'Have you charged him yet?'

'He's not talking.'

'I need more than "unnamed man in custody". I'm fielding calls from all the majors here.'

There was a brief return to the studio then they cut away to a street Zigic recognised, London Road, near the Peacock pub. Richard Shotton in a grey overcoat, standing in front of a billboard bearing a blown-up version of himself, the English Patriot Party logo looming large.

Zigic closed the screen before he started talking.

'Just do what you can please, Nicola. As soon as I've got something I'll let you know.'

'Make sure you do,' she said. 'And, orders from above, there's a vigil this afternoon at three on the cathedral green, you should be there.'

'We're in the middle of an investigation.'

'This is coming from the Chief. Take it up with him if your schedule's too hectic.'

Wahlia knocked on the open door. 'We've got an ID on the victim.'

He ended the call and followed Wahlia back to his desk, saw the young man's file open on his computer screen.

Asif Khalid. He was twenty years old, boyish-looking with a slim, fine-boned face and black hair voguishly cut and carefully styled, a diamond stud in his right ear, wearing a pink polo shirt with the collar turned up. He stood a little under five six by the lines on the wall behind his head, but he had a short man's air of studied insouciance which the situation hadn't wiped away.

'What was he arrested for?'

164

'Speeding,' Wahlia said. 'A lot of it.'

'Did he do any damage?'

'No, he just seemed to like duelling police cars.'

He was only a kid. Stupid and cocky but who wasn't at that age? Zigic thought. He probably imagined he'd die behind the wheel, harboured some boy-racer fantasy of topping 220 in a gleaming super-car. Music pounding, machine gliding, then a sudden swerve, a crash and a fireball and instant, painless death in a spectacular blaze of glory.

What he got was a commonplace exit, dying half in the gutter under the boots of a pair of fascist thugs.

'Was he local?' Zigic asked.

'Yeah, he lived on Gladstone Street,' Wahlia said, scrolling down his file. 'Guess he was on his way home, got jumped.'

'Alright, I'd better go and break the news.'

Ferreira looked up from her computer. 'Do you want me to come with?'

'No, stick with what you're doing.' He grabbed his parka from the hook. 'Keep me updated.'

25

The city centre was quiet despite the lure of the shopping centre and the Saturday market. The bright spring sunshine was beating down on the ugly 1970s buildings, unbroken by clouds. He'd had a vague notion of pottering in the garden today, clear some of the rubbish from the flower beds, mow the lawn, turn the compost heap. Anna had bought a swing for the boys which needed putting together, he was going to fix it to the gnarled old chestnut tree in the back, but that would have to wait.

Zigic turned onto Bright Street, passing the car park which had been filled with gawkers last night but now only held a few cars. In the far corner a team of men in a white van had their ladders propped against the billboard overlooking Cromwell Road, covering an old, heavily graffitied advert for home insurance with one for payday loans.

Forensics had been and gone and now a yellow street sweeper was trundling along between the parked cars, driven by a man with thick, blond dreadlocks and mirrored Aviators. It gathered up the thrown cans and the broken glass, the shreds of clothing ripped away during the riot and the ephemera which had spilled out of pockets. Anything which forensics had deemed unworthy of pursuing. A strand of striped police tape fluttered into its path and snagged in the brushes, trailing like a banner.

Zigic followed the one-way system up Cromwell Road and past the Faizan-e-Madina Mosque, the sunlight glinting off the building's arched windows. A small group of men were standing talking at the gate and he noticed Mr Shahzad among them, leaning on his walking stick, listening patiently.

He turned onto Gladstone Street. It was narrow, single-lane, the terraced houses in various states of disrepair behind their low front walls, a patchwork of buff brick, pebble-dash and grey paint, double yellow lines up both sides but a few cars were parked on the kerb, hazard warning lights flashing. More men walking home from morning prayers, women with kids in tow, weighed down with shopping bags.

The street hadn't changed much since his grandparents lived there in the late fifties. It was the first stop for new migrants and across the years the Slavs and Italians had given way to people from India and Pakistan, still the majority in the area. The most recent arrivals from Eastern Europe were making their presence felt on the neighbouring streets, opening cafes and beauty salons, but they hadn't reached Gladstone Street, and as he slowed, checking the house numbers, he passed shops selling Islamic books and clothing, halal butchers and grocers with crates of fruit and veg on trestle tables, shaded by striped canopies, a bakery with its windows open, filling the air with a warm, sweet smell.

It was the kind of place a right-wing extremist would want to strike at, Zigic thought, slowing to let a woman in a niqab cross the road ahead of him. This was exactly what the ENL were raging against, with their dialogue of cultural dilution and restoring traditional English values.

They were easy to shrug off as harmless cranks, only interested in getting together in scuzzy pubs to talk about a revolution they would never manage to provoke, more likely to fight among themselves than raise a concerted attack on the minorities they were so opposed to.

But all it took was one man more committed than the rest.

Or two.

He pulled up outside Asif Khalid's house. It was the same as all the others, painted white but grubby from exhaust fumes, one window up, one window down, a plastic front door with a patterned glass panel, a concrete standing with the bins lined up and a small trough with a few bulbs about to flower. The Victorian-style light next to the front door was still on and as he rang the bell he thought of the people inside, leaving it on for when Asif rolled in, not wanting him to come home to darkness.

A young woman in jeans and a linen tunic opened the door, hair tied back from a round face and a feather duster in her hand.

'Miss Khalid?'

'Mrs Khalid,' she said, eyeing him suspiciously, moving slightly, ready to slam the door shut. 'What do you want?'

'Detective Inspector Zigic,' he said, showing her his identification. 'I'm sorry, but do you think I could come in?'

'Is this about Asif?'

'Yes.'

'Don't tell me he's been arrested again.' She shook her head. 'I told him he couldn't keep driving without his licence. Does he listen to me? Does he hell. Now he'll lose his job –'

'Mrs Khalid, he hasn't been arrested,' Zigic said softly. 'Please, can we discuss this inside?'

He followed her into the living room and she sat down on the cream leather sofa, threw the duster into an armchair, large brown eyes fixed on him, tears already springing up.

'What's going on?'

'I'm sorry, there's no good way to tell you this –'

'No.'

'Asif was attacked last night –'

She pressed her face into her hands. 'Is he – he's not dead? Please. He can't be dead.'

'I'm sorry, but I'm afraid he was killed.'

'Why? Was it a robbery?'

'No,' Zigic said, feeling useless, standing there in her neat pillar-box-red living room, unable to do anything to help, knowing there was nothing he could say or do to soothe the pain on her face. 'We've arrested the man who did it. He's in custody.'

She cried quietly, shoulders shaking, her arms wrapped around her middle. He asked if there was anyone he could call for her and she shook her head. Asked if she'd like a family liaison officer to come round, was told no. And what would they do anyway? he thought. Make her tea, explain the slow, horrific process she would have to face, the trial and media intrusion.

He went into the kitchen at the back of the house, all gleaming chrome surfaces and black tiles, the washing machine humming to itself behind a cupboard. He gave her a couple of minutes alone, looking out across their small garden where a tabby cat was sunning itself on the decking, thinking of how this would change things.

Didi's and Ali Manouf's murders had gone largely ignored, no community to speak for them, nobody to vent a righteous fury that they had been killed so brutally, so casually. But Asif Khalid had a young wife, likely parents and siblings in Peterborough, and they would demand the men responsible were caught. Both of them, not just the sullen thug currently eating his breakfast in a cell at Thorpe Wood Station, gathering his strength for another round of one-sided interrogation.

They would want blood. And Zigic couldn't blame them.

By now it was likely that word of the second attacker was out, circulated at morning prayers, shared across the counters of the local shops. The presence of the ENL at the crime scene too. Reprisals were a definite possibility. Something the ENL might welcome, stir up even, to make themselves look like victims. It was a well-worn tactic of theirs, good for drumming up support.

He poured a glass of water and returned to the living room. Mrs Khalid took it from him, her hand shaking, but didn't drink.

'Can I see him?'

'Asif was beaten quite badly.'

'I don't care, I want to see him.'

Zigic squatted down in front of her. 'Mrs Khalid, it really wouldn't be wise. Asif sustained serious injuries. Multiple, serious injuries to his face and head. I'm afraid he is no longer recognisable.'

She straightened. 'Then it might not be him.'

'We've matched his fingerprints. I'm sorry, it's definitely your husband.'

The glass slipped from her hand and bounced on the thick carpet, water splashing across her bare feet, soaking Zigic's jeans.

'I don't understand why this happened,' she said. 'Why him? Asif was a good man, he didn't drink, he didn't start fights with people. Why would anybody want to hurt him?'

Zigic righted the glass, retreated to the armchair opposite her.

'The man responsible didn't know Asif. At least we don't believe he did at this stage. It's highly likely he targeted Asif purely because of his skin colour.'

She swore under her breath. 'But you've arrested him.'

'Yes.'

'And you can prove it was him?'

'We've got solid witnesses, Mrs Khalid. He's not going anywhere.'

She asked no more questions and after a couple of minutes' silence, with only the sound of the cat flap banging in the kitchen and the laughter of children out on the street, he realised there was nothing else he could say to her.

He gave her his card as he left, told her that if she had any questions, if she needed anything, she could call him. She nodded and retreated into the house, closed the door and switched off the light glowing next to it.

26

They stood in front of the forty-six-inch flat screen, Shotton, Selby and Marshall, who was no longer watching it, focused instead on his iPad. Like Google could give him the name of the man they were looking for if he knew exactly how to phrase the question.

It wasn't a matter of how you phrased it, Shotton knew, but who you asked.

He dialled Ken Poulter's number and when he answered said, 'I need a taxi at my place. Immediately.' Hung up without waiting for a reply.

Sky News was playing the same two minutes of footage on a loop, concentrating on the moment the ENL stormed the barricade of heavily armed Asian men, a plain-clothes policeman hitting the ground and being dragged away.

Then it got really ugly.

Scenes Shotton had paid good money to make sure wouldn't happen. Big, drunken men throwing their weight about, saluting the onlookers whose phones had captured this PR disaster. He could feel power slipping away from him as the seconds passed, knew how the voters he was courting would recoil from the sight of uniformed officers wading into the filth who peddled the most noxious version of his policies.

'You were there,' Shotton said.

Selby inhaled sharply. 'No, I wasn't.'

'You were supposed to be talking to this lot, don't tell me you didn't run along with the rest of them.'

'I wouldn't be here now if I was, would I?' Selby said, his voice rising. 'I was in the Red Lion when the messages started coming through and they all took off.'

The sound was muted but Shotton knew what the newsreader was saying, had heard it half a dozen times already, could recite it word for word. *Police in Peterborough are calling for calm today after a riot broke out at the scene of what is believed to be the third in a series of racially motivated killings in the city. The latest death comes less than a week after forty-six-year-old Ali Manouf, an Iranian asylum seeker, was brutally murdered, but a spokesperson for Cambridgeshire Constabulary denied that the situation has moved beyond their control. We are currently awaiting a statement on the arrest of a man at the crime scene.*

In the background he could see the corpse, covered in a white sheet, an elderly man standing next to it, and knew that in a moment the newsreader would break away to a reporter in the field, a pre-recorded package with the local imam, outside his mosque. He would make the same appeal for calm that the police had, but Shotton had watched him carefully twice already and saw that his blood was up. He didn't want calm, he wanted reprisals, and they would come tonight.

It might undo some of the damage, Shotton thought. Balance the books.

'What did you get out of them before they left the pub?' he asked.

Selby dragged his eyes away from the screen. 'I don't think they're behind it.'

'My God, man, look at this fucking mess. Some bloke gets killed and your ENL friends are at the scene before the police and you don't think they're responsible?'

'They're too talkative,' Selby said. 'They only mouth off when they've got nothing to hide.'

'What are they saying then?'

'They're bigging up whoever did it, saying what a hero he is, that he deserves a medal, that sort of thing. They're acting like it could be the beginning of something but it's all just talk. Believe me, I know these blokes, I know how they think. When something's in the offing they clam up. They're paranoid when you get right down to it.'

'What about Poulter?'

'He got funny, wanted to know why I was so interested.' Selby shrugged. 'Once he asked that it was like I didn't exist, they started talking about the football. End of discussion.'

Shotton's mobile phone rang and he checked the display. Walter again. He let it ring out, in no mood to take a earful of abuse which he had no answer for.

He told Selby to go home for a few hours, he wouldn't need him until this evening, and retreated to his desk, copies of the Saturday papers strewn about, including the weekend edition of the local rag, which featured the smiling face of the young woman who'd died in the hit-and-run on its front cover, an interview with her sister inside. The riot had happened too late to get any coverage but he knew the Sundays would have a field day with it.

Marshall had already given a statement to several journalists, a blanket condemnation followed by full support for the police, the same sentiment, but in different terms, to the quote he'd given *Look East* this morning after they caught him on walkabout in Peterborough.

The ENL were hijacking him at every turn.

He lit a cigarette and waited for Ken Poulter to arrive, wishing there was a button he could press which would instantly vaporise the whole lot of them.

As damaging as the riot was he tried to take some encouragement from the onlookers who had joined the fray. A few dozen potential voters swayed in his direction and with turnouts as low as they tended to be those people could make a difference.

He just needed to create distance between the ENL and his party. It had been a problem right from the off and he calmed himself with the knowledge that any political movement would initially be limited by its hardcore early adopters, the classic lunatic fringe. It happened across the spectrum and it was a sign of the English Patriot Party's potential that they were suffering it too.

Fifteen minutes later Ken Poulter's minicab pulled onto the driveway and he marched across the driveway towards the office like a man bent on losing his temper.

Marshall showed him in and tactfully retreated.

'Things not working out with your driver?' Poulter asked.

He stood with hands curled by his sides, simian-looking with his long arms and slightly stooped posture, earned by spending years hunched over in his cell, Shotton guessed.

'Sit down.'

'I'll stand.'

If he thought that constituted an advantage he was much mistaken.

'Back to your old tricks, Kenneth,' Shotton said, keeping his own anger smothered for the time being. 'We talked about that, didn't we?'

'Nothing to do with me, boss.'

'You've got ten grand of my money that says otherwise.'

Poulter smiled. 'Exceptional circumstances.'

'It was a fucking riot.'

'Out of my control. I was at work last night. Can't do much about it if I'm not there. Got to earn a living, you know.'

He was jumpy behind the bravado, Shotton saw. Couldn't keep his feet still, couldn't control the nervous energy which made his fingers twitch.

'No public displays, we agreed on that.'

'I didn't sanction it,' Poulter said, shoving his hands in his pockets, hiding the knuckleduster rings and the prison tattoos. 'And if I could have stopped them, I would have. I want the same thing you do.'

'I want whoever killed those men arrested and charged,' Shotton thundered. 'You're as much at risk as I am now. Do you understand that?'

'None of my boys are responsible for those murders.'

174

Shotton carried on as if he hadn't spoken. 'Do you want the ENL to become an outlawed terror group?'

'No.'

But the idea seemed to amuse him.

'How about another spell in Littlehey?' That killed the amusement. 'Because when the police catch your man, it'll reflect very badly on you as leader. And I doubt they'll buy whatever rubbish you give them about being ignorant of his actions.'

'I don't know who's responsible,' Poulter said.

'Then find out.'

'Isn't that Selby's job?'

'It's your job now.'

Shotton stood up and moved around his desk. The muted television was still playing, showing the steps outside Thorpe Wood Station, a young blonde woman standing in front of the gathered press.

'I want you to find him and turn him in.'

Poulter eyed him suspiciously. Wet his lips. 'Why would I do that? Even if I could.'

'Because you're getting on and I imagine you don't have much in the way of a pension provision.' Shotton smiled slightly, seeing that he was right. 'Thirty grand goes a long way in Turkey, I hear.'

Poulter's expression hardened in an instant.

'You think I'm going to sell out the cause for thirty fucking grand?' Poulter stepped up and Shotton forced himself to hold firm against the wave of aggression rising off the man. 'This is why you'll never get anywhere. You don't believe in what we stand for, you just want a cushy job and a fucking expense account.'

'Thirty grand is more than fair.'

'You jumped-up Tory cunt,' Poulter spat. 'What do you think the press would make of your pay-offs? Won't hurt us if it gets out, will it? But I reckon your political career would be properly fucked.'

'Forty then.'

'You can't buy me.'

'I already have,' Shotton barked.

Poulter's face darkened. 'The deal's off. And if you send any shit in our direction I'll go straight to the papers.'

He stormed out of the office and Shotton returned to his desk on uncertain legs, seeing his carefully laid plans, all of the whoring and finessing, ground to nothing under the heel of a heavy black boot.

27

'You're going to get wrinkles if you keep doing that,' Wahlia said.

Ferreira glanced up from her computer, footage of the riot playing, chanting coming through the bud she'd plugged into her right ear.

'Doing what?'

He pulled a face like an angry kabuki mask.

She smiled, felt the tension leave her forehead, her jaw unclench. 'What're you doing?'

'Forensics have just come through,' he said. 'Preliminary stuff. About what we expected. Blood type match from Khalid on the guy's boots, fibres from his jumper on Khalid's jacket.'

Ferreira stretched in her chair, rolled her shoulders and heard something crack in her neck. 'Have they found any sign of our second attacker?'

'Jenkins has retrieved a couple of unidentified hairs but they're blonde, very long and dip-dyed.'

'We could be looking for a woman.'

'I think we both know how they got down his shirt,' Wahlia said, unwrapping a stick of gum.

'You Asian boys and your dirty blondes.' Ferreira swivelled in her chair, looked towards Grieves, who was dunking a biscuit in her tea, keeping her cup under it so it wouldn't drip on her keyboard. So neat and careful. So fucking conscientious.

Ferreira thought of her sitting outside the inspector's office, bolt upright, her uniform just as immaculate that day as it was on any other, despite the fact that she'd spent the previous fifteen minutes down in the cells performing pointless CPR on a dead boy.

'Grieves, have you got hold of the CCTV footage yet?'

'There's no sign of a woman with Khalid,' she said. 'I've traced him right back to when he left the Yates's on Long Causeway.'

'Anything on Cromwell Road?'

'I'm still trying to get in touch with the company whose camera it is,' she said, turning away from her desk, brushing a few crumbs from the thighs of her charcoal-grey trousers. 'They obviously don't answer work calls over the weekend.'

'So get the owner's address and send a couple of uniforms round there,' Ferreira told her. 'You do this shit in CID, don't you?'

Grieves mumbled a 'Yes, ma'am', and picked up her phone.

Across the desk Wahlia shook his head at her, more amused than disapproving. She was glad Zigic wasn't there; his reaction wouldn't have been quite as indulgent, she suspected.

He was impressed with Grieves. She was just the kind of DC inspectors loved, all yes sir, no sir, perfectly deferential and incapable of independent thought.

'What else?' she asked Wahlia. 'Has Jenkins run our attacker's samples against what we got off Manouf's body?'

'Yeah, same blood type. DNA to follow. The usual.' He snapped the gum between his teeth, popping it with a sharp crack. 'It's all looking pretty neat.'

Ferreira paused the footage on her screen, faces frozen in wild contortions. 'I don't like this. How hasn't he got a record? The man's like forty years old and he's never been arrested once. There are no dead starts for psychos. It doesn't make sense going straight to serial murder.'

'You can't argue with the evidence, Mel.'

'I'm not arguing with it, I just don't think we're getting the full picture.' She picked up the half-smoked stub of her last cigarette and relit it. 'And why isn't he talking? He salutes a CCTV camera – for us to see – he's telling us everything about his motivation right there. He should want this platform.'

'I don't know,' Wahlia said.

'We put the crime-scene photos in front of him and he beamed. He's proud of what he's done, he's got a captive audience. He should be boasting.'

'I don't know,' Wahlia said, a hint of annoyance creeping into his voice. 'You're the one with the psychology degree, you tell me why.'

Ferreira drew deep on her cigarette, eyed fixed on the computer screen, all of that rage held static, poised to flare again. 'Maybe he's scared of his little buddy. If he starts talking it becomes a negotiation, doesn't it? We offer him consideration if he turns the bloke in, maybe he gets tempted to take it.'

'He's kicked three men to death,' Wahlia said. 'I doubt he's scared of much.'

'We don't know what his situation is. What if he's got a family? You want someone to keep their mouth shut, what do you do? Talk and we kill your kids.'

Wahlia ran his fingers through his hair, face twisted in thought. 'It happens, I suppose. But not with this sort of crime. If it was drugs or something, yeah, maybe.'

'What makes this any different? Fear's fear.'

'And it's usually exercised on unwilling participants,' Wahlia said. 'Drug mules, prostitutes. Nobody falls into a racist killing spree by accident. He knew what he was doing. Nobody forced him to kill those men.'

Ferreira sucked the last breath out of her cigarette, felt the burn touch her lips and stubbed it out angrily. 'We'll see.'

She unpaused the footage and watched the final few minutes play through, knowing exactly what was coming. She'd watched the same scene from a dozen or more, very slightly different angles, but saw nothing she hadn't noticed at the time. Everything on YouTube had been uploaded by people in the car park, not ENL players, just civilians who were more interested in the dead body and the murderer being escorted out of the house.

One person had focused solely on her and Zigic though, and it made her uncomfortable now, sitting at her desk in the contained environment of this office, to know someone had zoomed in on her face as she lifted the sheet from Asif Khalid's corpse, wanting to see her reaction more than anything else. They'd been watching her and she hadn't felt it, too wired from the violence in the air and the adrenalin singing in her veins.

This was the wrong place to look, she thought, as she clicked through to another account and watched the same things happening yet again. Zigic walking out through the police cordon, her behind him. He tries to reason with them and fails, then falls as he's hit on the head. She saw herself haul him away and plunge into the clash of bodies, take a blow to the back she couldn't remember feeling at the time.

The camera panned away to the right, trained on the men grappling at the mouth of the road, and Ferreira hit pause.

Ken Poulter. ENL commander-in-chief. Standing well back, looking like any other passer-by, uninvolved and unobtrusive in his black shirt and trousers, a black wool beanie pulled low on his forehead.

He wasn't among the men they arrested.

Sure enough when she unpaused the footage she saw him turn away from the riot and disappear up Westgate like it was nothing to do with him.

She opened up Facebook, signed in and went to the ENL Peterborough Division group, a St George's Cross emblazoned across the top of the screen.

'Mel, coffee?'

'Thanks.' She passed her cup across the desk in the gap between her and Wahlia's computers. 'Find me some chocolate, would you, Bobby? There's change in my jacket.'

There were a few new members since the last time she'd visited the site, a week ago, and she guessed they'd been drawn in by the attacks. That or Richard Shotton's campaigning had attracted some fresh bodies to the militant arm of the cause. She recognised a couple of the names, both petty offenders, a car thief and a small-time dealer. There was another woman, or a woman's name at least, attached to a profile picture which showed nothing more than a pair of red glossed lips cut from a cosmetics advert.

The photograph Ferreira had used to gain access to the closed group was just as fake, plucked from a amateur porn site, a bleach blonde with a bust bigger than her head. It took over a month to position 'Tracey Holland', make the right contacts, say the right things. A delicate job among people who believed they were constantly under surveillance by the police and MI5, with 'reds' trying to infiltrate them from all angles. Tracey was supportive but not pushy, flirty but 'in a relationship', and she categorically was not a racist. She just didn't like what was happening to her country.

When the invitation had finally hit her inbox Ferreira punched the air, shouted 'Suckers!' in the middle of Topshop.

Now she could see all the stuff the ENL didn't think fit for public consumption.

More photographs of the riot, ones of the cordon Mr Shahzad's men had formed at the mouth of Cromwell Road – 'Paki patrol in PBO' – then a shot from this morning, three ENL members on the steps of Thorpe Wood Station, smiling stupidly with their black eyes blooming.

Left the copshop. Off 4 a full english. Yolo.

Tracey 'likes' this.

1 *muzzi down,* 1,999,999,999 *to go.*

Twenty messages of support for that. Seventy-eight 'likes', almost everyone in the group showing their approval.

More of them. She kept scrolling, stopping at an image of Asif Khalid dead on the pavement before he'd been covered with a sheet. Three Asian men were standing nearby, the front door of the house they'd come from open to the street, lights on inside.

It had been filmed from the car park. Posted by Ken Poulter at ten forty-two.

Ferreira felt her pulse quickening. Poulter was there before the police, before Shahzad arrived and organised his men.

'Coffee and chocolate.' Wahlia put them down next to her keyboard. 'What's that? Is that Khalid?'

'Yeah.'

'How did you get into a closed group?'

'Ingenuity,' she said. 'Look, Ken Poulter was at the scene within minutes of Khalid being killed.'

'You need to get a screenshot before they take it down.' Wahlia reached over her to make the grab himself. 'I can't believe he'd post that if he was involved.'

'He didn't think anyone but the faithful would see it.'

'He can't be that stupid.'

'So it's just a coincidence?' she asked. 'Out of all the places he could be, he just happens to be standing within spitting distance of a dead man, minutes after he's been murdered?'

Wahlia retreated to his own side of the desk. 'He's dressed right, I'll give you that.'

'This has reeked of the ENL right from the beginning.' Ferreira found her mobile, dialled Zigic's number, eyes on the photograph, which received another 'like' as the phone rang in her ear.

'What've you got, Mel?'

'Ken Poulter,' she said. 'He was there when the attack took place.'

'Hold on, I'm just pulling into the station.'

The phone went dead and she pushed away from her desk, paced to the window and back again, went to the murder board and stared at the mugshot of their mute suspect, praying this would be enough of a threat to get him talking. It was the best chance they had, play him and Poulter off against one another. No honour among thieves was a cliché for a reason and she hoped it would hold good for racist murderers too. Poulter was more likely to break, if he was only an observer; if he could convince them of that, he might turn Queen's evidence.

It wasn't what she wanted but it might close the case and that was all that mattered.

Zigic came into the office, looking hollowed out by the grim task of passing on bad news, an uncharacteristic trudge in his step.

'OK, let's see it.'

'It's on-screen,' she said.

He dropped into her chair and she watched the realisation play across his face, eyebrows lifting, then he frowned.

'Alright, bring him in.'

28

Ferreira tracked Ken Poulter down to the taxi rank outside Peterborough train station. Saturday lunchtime and the place was crowded with football fans heading to Posh's away game at Wolves, people laden down with shopping bags arriving back from London and Cambridge, moving quickly, eyes averted, skirting the throngs of men with beer bottles and cans chanting as they made their way through the main building and out onto the platform.

Poulter was leaning against the bonnet of his cab, flicking through a copy of the *Daily Express*, waiting for a customer. He'd got a tan since the last time Ferreira picked him up, four weeks ago, just after the first murder, and his skin looked like leather, hanging slack on his gaunt face. He was built for brawling, with a compact, wiry frame and a low centre of gravity, well-seasoned fists tattooed across the knuckles, wearing gold sovereigns which she guessed had split countless lips.

Pushing fifty now. A veteran. Just like the man they had already arrested.

Ferreira crossed the road in front of the Great Northern Hotel, two uniforms behind her, peeling off left and right, forming a pincer movement in case Poulter decided to make a run for it.

'Been somewhere nice?' Ferreira asked.

He glanced up from his paper. 'Turkey.'

'Lot of Muslims in Turkey.'

'I've got no problem with them in their own country.' He closed his paper, rolled it up tight. 'What do you want?'

'A word.'

'I'm listening.'

'At the station,' Ferreira said.

He tapped the newspaper against his thigh. 'This about last night?'

'Unless you've done something else you shouldn't have.'

The two uniforms had moved in close, leaving him nowhere to go. Poulter eyed the pair of them up, big men but most of it was fat, and Ferreira could see him make the calculations, knowing he could probably take them, but then what?

'Alright,' he said. 'I'll follow you.'

'This isn't a request, Poulter.' Ferreira gestured to the uniforms and they were on him fast; turned him round and cuffed him, held him sprawled over the bonnet of his cab while she cautioned him. 'You understand that?'

'Yes.' Through gritted teeth. 'What about my cab? I can't leave it here. I'll get fined.'

'Funny, you've never worried about breaking the law before.'

He kept protesting as the uniforms walked him across the road and shoved him into the back of the patrol car, watched all the way by the other drivers on the rank.

Ferreira climbed into the taxi, a cream Skoda five years old. No chance of a hackney licence with his criminal record. He'd left the keys in the ignition and the radio was playing, voices arguing hotly on TalkSport, picking apart the legality of a tackle. She switched it off, pocketed the mobile phone he'd left on the dashboard, and deciding to do the decent thing, locked the cab up before she left.

At the station Poulter demanded a solicitor, started running his mouth about the rough treatment and the loss of earnings he was going to incur, saying he'd sue for the fine the council would levy on him over blocking the taxi rank.

Ferreira had him celled and went back up to Hate Crimes, took the stairs at full pelt, almost floating. This could be the end of the ENL. Three murders, a chorus of approval from within their ranks. It would be enough to have them officially deemed a terrorist organisation, and sure, the remaining members would form new groups, but there would be no more hiding behind the rhetoric of patriotism. All pretence of politics wiped away by the innocent blood those men had spilled.

The office was a wall of backs when she arrived, everyone crowded around Grieves's desk, listening as she talked in a high, animated tone.

'. . . come out through the bus station and get onto Cromwell Road that way.'

'The techies should be able to do something with it,' Zigic said, leaning over her shoulder to peer at the screen, like that would make the image clearer. 'Good work, Deb. Send it up and tell them to get a hurry on.'

'Progress?' Ferreira asked.

'We've got two men approaching the crime scene,' he said, heading for the coffee machine. 'Still no sign of our second man leaving it though.'

He shook the pot at her.

'No thanks, I'm all coffeed out. Does it look like him?'

'It doesn't look like anyone much right now,' Zigic said, shrugging slightly. 'But it's a start. Did you get him?'

'He wants a solicitor before he'll talk.'

Ferreira sat down and prepared for the wait.

'Call came for you while you were out,' Wahlia said, eyeing her over the top of his computer. 'A bloke.'

'Does this bloke have a name?'

Wahlia shoved his hand across the desk, a pink Post-it note stuck to his fingertips. 'Embarrassing when one of them tracks you down at work, isn't it?'

She took the Post-it and the jokey reply died on her tongue.

'He sounded married,' Wahlia said.

He probably was by now, she thought. It was what he wanted. Even when they were at university he didn't act like everyone else, was steady and reliable, no bed-hopping for Alex, no heavy drinking, the kind of boy who wouldn't even pretend to inhale. His life was plotted ahead of him in a predictable line; PhD, lecturing, wife, kids, dogs, a nice little house in a nice little village somewhere within a ten-mile radius of Cambridge, close enough to cycle in every day.

'What did he want?' she asked.

'He wouldn't say. Just told me to get you to ring him.' Wahlia rocked back in his chair, work forgotten, his full attention on her now. 'So, who is he?'

'An old mate.'

'A "mate"?'

She heard the quote marks he threw around the word and either interpretation fitted. Alex was the first friend she made when she arrived at university, painfully aware of how out of her element she was. She didn't talk like the other girls, didn't dress like them, not enough money from Mummy and Daddy to pull off that expensively anti-fashion look they had, all designer denim and moth-eaten cashmere. She could barely afford the textbooks, ended up buying half of them from a bloke in a pub on the market square who shoplifted them to order from Waterstones. Not a good start for someone who knew she would be heading to Hendon when her three years were up.

Alex was going out with the girl she shared a room with, four years older than both of them, well into his doctorate by that point and tutoring on the side for some extra cash. It was such a cliché that Ferreira blushed when she remembered it, the long, earnest conversations, the rigorously platonic tone, months of pretending the chemistry didn't exist before she realised he would never make the first move and pretty much pounced on him.

'You want me to find you some whimsical memory-lane music?' Wahlia asked.

Ferreira looked up from the desktop, smiled back at him. 'No, you're alright, I'm done now.'

She tapped Alex's number into her phone and went out into the corridor, not wanting an audience for this. She paced a few steps waiting for him to pick up, looking at the posters for knife crime and identity theft, wondering why they were even up where no civilian ever ventured.

'Alex Cator.'

She stopped pacing. 'Alex, hi, it's Mel. You called me –'

'Yes, God, it's been forever, hasn't it?'

'I guess it has, yeah.' She watched her feet start moving again across the carpet. 'How are you?'

'I'm good, thanks. Yeah, I'm great.' Did his voice sound slightly strained, the lightness forced? 'So you're a sergeant now? How's that working out?'

'It's what I wanted.' She winced at the hard tone, knowing those conversations were long done with, that his disapproval shouldn't matter to her any more. 'Look, Alex, things are a bit hectic here –'

'I've just seen the news,' he said. 'That's why I'm calling. I think we should talk.'

For a moment she didn't answer, processing the unexpected sense of disappointment then the randomness of his suggestion. In the background she heard music playing softly, a woman's voice singing, the chink of a cup hitting a saucer, and imagined him sitting in the cafe on King Street where they used to go for breakfast. She pushed away the memory of his sleepy smile and their fingers intertwined on the melamine tabletop.

'Have you got some information?'

'You could say that.'

Ferreira glanced back into the office, saw Wahlia looking at her and turned away.

'About the murders?'

'Possibly,' he said, drawing the word out. 'It's complicated, Mel.'

'So explain.'

'This isn't really an over-the-phone kind of thing.' A bell sounded at his end and then she knew he was in the cafe, recognised the distinctive chime. 'Can we meet up for a drink?'

'Alex, if you know something useful we can't fuck about, I need the information now. This situation is already getting out of control. Where are you?'

'No, I'll come to you.'

Wahlia was right, he did sound married.

'Or maybe we could meet in the middle,' Alex said quickly. 'There's a place on the side of the A1, near Huntingdon.'

'I know it.'

'Seven? Is that OK for you?'

'I'll see you later.'

Ferreira ended the call without saying goodbye, annoyed with him in some vague way she didn't want to examine, but as she slipped back into her chair and started to roll a cigarette the irritation festered.

Was it his insistence about meeting on neutral ground and the obvious implications behind it? Or how careful he was not to call the place what it really was, a hotel? Allowing them both to pretend that the potential didn't exist. She should have pushed him harder for an explanation, she thought, as she went to the window and lit her cigarette, and she realised she wasn't annoyed with him but with herself, because she wanted to see him again, and she had played along with his stupid teasing game to make that happen.

What could he possibly know that would have any relevance?

He was a psychology lecturer for Christ's sake. The best he could offer was an offender profile for a racially motivated murderer, nothing she didn't already know and couldn't have worked up herself.

He couldn't have anything useful. He'd seen her on the news and got a nostalgic itch which needed scratching so he called the station. It was that simple.

'Mel.' Zigic was standing in front of her, arms folded. 'Is there something I should know?'

'It's probably not relevant.'

'Meaning maybe it is.'

189

She pitched her spent butt out of the window. 'That was an old friend from uni, he said he's got information which might be useful. I'm meeting him later to discuss it.'

'He's not a hack, is he?'

'Alex is a lecturer.'

'Well, watch what you say, alright? These kinds of high-profile cases bring out all sorts of cranks.'

'I'll be careful.'

The telephone on her desk rang and she went to answer, glad of the excuse to end the conversation before it went any further.

'Poulter's solicitor's here.'

29

Ken Poulter sat back from the table with his arms crossed over his chest, dark smudges of old tattoos faintly visible through the thick hair on his forearms. They were not as crisp as the recently inked ones on his fingers, very black against the straps of white skin where his rings had stopped him tanning.

Zigic only knew him by reputation, most of that second-hand from Ferreira, but he was every inch the ageing thug, weathered and battle-hardened with old scars visible above his eyes and across his cheeks, a strange spray down the left side of his jaw which might have passed for acne pockmarks until you looked closer and saw the shape of them was more consistent with shards of broken glass, a souvenir from his time with a Luton football firm. And Zigic imagined whatever he'd received he'd given out three-fold, an unmistakable air of competent aggression around him, the confidence which came from knowing you'd taken the hardest blow that could be thrown and climbed to your feet again.

He saw the same thing on their unnamed suspect and thought what a perfect team the men would make. He could see them swapping war stories and propaganda, both knowing their years in the cause were for nothing, that they were fighting a losing battle against multiculturalism and liberal values, small men in a changing world wanting to make a mark while they were still capable.

Because wasn't that what terror came down to, a toxic blend of narcissism and fear and self-righteous indignation?

Poulter glared at Ferreira as she set up the recording equipment, stated his name in a clear, hard voice. Which was more than you could say for his solicitor, Mr Hall, a fresh-faced young man who seemed to be suffering from stage fright and had to repeat his name twice before Ferreira was satisfied.

Zigic took a deep breath, placed his hands on the file in front of him.

'Mr Poulter, why don't you start by telling us where you were between ten o'clock and eleven last night?'

'I was down Midgate,' he said placidly. 'Watching you lot getting your arses handed to you.'

'Did you join in?'

He snorted. 'I leave that stuff to the young lads these days.'

'How did you know it was kicking off?' Zigic asked.

'Jungle drums. Something like that gets about.'

'So things were in full swing when you arrived?'

'Gearing up to it, I'd say.' Poulter smiled, showing very white teeth, a chipped incisor. 'Didn't really get going till you tried to calm things down, did it? Fine job you did there. Thought they trained you for that sort of thing.'

Zigic fought the urge to touch the cut in his hairline. 'Where were you before that?'

'Where d'you think I was? I'm a cabbie,' Poulter said. 'I was driving people round town.'

'And then someone called you and you headed down to Midgate for a gawp?'

'Bout the size of it, yeah. Not a crime, is it?'

'No, it isn't. It's ghoulish and distasteful but that's all I'd expect from someone with your record.' Zigic tapped his fingertips against the file. 'So you arrived once the area was sealed off?'

'That bunch of Muzzis, you mean? Seems unlawful to me, letting a group of armed civilians close off a road. Have them threatening anyone who comes up. This isn't fucking Syria.' He smiled. 'But you're the inspector, sure you had your reasons.'

'You believe in community action,' Zigic said. 'I've seen your literature. If a young man was murdered outside your front door, wouldn't you want to protect the crime scene from gangs of marauding drunks?'

'Wouldn't happen where I live. It's a nice street.' He puffed his chest out as he spoke, as if he didn't live on one of the roughest squares on the roughest estate in Peterborough, surrounded by drug dealers and petty thieves and dozens of kids who couldn't move beyond their front doors without their electronic tags going off.

It was fairly white though and that would be enough for Poulter.

Zigic opened the file he'd brought with him, took the top photograph from the pile and closed it again.

'If you only arrived once the scene was cordoned off maybe you could explain how you came to take this.' He placed a still they'd lifted from the video on Poulter's Facebook page in front of him. 'You filmed this after Asif Khalid was murdered.'

Poulter swallowed hard and stared at the photograph.

'Well?'

'That doesn't prove anything.'

'It proves you were at the scene.'

'I didn't kill him.' Poulter unfolded his arms and leaned across the table, covering the photo with both hands, trying to block out its existence. 'You arrested the bloke who did it already. You can't put this on me.'

'We've arrested one of the men responsible.' Zigic leaned forward too, their faces inches apart, close enough to see the fear in Poulter's eyes. 'And when we're done with you we're going to bring him in here and he's going to try and get himself off by laying the blame on you.'

Poulter was breathing fast now, his mouth hanging open, wanting to say something, anything, which would get him off, but the evidence was there in front of him. Undeniable.

'I was there,' he said. 'But I didn't kill the lad.'

'You just happened to be passing the scene within minutes of a murder?' Zigic asked, incredulous. 'How stupid do you think we are?'

'How stupid do you think I am?' Poulter snapped. 'Would I have taken this picture if I was guilty?'

'You'd be surprised how many idiots post the evidence of their crimes on Facebook,' Zigic said. 'You're not unique.'

'I didn't do it.'

'OK.' Zigic leaned back in his chair, let the silence stretch for a few seconds, watching Poulter, waiting for him to relax as well, but he didn't. 'Maybe you didn't actually kill Khalid, maybe it wasn't your boots which kicked his head apart, but you were there, which makes you an accessory.'

'I was passing,' Poulter insisted. 'Afterwards, right. I didn't even see him get killed.'

Zigic blew out a sigh, turned to Ferreira. 'That sounds like a lie.'

'Yeah, he's definitely lying.' She shifted forward in her seat. 'We've got CCTV showing two men following Asif Khalid onto Cromwell Road but after the attack neither leave. One of them was detained until we arrived and the other one . . . well, he hung around.'

'It wasn't me.'

'The photograph shows you were in the car park, which, incidentally, is not passing, it's loitering.' She snatched it out from under his hand. 'Where was your cab?'

He hesitated, dropped his gaze.

'We'll check, so don't bother lying.'

'On the rank,' he said. 'Out the back of John Lewis.'

'That's a hundred yards from the car park, at least, so you weren't passing.' Ferreira dipped her head, getting into his eyeline. 'But Khalid passed you. He comes down Westgate, walks right past your cab, and you think "yeah, he's small, we can take him".'

'That isn't what happened,' Poulter said, a flush burning through his tan. 'Fucking hell. I was getting a blow job, alright? That's why I was in the car park. You happy now?'

'You left your cab on the rank and went to get a blow job?'

'I'm not fucking proud of myself.'

194

Ferreira put her hands up. 'I'm not judging you, Poulter, I just don't understand why you didn't do it in your car like a normal person.'

'My wife cleans the cab.'

'We need a name,' Zigic said.

Poulter deflated where he sat. 'Heather. She works the bottom end of Lincoln Road.'

'We'll talk to her.'

'I don't know where she lives,' he said quickly.

'Don't worry, we'll find her.'

'She didn't see anything.'

Ferreira smiled at him, cocked her head. 'How long did it take you?'

'What?'

'To come.'

Poulter's solicitor cleared his throat like he was going to complain but thought better of it. It was a fair question, Zigic thought, seeing where she was going.

'None of your business,' Poulter said and turned to Zigic. 'What the fuck is this?'

'Answer the question please.'

He shook his head, couldn't look at them. 'I don't know. What's it matter?'

'It matters because you took this photograph when you were done,' Ferreira said, steepling her fingers over it. 'Which means you and Heather were in the car park, a few yards away from the murder when it happened.'

'We were right over the other side, we didn't see anything.' His voice rose as he spoke, finishing near a shout, and the final syllable hung in the air, loaded with desperation.

Maybe he was worried about it all coming out in court, being forced to give evidence with his wife sitting in the public gallery. Zigic had seen people come close to conviction for the sake of hiding an infidelity, but he didn't think that was the case with Poulter, suspected

195

he'd seen far more than he wanted to admit, and maybe Heather had too. Someone Poulter knew personally, one of his ENL cronies.

Zigic brought another photograph out of the file, the man they had already arrested.

'Tell us about him.'

Poulter looked at the mugshot, frowning deeply. 'Don't know him.'

'Come on, you're a well-connected man,' Ferreira said. 'You must know every far-right player in a hundred-mile radius.'

'I do,' Poulter said, throwing his chin up, some composure regained. 'And he isn't one of them.'

'He killed Asif Khalid,' Zigic said. 'And we believe he's responsible for two other murders in Peterborough.'

'He's not one of us.'

'Because you'd tell us if he was, right?' Ferreira said, sneering at Poulter, who loosened a thin smile at her.

'What do you think he's going to say when we show him your mugshot?' Zigic asked. 'Do you think that loyalty cuts both ways?'

'He won't say anything, because he doesn't know me.'

Zigic studied Poulter's face, trying to read the meaning behind the remnants of his amusement. Was it defiance or arrogance, or did he already know the man wasn't talking because they had arranged a vow of silence in the event of getting caught? Old soldiers might do that.

'Interview terminated two thirty-seven.'

Poulter rose from the table and started towards the door, muttering under his breath about them wasting his time, and almost bounced off the chest of the uniform standing guard.

'You know the drill better than that,' Ferreira said. 'Take him down.'

Poulter took a few hurried, backward steps. 'Now hold on. You've got no right to keep me here.'

'We can keep you for at least twenty-four hours.'

'Listen to me, I didn't do anything. I'm fifty years old for fuck's sake.' He clenched his fists, muttered under his breath. 'Talk to Joe Selby. You want to know who killed those blokes, talk to Joe.'

Ferreira stepped up to Poulter. 'Why him?'

'He's been skulking around asking questions, wanting to know who you lot have pulled in, what they told you. I'm telling you, he's shit-scared.'

'Keep talking.'

30

Back in the office Zigic told Wahlia to run the name Heather through the system, check for recent soliciting arrests, hoping they would get lucky and she was using her real name. It wasn't the kind women assumed for business purposes, not flashy or sexy enough.

Parr was still out canvassing the area around the earlier murders, no new developments from that direction. Grieves had gone off to the canteen.

When Zigic checked his mobile he found three messages from Nicola Gilraye, increasingly impatient, wanting something for the evening news bulletin. He called her back, heard pub noise in the seconds before she spoke, voices and laughter, a quiz machine beeping.

'The Sundays are bombarding me with requests,' she said. '*The Times* are running a profile on Shotton in their magazine. A very sympathetic one from what I can gather.'

'His PR team are doing good work.'

'Which is bad for us.'

'It has nothing to do with us,' Zigic said.

The sound of tonic fizzing into a glass at her end. 'Please tell me you've identified the victim at least.'

'I'll send you over the details.'

Zigic ended the call and told Wahlia to give her the basics, nothing more, no matter how hard she pressed him.

Ferreira was pulling her jacket on, grabbing her bag with her free hand.

'Where are you going?'

'For Selby.' She pocketed her tobacco, snagged her keys from the desk. 'Are you coming?'

Zigic crossed his arms and she froze.

'What?'

'So you've thought this through,' he said. 'You're confident you've got enough of a reason to drag him in here?'

'He's involved,' she said. 'You heard Poulter. Why else would Selby be asking questions if he didn't have something to hide? He's worried one of them's implicated him.'

'Which they haven't.'

'Poulter has.'

'He's told us nothing,' Zigic said. 'He wanted kicking loose so he gave us a name off the top of his head, hoping we'd be stupid enough to believe him.'

'Selby's involved in this.' Her hand shot away towards the murder boards. 'Poulter said he was with him in the Red Lion last night, that's a very short walk through the centre of town to Cromwell Road.' She went over to the board, stabbed a point on the map. 'He's less than half a mile away forty minutes before the attack.'

'Did you see him on any of the footage?' Zigic asked.

'No. And that's suspicious in itself. First sign of trouble he should have been wading in with the rest of the wankers. But he wasn't. Don't you find that strange?'

Zigic gave a non-committal murmur, knowing Selby's absence from the scene was strange but not wanting to encourage her any further.

It would be easy to get sidetracked now. Selby was a decent fit but so was every other ENL foot soldier they'd pulled in, now that a second man was implicated in the murders. They wouldn't know for sure until they had a DNA match but it looked highly likely that the mute in the cells had left his spit on Ali Manouf's dead face. The evidence which had blacked out every name in their suspects list was suddenly meaningless and they were all back in the frame. Dozens of men with the same form and prejudices as Joe Selby, and the only thing that distinguished him right now was Ken Poulter's say-so.

Poulter, who looked by far the most likely suspect.

'Got an address,' Wahlia said. 'Heather Crane, multiple solicitation charges, lives on Midland Road. That's got to be her.'

'Selby can wait,' Zigic said.

Ferreira hitched her bag onto her shoulder. 'You're the boss.'

It was good to hear her say it, because sometimes he wasn't sure if she realised that.

A degree of friction was necessary during any investigation, questions needed to be asked, certainties challenged, and more often than not Ferreira was the one who did it, but as much as he valued her judgement she was prone to pursuing avenues of inquiry which had nothing more to recommend them than personal annoyance.

She'd probably call it instinct but Zigic had seen too many investigations derailed by an officer's unshakeable belief in their gut to trust anything so nebulous.

Midland Road was a short drive from the station. A row of Victorian houses built in the shadow of the derelict hospital, opposite the abandoned and decaying hulk of the old Dairycrest lot and a run of corroded, corrugated-steel sheds which had once been a bakery. Sunlight glinted on the broken windows and the metal security fencing that had been erected to keep out vandals and the graffiti artists who had scrambled up to tag the most challenging spots. Beyond that was the wasteland around the railway, weed-strewn sidings and maintenance yards, and as they climbed out of the car a train barrelled through, its warning sounding.

'This one,' Ferreira said, pointing at a narrow terraced house with bleached net curtains up at the windows and a glossy red front door. 'It's a fast commute for her anyway.'

The parking area where Heather Crane had taken Ken Poulter was a couple of minutes' walk away over the bridge, but it felt distant just then, with the birds singing and an unseasonal ice-cream van parked a few houses up filling the air with jangling music.

Zigic knocked on the front door, hearing a vacuum cleaner running inside. Waited a minute and knocked again, harder.

The vacuum cut dead and moments later Heather Crane opened up, just as far as the security chain would allow, a wedge of scrubbed face and scraped-back hair showing in the gap.

'What do you want?'

Zigic held up his ID. 'Could we have a word, Ms Crane?'

'What's this about?'

'There was a murder last night. We need to ask you a few questions.'

She closed the door sharply and for moment there was no sound from her side, as she weighed up her options. Zigic imagined she knew better than to think this would just go away, and sure enough a few seconds later the chain slid off and she opened the door.

'You'd better come in then.'

The vacuum cleaner sat in the centre of the small, square living room, the noxious aroma of lemon polish thick in the air and a feather duster propped against the foot of the stairs.

Her kids were playing in the back garden, laughing as they jumped up and down on a trampoline, and Heather Crane went to the window to keep a watchful eye on them, clearly not wanting them to rush in and hear what was going to be said.

She was older than he expected, approaching forty, plain and rounded in her grey tracksuit, bare feet gnarled from too many hours walking the streets in cheap, high shoes. It would be a challenge to make a living, he guessed. What with the ever-increasing, ever-renewed pool of foreign girls brought into the city to satisfy the wants of men who wouldn't care how unwilling or mistreated they were.

The ages went down, the prices went down, and women like Heather Crane were pushed to the edge of the market by more exotic alternatives. Even the Eastern Europeans were falling out of favour, replaced by women trafficked over from China and Malaysia. It was a trade which thrived on novelty.

Ken Poulter's politics obviously dictated his sexual preferences though.

'I didn't see anything,' she said, her voice wavering already.

'But you were in the car park when the murder happened,' Zigic said, keeping his tone neutral, wanting her to know she wouldn't be judged. 'Your client told us that much.'

She smiled grimly. 'I had my head down, didn't I?'

Zigic moved closer to the window, wanting to see her face. 'Just take us through what happened please.'

She folded her arms and looked away from him, into the garden where her kids had got bored with the trampoline and started playing with a pair of water pistols, screaming as they chased each other, two little girls in matching dungarees.

'Ken rang me and said he was down Westgate, he wanted some . . . attention. He won't let me in his cab so we went to the car park as usual.'

'Were there many people about?' Zigic asked.

'A few. The pub crowd. It was pretty quiet, though.' She tucked her chin into her chest, clearly uncomfortable about having this conversation when her kids were just a pane of glass away. 'We went right into the corner, far away from the road as you can get. I heard some shouting but it sounded like the usual shit, you know? And Ken always takes a fair bit of warming up so I was concentrating on him.'

'Men shouting?'

'Yeah.'

'What were they shouting about?'

'I don't know. Ken was talking to me, there was music from the pub. You just tune all that stuff out. You have to.' She bit her lip. 'I was kind of aware of it. I heard it stop. I think I heard some banging. Like a door maybe.'

'A car door?'

'No, a house door.' She took a deep breath. 'Like a minute later Ken finished and we started walking back over the car park. Then there was a load more shouting, doors going, and I wanted to get out of there sharpish.'

'Why?'

'They don't like girls working on their streets,' she said. 'I know a couple who've been beat up the last few months, told if they go back it'll be worse.'

'But you keep working there?' Ferreira said.

'I'm careful,' she said. 'The others look like whores.'

Zigic glanced at Ferreira, got the merest shrug from her and wondered if she was thinking what he was now. Whether Heather's experience was colouring her recollection, deliberately or otherwise. If what she said was true she might be sympathetic to Poulter's way of thinking.

'What did you see?' Zigic asked.

She didn't answer.

'We've spoken to Ken, we know he saw the body. Were you still with him?'

'He wanted to take a picture of it.' She closed her eyes. 'Sick bastard – can you believe it? He made me stand there while he did it.'

'Why did he make you stay?' Ferreira asked.

'There were men on the street, I guess Ken thought they'd notice him if I walked off.'

'How long did you stay there?'

She frowned. 'It can't have been more than a couple of minutes. A load more Asian blokes came out of their houses and Ken started getting twitchy. He said we should clear out before they got aggro.'

Zigic took out their mute suspect's mugshot.

'Do you recognise this man?'

'Who is he?'

'He killed the young lad whose body you saw. Asif Khalid. He was twenty years old, just walking home from a bar, minding his own business.'

'It said on the news you arrested someone.'

'This man, yes. But we have reason to believe he wasn't acting alone. There was a second man involved but he ran off. You and Ken were the closest people to the scene when that happened, so it's very important that you think now, did you hear or see anything, anything at all, which might help us identify him?'

'No.'

Just like that. Snapped out, no thought given to it at all.

'You said you heard shouting. Maybe a name . . .'

'I wasn't paying attention.'

'What about earlier in the evening?' Zigic asked, taking the photograph as she shoved it back at him. 'You work around there, did you see anyone acting strangely?'

She laughed. 'In Peterborough? On a Friday night? Are you joking?'

'Do I look like I'm joking?' Zigic said, dropping the neutral tone.

'Maybe Ms Crane would be able to concentrate better at the station,' Ferreira said, taking out her mobile. 'I'll call social services and have them send someone over for your kids.'

Heather turned on her, face wild. 'Don't you dare threaten my kids.'

Ferreira held her phone up. 'Tell us what you know and we'll leave you to the rest of your weekend.'

There was a moment of charged silence as they stared each other down. Zigic didn't like operating this way, was sure that reasoning with people yielded better results than bullying them, but sometimes it was the only option.

'Look, I didn't see anything. All I know is I heard a couple of blokes shouting. I thought it was a robbery or something.'

'What made you think it was a robbery?' Zigic asked.

'One guy was saying "no" over and over. Then there was some scuffling.'

'What about the other guy?'

'I couldn't understand him. He wasn't speaking English, but he was doing most of the shouting.' She looked at Ferreira. 'Satisfied now?'

'Where were you when you heard this?'

'It wasn't long after we got there. I was too far away to make out what was going on properly,' Heather said. 'All I know for sure is that he wasn't English.'

'What did he sound like then?'

She shrugged. 'Foreign. I don't know.'

The back door opened and her kids ran in through the kitchen, into the living room, both drenched, the older girl still squirting her sister with the water pistol. Heather shouted at them not to mess the house up and they shrank back, stood in the doorway looking at Zigic and Ferreira, water dripping off them into the spotless cream carpet.

'That's all I can tell you.'

They returned to the car, the sound of an alarm going off a couple of streets away cutting through the air, off-key but insistent. Zigic pulled away from the kerb, turning around what Heather Crane had said, trying to find something more hidden between the lines.

'Did you buy that?' Ferreira asked. 'She's basically alibied Poulter.'

'Why would she lie for a client?'

'It's a saturated market, she needs to keep the regulars she's got. And let's face it, she's biased. All that about "them" not wanting working girls on their streets. She's got her own axe to grind.'

'Poulter does have alibis for the other murders,' Zigic said. 'And they're pretty solid ones at that. Maybe he was just in the wrong place at the wrong time.'

'It doesn't feel right.'

'No, it doesn't.' He slowed as he hit a line of traffic on the railway bridge, shunting out of the city centre. 'It feels like too much of coincidence, but think about it for a minute, do you really believe Poulter would set up a prostitute for an alibi? If it was him and he was planning to murder a third man in a matter of four weeks, with an accomplice, would he really use her to cover for him?'

'Depends how well they know each other.'

'No, Mel. It doesn't stand up. Especially when you factor in him posting that photograph on Facebook. Nobody is that stupid. Not even Poulter.'

She blew out a sharp sigh and he felt the same frustration. Right from the very beginning, within hours of Didi's murder, they started hitting dead ends. Inevitably it happened in every case, because no matter how many enemies a person had they couldn't all be guilty, but this case was different. No matter how diligent they were, no matter how determined, the shutters kept coming down around them. They get CCTV of the culprit. He's wearing a balaclava. They get DNA. There's no match on the system. They arrest the murderer, finally, literally red-handed. It turns out he isn't working alone.

One step forward. Two steps back.

'He must know more than he's admitting though,' Zigic said. 'If she heard shouting, he heard it too.'

'Foreign shouting,' Ferreira said, like she didn't believe that either.

'It could have been Khalid.'

'Or she was lying, trying to lead us away from Poulter's boys.'

31

It was the wrong weather for a vigil, Zigic thought, as they entered the cathedral precincts through the western gateway. The wrong time of day. Four o'clock on a Saturday afternoon with the spring sun shining down on the green, promising regeneration and growth, almost taunting the gathered crowd with its permanence in the face of their loss, rendering the candles they held invisible.

It was the wrong location too. They were all here to pay their respects to the victims of the hit-and-run, and by rights they should be standing on the spot where it happened, but that would have meant closing down Lincoln Road for the second time in four days and the council had evidently decided that was too disruptive.

Tough to make space for all the dignitaries on that stretch of pavement as well.

They'd come out in force, the mayor in full regalia and a few members of the city council, Chief Constable Weir and a trio of priests Zigic recognised from St Mary's Church; they held services in several different languages now and they'd obviously decided to make sure everyone was catered for. Despite the fact that Jelena and Sofia Krasic didn't seem particularly religious and who knew what Pyotr Dymek believed in.

The crowd was fifty or sixty strong, more women than men, mostly young, around the same age as the Krasic sisters. Co-workers perhaps or aquaintances from the neighbourhood. They stood in silence as Father Piec addressed them, his words prompting occasional group responses and flurries of sombre crossing.

Zigic noticed Ferreira's hand twitch but she managed to keep it by her side, fighting the old Catholic impulses she'd deny having.

Beyond the core group a steady stream of shoppers made their way through the precincts and into the courtyard, a few slowed to see what had the local press so interested but most kept walking.

The TV crews maintained a respectful distance, placed to capture both the small raised platform outside the cathedral's main doors and the faces of the men and women waiting to take their turn on it.

Under other circumstances there would be police cameras here too, more discreet and roving, capturing every person in the crowd for later analysis, just in case the man responsible for the hit-and-run had come to feed off the misery he'd caused, but it wasn't that kind of crime.

A young man came over and offered them candles from a tray, looked disappointed when they both declined, then moved on to an elderly couple weighed down with shopping bags, who had stopped on their way back to the car park nearby. They took the candles and shared an uncomfortable moment as the young man lit them, then stood awkwardly watching, as if they felt they'd been pulled into something which was none of their business.

'I hate all this,' Ferreira said.

'You hate grief?'

'The public spectacle. It's so fake.' They were walking slowly now, moving to a good vantage point in the lee of the graveyard's high stone wall. 'How many people here actually knew Jelena or Dymek?'

'Does it matter?'

'Of course it matters,' she said. 'If they didn't know them then they're tourists, wallowing in someone else's suffering.'

Zigic scanned the faces in the crowd, saw tears and clasped hands, eyes lowered to the ground.

'They don't look like they're faking it.'

Ferreira threw her chin up towards the platform. 'How about him?'

Zigic followed her gesture to the man helping Father Piec down from the makeshift podium, lending the elderly priest a much needed arm. It wasn't unusual for a local MP to attend a vigil – PR was PR – but it was unlikely that a single person here had voted for Richard Shotton or ever would. Despite his trumpeted manifesto policy of extending an amnesty to all existing EU migrants once his party pulled the UK out of the European Union.

How he manoeuvred himself into a position to do that was anyone's guess.

There was no discernible negative reaction among the crowd and it occurred to Zigic that few people here knew who he was. Many wouldn't be registered to vote and even if they were it was unlikely that his team had gone canvassing on their streets.

'Don't you just want to punch him in the face?' Ferreira said.

'I'd wait until the Chief Constable isn't around if I were you.'

Shotton spoke in a calm, measured voice which carried effortlessly across the crowd, expressing his sympathy to the friends and family of those who had died, managing to sound almost like he meant it, the rhythm of his speech familiar from all of those turns on *Question Time*. The little verbal tics, the movements of his hands, each artful pause. All of it carefully crafted.

Zigic could see why he was dangerous. He didn't look like a right-wing zealot or a crackpot, in contrast to the long line of fascist politicians who'd gone before him. The ones who'd tried and failed to move their ideology into the mainstream.

In the three years since he'd taken control of the English Patriot Party he'd won over the media with his flawless record of military service, his much vaunted but lightly worn erudition and his ability to 'connect with the common man'. That was the official line the papers took anyway.

But it was Shotton's appearance which kept him in the public eye, Zigic suspected. He was handsome – by political standards – lean and square-jawed, rugged but slick; every inch the ex-RAF silver fox. When floating voters with no interest in policies could be swayed by a trustworthy face that might be enough to make the EPP a significant political force come the general election in May.

On the podium he'd moved into sombre entreaty mode.

'It is at times like this, when a terrible tragedy strikes at the heart of our community, that we find ourselves to be strongest.'

Zigic tried to tune him out, watched the mayor resettle his chains around his neck, while Chief Constable Weir stood next to him with his hands clasped, eyes fixed on Richard Shotton, wearing an expression which looked like admiration even at that distance. No surprise really, when Shotton was so vocal on cutting red tape for the police and boosting their budgets.

Ferreira swore under her breath. 'This isn't about the hit-and-run.' She was obviously paying more attention than him. '"Social cohesion"? He's using a vigil to smooth over last night's riot.'

'It's the wrong audience if that's what he's up to,' Zigic said.

'He's playing to the cameras. That's the only audience he cares about.'

Shotton stepped down and returned to his wife's side, finding her gloved hand, their fingers interlinked throughout the minute's silence which followed. It was perfectly observed by the crowd but voices blew in from Cathedral Square, kids squealing, parents shouting after them, a *Big Issue* seller calling his wares, drowned out by music from a fast-food van.

Father Piec gave a final blessing and as the crowd began to break up, Weir gestured at Zigic.

'Come on, Mel, the boss wants us to pay court.'

She fell in step behind him and he hoped she realised what the situation demanded, deference to Shotton if she could muster it, silence if not.

Shotton was watching them approach, nodding at whatever Weir was saying to him, and he favoured them with a politician's warm but meaningless smile as they drew close.

'Detective Inspector Zigic and Detective Sergeant Ferreira,' Weir said, stiff and formal as ever.

They did the handshakes, the nods, and Zigic heaved a silent sigh of relief when Mrs Shotton engaged Ferreira in conversation, addressing her in Portuguese. She was Brazilian, he remembered, ex-UNICEF, the perfect way to complete a power couple.

'Sorry to be meeting you under such terrible circumstances,'

Shotton said. As if they'd meet under any others. 'But it's good to see the community pulling together at a time like this.'

'It's a tight-knit area,' Zigic said.

'I dare say the rest of Peterborough could learn a thing or two from them. Strictly between us.' Another smile, very thin. 'How's the young woman doing now? The one who survived?'

Zigic thought of Sofia Krasic, back in hospital, under guard. 'She's recovering well.'

'Good.' He pointed at Zigic's head. 'Looks like you took a knock yourself, Inspector.'

The cut was throbbing from the cold but he resisted the urge to touch it. 'Not all community gatherings are this peaceful unfortunately.'

Weir cleared his throat, a low warning rumble.

'I hear you've made an arrest.'

'We made several,' Zigic said. 'But I doubt that will stop them. Most of them have long histories of racially motivated violence and public order offences. A night in the cells won't alter their thinking.'

Shotton tucked his hands into the pockets of his grey wool overcoat, the bulge of his fists visible through the soft fabric. 'And what about the man responsible for the murders?'

'He's in custody,' Weir said, voice firm, eyes on Zigic.

'Has he told you why he did it?'

Zigic didn't answer, looked back to Weir expecting him to make the standard comment on not discussing operational issues, but he didn't.

How far would the Chief Constable go to curry favour with Shotton? Zigic wondered. Lay it all out for him over an expensive lunch on Shotton's tab? Name names? The desperation was there in Shotton's eyes, the need to know exactly who they had locked in a cell and how much bad press it might generate.

Luckily they had nothing for Weir to pass on, only a suspect who wouldn't talk and who they hadn't yet identified.

'We're in the process of questioning him,' Zigic said. 'It's a complicated matter, as I'm sure you can appreciate.'

'Of course.' Shotton's gaze slipped away from them, moving across the last few stragglers leaving the green. 'And you'll want to be getting back to it.'

Weir gave him the barest gesture of dismissal, his displeasure at how the conversation had progressed clearly marked on his face as the group broke apart, Ferreira and Mrs Shotton saying their good-byes in a warmer manner than Zigic would have expected.

He waited until they were out of the courtyard, crossing Cathedral Square, before he asked what they'd been talking about.

'She's setting up a mentoring programme for the daughters of local immigrants,' Ferreira said, her voice laced with bitter humour. '"To give them the opportunities that their mothers didn't have."'

'That sounds very worthwhile.'

'Yeah, it's going to be hugely worthwhile to his campaigning.' She slowed as they passed a chrome fast-food van but kept walking. 'She thought I might like to get involved.'

Zigic laughed. 'I can just see it – your face all over Shotton's election brochures.'

She grinned. 'Shut up.'

'Melinda Ferreira – the poster child of New British Facism.'

32

The place that Alex had so carefully avoided calling a hotel was a Premier Inn on the side of the A1, ten minutes south of Peterborough. Nothing much around it but sleepy villages and a rubbish dump which blanketed the area with the scent of smouldering plant matter and melting plastic. The car park was large but quiet, a dozen vehicles clustered together in the spaces closest to the main doors, where a woman in a tight cobalt-blue dress stood smoking, glancing at her watch every few seconds.

Waiting for a man, Ferreira thought, as she locked her car. All dressed up and wondering if he was still coming.

She hadn't made as much effort herself. Debated it for about two minutes, standing in front of her wardrobe with her hair damp from the shower, before she pulled out a pair of jeans and a slouchy black jumper. If Alex wanted to pretend this was purely about work then she would too.

She hated the ambiguity though.

It was just like him. He drifted and dithered, was never one to take control and make something happen. Which was why it had ended between them. He didn't want her to go to Hendon but he never attempted to stop her, insisting he respected her decision to join up even though he thought the police were institutionally racist and sexist and rotten at some deep, unreachable level which could never be cleaned out. Maybe he knew her well enough to realise he couldn't change her mind but she wanted him to try, make a stand for once, be a man.

Ferreira scanned the bar area as she went in, one fast, practised sweep that took in everything; the bland art and the migraine-inducing carpet, a couple in an alcove having a fraught conversation, the guy on the next table pretending absorption in his laptop as he cocked his head to eavesdrop, a few more lone men scattered about, all eating without pleasure, none of them Alex.

She ordered a dark rum and took it to an out-of-the-way table, sat opposite the flat screen bolted to the wall. The seven o'clock bulletin was just starting, leading on Syria, then it was a series of weekend-friendly puff pieces, no mention of the riots, and she knew Zigic would be breathing a sigh of relief, a couple of days' respite from Gilraye's demands.

It bothered her how quickly they got bored though. Three men brutally murdered, the city descending into racially motivated anarchy, and a film premiere in London had made third spot in the running order.

With no compelling reason to hold him Zigic had released Poulter when they got back to the station. Within half an hour he was on Facebook, soapboxing to his followers about the treatment he'd received, throwing around accusations of prejudice and harassment, ramming home his belief that as a white working-class man he had become an oppressed minority in his own country.

She was still convinced he knew more than he was saying, but without some kind of leverage he wouldn't give it up.

Their suspect was maintaining the silent treatment too. An hour and a half they spent needling and cajoling him this afternoon, and he remained upright and tight-lipped, let them talk themselves hoarse without giving them so much as a change in expression.

He was inhuman. She had never seen anyone so completely blank in an interview room. A few she'd come across had started out that way, thinking they were tough enough to weather a barrage, but they all cracked eventually, out of fear or weariness or sheer boredom at having the same questions thrown at them dozens of times. Not this one though. He was going to protect his partner right to the end, ensure his continued liberty and take satisfaction from knowing he would be partly responsible for any further crimes the man committed.

It killed her that there was nothing she could do about it.

She sipped her rum.

When she looked up again Alex was coming round the corner, eyes fixed on her, that sweet, lazy smile making her smile right back like it always had. It was the only thing about him which hadn't changed though; the grungy boy was now a smart man, dressed like he'd just stepped down from a Gap advert, the beard gone, the Afro cropped close to his skull. He'd lost the piercings from his ears but acquired a wedding ring.

She stepped round the table and into a hug, felt the hard body she remembered and backed away before she began to think about it.

'It's great to see you again, Mel.'

'Yeah, you too,' she said, returning to her seat. 'You look different.'

He sat down. 'You mean older?'

Both still smiling.

'More mature.'

'You look just the same.'

She reached for her drink. 'You know us Portuguese girls, we don't go to seed until forty. Then it gets really bad, really fast.'

'I don't know, your mum was pretty hot as I remember.'

'I'll tell her you said that.'

Alex leaned back in his chair, crossed his legs, settling. 'How are they all? Did they stay over here? Your dad was talking about leaving.'

'They stayed. I don't think they'll go home any time soon, not with the way the economy is over there. Although Peterborough's getting kind of inhospitable lately.'

'Everywhere is,' Alex said. 'Right across Europe. They might as well be here. At least we're trying to deal with the problem.'

She almost jumped on the 'we', decided not to. It would be easy to fall into the old argument, him thinking the best way to make a difference was educating people, her certain a tougher line needed to be taken. They'd been through it a hundred times without softening each other's positions and she imagined that the intervening years wouldn't have changed him.

It hadn't changed her.

'So, you're lecturing?'

'No.' He took a mouthful of his wine, put the glass down very carefully but held onto the stem, turning it between his fingers. He gave her a wry smile. 'Things didn't quite work out how I planned. I got, let's say, distracted.'

'By what?'

'An offer I couldn't refuse.'

'You're in the mafia then?'

His eyes lit up. 'Something like that.'

'Were you always this annoyingly vague?' Ferreira said.

'I'm not being vague, you just think I am because you're one of those ball-busting lady coppers now.' He moved forward, elbows on his knees, filling the space between them. She could smell his after-shave, warm and leathery. 'That was some impressive riot-breaking you did last night. Leading from the front like a good general.'

'The general was down,' Ferreira said. 'But you know how much I love to tussle.'

Alex leaned back again, retreating from the moment.

'What's he like, your boss?'

'Why?'

He smiled but this time it looked forced. 'I'm just wondering what kind of man could keep you under control.'

'What makes you think he's got me under control?' she asked and her own smile felt just as fake. 'He's decent. Doesn't throw his rank around, which is rare. But I think he's too nice for the job sometimes. He won't push people hard enough. It's almost like he's uncomfortable wielding the power he's got.'

'So why's he a DI?'

She swirled her rum around, looking into the dark liquid. She was already regretting what she'd said, felt like she'd betrayed Zigic and the faith he'd shown in her. Five minutes with Alex and she was sharing confidences he didn't deserve to have, falling back into the old dynamic, wanting him to validate her opinions.

She was past that now.

'Zigic is smart,' she said. 'He doesn't need that macho bullshit the others get by on. I've learned a lot from him.' She held Alex's gaze, watching him just as closely as he was watching her. 'Like spotting when people are trying to sidetrack me.'

Alex looked away, toyed with his glass some more, letting his wedding ring chime against the bowl. Once, twice, the sound almost lost in the background chatter and the music pumping from the speaker nearby.

'Is that subconscious?' Ferreira asked. 'Or do you want me to ask about it? How you met, what she's like, show me some pictures of your kids.'

He lifted his hand away, settled it on his thigh. 'Normal people catch up when they haven't seen each other for five years.'

'Normal people don't call out of the blue dangling a promise of information about a serious crime which they don't actually have.' She brought her voice back down, aware of the women on the next table who had fallen suddenly silent. 'Let's cut the bullshit, Alex. You've either got something or you want something, so which is it?'

He shook his head. 'You never change, do you?'

'No, I don't. Now you answer my question.'

'I wanted to see you again.'

She thought of all the empty rooms piled above them, the big beds and the fresh sheets and if the man fucked different to the boy.

'But we need to talk about your case.' He drew his chair up closer, hunched forward to the edge of it. 'You're looking into the ENL, right?'

'I can't discuss this with you, Alex. It's an ongoing investigation.' She pushed her hair away from her face. 'Why are you interested anyway? Christ, don't tell me you're a journalist now.'

'Give me some credit,' he said, trying to sound light, but there was tension around his eyes and a hesitancy in his manner which was beginning to make her uncomfortable. 'I'm, uh, I got headhunted, I guess you could say, after my PhD. They were very impressed with

217

the material I'd uncovered, said they were developing an operation in a sympathetic sector and they thought I'd be an asset.'

Ferreira saw where he was going but couldn't quite believe it. The bashfulness, the embarrassment, his PhD on the growth of far-right groups in young offenders' institutions.

'You're a copper?'

'Not exactly.'

'Then what? Exactly.'

'I'm with the Domestic Terrorism Unit.'

A laugh broke out of her, dark and malicious, and she enjoyed how uncomfortable it made him. 'You massive fucking hypocrite. All that shit you gave me about joining up. You made me feel like I was betraying my people and my politics.'

'But you were right,' he said. 'It isn't enough to just talk about changing things. We need to take action. They need people like us, outsiders, to raise the problems nobody else is interested in tackling.'

Now he looked like the boy again, animated and optimistic, his body swelling with a convert's fervour. She tried to picture him in some anonymous office in that big, ugly building on the side of the Thames, surrounded by Oxbridge grads and grey old veterans twisted by knowing too many secrets, everybody very white. She couldn't see it.

'So what are you doing?' Ferreira asked. 'Domestic terrorism, that's like, radical Islamists and animal rights protesters?'

'And anti-capitalists,' Alex said. 'They're very big on that right now. But no, I've got a small team, very small, and we've been tasked with monitoring the neo-Nazi movement. The ENL and their brethren, scanning for new cells, observing how the alliances are working out, liaising with our European counterparts.'

Ferreira picked up her glass, found it empty and put it down again. 'Should you even be telling me any of this?'

'It's OK, I'm going to get you so drunk you won't remember any of it in the morning.'

He walked off towards the bar and she turned over what he'd said, the shock settling quickly. He was the perfect person for the job really, astute and highly analytical, endlessly patient. She thought of how carefully he had pursued sources for his PhD, tracking down ex-offenders who'd been radicalised inside, the kind of half-feral thugs who shouldn't have been willing to talk to an educated black guy who hated everything they stood for. But somehow he had got close to them, brought out their stories.

Alex returned a couple of minutes later with a fresh glass of wine and tumbler packed with ice, what looked like a treble rum.

'I saw that you've made an arrest,' he said.

Ferreira filled him in on the details, keeping it brief. 'The problem we've got now is the accomplice. We're thinking he's ENL but nobody's talking.'

'Suspects?'

'Plenty,' she said. 'But if you want to throw a name into the ring I'm listening.'

'What about Joe Selby?'

'He's been mentioned. We haven't spoken to him yet though.' She sipped her rum, the burn flattened out by all that ice. 'Is he on a watch list?'

'That's not how we work,' Alex said. 'But Selby's come to our attention recently.'

'Why?'

'About six months ago Selby was hired by Richard Shotton.'

'What does Shotton want with someone like Selby?'

Alex shrugged. 'Officially he's a driver.'

'And unofficially?'

'We're not sure yet.'

Ferreira took another sip of rum. She wondered why Shotton would undermine his carefully constructed image by involving himself with Selby though. He wasn't exactly the worst ENL offender on file but any link to the group was bad PR.

'How do you know about this?' she asked.

'We've got a man inside Shotton's operation.'

She straightened in her chair. 'I knew it. I knew he was involved in this shit.'

'He isn't involved,' Alex said firmly. 'If he was, we'd know about it. Believe me, we're watching him very carefully. Something of this magnitude wouldn't have gone undetected. And how would it serve him anyway? This is a PR nightmare for Shotton – think about it, he's working his balls off to try and rehabilitate the image of the ultra-right movement and then you have three murders in quick succession, plus a riot, not to mention that hit-and-run.'

'The hit-and-run's a separate case,' Ferreira said.

'But it's created a sympathetic mood towards migrant workers, his potential voters are looking on them as innocent victims. Instead of greedy foreigners over here poaching the jobs their kids want.'

'I'm not seeing a hell of a lot of sympathy on the street.'

'Shotton isn't involved, Mel. If I thought he was, I'd tell you.'

'Would you?' she asked. 'You're in there for some reason and I bet it's a hell of a lot more important than some dead immigrants.'

'I told you, it's a watch brief.'

'Watching for what?'

'I can't tell you that. Obviously. But –' Alex stopped as a man walked past their table, heading for the complimentary newspapers, waited for him to pick one and return to his seat, eyeing the man like he didn't trust his motives. 'Look, there's a feeling that Shotton will emerge as a major political force in this country over the next few years.'

Ferreira rolled her eyes.

'Yes, I thought it was unlikely too, but the numbers are moving that way and he's attracted some very influential backers. The next election will likely result in a hung Parliament and a Conservative/ English Patriot Party alliance is a very real possibility.'

Ferreira reached for her glass, thought better of it. 'Your bosses won't have a problem with that, will they? He's only saying what a lot of them think.'

'Governments come and go,' Alex said. 'But the service never changes.'

'And they want to know who they're dealing with?' she asked. 'Where the bodies are buried?'

Alex gave the barest nod.

'And what are they going to do when you find those bodies?'

'That all depends on whose they are.'

'I can't believe you, Alex. Are you seriously prepared to cover for this piece of shit? He'd have me and you and everyone like us deported in a heartbeat.' She snatched her handbag from the floor and took out her tobacco. 'You know what kind of arseholes are in that party? Ex-BNP, ex-Combat 18. That's who you're helping get into power.'

'I am fully aware of who Shotton's in bed with,' he said.

Ferreira started to roll a cigarette, badly, angrily, scattering strands of tobacco across the table. 'I actually thought you had principles.'

'It isn't that simple.'

She sealed her cigarette and slipped past him, strode through the rest of the bar where the music was hammering now, too loud for the space, voices raised, laughter crackling. She lit up as she pushed out of the main doors into the car park, took a deep, furious drag and held the smoke in her lungs for as long as she could, needing every molecule of nicotine to calm her down.

She knew what was coming next. There was only one logical explanation for Alex bringing her here and she wanted to run away from it, get in her car and leave, pretend their conversation had never happened. She could fob Zigic off if he asked, say it was just sex, he wouldn't push her after that.

There was a surge of music and warm, food-scented air as the door opened again and Alex came over to the wall where she was sheltering from the wind, stood towering over her.

'I'm not covering for Shotton,' he said. 'If we find something which can take him down we'll use it.'

'How stupid do you think I am? If you find something it'll get kicked straight up to your boss, then his boss, and however many pay grades there are until it reaches somebody with real power, who'll slip it away in a drawer for when they need a favour from Shotton.' She took another long drag on her cigarette. 'That's what all this is about, right? You don't want us stirring up shit around him.'

'I want you to be careful, that's all. I understand that you've got to pursue Selby if he's a legitimate suspect, but I would appreciate a low-key approach until you know for sure.'

'I didn't even know he was with Shotton until you told me.'

'You'd have got there.' Alex plucked the cigarette from between her fingers and took a shallow hit. 'I need Shotton to feel secure. I can't afford for him to start doubting his people and if you barrel in there after Selby he'll get jumpy. He's paranoid, Mel, and I need to protect my source.'

She leaned against the wall, feeling the brickwork grazing her skin through her jumper. 'Is Selby yours?'

'No.' He passed the cigarette back. 'He's a problem actually, too much of an unknown quantity. We're not even sure how Shotton found him yet.'

'ENL contacts,' Ferreira said.

'That's the current thinking, but we don't know who. Shotton has been cutting deals all over the place, meeting with the heads of dozens of splinter groups. He's paid out tens of thousands in cash – protection money basically – to stop them doing anything which would lead to adverse press for him.'

Ferreira straightened. 'What about Ken Poulter?'

Alex nodded. 'The ENL have had their bonus.'

'We've still got three murdered men though,' she said. 'Shotton's bribe didn't stop that happening. Or the riot.'

'And he's about as furious as you'd expect.' Alex nodded towards the doors. 'Come on, let's go inside and talk about this. Have you eaten?'

Ferreira flicked her cigarette away and followed him back

through the bar, to the table where their drinks were still waiting. The ice had melted into her rum, making it weak and watery, and she threw it down while he went to fetch a menu, feeling the heat settle in her chest, beginning to soften the ugly edges of the place.

DAY FOUR

33

Is there anywhere bleaker on a Sunday morning than a hospital cafeteria? Zigic wondered. He was the only customer in there, on his second cup of coffee already, a newspaper read and discarded at his elbow. The riot had made page 5 of the *Observer*, a mention of the murder tacked on almost as an afterthought. He glanced at his watch and called Ferreira again.

She answered quickly, the sound of wind rushing through a cracked window and the stereo blaring when she spoke. 'I'm five minutes away.'

'You said that fifteen minutes ago.'

'I'm just pulling off the A1. I'm almost there.'

He picked up the arts section and scanned the articles; an interview with a singer he'd never heard of, reviews of books he wouldn't get a chance to read and films he never had time to watch. Anna had bought him a Jean-Pierre Melville box set for his birthday last month but it was still in the cellophane thanks to a series of long days and stolen weekends and the boys' current addiction to wrestling, which had to be watched on the big TV.

The automatic doors opened and Ferreira strode over to him, dropping her sunglasses into her bag. She looked shattered, eyes small and bloodshot under traces of last night's make-up, but he noticed her hair was damp in its ponytail and she smelled of some sweet, floral soap.

'How did it go with your friend?' he asked.

'Not as expected.' She smoothed her hand back over her hair. 'I'll tell you about it later.'

They went up to Ward 7, everything washed in bright morning

sun, the aroma of burnt toast and scrambled eggs lingering in the air. A nurse in baggy blue scrubs was pushing a trolley between the bays, handing out medication in an unnaturally cheery voice which carried from one end of the ward to the other.

Anthony Gilbert was in a private room, a guard on his door.

In another part of the hospital, at a safe distance, Sofia Krasic was in bed. Another uniformed guard was stationed outside her room in case she somehow slipped free and came looking for Gilbert to finish the job she had denied starting on Friday evening.

It was a precaution for her as much as him. Protecting her from herself.

The PC stood as they approached and Zigic told him to go and get a drink or something while they were in with the suspect, stretch his legs.

Anthony Gilbert was sitting up in bed, as pale as the sheets he had kicked off, except for the skin under his eyes which was a bruised purplish-grey. He looked dehydrated, despite the drip, his lips cracked, cheeks stubbled and hollow, and Zigic saw that he hadn't touched his breakfast, which sat on the table pulled across the foot of the bed.

There was no sign of Sofia's visit on him.

'Mr Gilbert, I'm Detective Inspector Zigic, this is Sergeant Ferreira.' He closed the door. 'We're glad to see you've pulled through.'

Gilbert licked his lips. 'I didn't kill Jelena. Whatever Sofia has told you, she's lying.'

Zigic pulled a chair over to the bed and sat down, while Ferreira moved away to the window and perched on the sill, her attention fixed on Gilbert who didn't know who to focus on now, kept darting between them, wondering who would be most sympathetic.

'We're aware that the situation was complicated,' Zigic said.

'No, it wasn't. Jelena wanted to move in with me and Sofia wouldn't let her.'

'So you killed her,' Ferreira said.

'No.'

228

'Or maybe you didn't want to hit Jelena. Maybe it was Sofia you were trying to take out and you fucked up. Is that why you tried to kill yourself?'

Gilbert turned back to Zigic, tears in his eyes. 'I heard it happen, that's why I did this. Jelena was on the phone to me when that car hit her. I heard her die.'

He wept quietly, shoulders shaking.

Zigic glanced at Ferreira, got a shrug.

Gilbert sniffed, his voice thick when he spoke again. 'I can't live without her. When I get out of here I'll do it again and nobody can stop me. I need her. I can't – I loved her so much.'

'She obviously didn't feel the same way,' Ferreira said. 'She'd have stood up to Sofia if she did.'

'You don't understand.'

'We've seen your record, Gilbert. We understand exactly what kind of man you are. I think it's fair to say you don't take rejection well.'

'Jelena didn't reject me,' he snapped. 'We were going to be together, we were just waiting for Sofia to come round.'

'Why did it matter what Sofia thought?' Zigic asked.

'They only had each other, Jelena didn't want to lose her. She'd have come round eventually.' His voice hardened, 'She didn't have any choice.'

His words hung in the air for a moment, with the sound of the heart monitor beeping, his pulse rising, and the nurse's too bright voice bleeding in from the corridor outside. Zigic watched him tug against the restraint shackling his left wrist to the bed's raised bar, a sudden surge of anger directed at Sofia. In his head this was all her fault and that could only be the case if he was guilty.

'If you weren't driving –'

'I wasn't. I told you. I was at home when it happened.'

'If you weren't driving the car then why does the blood on the airbag match yours?'

Gilbert twisted where he sat, like he wanted to get up, but the restraint held him. 'It can't. It wasn't me. You're lying.'

Not lying, but not quite telling the truth either. They only had a type match but Zigic wanted to see how he reacted. Gilbert was weakened by the overdose and this would be their best opportunity to study him before they got him into an interview room, with the reassuring presence of his solicitor. He decided to push a little harder.

'And if you weren't driving, why does CCTV at the place where the car was bought show a man who bears a striking resemblance to you handing over the money for it?'

Gilbert clutched his head with his free hand, fingers tugging at his hair. 'This is insane. I haven't done anything.'

'It's not the first time you've tried to run someone down who got in your way,' Ferreira said. 'That woman's boyfriend a couple of years ago.'

'That was an accident.'

'The judge didn't think so.'

'He ran at me, I tried to swerve.'

'Well, you did a much better job this time,' Ferreira said. 'You've killed two people – you would have killed Sofia too but she got lucky. Was it her you wanted to hit?'

'I don't want to talk to you any more.'

'Why go after her like this?' Ferreira asked, straightening up off the windowsill. 'You could have stabbed her while she was alone, broken into the house and made it look like a burglary gone wrong . . . you might have got away with that.'

Gilbert kicked out at the table, sending his breakfast to the floor, cold baked beans and tea spattering the lino. 'Get out. I'm not going to say anything else without my solicitor. I know my rights.'

Zigic stood up. 'Gather your strength, Mr Gilbert, we'll be back tomorrow.'

They left him muttering under his breath, a combination of denials and disbelief, and went back out through the silent corridors and the grey stairwell, a few early visitors arriving in the reception area as they left.

'What do you think?' Ferreira asked.

'We need those DNA results back before we can do anything more.'

'Should be in tomorrow.' She stopped to dig in her handbag for her sunglasses. 'A guilt-induced overdose makes sense though. He's going for Sofia, he gets Jelena.'

'We'll see.'

'We're screwed if it isn't him,' Ferreira said.

They crossed the road to the almost empty car park, their vehicles parked next to each other.

'What happened with your friend then?' Zigic asked. 'Did he give you anything useful?'

Ferreira slowed her pace, frowning. 'I don't know how useful it is, but short version – Joe Selby is working for Richard Shotton now and Shotton has paid off the ENL and a bunch of other groups to behave themselves until after he's elected.'

'How does he know all this?'

'Alex is MI5. They're monitoring Shotton.'

'Why?'

'He wouldn't go into details.'

Zigic's mobile peeped and he took it out of his pocket, wondering why Ferreira's friend had given them that information and what he would expect in return.

He opened the text message. Grieves. *I think I've found our mystery man.*

34

'I thought I told you to take the day off.'

Grieves spun away from her desk and stood up, looking justifiably pleased with herself. 'Dan's got his kids this morning, so I thought I might as well come and put a few hours in on the CCTV. There's so much of it.'

Zigic heard Ferreira snort softly behind him and felt a prickle of annoyance at her attitude. While she was sleeping off her hangover Grieves was in here diligently ploughing through hours of mind-numbing, eyeball-furring footage of the streets around New England. And now it had paid off.

'OK, let's see what you've got.'

She tapped her keyboard, brought up a still lifted from the video. It showed a Polish cafeteria on Lincoln Road, a few people sitting out front in the sunshine, their faces blurs of movement as they held animated conversations. All except the two men at the table furthest from the door, who were both staring out across the road, faces still and crisp enough to make a positive identification.

One was the man they had arrested for Asif Khalid's murder, but it was his drinking buddy who made Zigic swear under his breath.

'What?' Ferreira asked.

'That's Sofia's boyfriend. Tomas.'

'Are you sure?'

He leaned across Grieves's shoulder, needing to be certain. Tomas had a distinctive appearance, broad-shouldered and heavily muscled, with a lean bony face and light blond hair worn long on top and shaved at the sides. Zigic thought of the photos he had seen in Anthony Gilbert's house, the ones of them all together on Jelena's Facebook page, and knew he was looking at the same man.

'It's him. I'm positive.'

His eyes drifted down to the time code at the bottom of the screen. The footage had been taken four weeks ago, a Friday afternoon.

'This is the day before Didi was murdered.'

'Wasn't that around the time Gilbert and Jelena were talking about him leaving Sofia?' Ferreira asked. 'Do you think she's covering for him?'

'I don't know. Gilbert and Jelena seemed to think he'd dumped her – that was a private conversation, so we have to assume it's legitimate.'

He thought of how flustered Sofia became when they discussed Tomas, and he'd put it down to embarrassment at the time, a desire to conceal the fact that she'd been dumped, but now he wondered if it was a tactic to stop him pursuing the subject.

'If anyone knows where to find Tomas, it's Sofia.'

'Maybe this is why they split up,' Ferreira suggested. 'She finds out what he's done, doesn't like it, they argue, she throws him out.'

'Why wouldn't she report it to the police though?' Grieves asked.

Ferreira laughed. 'Seriously? I don't know if you've noticed but we're not exactly popular around that neck of the woods.'

Grieves looked away, cheeks burning. 'Maybe she's scared of him.'

'No,' Zigic said. 'She's scared of us.'

'She didn't act like it when we pulled her in.'

'That was about avenging her sister. Her own safety wasn't a consideration. But she wouldn't have risked exposing herself to report Tomas. She can't afford the scrutiny.'

'Why?'

'Her papers are dodgy.'

'Good, that gives us leverage.'

Zigic looked again at the two men, relaxing in the afternoon sun, and wondered what conversation they'd been having. Was it the usual work and women and football stuff? Or was it something altogether more serious?

'Have you found any more footage of them together?'

Grieves looked back at the screen. 'Not yet – this is the first thing I found. I thought you'd want to know right away. They stay at the cafe for about twenty minutes then they walk south down Lincoln Road and turn off onto Green Street, but there's no cameras on the road so I don't know where they went afterwards.'

'Sofia and Jelena's house is on Green Street,' Zigic said.

He walked over to the whiteboard with Didi's photograph at the top, picked up a marker pen and added 'Tomas' to the suspects column, then did the same for Asif Khalid's and Ali Manouf's.

'Deb, see if they're using that cafe regularly, we can chase up on that then. And concentrate on the next thirty-six hours of footage. Didi was killed a couple of streets away, it's possible you'll spot them now you know what we're looking for. And print a copy of that, would you?'

'Yes, sir.'

He turned away from the board. 'Mel, make a file up, you know what we need.'

'Gore?'

'I'm not sure that will have much effect on Sofia, but we'll try.'

On Wahlia's desk he found the mobile phone number they had for Tomas, dialled it and heard it go straight to voicemail again. He was keeping it switched off or he'd discarded the SIM card for some reason. If he was involved, the latter was most likely. Especially since his partner had been arrested.

Zigic tried not to get ahead of himself. Having a beer together didn't make them brothers in arms, but Tomas's sudden disappearance and Sofia's reticence bothered him.

Ferreira came over with a cardboard file tucked under her arm.

'Back to the hospital then?'

The car park was busier now, Sunday visiting duties to be done.

234

As they walked up to the ward where Sofia was they passed people with bunches of flowers and arms full of magazines, bags of food and books to help ease the annoyance of confinement.

Sofia had none of those luxuries.

When they went into her room she was lying with her back to the door and she didn't stir at the interruption. Zigic walked round the bed and saw that she was sleeping, but not peacefully. Her face was drawn into a tense frown, her hands curled into tight fists, ready to fight despite the restraints.

Gently he shook her shoulder and she came round with a start, snapping upright so quickly that she gasped and pressed her hand to her ribs. Three days on from the hit-and-run she was still delicate and he wondered if her injuries were worse than she'd made out. The doctors had her on what looked like a morphine drip, a button attached to it so she could self-medicate. But she didn't reach for it, only settled back slowly against the pillows, biting down on the pain.

Zigic held his hand out to Ferreira and she passed him the file. He found the photograph of Asif Khalid's murderer and showed it to Sofia.

'Do you know who this is?'

She glanced at it, no change in expression. 'Why do you want to know?'

'He's a friend of Tomas's, is that right?'

'What has he done?'

'Who is he?'

Sofia scowled at him. 'Lukas.'

'Lukas what?'

'I do not know his other name,' she said. 'What has he done?'

Zigic slipped the photograph away, found one of Asif Khalid dead on the pavement in Cromwell Road. 'This.'

Sofia looked at the image for a couple of seconds without any discernible change in expression. He didn't expect her to be shocked – she had grown up in a war zone, seeing people dead and dying on the streets, shot by snipers, bodies shredded by shell debris, this photograph was too remote to provoke a reaction.

'I did not like him. Tomas brought him to the house once. I told him I would not have him in my home again.'

'Why?'

'I have seen men like him before. I knew what he was.'

'And what was that?'

'A soldier. I could see it in his eyes that he has killed people. When I ask Tomas he says, yes, Lukas was in the army but a medic. I did not believe him.'

'We need to speak to Tomas, he's the only link we have to Lukas right now and there's a chance he'll have vital information.' That got a reaction. She tried to fold her arms but the restraints stopped her. 'Where is he now?'

'I told you, he went home.'

'His phone's switched off,' Zigic said. 'It's been switched off for days.'

'I know. I have tried to call him to tell him about Jelena.'

'And we have reason to believe he hasn't left the country. We think he's likely still in Peterborough.' Zigic held her gaze, seeing something like fear in her eyes. 'He's been in touch with you, hasn't he?'

'No.'

'We only want to talk to him about his friend, Sofia. He isn't in any trouble.'

'Why would I care if he is in trouble?' she said, spitting out the words. 'He is nothing to me now.'

It sounded like bravado, the same behaviour Zigic had observed in her right from the start, denying weakness, rejecting comfort. She did care though, and she couldn't hide it; her shoulders lifting defensively, her chin dipping. She stared him down, defying him to contradict her.

Zigic knew there was no point attempting it, but she was hiding something and he wouldn't leave until he'd teased it out of her.

'Why did Tomas leave you?'

236

'Money. He did not want to pay his part of the bills. I said I would not keep him. So he left.'

'How long were you together?'

'Three years.' She sucked her bottom lip into her mouth. 'Nearly three years.'

'Did you meet over here?'

'Of course over here. I have lived in Peterborough since I was twenty.'

'What about Tomas?' Zigic asked. 'When did he arrive?'

'Why are you asking me these questions?' Sofia demanded. 'They will not help you find him. He has gone back to Poznań. Ask people there.'

'We're asking you,' Ferreira said, her voice low and hard.

She moved to the foot of Sofia's bed, stood with her hands curled around the bars.

'In case you've forgotten, you're in custody here, Sofia. You've assaulted a police officer.' Sofia bristled visibly, folded her free arm across her abdomen as Ferreira went on. 'It's an offence we take very seriously. Three years in prison seriously. Followed by deportation to . . . where is it you're from again?'

Sofia turned to Zigic, switching into Serbo-Croat. 'You are a traitor to your people.'

Zigic ignored the comment. 'We want to help you, Sofia, but we need you to help us.'

'So you threaten me? You are no better than the police at home.'

'I don't want to see you sent back there,' he said. 'But we believe Lukas has killed three men and Tomas is the only person who seems to know him. We need to speak to him and one way or another we'll find him. It would be best all round if you're the one who tells us where he is.'

She looked down at her stomach, her arm pulled defensively across it, bruised from elbow to wrist. 'If I knew where he was I would tell you.'

But Zigic didn't believe her.

'Has he threatened you?'

Her face flushed. 'He would not dare.'

'What about Lukas? Do you know where he lives? Where he works maybe?'

'I only saw him once.'

'OK. Tomas probably has gone home,' Zigic said. 'We're going to need some details on his family, friends over there. What's Tomas's surname?'

'Kaminski. I do not know anything of his family.'

'Do you seriously expect us to believe that you lived with him for three years and you never met his family?'

'He would not be here if they were important to him,' she said.

'Then why did he go home to them?' Ferreira asked.

'You must ask him this.' Sofia rearranged her pillows and burrowed down the bed, pulling the cover up to her chin. 'I am tired. My doctor says I am to rest. You must leave.'

Ferreira shot him a questioning glance but Zigic stood up and gestured towards the door. They left without another word.

What else was there to say? Zigic felt he could sit in that small, dim room for hours without breaking through the wall of denial she had constructed. He didn't believe for one second that Tomas had gone back to Poznań and, despite her grudging explanation of an argument, he felt sure Sofia knew his whereabouts.

'If we're seriously considering Tomas as a suspect we need to move fast.'

'Call Bobby and Parr, get them into the office.' Zigic opened the stairwell door and she slipped through ahead of him, eyes on her mobile. 'We need to make sure Tomas hasn't actually left the country.'

Maybe Tomas had fled back to Poland after killing Didi – if he was involved – but it was Asif Khalid's murder they needed to focus on now, and if he'd returned to the city to take part in that attack, with no knowledge that he was a suspect, there was only one place he'd be staying.

35

Early afternoon on Green Street was quiet, some of the residents out on their second or third jobs, the rest enjoying a few hours' leisure before the evening made its fast march towards night and bed and everything starting again on Monday. A man was washing his car on the pavement opposite Sofia and Jelena's house, alternately soaping the bonnet and flicking water at his small daughter as she squealed and laughed, ducking away behind the rear bumper.

As the uniforms climbed out of the patrol car he called to her and sent her back inside, following a few seconds later, bucket in hand, only to reappear at the front window with his wife.

Zigic sent PC Hale down the side of the house, heard him fighting with the gate for a moment before it opened creakily. He looked up to the bedroom windows where the curtains were drawn, no indication whether Tomas Kaminski was inside or not.

He couldn't believe the man would be stupid enough to hang around if he was guilty. Couldn't believe they would get that lucky either, but his nervous system ignored the argument and he felt adrenalin surge through his veins as he unlocked the front door.

PC Moore charged straight up the stairs, Ferreira headed for the kitchen, baton held low by her side, and a few seconds later Zigic heard the back door open, PC Hale blundering in, Ferreira snapping at him. Then a call of 'clear' sounded from the top of the stairs and the expected feeling of disappointment sucked all the tension out of the moment, leaving the four of them standing in an otherwise empty house, chilled by its lack of recent occupation and the lingering shadows of Sofia's grief.

Zigic dismissed Moore and Hale, who looked irritated that they'd been brought out for a scuffle which never materialised. Their radios were going as they left the house though and from the sound of the report they would get one soon enough.

'Wouldn't be fun if it was easy, hey?' Ferreira said.

Zigic smiled. 'It's like you don't want a weekend.'

'Shall we toss the place then?'

'What do you want, up or down?'

'Down.'

He started up the stairs. They were steep and narrow, with treads that creaked underfoot, betraying how old and badly maintained the house was despite the care Sofia and Jelena had gone to in decorating it. The landing was laid with striped runners, abstract prints in box frames on the walls, everything bright and clean.

The master bedroom was at the back of the house and the tidiness stopped at the door. The double bed was unmade, clothes on the floor, shoes sitting where they had been kicked off. He opened the wardrobe and found enough of Tomas's things inside it to suggest that he hadn't actually left Sofia. He could have packed a bag to go home for a few days and left so much, but this didn't look like the aftermath of a broken relationship.

Unless Sofia was the sentimental type, which he had seen no evidence of.

She was the kind of woman to throw clothes out of the window, he thought, pile them up in the back garden and start a bonfire.

No, Tomas hadn't left her, Zigic felt certain of that.

In the bedside cabinet, a shiny white thing from IKEA, he found men's underwear and socks, a few condoms dropped in among them, a heavy metal watch still in its box. It was relatively decent, perhaps two hundred pounds' worth. Would Tomas have left that here?

Zigic checked under the bed, found nothing but dust, tried the chest of drawers, carefully searching the folded jumpers and T-shirts, a mix of Tomas's and Sofia's, hoping to come across a badly hidden passport, something which would indicate where Tomas was, but closed them again empty-handed.

Beneath him he heard Ferreira rattling around in the living room. 'Anything?'

'Not yet,' she shouted back.

He went into the bathroom; more of Tomas's personal items in there too, a navy-blue bathrobe hanging from a hook, shaving things and cologne, antibiotics with his name on the sticker, the prescription four months old.

As he went back across the landing he heard Ferreira open the cupboard under the stairs and begin riffling through its contents. She was good at this. He didn't know how she did it but she seemed to magnetise towards things which didn't want to be found. He guessed it was growing up with three brothers, always having to hide her most precious belongings from then. When you knew how to hide things you knew where to find them.

The smaller bedroom at the front of the house was like a teenage girl's, painted hot pink, with patterned curtains drawn against the street, candy-stripe bedding and sequinned cushions. It seemed far too young for Jelena but perhaps it was partly Sofia's doing, another way to infantilise her little sister and keep her close, convince her she wasn't ready for a serious relationship, that Anthony Gilbert was too old for her.

He'd crept into the room though.

On the floor around a wicker bin he found the ripped-up remains of bouquet notelets and cinema stubs for romcoms, lots of pieces of glossy print which a few minutes' patient reassembly revealed to be photographs of Jelena and Gilbert.

It was the group one including Sofia and Tomas which drew his attention though. An overlit bar, everyone drunk and grinning madly, and they looked genuinely comfortable with one another. Close. Sofia's arm around Gilbert's waist, his draped across her shoulder, the other holding Jelena tight to him.

Sofia hadn't hated him right then, Zigic thought. She might have been play-acting for Jelena's sake but he didn't think so. Her eyes were red, her face slack, too much drink inside her by that point in the night to keep up the pantomime.

What had happened to break the link? he wondered, as he left Jelena's bedroom and headed back downstairs. Had Sofia seen something in Gilbert she hadn't noticed before? Something she didn't like? Or was it the opposite – did she get a little too close to Gilbert? Was it a simple case of sibling rivalry?

They were missing something.

Zigic went into the kitchen, found the back door standing open, letting in a chill breeze which carried the scent of woodsmoke and recently mown grass, and went out to where Ferreira was standing at the foot of the garden, peering into a wheelie bin.

As he approached she stepped back, a plastic carrier bag in her gloved hand.

'We've got blood,' she said, holding it open for him.

The bag was stuffed with clothing, too much for the size of it, balled up and crumpled. On the top was a pair of dark green combat trousers, heavily stained with telltale brown-red marks.

'There could be an innocent explanation,' he said.

Ferreira nodded. 'There could.'

'It's a lot of blood though.'

'That's just what I was thinking.'

Carefully she lifted the waistband of the trousers to expose the label inside. H&M menswear, a thirty-four-inch waist, thirty-six-inch leg.

'This has to be Tomas's clothing,' she said. 'Neither of the women would be wearing this size.'

On the other side of the fence something clanked and they both looked towards it, but the person was already moving, feet crunching along a gravel path back towards the house.

'Put it back and call forensics,' Zigic said. 'Tell them this is top priority.'

His phone rang as he was passing through the hallway. Grieves.

242

'I've found them, sir. Half an hour before Didi was murdered they show up on Lincoln Road, near the junction with Green Street, they go into the same cafe we saw them at earlier, they have a drink, then they head north towards the locus and that's the last I can find.' She swallowed. 'They don't appear again on any of the surrounding streets.'

'Have you found them leaving the locus?' Zigic asked, pausing with his hand on the newel post.

'Yes, there's a ten-minute gap then Tomas reappears –'

'Alone?'

'Yes. He takes the same route, minus the cafe, and disappears again at Green Street.'

'Great work. Thanks, Deb.'

Zigic went outside, thinking of Tomas and Lukas setting out through this same door the night they killed Didi, leaving Sofia and Jelena at home, watching TV or already in bed, no idea what they were planning. And then Tomas returning alone? In bloodstained clothing, high from the kill?

He wondered which one of them had actually killed Didi, because the CCTV footage proved it wasn't a joint endeavour. Which one of them had looked on, admiring, enjoying his friend's brutality? Which of them was the man who had then turned to the camera and raised a Nazi salute?

The state of Tomas's clothes suggested he was the likely perpetrator but until forensics had been over them everything was open to debate. Maybe they weren't Tomas's clothes at all.

Zigic knocked on the neighbours' door and it was answered quickly by a small, moon-faced woman with a floral apron over her clothes.

'Mrs O'Brien? Detective Inspector Zigic. You spoke to one of my colleagues a couple of days ago . . .'

'Oh, Nicola, yes, lovely young woman.' She beamed, showing a set of false teeth slightly too large for her mouth. 'Will you come in, Inspector?'

He followed her into the hallway, past the living room where a television was playing with the sound up high, the roar of a football crowd crashing over the muttered commentary of an elderly man. He glanced towards the door as Zigic passed, put his hand up in a vague greeting or dismissal.

'Best we go in the back,' Mrs O'Brien said. 'Himself won't stand any blather when the match is on.'

A stew was simmering on the hob, filling the kitchen with a salty, sour aroma. There was stout in there, Zigic thought, and sure enough he saw a small glass of it on the kitchen table where Mrs O'Brien had been sitting, flicking through the *Sunday Mirror*.

'Would I make you a cup of tea?'

'No, thank you. I won't keep you long, but I wondered if I could ask you a few questions.'

'It's no bother.' Mrs O'Brien sat down at the table and waved him to join her. 'How's Sofia? The poor dearie's back in hospital, is she?'

'Yes. But she's recovering well,' Zigic said.

'Strong young woman, that one. And she was devoted to Jelena, like a mother to her she was. Lovely thing, so pretty.' She closed her newspaper. 'And now Sofia's all alone. Breaks my heart to see her like that.'

'Hasn't Tomas been back?'

'No. She phoned him a couple of days ago to tell him the bad news but . . . well, they've gone their separate ways now, haven't they.'

'When was the last time you saw Tomas?'

Mrs O'Brien turned a beady eye on him. 'Why? You don't think he was the one who hit them?'

'No, it's an unrelated matter,' Zigic said. 'A friend of Tomas's is in trouble and we need to speak to him, but nobody seems to know where he is and Sofia isn't in a fit state to help us yet.'

'I've not seen hide nor hair of him since he took himself off.'

'And when was this?'

She tapped her finger on the table. 'It was the second of last month.'

'That's very precise,' Zigic said. 'Are you sure?'

She bristled. 'Of course I'm sure. I might be getting on but I've not gone soft in the head yet.' She pointed at him. 'Now, I remember because it was Willy's – that's my husband – it was Willy's birthday and I was in here icing his birthday cake and I heard an almighty carry-on from next door. They were shouting and throwing things. Well, the walls in these houses are so thin . . .'

Zigic thought of her loitering in the back garden and imagined she hadn't exactly tried to ignore it, but he was grateful now. Police work would be ten times harder without 'concerned' neighbours.

'Then it all went quiet.' She paused, looking away at the party wall. 'And a few minutes later the front door slammed so hard I'm surprised it didn't fly right off its hinges.'

'And you didn't see Tomas again after that?'

'No. I only know because he was supposed to come and fix my tap.' She gestured towards the kitchen sink, where the hot tap was dripping rhythmically, pinging against the stainless steel. 'He was very handy with that sort of thing. I asked Sofia if he wouldn't mind coming round and having a wee tinker with it and she said Tomas was after going home for a bit. She said she'd send him round when he came back but –' She shrugged. 'He never did.'

'Did you ask her about the argument?'

Mrs O'Brien looked at him like he was mad. 'You don't ask a woman a question like that. But that *other* one was there. Jelena's boyfriend. Although I can't see as he'd be much help to you after what he's gone and done.'

'We'll try him.' Zigic took Lukas's mugshot out of his pocket and handed it to Mrs O'Brien. 'Have you seen this man visiting the house at all?'

She put on a pair of reading glasses and frowned at the photo. 'I remember this one. Sure, you don't forget a face like that. Fearsome-looking creature, wouldn't you say? He used to come round when the girls were out at work.'

'Often?'

'A few times that I saw.' She gave it back to Zigic. 'What's he done? No good, I bet.'

'You're a fine judge of character, madam.' He tucked the photo away again and stood up, pushed the chair back under the table. 'Thank you for your time, you've been a great help.'

'Oh, it's no bother.'

She saw him out, asked him to pass on her best to Sofia when he saw her, no idea of how serious the next conversation they had was going to be.

Back to the hospital. Again. Three times in four hours and Zigic was beginning to feel like he'd spend the rest of his life in the place, walking endless claustrophobic corridors, pushing through infinite sets of swings doors then sanitising his hands, nose full of bleach smell and sickness and pollen from the flowers already wilting in their plastic vases on the nightstands.

Visiting hours were over and dinner time not yet started, the minutes between stretched, with nothing to do but watch the sun creep across the sky and think about what was happening inside your broken body, completely out of your control.

He'd been there himself. Last year when a fight with a suspect ended with him on the wrong end of a handgun, only the bulletproof vest saving him from being shot in the heart at point-blank range. It was a minor injury but they kept him in for a few hours which felt like days, tests and pills and 'you're a very lucky man, Inspector, a few inches higher . . .'

In the end he discharged himself, not wanting to lie there any longer like a victim.

Sofia was struggling with it too, he realised. She thought she was strong, she'd been through enough in her life to prove it, and yet here she was. Sedated the nurse said, explaining how agitated she'd become since their last visit, wanting to leave, shouting and cursing, threatening to hit the doctor when he tried to examine her.

She looked small under the sheets and very fragile, stripped of her defences.

Zigic stood in the doorway for a few minutes, watching her sleep, wondering how much information she had locked away in her head, and whether he would be able to get it out of her. She was protecting Tomas, through fear or loyalty.

Fear, he thought.

If Tomas had kicked Didi to death, stamped on his skull until it no longer resembled one, what on earth was he doing to Sofia? Men like that didn't save their psychopathic behaviour for strangers. He might consider himself a soldier and claim there were battle lines scratched in the sand, but the moment Sofia did something he didn't like he would have lashed out. So much rage couldn't be neatly compartmentalised.

Zigic closed the door and went up to the ward where Anthony Gilbert was.

'What do you want?' Gilbert said wearily. 'I've already told you I'm saying nothing else without a solicitor.'

'This isn't about you.'

Zigic switched off the television opposite Gilbert's bed and sat down in the chair next to the window, sunlight washing the room, throwing his shadow across the twisted sheets.

'I want you to tell me about Tomas.'

'What about Tomas?' Gilbert licked his cracked lips. 'What's he got to do with anything?'

It would come out soon enough and Gilbert wasn't in a position to tell anybody what they were going to discuss; shackled and under a police guard, he might not talk to another civilian for days.

'Have you see the news today?'

Gilbert nodded hesitantly.

'The young man who was murdered on Saturday night,' Zigic said. 'We've arrested one of Tomas's friends. We think he might have been involved too.'

'That's impossible. Tomas went back to Poland weeks ago.'

'Did he?'

'Didn't Sofia tell you?'

'Maybe she believes that. We don't.'

'Well, I don't know where he is, if that's what you're here for.' Gilbert reached under the sheets to scratch his leg, eyes fixed on the dead television screen. 'Tomas and me weren't friends. If it wasn't for Jelena I wouldn't have had anything to do with him. Either of them.'

'You didn't get on?' Zigic asked and still Gilbert wouldn't look at him. 'Why was that?'

'He didn't like Jelena going out with an English guy.'

'Any English guy? Or just you?'

'Maybe just me,' Gilbert said. 'I don't know, it's just what Jelena told me. It's not like he came out and said it to my face, but he made it pretty clear he didn't think I was good enough for her.'

Gilbert closed his eyes for a moment, lost in memories of Jelena and him. Zigic had seen guilty men make elaborate displays of innocent grief before though, and he didn't let this one colour his judgement. Gilbert might not have wanted to kill Jelena – Zigic was convinced that the man genuinely loved her – but he was still their only suspect and his regret changed nothing.

'What kind of man is he?' Zigic asked.

Gilbert gathered himself again, but when he spoke he picked his words carefully, wary of saying anything which might further implicate him. 'He's your typical East European meathead. Not very clever and he hates anyone who is. You know, the type who thinks being physically strong's the only way you can be a real man.'

'He looks like a powerful guy.'

'He used to pick Sofia up and carry her around the house over his shoulder. She hated that.' Gilbert's face darkened. 'He did it to Jelena once. Sofia screamed at him to put her down and he just laughed at her.'

'Did they argue a lot?' Zigic asked.

'Not really.'

248

'But he left her,' Zigic said, trying to catch Gilbert's eye, which had wandered again and settled on a spot in the corner of the room, near the sink with its pink hand sanitiser and plastic-wrapped medical supplies. 'Or did Sofia throw him out?'

'I don't know.'

'But you were there when it happened?'

Gilbert's attention snapped back to him. 'When what happened?'

'The fight,' Zigic said. 'Sofia's neighbour reported hearing an argument the night that Tomas left the house. She told me you were there too.'

'I don't know what the fight was about, I was upstairs. It got heated. Jelena wanted to go down. I said we should stay out of it. Then the next thing I know Tomas is coming up and Sofia is still shouting at him but he doesn't answer her. Jelena got up to see what was happening – I tried to stop her but she was worried about Sofia. Tomas had packed a bag by then and he was leaving.'

'Did Sofia try to stop him?'

'No.'

She wouldn't have given him the satisfaction of begging, Zigic imagined.

'Has she been in contact with him since?'

'No.'

'Would she tell you if she had?'

'No,' Gilbert said. 'But she would have told Jelena.'

Zigic considered it for a moment, something niggling away at the back of his mind that he couldn't quite catch hold of. Was Sofia the forgive-and-forget type? He didn't think so, but he had very little to base that assumption on, only the impressions he had gathered during a couple of conversations. There would be whole swathes of her character he hadn't seen.

'This was around the time you and Jelena had to cool things off.'

Gilbert didn't reply. His eyes were shining wet.

'Sofia didn't want you in the house any more?'

'No.' A croaky whisper.

'Why was that? She must have given Jelena a reason.'

He just shook his head and gave in to the tears.

There was only one reason Zigic could think of, and it was speculative at this point, based on incomplete evidence and gut instinct, but when he looked at the situation as a whole it made perfect sense. Tomas came home covered in blood; Sofia challenged him. Perhaps she knew exactly what he had done; worked out the link between his behaviour and the murdered man all over the local paper. Perhaps only that it was something which might bring trouble to her doorstep, but she would want him to leave for a while until the danger passed.

Tomas could have spun her a line, called Didi's murder self-defence. If she loved him she would want to protect him and eventually she would want him to come home to her.

It would be risky though, and the fewer people who knew he was back in Peterborough the better. So Jelena would have to end it with Gilbert.

Or was he misjudging Sofia? She'd shown so little emotion he found it hard to get a handle on her thought process. Did she seem like a woman in love? Or a woman in fear?

Nobody had been able to give Zigic a satisfactory reason for the sudden, enforced break in their relationship and that bothered him, smacked of guilty secrets. This explained it. Explained the vagueness too.

But it didn't tell him where Tomas was now.

Only Sofia could do that.

36

Ferreira was getting out of a cab as Zigic pulled into the station car park and she waited on the brown brick steps for him, hands shoved down into the back pockets of her jeans.

'Make sure you claim for the taxi,' he said.

'I can't be bothered with the paperwork. Not for a fiver.'

They went in through reception, empty on a Sunday afternoon, everyone with better things to do than raise hell. Zigic debriefed her on his conversation with Anthony Gilbert as they climbed the stairs, answered her questions, which were the same ones he'd asked himself, and felt reassured that his theory sounded more solid out loud than it had in his head.

'Do you think Gilbert knows more than he's saying about this?' she asked.

'He's got no reason to lie.'

'We're getting ready to charge him with multiple murder. I wouldn't help us if I was him. Not without getting something in return.' She stopped at the vending machine and shoved a handful of change into it. 'Do you want anything?'

Zigic shook his head and she started punching the buttons.

'Because it sounds like he's trying to keep Sofia in the clear,' Ferreira said. 'She bullies Jelena into dumping him, tries to kill him and he insists she doesn't know where Tomas is. It's like he's protecting her.'

'Or he genuinely doesn't know.'

She gathered her Coke and chocolate from the tray, then leaned against the machine. 'I had a look around the house while I was waiting for forensics, there's a sleeping bag in the loft. Pillows and stuff.'

'Did it look recently used?'

'Tough to say. It's pretty clean up there.' She opened her Coke. 'I found Sofia and Jelena's stash too. A shoebox hidden in an old chest of drawers. There's twelve grand in it.'

It was a crazy amount of money to leave lying around the house, even if it had been well hidden, but a lot of migrant workers didn't trust the banks or were employed on the black. Some didn't have the right paperwork to open accounts; more still had been forced from their homes by warfare or ethnic cleansing, driven out with whatever possessions they could carry. It was a lesson you didn't need to learn twice. After that you would keep your money portable and to hand.

That was why they'd seen a steep year-on-year rise in burglaries in predominantly immigrant areas, they were lucrative places to hit, no need to find a fence, no trail left through pawnbrokers, just anonymous cash.

'So maybe it's clean because they were going up there to stow their savings.'

Ferreira shrugged. 'Maybe. It's not a great place to lie low, is it?'

'Didn't take you long to find it.'

'He'll be well away by now,' she said. 'If he was with Lukas when he murdered Khalid he'll know they're caught. You wouldn't hang around and chance him giving you up.'

'It depends whether they agreed not to talk if they got caught. Tomas might know Lukas has no intention of telling us anything.'

'He can't know it for sure. Let's say they made a pact, spat on their hands, did the blood-brother thing, whatever. Would you trust the strength of that promise if you were Tomas?'

'I'd clear out,' Zigic said.

In the office Grieves and Parr were standing in front of Asif Khalid's board while she brought him up to speed on the recent developments. He nodded, mumbled, but didn't look as if he was paying much attention. When she led him back to her computer he stifled a yawn.

Wahlia was hunched over his desk, eyes fixed on the screen, columns of print reflecting off his glasses.

'OK, what've we got on Tomas Kaminski?' Zigic asked.

Grieves piped up first. 'I've found three more instances of him and our unidentified man –'

'His name's Lukas,' Zigic said, dropping into a seat at one of the unmanned desks. 'No surname and it's not for definite, but we can stick with it until we know better. Go on.'

'Tomas and Lukas were regulars at that cafe so I thought perhaps one of the staff might know something about them.'

'Did you send someone round there?'

She hesitated. 'No, sir. Not yet.'

Zigic turned to Wahlia. 'Bobby, anything from customs?'

'Still waiting,' he said. 'It's Sunday, you know the deal. I said it's a priority but every appeal they get is. Best guess, we won't hear back until tomorrow morning.'

'Unfortunately we don't have the luxury of waiting,' Zigic said. He rose from the chair again and went over to Asif Khalid's board. There was a photograph of Tomas Kaminski tacked up there, lifted from Facebook judging by the beer in his hand and the idiotic grin. 'Tomas is our only viable suspect right now and given the evidence from the CCTV on the night of Didi's murder he's looking solid, so we need to concentrate on tracking his movements.'

'Does Sofia know where he is?' Wahlia asked.

'If she does she isn't saying, but we'll try and put some pressure on her tomorrow. Right now I want a thorough canvassing of the hotels and dosshouses around the city, concentrating on New England first. And this cafe they were using. Parr, that's you.'

He didn't look too happy with the job.

'I know it's Sunday and I know you'd rather be at home. So would the rest of us.' Parr shifted uncomfortably in his seat. 'The sooner you get started the sooner it's done. Take what you need, grab some uniforms and get cracking.'

Parr drew himself up slowly and trudged out of the office.

'Bobby, check back through Jelena and Gilbert's Facebook messages and see if you can pin down when exactly Tomas is supposed to have left Sofia. Also, look for anything that suggests why it happened and how Sofia reacted.' Wahlia nodded. 'The line I got from Gilbert is that there was a fight but I think he's hiding something. We need to know if Sofia is genuinely pissed off with Tomas or if she's covering for him. Find me something to get her talking please.'

'On it.'

'Deb –'

'Yes, sir?'

'Bank records, employment details, all the basic stuff on Kaminski,' Zigic said. 'He was working through Pickman Nye but you'll have to leave that for the morning. And track down his phone logs – Bobby can give you the number.'

He turned to Ferreira, saw her playing with her mobile, feet up on the bottom drawer of her desk.

'Mel.'

'Yeah?' The phone on her desk started ringing. 'Hold on.'

She answered it and immediately stood, listened for a few seconds, then swore towards the ceiling and slammed the receiver down again.

'Lukas,' she said, starting for the door.

Rita, the custody sergeant was waiting for them, red-faced in front of the main desk, one hand at her throat, clutching the gold crucifix which was usually tucked safely away inside her uniform shirt.

'I don't know how this happened.'

'Wasn't someone watching him?' Zigic asked, already heading for the cells.

She fell in step behind him. 'Lee collected his lunch half an hour ago and he was fine.'

'Had he eaten it?' Ferreira asked.

'No, but we didn't think anything of it. He hasn't eaten anything for a couple of days. We thought it was just the food. I asked if he was vegetarian or something but he didn't answer so we kept giving him the usual. What else was I supposed to do?'

The corridor was long and brightly lit, despite its basement location, cell doors standing closed on the left, the names of their occupants on whiteboards. They were kicking up a racket now, alerted by the alarm which had been sounded too late, shouting and banging. There was a smell in the air, stale bodies and dirty hair and the tang of alcohol sweated out overnight into the confined spaces, then urine, as they approached the final cell, where Dr Hopkins was standing with one gloved hand on his balding head, looking in through the open door.

Hopkins moved aside as they approached, letting them see Lukas's naked body, lying flat on the floor, arms outstretched, head still tilted back from the failed attempt at resuscitation. His lips were blue, drawn back from his teeth, eyes closed. The ligature, formed from the ripped and knotted fabric of his shirt, had been cut away and thrown aside, the other end of it still tied off around one of the metal brackets which supported the bunk. The rest of his clothes were neatly folded and piled up on the thin pillow.

'What happened?' Zigic said. 'Exactly.'

'I tried to revive him,' Rita said, getting her defence in quickly.

'Before or after you called Dr Hopkins?'

'I was attending to another guest,' he said. 'Your man was dead by the time I got here. I performed CPR but there was very little point. Choking takes a high degree of willpower. It isn't like hanging, you can stop at any point, but he didn't. It would have been drawn out and very painful. He was clearly determined to end it.'

Zigic looked at the scrap of striped fabric secured around the metal bracket, no more than two foot above the floor. Lukas must have knelt down and leaned forward until the makeshift noose began to bite, felt his lungs burn and scream, heard the blood rushing in his head as his vision shimmered and broke apart. Maybe he pulled back once or twice, a change of mind, a surge of self-preservation, but he kept going, pushed through the fear and the pain until he passed out, then his bodyweight would have done the rest, holding him in that position until he finally died.

Zigic turned on Rita, trying to make herself as small as possible in the corner of the corridor. 'Who cut him down?'

'Lee. He found him on routine inspection.' She wouldn't look at Lukas's body, kept her eyes fixed firmly on Zigic. 'We did a full assessment, he didn't present any of the characteristics for a suicide risk.'

'And yet there he is,' Zigic said.

'There was no way to predict he'd kill himself.'

Zigic thought of his behaviour during the interviews, that absolute refusal to interact, the upright and defiant stoicism. He'd interpreted it as strength but now he wondered if he'd been wrong. Was the man scared? Did he sit in this cell imagining what the next thirty years of his life would be like, locked up in a prison with men as tough as him, ones who would be queuing up to stick a knife in the ribs of a racist serial murderer? Motivated by their own ideas of vengeance or the desire for the kind of kudos which came with killing a high-profile hard man.

Ferreira was laying into Rita, asking her precisely when the previous inspection had been made, questioning the length of the interval against the time it would have taken for Lukas to choke himself to death. The woman struggled to give her a satisfactory answer, first mumbling then becoming increasingly hostile.

Sunday afternoon was a soft shift in the custody suite; they used it like paid downtime and he wouldn't be surprised if the usual protocols had slackened for a few hours.

'What do you care?' Rita snapped defensively. 'Everyone knows you couldn't get him to talk.'

Zigic turned from the cell. 'We care because the men he murdered, and their families, have a right to see him punished. And thanks to your negligence they will never get that.'

'We did everything we had to.'

'You better hope the IPCC agrees with that assessment.'

37

It was gone seven by the time Zigic got home, the sun dipping low, throwing long shadows across the front garden, where Anna was fiddling with the honeysuckle around the door, tucking the slim, whipping strands back into the wire supports so it wouldn't attack them every time they went in or out. She'd been out there a while, he noticed, gathered a binful of weeds stripped from the flower beds under the windows, leaving the earth bare between the evergreens.

'You look shattered,' she said.

He bent to kiss her, smelling the sap on her skin.

'It's not been a good day.'

'I can see that.' She took hold of his shoulders and scrutinised his face. 'What's happened?'

'I need a shower first.'

He went inside, threw his parka over the newel post and kicked his shoes off under the console table. As he trudged upstairs he regretted saying anything. He didn't want to tell her about Lukas's suicide. That was work and this was home and he knew that it was best for everyone's sanity if the two things were kept separate.

Through the bedroom window he saw Milan and Stefan playing in the back garden, running around the chestnut tree with their lightsabres glowing in the shade from the sagging branches. Stefan's was dragging along the ground through the grass as he shouted out commands. Milan's heart wasn't in it and Zigic wondered how much longer he would go on playing these games with his little brother, occupying a fantasy world which wasn't as real for him as it was to Stefan.

He went into the en suite and turned on the shower, stripped off his work clothes and stepped into the cubicle. He closed his eyes and turned his face into the water, trying to think of nothing, wanting just a few minutes' respite from the continuing cases and the looming prospect of an investigation into Lukas's suicide. It wasn't his fault but Lukas was his suspect and he knew he would be touched by the process, tainted by association even if he faced no official censure.

It was just another problem to add to all the others and he could have done without it.

He thought of Asif Khalid's young widow, the grief she was going through, and hoped her friends and family were looking after her. How was she going to feel when she discovered that the man who'd murdered her husband had evaded justice by killing himself? If she was devout she might regard it as Allah's will and be satisfied that Lukas's greatest punishment had come to him early, but still, some part of her would have wanted to see him rot in jail, Zigic imagined.

There would be no respite from these thoughts tonight.

He switched off the water and dried himself, pulled on his oldest jeans and a jumper and went downstairs into the kitchen. There was chicken marinating in a bowl in the fridge, salad in another. He ate a couple of fat green olives stuffed with lemon zest, picked out some feta, then poured a glass of Żubrówka from the bottle in the freezer.

The Sunday papers were piled up on the kitchen table, read and refolded, the glossy sections on top. He sifted through them as he sipped his vodka, found a magazine with Richard Shotton's tanned and serious face staring out from the front cover, the English Patriot Party's red-and-white rosette pinned to the lapel of his cashmere overcoat.

Inside, the piece ran across six pages, light on political interrogation and so heavy on flattery that it might have been written by Shotton's PR people, focused on his military career and his charity work. There was much mention of his wife of eighteen years, a corporate lawyer and art collector, Brazilian by birth and always impeccably turned out. The implication being that of course he couldn't be a racist and he must have leadership potential or why else would this alpha female be with him?

Zigic closed the magazine in disgust then shoved it in the bin.

There would be more in the rest of the papers, editorials about the social implications and underlying causes of the ENL riot, skewed to suit the perspective of intended readers, and columns on the murders which would focus on the most gruesome aspects. Everyone interested now. It seemed impossible that a few days ago he was pushing Riggott for more press coverage, hoping to stir some reticent member of the public into coming forward with information.

When news of Lukas's suicide was formally announced tomorrow it would only get worse, accusations of negligence and incompetence thrown into the mix, his name attached to it because who cared who the custody sergeant was? She hadn't given a press conference. They didn't know her.

He put a cast-iron pan on the heat, slammed it down harder than he meant to, and started to fry the chicken, the smell of tomato and oregano filling the kitchen as it sizzled.

Anna came in through the back door, pulling off her spotty gardening gloves.

'I was just about to do that.'

He offered her the tongs. 'Do you want to take over?'

'No, you look like you've got it under control.' She took his glass out of his hand and gave it back refilled. 'How many more are you going to need before you can tell me what happened?'

'There's no point talking about it,' he said, concentrating on turning the meat. 'It's getting frustrating, that's all. We seem to be making progress then something swims up from nowhere and sets us right back where we started.'

'Is this the hit-and-run?'

'No, the other thing.'

'But you charged the man responsible?' she said. 'It is him, isn't it?'

Zigic took a long mouthful of vodka and looked down into the pale green liquid when he spoke, telling her about the second attacker and this afternoon's suicide, how it complicated the matter and how much new pressure it would bring down on them.

'We've identified another suspect but we've got no idea where he's hiding. He's probably out of the country by now.'

Anna rubbed his shoulders, concerned, but he could tell she didn't want to hear any more about it, and he could understand her reaction, she wasn't living inside it like he was.

'Why don't you try and forget about it for a couple of hours? You can't do anything else tonight.'

They ate dinner in the kitchen, Anna talking about the new development being planned for the edge of the village, a hundred houses she was convinced would spoil the community. He knew she was right, this was an oasis compared to most of the places around Peterborough, small and close-knit, with a good primary school and nice pubs, but there was a ulterior motive to her bringing it up. She was already looking for their next house, wanted a bigger garden for the boys and an extra bedroom in readiness for when she got pregnant again.

Life moved in a straight line for Anna, always progressing, always improving, and he wondered if she realised how lucky they were to be so comfortable. She'd never known anything else though, didn't want to think about how close they were to people with radically different lives.

Four weeks earlier, a five-minute drive away from where they sat now, a young Somali man had left the dingy flat he shared with three virtual strangers, hopped on a bus into the centre of Peterborough and, just by pure chance, a moment of terrible luck, he crossed paths with a pair of men who kicked him to death for the colour of his skin.

If he pointed that out to her, she'd say, 'Well, we definitely need to move further out then.' And perhaps she'd be right; the new development being planned would link the village to the chaotic sprawl of Bretton, with its low-rise flats and no-go areas, and slowly this would become the kind of place he would worry about his children growing up in.

His boys with their foreign surname to mark them out in the classroom and the playground. Their fourth-generation status wiped away by their Slavic Christian names. That was Anna's idea but he'd gone along with it, wanting to maintain a link back to the country of his grandparents' birth, even though it meant little to him now. No more than a fading oral history and a series of villages which had been bombed out of existence long ago.

Why had he tied his sons to that?

He wasn't patriotic, didn't trust the concept. It kept unpleasant company; nationalism and xenophobia and dangerous ideas about racial supremacy which didn't belong in the twenty-first century.

Soon Croatia would join Europe and when they started to arrive in the UK they would bring a fresh wave of sectarian hatred with them, old scores to settle in a new country. It was a hidden racism, something the English barely conceived of, the festering, blood-borne conflicts of Eastern Europe which lay at the heart of so many incidents they dealt with. The Poles hated the Lithuanians, the Bulgarians hated the Romanians, everyone despised their respective Roma. White-on-white racism predicated on name alone.

So much pointless contempt and nothing he saw suggested it was fading. The world became smaller and yet less intimate, homogenised on a superficial level only, and it seemed to him that the further people moved from home the more aggressively they defended the perceived uniqueness of their own culture.

DAY FIVE

38

Monday morning's workload picked up where Sunday night's left off, tasks unfinished on desks returned to smoothly, everyone kicking into gear fast, knuckling down straight after the most perfunctory of briefings.

Zigic stood at Asif Khalid's board, looking through a list of hostels and hotels which Parr had compiled the day before. He recognised most of the names but a few places were new. They sprang up monthly, went in and out of business, changed hands according to arrangements it was impossible to fathom, retaining the same staff and occupants, only the title deeds moving from one solicitor's office to another. It was an area of sketchy regulation and grey economics, occasional council inspection and unchecked expansion, the kind of places where nobody asked too many questions because the owners were often as dodgy as the residents, running women or illegal labour or any of a dozen other scams under the cover of 'rooms for rent'.

Parr had struck through a third of the list, was on his way into the city centre now with a couple of uniforms in tow to work through the remainder. So far nobody had any knowledge of Tomas Kaminski or Lukas. Or if they had they hadn't admitted it.

He trusted Parr to make clear the benefits of cooperating and what the cost of lying would be if either man was later found to have been staying with them. The threat of a charge for assisting an offender might prompt an act of good citizenry, but the heat they could bring down from the taxman and environmental health would be the killer.

Parr had been shocked by the living conditions he'd seen, dingy, overcrowded rooms with a dozen types of mould climbing the walls, leaky windows and sagging ceilings and infestations. He said he'd stood under a scalding hot shower for an hour when he'd got home last night, trying to scrub off invisible spores and the tickling sensation of fleas and ticks which weren't really there.

It was a long-overdue wake-up call, Zigic thought. If Parr was going to be a copper in Peterborough these were the streets he needed to walk.

At the very least it would make him grateful for his lot when he returned to CID in a few days' time.

Or weeks, Zigic realised, with a sinking feeling.

'Got the number you wanted,' Wahlia said.

Zigic went into his office and told him to shout it, dialling as he did so.

He waited, looking at the mess of paperwork across the desk, time sheets he should have filed yesterday and notes which needed turning into reports, thinking how good it would be to have a secretary for this stuff.

A gruff-voiced man answered. 'Strug.'

Zigic introduced himself, continued in Polish, hoping to keep things simple. 'Inspector Strug, I'm looking for information on a suspect from your city. We think he's gone home.'

'You speak Polish like a peasant, Inspector.' Strug laughed, low and rattling. 'But you are the first English policeman who has made an effort and, for that, I thank you.' A lighter flicked at his end, the sizzle of cigarette paper catching. 'Now, who is this suspect and what havoc has he caused?'

'His name's Tomas Kaminski.' Zigic spelled it out. 'He's wanted in connection with a murder.'

'A domestic?' Strug asked.

'No. Why, has he got form?'

'Usually it is a domestic when one of your people calls us. They knock the girl around, you get involved, they run home to Mama and Papa.'

266

'This was racially motivated,' Zigic said. 'And there's high probability it isn't the only one he's been involved in.'

'Then you will be under pressure.'

'We are, yes.'

Strug blew out a long breath and Zigic imagined him in an office just like this one, the same filing cabinets and corkboards, photos of his family on another chaotic desk.

'Let me see what I can do,' Strug said. 'I will be in touch.'

He put the phone down before Zigic could thank him.

Through the open door he saw Kate Jenkins come into the department and make a beeline for Ferreira, who was underneath her desk fiddling with the guts of her computer. By the time she was upright Zigic was out there too.

'What have got for us, Kate?'

She brandished a folder at him. 'DNA results are back for the hit-and-run.'

'You didn't have to come down for that.'

'Thought I'd best deliver the news personally.' She frowned as he took the folder from her. 'It's not Anthony Gilbert's blood on the airbag.'

'It must be,' Ferreira said. 'You need to double-check.'

'We run multiple tests, Mel.'

'Maybe the samples were contaminated.'

Jenkins crossed her arms. 'I know this is the last thing in the world you want to hear right now but I'm afraid it's definite.'

'Who is it then?' Ferreira asked.

'He's not on the system. No previous at all.'

Zigic sat down on the edge of Ferreira's desk, seeing the bottom drop out of the case in one swift movement. Jenkins apologised but he barely registered it, looking at the yawning void in the suspects column underneath Anthony Gilbert's name.

They'd been too quick to jump on him. Too keen to shift the hit-and-run onto the back burner so they could return their main focus to Didi's and Ali Manouf's murders.

'We are so fucked,' Ferreira said. She took the file out of his hands, as if looking at it herself could change the results. 'Why did he try to kill himself if he wasn't guilty?'

'He said he heard it happen while he was on the phone to Jelena – wouldn't that be enough to tip you over the edge if you loved someone?'

'Just because he was on the phone to her doesn't mean he wasn't driving.'

'No, the DNA results mean he wasn't driving,' Zigic said sharply. 'Have you got anything we can use, Kate?'

Jenkins made a non-committal gesture with her hand. 'The car was cleaned very thoroughly prior to the incident. We recovered a few items from the boot but the only fingerprints on them belong to the previous owner, your Mr Devlin. The shovel was new, no prints on that at all. The actual interior was vacuumed and washed down, every single surface. He was careful.'

'Meaning this was definitely premeditated?'

'Seems like it. If anything else turns up I'll let you know.'

Jenkins left the office, her promise a meaningless act of kindness. There would be nothing new recovered from the car. Zigic knew she was too much of a perfectionist to let anything slip her beady eye.

Ferreira dropped down into her chair and picked up a half-smoked cigarette, held onto it without lighting up.

'Maybe we're not as wrong as we think we are,' she said slowly. 'We thought this was personal. It might still be.'

'Tomas, you mean?'

'We know him and Sofia have a volatile relationship, we know she threw him out. And he seems to have a propensity for violence.'

'She wasn't the only person at that bus stop,' Zigic said.

'No, but she's the only one who's pissed somebody vicious off lately.'

'What about Dymek?' he asked. 'When I spoke to his wife she said "he was not a good man".'

Ferreira shrugged. 'That can mean a lot of things.'

'He wasn't supposed to be there,' Zigic said, thinking of the CCTV footage, Dymek in the wrong place at the wrong time, pausing to light up as the car cut across the road. 'If this is as premeditated as it looks, Dymek is a pretty unlikely target.'

'Exactly. How would anyone know he was going to be there?' Ferreira straightened in her chair, the idea taking hold. 'No, forget about Dymek. He's collateral damage. Everything we thought about Gilbert and Jelena is applicable to Sofia and Tomas. It actually makes way more sense because they hadn't split up after all but Sofia and Tomas had; he's got cause to go after her.'

'Like this though? Tomas is a very different kind of man to Anthony Gilbert. He wouldn't need a car to do his dirty work.'

'But the same logic applies. You stab someone, or strangle them, or whatever, it looks personal. And who gets arrested first in a case like that? The boyfriend. A hit-and-run is messier, it might be an accident, it might be deliberate, and instead of one victim you have several, any of who could be the intended target. It muddies the water.'

Zigic looked at the diagram of the accident tacked up on the board, seeing how the driver had struck Jelena first, straight on, almost dead centre of the bumper; but Sofia had been standing directly behind her. The only way to be sure of hitting her was to go through Jelena. If it wasn't for Dymek shoving Sofia away at the last second she would have died too.

'If Sofia is protecting Tomas this should be enough to get her talking.'

39

Outside on the ward the visitors were arriving again, bringing bright voices and kind words, and Sofia pressed her face into the pillow, jaw clenched, willing herself not to cry.

Everybody had someone. Except her.

She wanted the door to open and for Jelena to walk in, no flowers, no gifts, just herself, and sit down in the seat at the foot of the bed, but even in her dreams she couldn't pretend it was possible.

She thought of Tomas, her big bear, remembering the moment they met. It was his first day at the farm and he was trying so hard to make a good impression, doing twice the work of the other men shifting crates in the pack house, carrying one on each shoulder, muscles flexing against his T-shirt. She'd told him off, quoted the health and safety regulations at him, and he just smiled, said she was a tough woman to please, like it was the highest compliment he could give.

A week later they slept together. A month later he moved in. For the first time in her life she could see a future she actually wanted to live rather than one she could simply endure. They would work hard, save money, start their own business. Her and Tomas and Jelena. Maybe they would have children; they'd stopped using protection, leaving it to fate.

Some nights, lying awake in bed beside him, imagining a baby growing inside her, she would panic, fearing what kind of mother she would be, afraid of repeating the mistakes her own mother had made. Not mistakes, her behaviour was more deliberate than that. She was a bad woman, cold and distant, incapable of love. What if she was no better when the time came?

But in the morning she would see Jelena and the fear would go. She'd raised her little sister, nurtured her like a mother should, protected her from the boys, then the men, who wanted to exploit her, all the Anthony Gilberts of the world who saw her as a pretty thing to be used up and discarded. None of them were good enough for her and him least of all.

Jelena wouldn't accept it though.

If she'd survived Sofia was sure she'd still be making excuses for him.

She was like a child. In so many ways. Incapable of seeing Gilbert for what he really was. A control freak and a manipulator who watched and waited and when he saw an opportunity, a moment of weakness, tried to take over their lives.

He'd underestimated her though.

Even at her most vulnerable Sofia was stronger than him.

On the other side of the door she could hear the policeman who was guarding her talking to a nurse. The one she hated more than the others, a skinny, mean-faced bitch who spoke out of one side of her mouth and acted like she was above her job. The man laughed and Sofia was sure he was laughing at her.

She looked at her wrist, wrapped in a padded restraint, shackled to the bed frame.

Gilbert would be held down by the same kind of restraint, locked away in a room like this on another ward, gathering his strength, waiting to speak to the police.

There was one route out of this for him and she knew he would take it.

The door opened and the nurse came in, the policeman with her. Not the one who'd pulled Sofia away from Gilbert's bed just as his eyes finally opened, but not so different to him either. This one would have done the same, dragged her to the ground and punched her in the ribs to stop her struggling, knowing that his uniform gave him the right to act however he saw fit.

A few more seconds and she would have known. That was all

271

she'd needed. A single question and a single answer and it wouldn't have mattered if Gilbert lied because she could see through him. Had done right from the start.

'Time to clean you up,' the nurse said, an acid smile on her pinched face.

The policeman unfastened the restraint and locked it around his own wrist. As if she would make a break for it, barefoot in her pyjamas, unsteady on her legs from so long lying down.

They led her into a beige-tiled room with bars on the walls and a pulley on tracks which could be moved between the toilet and the bath. It smelled of cleaning fluid and shit, the stench of sick bodies. The bath had been run already and the extractor fan was humming, sucking the steam out of the air.

Once again the cuffs came off and the policeman retreated to the door. Was he going to stay there? Watch her strip down and wash herself?

'You've got ten minutes,' the nurse said. 'Towels are there, soap's in the pump.'

The policeman pointed at her. 'And we'll be right outside the door so don't get any funny ideas.'

They went out again but didn't fully close the door. Sofia shoved it so hard her ribs screamed and she swallowed the cry which threatened to break out of her mouth, bracing herself against the door frame until the pain subsided.

She didn't want to wash but she knew she needed to, could smell how sour her body was, the sharpness of sweat tinged with fear and hurt, different to the sweat of exertion. Soon she would be at the police station again and she would not have them see her so filthy.

That was why she was being told to wash, she thought, because Zigic was going to question her again.

Which meant Gilbert had talked already.

In the mirror she saw a face she barely recognised, grey and tired, but it wore an expression more fierce than she felt. She had to keep her fear in check, not show weakness, not let them bully her into admitting anything about Tomas.

Slowly she eased her arms out of her pyjama top, goosebumps rising across her bare skin, and examined the bruises on her ribs, faded to yellow and brown. Except for the fist-shaped mark which the policeman had left behind.

Sofia slipped off her pyjama bottoms and stood looking into the bathwater, wondering if they'd put other people in it before her. The thought wrinkled her nose but as she peered closer she saw that it was clean and she climbed in carefully, settling on her knees because she knew from experience that she wouldn't be able to lower herself in fully with her ribs broken.

She cupped the warm water in her palms and washed her face, thinking of Tomas standing in the kitchen, blood on his clothes and his boots, smiling but only with his eyes, as he explained it away.

Gilbert would tell the police about Tomas.

It was all he had left to bargain with.

40

Zigic had a patrol car collect Sofia from City Hospital and bring her into the station for questioning. He wanted to make it absolutely clear that her entire future was hanging in the balance, give her a preview of what prison would be like.

She needed to understand that the only way out was helping them find Tomas, and Zigic was certain he couldn't get her talking with kindness, which only left one option, as much as he hated it.

He had her taken down to the cells for an hour, told the custody sergeant to place her in the one where Lukas had committed suicide. It had been cleaned up and put back into use but no amount of bleach could wash away the invisible traces of a death which thickened the air and dulled the brightest of lights, something intangible but insistent.

Zigic didn't believe in ghosts and he'd bet Sofia didn't either, but there was no denying the shift in energy which dampened a room for a few days after a violent death.

Inspector Strug called while he was sitting in his office, scanning through a printout of Jelena and Gilbert's private Facebook chat, wanting to read it himself, see if there was some nuance or allusion which Wahlia had missed.

'Inspector Zigic, I have found your man.'

Zigic felt a jolt go through his body. 'Where? Have you got him?'

'Sorry, my English is bad,' Strug said. 'I have found him in our records.'

Zigic sagged in his seat. Of course it wouldn't be that easy.

Strug went on, 'Tomas Kaminski, born January fourth 1983, in

274

Poznań. He is well known to us, many minor charges. He has quite a temper when he has been drinking.'

'Anything more serious than bar fights?'

'In March 2002 he was involved in a very bad incident in Drweskich Park. He and his brother attacked two Turkish gentlemen with iron bars.'

'Was he arrested?'

Strug snorted. 'More than arrested, Inspector. The Turkish gentlemen were both armed – they are a knife culture, you understand. Tomas's brother was killed. His throat was cut. Tomas suffered serious injuries but the doctors saved his life.' Strug muttered to himself in Polish, 'Some lives are not worth the trouble.'

Was that it then? An act of revenge for his brother's death? Three entirely innocent men murdered because one night the Kaminski boys decided to throw their weight in the wrong direction?

'Did you catch the men?' Zigic asked.

'Of course we caught them,' Strug said, sounding wounded. 'They are both in prison still. They have one or two more years to serve and then they will be deported.' He laughed. 'You will probably have them in England then.'

Zigic ignored the jibe. 'What happened to Tomas? Was he charged with anything?'

'Yes. Assault. He was given two years – not enough time in my opinion but the judge thought the injuries he received would make him think before acting that way again.'

'Did it?'

'He did not serve two years,' Strug said, then broke away to shout at someone at his end, the words fast and clipped. 'Sorry, Inspector. Tomas Kaminski killed an inmate – another Turk – and was given four more years.'

Zigic worked the numbers out quickly, finding that almost as soon as Tomas got out of prison he came to England, to Peterborough, and began a relationship with Sofia. He wondered if she knew about any of this.

'Four years isn't very long for a murder,' Zigic said.

Strug sighed. 'It is not. But Tomas pleaded self-defence and several witnesses came forward to swear that the Turk had a razor.'

Zigic detected a new strain of disgust in Strug's tone.

'When you say witnesses . . .'

'They were not reliable men,' Strug said darkly. 'I do not know how it is in England but here we have a very bad situation with gangs in our prisons.'

'We have that too,' Zigic told him.

'Then you will understand this. Because of Kaminski's crime and the murder of his brother he was sought out by a powerful neo-Nazi group who offered him protection. He was only nineteen years old, scared I would think, and he shared their beliefs before he went in. He became something of a mascot for them. Maybe the man did have a razor,' Strug said. 'But maybe one of Kaminski's White Brethren put it in his hand after he was dead.'

'This White Brethren, what can you tell me about them?'

'Very little. They are a prison gang, I have no dealings with them, but they have chapters on the outside too. I will send you Kaminski's file, maybe your people can use it.'

Zigic thanked Strug, gave him his email address, and thanked him again, feeling the pieces beginning to lock into place. The dead brother, the teenage bravado, his neo-Nazi family drawing around him in his moment of need.

He went out into the main office and debriefed the rest of them on what Strug had told him, standing in front of the murder boards, thinking how good it was to be adding information for a change, rather than asking questions nobody had answers for.

'Mel, check up on this White Brethren.'

She was looking at her computer screen. 'Yeah, I googled it as soon as you said it. There's a few hundred hits, mostly in Polish. You might have to take this job yourself.'

He glanced at the clock; forty-five minutes since Sofia was celled.

'OK, later. Let's see what Ms Krasic has to say for herself first.'

Zigic went down to the custody suite. A lone man was waiting on the chairs, handcuffed and silent, his skin ashen, dressed in his best suit ready for court, and a pair of white trainers. At the desk a PC was talking to the custody sergeant, their conversation nothing to do with work, and Rita flushed when she saw him.

'Sofia Krasic?'

Zigic nodded.

He followed her through the heavy metal door, waiting while she shoved her key card in the lock, swore when it didn't connect then pulled it out and turned it over. She was flustered. He knew the investigation into Lukas's suicide had been turned over to the IPCC already, everything being done fast to try and prove there was no wrongdoing on their part. It didn't pay to hold things up when you were guilty.

Most of the cells were occupied, only a couple of the whiteboards wiped clean, waiting for new names to go up on them. He wanted to see Tomas Kaminski printed there in blocky red letters. Sooner rather than later.

Rita opened the door to Sofia's cell and stood aside.

Sofia was sitting on the bunk, staring at the spot on the floor where Lukas's body had been laid out less than twenty-four hours ago, her expression pensive. She wore jeans and a hoodie, red tennis shoes with the laces removed. Out of the hospital bed she looked stronger, but he noticed her wince as she stood, her hand automatically going to her side.

'You have no right to do this,' she said.

'You're still under arrest, Sofia – being in hospital changed nothing.'

She threw her chin up. 'I am innocent.'

Zigic leaned against the door frame. 'Do you know who the previous occupant of this cell was?'

'How would I know?'

'Lukas,' Zigic said. 'Yesterday afternoon he tore his shirt into strips and he choked himself to death on that bracket. He died right where you're standing now.'

Sofia loosened a contemptuous smile on him. 'What do I care about this?'

'The fear got hold of him, Sofia. He sat in this cell and realised that the rest of his life would be spent locked away in a small room, surrounded by people much harder than him, with no freedom, no privacy, no pleasure of any kind, ever again.'

The smile had faded to a thin, hard line.

'And Lukas was tough. Tougher than you are.'

'You do not know what I am,' she said, switching to Serbo-Croat. 'I have seen my friends dead in the street being eaten by dogs. Lukas was a thug and all thugs are only cowards at heart. You cannot scare me with prison.'

'And deportation?'

She lowered her eyes, shook her head. 'I thought you were a decent man, Dushan Zigic. You must have some Turk in your blood to behave like this.'

Her words stayed with Zigic as they went up to the interview rooms, wondering if it was just a throwaway comment or something more significant. 'Turk' was a basic racial slur among Serbs and Croats, applied to Muslims from anywhere in the former Yugoslavia. If he hadn't spoken to Strug he would have shrugged it off, but now it made him uncomfortable, like she was taunting him with something she didn't think he knew. Amusing herself.

Ferreira was waiting for them in Interview Room 3, the most comfortable of the rooms, the one reserved for witnesses and grieving parties, and he guessed she wouldn't have chosen it unless the others were in use already. She'd brought a bottle of water in for Sofia though, so maybe she still thought they could finesse the information they wanted.

They hadn't discussed how to play this, too used to falling into rhythm naturally, and he regretted that now. Ferreira thought it was fear keeping Sofia silent but Zigic wasn't so sure any more.

'Do I need a solicitor?' Sofia asked, her attention on Ferreira.

278

'No,' she said. 'This is just a chat. But if you feel you'd like one at any point just say and we'll break to organise it.'

Zigic slid into the chair next to her, Sofia diagonally opposite him, not looking in his direction. He could see the scar on her neck more clearly in here, and thought it looked a few years old. After she came to England perhaps. As if sensing his gaze she dragged her ponytail around her neck, hiding the mark.

Ferreira leaned forward. 'I have to tell you that we've received the DNA results back from the hit-and-run this morning and, consequently, we no longer consider Anthony Gilbert to be a suspect.'

Sofia blew out a long, controlled breath and it looked like relief, but Zigic couldn't imagine why the news would be welcome to her. She hated Gilbert and despite distancing herself from her initial certainty over his involvement, Zigic was sure she had believed him responsible.

'So, now we have a problem,' Ferreira said. 'If it wasn't him, who was it?'

'Where's Tomas?' Zigic asked.

'It was not him,' Sofia said.

'The driver was aiming for you. You were the target.'

She held his gaze, something stirring in her eyes which looked like fear.

'We know you and Tomas had a fight and we know you threw him out. When we see a situation like this the ex-boyfriend is always a suspect. And given Tomas's history of violence he is a very cred-ible suspect.'

'He was not violent,' Sofia said flatly.

'I've spoken to the police in Poznań. Maybe Tomas hasn't told you about it, but before he came to England he served six years in prison for murder and attempted murder.' She looked down into her lap. Didn't ask for details. 'And we have reason to believe that Tomas has been up to his old tricks over here too. Lukas didn't act alone when he killed the young man we told you about. Tomas was involved in that murder, maybe others too. So we know exactly what he's capable of.'

'He would not do this to me and Jelena.'

'Why are you protecting him?' Ferreira asked. 'He killed Jelena. He tried to kill you. Don't you want to see him punished?'

'I do not know where he is,' Sofia said, that same flat tone. 'If I knew I would tell you.'

'Has he been back since you threw him out?'

Sofia shook her head. 'I have not seen him.'

'We found bloodstained clothes at your house,' Zigic said, and she looked up at that, eyes wide. 'They're Tomas's clothes and they were in the bin. I imagine you put your rubbish out every other week like the rest of us, so those clothes are two weeks old at the most.'

'I threw them out last week,' she said.

'Whose blood is it?'

She stuttered, 'There was an accident, at the pack house, last month. A man was injured, his hand, Tomas tried to help him. It is his blood, check with the farm, they will tell you.'

'We will check,' Zigic said. 'But none of this is helping us find Tomas.'

Sofia blinked at a few strands of lank brown hair poking in her eye and when she moved to brush them away he saw that her hand was shaking.

'The night you threw Tomas out, what did you fight about?'

'I told you this already – money.'

'I don't believe you,' Zigic said. 'I think you knew Tomas was getting involved with something bad and you didn't like it.'

She said nothing, looked at the bottle of water but didn't reach for it.

'The night before you threw him out a young man was kicked to death a few streets away. CCTV places Tomas and Lukas near the crime scene at the time of the murder.' Zigic tried to catch her eye; failed. 'Do you remember that night, Sofia?'

'No.'

'Tomas would have come home covered in blood.'

'I do not remember,' she said. 'Me and Jelena must have been at work.'

'We checked your time sheets – you weren't working.'

'Then we must have been out.'

'Maybe you were at Anthony's house,' Ferreira suggested. 'Or had you made Jelena dump him already?'

Sofia glared at her. 'We were not with him.'

'You seem very certain about that, considering you couldn't remember where you were ten seconds ago.' Ferreira shifted in her seat and Zigic realised she was on to something. 'Maybe Anthony's memory's better than yours. Maybe he remembers what you two were fighting about.'

'He wasn't there. Anything he tells you is a lie.'

'He told us Tomas was getting a bit too close to Jelena for your liking,' Zigic said. 'Was that a lie?'

Sofia's face coloured and she spoke through gritted teeth. 'Tomas was like a brother to her.'

For a moment nobody spoke and there was only the sound of the strip light humming and the pipes ticking behind the walls. Gilbert had insisted he was there the night Sofia threw Tomas out, Mrs O'Brien had said the same, and now Sofia was denying it.

Sofia would keep lying until they put incontrovertible proof in front of her, Zigic thought, but now that he was in the clear maybe Anthony Gilbert would be more forthcoming.

4I

'Take the cuffs off him,' Ferreira said.

Relief washed across Gilbert's drawn and stubbled face as the PC who had been stationed outside his room walked round the bed and unlocked the restraints at his wrist. He rubbed his skin, even though the cuffs were padded, and looked for marks which they hadn't left behind. The only damage showing on the man was self-inflicted and even that was fading now.

The dark rings had disappeared from around his eyes, the swelling at his nose had calmed, and when he spoke to ask what had happened, the telltale rasp from the charcoal wash was gone.

'The DNA results are back. We know you weren't driving the car.'

'I told you I didn't do it.'

'Funny enough, a lot of guilty people say that too,' Ferreira said, closing the door behind the retreating PC.

Gilbert swung his legs over the side of the bed and stood carefully, none too sturdy, but he made it to the window and looked down across the small garden there, just a patch of grass and some flower beds dotted with tulips. He pressed his forehead against the glass and cried quietly for a few minutes.

Now he was officially innocent his pain would take over, Ferreira imagined, fill up every quiet hour until the hospital deemed him fit to return home, and then what? Pills again, but more this time, enough of them to kill what he was feeling once and for all.

His eyes were shining when he finally turned away from the window and he wiped them on the back of his left hand, a drip still plugged into his right.

'Who do you think did it?' he asked, voice thick. 'Was it an accident after all?'

'No,' Ferreira said. 'We're certain it wasn't. The car was bought with cash a few days before, the driver was very careful not to leave a paper trail, and he cleaned it thoroughly to be sure we wouldn't be able to get DNA or fingerprints.'

'But you got DNA.'

'Guess he wasn't expecting the airbag to punch him in the nose.'

'Well, is he on the system?' Gilbert asked. 'You've got other suspects, right? You're going to catch who did this.'

'We have somebody in mind, yes.'

'Who?'

'Tomas.'

Gilbert lowered himself into the chair next to the window. 'Is that all you can come up with up? Seriously?'

'Tomas has a long history of violence,' Ferreira said. 'Even longer than yours.'

He scowled at her then quickly looked away, back to the window, but she wasn't sure he saw the view any more. 'What makes you think this is anything to do with Sofia and Jelena? They weren't the only people there.'

'We believe that Sofia and Jelena were the target,' Ferreira said firmly.

'You can't know that. Not until you catch whoever did it.' He threw his hand up, brought it down on his thigh with a slap. 'I mean, these people come to Peterborough from all over Europe – the world – you don't know who they are really, what enemies they might have.'

'We're looking into that now.'

'Because you didn't do it before,' he said, disgust hitching the skin around his nose. 'You were so fucking convinced it was me that you didn't bother to look for another suspect. I've seen the paper. That other man there, who was he? What about if he was into something shady and someone wanted rid of him?'

283

'We're checking that out,' Ferreira told him, feeling her patience beginning to give already. As much because he was right as anything else. They'd had too much workload put on them with not enough resources and Zigic prioritised as best he could, following the clearest lead, what looked like a nailed-on certainty. Riggott had encouraged it too, knowing they needed a swift resolution, one which wouldn't stoke the simmering racial tensions in the area.

Everyone wanted Gilbert to be responsible.

If it was him it was terrible but understandable and it allowed them to concentrate on the murders which had been defeating them for weeks.

Had Zigic miscalculated? She didn't think so, but from the outside it looked bad on them, and with a press conference looming later this afternoon it was going to get worse, questions would be asked about his judgement and their capability as a department, especially when Lukas's suicide was factored in.

As of right now they had one missing suspect, still to be identified, one perpetrator dead by his own hand, and a hit-and-run with no known driver. Five murders unsolved.

Tomas was at the heart of it. She was in full agreement with Zigic on that, but the information which came in while they were questioning Sofia offered little hope of finding him. Nothing on the manifests from the local coach operators, nothing from passport control or customs. There were too many quiet ways to slip out of the city, or the country, for them to say with any certainty that he was still here. A fake passport was easily bought, especially if Tomas was as organised as the hit-and-run suggested. A different city could be driven to without leaving a trail – steal a car or hitch a lift, who would remember that?

Parr had finished canvassing the dosshouses by lunchtime, through them too fast to have done the job properly, and Ferreira regretted not speaking up when Zigic gave him the task. He didn't know the area or the people, and his mind clearly wasn't focused, judging by the amount of private conversations he was taking out into the hall, talking bottle temperatures and nap times and the colour of his new baby's shit. Could they really trust his claim that Tomas wasn't at any of the places he'd been to?

It was easy for ineptitude to slip by unnoticed in CID; with such a large pool of officers there was always somebody else to take up the slack. In Hate Crimes they didn't have that luxury.

She was confident that when they finally found Tomas it would be in one of the ninety-pound-a-week B&Bs off Lincoln Road which Parr had visited.

Ferreira went round the bed and sat on the windowsill, getting between Gilbert and the view he was finding so fascinating.

'Is there anything at all you can tell me about Tomas? Anything that could help us find him?'

'It isn't Tomas,' Gilbert said, his voice loaded with frustration. 'Is this how you work? You get fixated on someone and block out all other possibilities until you realise you've fucked up and move on to the next person?'

'We look at the most credible suspects,' Ferreira said, her own frustration bubbling up. 'And after you, Tomas is next on our list. Him and Sofia fought, she threw him out and then somebody tries to kill her. You don't think that makes him a likely candidate?'

He looked down at the floor. 'It wasn't Tomas.'

'Why not?'

'Because he went home.'

'Sofia says.'

'Why would she lie?'

'To protect him,' Ferreira said. 'Which I get, kind of. She's got some twisted sense of loyalty to him, or she's scared of him. Maybe she just can't handle the idea that he killed her sister because she loves the bastard. But you don't. By your own admission you hated each other.'

Gilbert swallowed hard, tears shining in his eyes again. He never seemed to be far from crying.

'You need to find who killed Jelena,' he said.

'We'll find him.'

'But you won't,' he said, almost wailing. 'It wasn't Tomas. You're wasting your time looking for him. You need to concentrate on finding out who was really driving that car before they leave the country and you can't touch them. You can't let them get away with this.'

'Him,' Ferreira said, low and hard. 'Tomas. And we are going to hunt him down wherever he's hiding.'

She stood up and inched past Gilbert, heading for the door. She'd done what she was told, passed on the news, released him from their custody, and it was obvious he had nothing useful to tell her. Another dead end.

'Wait.'

She sighed lightly and let the door swing shut again, blocking out the ward noise. Gilbert was on his feet now, one hand gripping the front of his hospital gown, a nervous gesture to match the expression on his face. He groaned, closed his eyes and almost whispered it.

'I know where Tomas is.'

42

It wasn't quite the middle of nowhere, but isolated enough that they missed it on the first pass. Zigic driving, Ferreira in the passenger seat scanning the countryside for the place Gilbert had described. The fens unfolded to the east, thousands of acres of bare earth, a few rippling green fields. The road was busy with agricultural vehicles, tractors with muddy ploughs overhanging that scattered the tarmac with sodden clumps of earth, lethal shears glinting in the afternoon sun. A couple of times Zigic had to pull onto the verge to let them pass, the cars behind him following suit, hedgerows scraping paintwork.

Peterborough fell away behind them, no longer visible in his rear-view mirror, the streets where they expected to find Tomas Kaminski becoming distant and remote.

Ferreira tapped on her window. 'There, that must be it.'

'Are you sure?'

He slowed and looked across her, saw a spread of dense woodland blocking off the horizon, a few of the trees coming into blossom. A dirt track led up to it, ungated, which was rare for the area, but there was obviously nothing worth stealing in the small, red-brick building which sat at the edge of the trees.

'Gilbert said there's a bunch of clapped-out machinery behind it.'

'I don't see it,' Zigic said.

'It's there.'

He squinted, made out a patch of yellow paintwork and the silvery glimmer of broken glass, almost completely obscured by a wild tangle of greenery.

'That's the place,' Ferreira said, reaching for the radio, passing it on.

Zigic turned onto the track, the patrol car swinging in behind him. The fields on either side lay fallow, tall grass swaying in the light breeze, stray stalks of rapeseed blown in from across the road making pinpoints of colour, everything perfectly serene and idyllic. Dust blew up from his tyres as he idled up the track and he punched the horn to scare off a cock pheasant strutting ahead of him. It sauntered away into the field, answering the call of a potential mate, the sound like a woman being strangled.

Up close Zigic saw that the old worker's cottage was half derelict, its roof sagging at the centre and missing a few dozen pan tiles where an elder bush had somehow grown up from the inside and punched through, striving towards sunlight. Its windows had been smashed in, only a few shards of glass clinging to the stone frames, the front door long gone, the entrance blocked by a rambling rose bush beginning to bud. ·

The hulk of an ancient tractor was parked a few yards from the side of the house, its fabric roof shredded and flapping in the breeze, its body more rust than not, just a strip of flaking yellow paint here and there which had survived the elements.

He stopped the car and they got out.

The air was heavy with pollen, but there was rain on the way, blowing in from the North Sea, ozone-tinged.

'How did Gilbert know about this place?' Zigic asked.

'He said he came here when he was a kid, there's a trail through the woods. Him and his mates used to bike over from the village and get stoned in there.'

Which explained the green plastic cider bottles nestling in the grass, he thought. If Gilbert and his friends came here years ago then other kids would have found it too, more recently, and done the same thing. There wasn't much else to occupy them in a place like this.

Nobody had been here for a while though. Or if they had they'd been scared off.

288

Moore and Hale climbed out of the patrol car, ready for action, hitching their belts and checking their radios. Ferreira shouted at them to get a torch.

Zigic picked his way through the tangled undergrowth in front of the house, seeing the remains of a garden in the chaos, a stone bird bath off its plinth, the brick outlines of what had once been flower beds. Behind him Ferreira swore as she stumbled and kicked out at a bottle, sending it flying into the track.

'You'd better hope that isn't evidence.'

He peered in through the doorway, not getting too close, aware of the wicked barbs on the rose bush. The cottage's interior was dark, very little of the afternoon sunshine penetrating the small windows, and all he could see was a patch of earth floor.

'There's another way in, sir,' Moore said.

It was at the side of the cottage and as he approached he saw that the grass was flattened in a wide path from the road, no sign of tyre tracks or clear footprints but that wasn't what they were there for. The door was closed but not locked and it opened with a quick shove, cool, stale-smelling air rushing out in a cloud.

Zigic stepped over the threshold, the ground level falling away six inches in one step, told Ferreira to watch herself as she followed. A torch beam came with her, sweeping the interior, catching on broken bottles and discarded needles and the quick yellow flash of a rat's eyes before it darted across the room and disappeared through a hole in the wall.

He could hear more of them though, scratching away in the shadows.

A feather brushed against his eyelashes and he wafted it away. There were too many of them, too white, to be from an odd stray bird which had flown in through one of the broken windows.

Then he saw it. In the furthest corner of the room, partially hidden by an old pine table turned on its side like a barricade, a scrap of floral fabric and a puff of white down from the duvet inside.

A grubby trainer lay nearby, no foot in it. No sign of the foot which had been inside it either.

'Give me the torch.'

Ferreira handed it over, followed him towards the table.

The body, or what remained of it, lay on its back. The duvet it had been wrapped in was shredded and pulled about by rats and foxes and feral cats, alerted by the scent of decay which would have wafted out of the broken windows and across the fields. Zigic knew they went for the softest tissue first, the eyes, the mouth, the sludge of liquefying innards, they nibbled on the extremities until the small, intricate bones of the hands and feet came apart, and those pieces would be spirited away to nests and coverts for the young.

All of that within the first couple of days.

Tomas Kaminski had been lying here for four weeks, kept cool by the earth floor, protected from the worst of the elements, but that hadn't saved his body from being picked near clean.

His hair remained, straw-coloured under the torch beam, and stained with dried blood, but his face was just a skull, missing its jawbone and sitting at ninety degrees from its proper position.

Through his ripped T-shirt Zigic could see ribs, but not all of them, scraps of flesh and clods of meat which the rats were still coming back to. The same with his jeans, which had proved a tougher proposition, not so badly destroyed but the limbs inside them were insubstantial now, misshapen, and he tried not to think of how the rats would have slunk up the hems, burrowed in and fed.

Ferreira was staring, wide-eyed at the body, her balled fist pressed to her mouth, as if to block out a rank odour. The body was past that stage though.

'Let's see Sofia deny this,' she said.

'We've only got Gilbert's word how it happened.'

'He's out of the frame anyway. Whoever was with Lukas when he murdered Asif Khalid, it sure as hell wasn't Tomas.'

43

Back at the station Zigic went up to Riggott's office, dreading the conversation they were going to have but there was no point delaying it. The case wouldn't break in the next couple of hours and there was a press conference slated for five. Riggott would have sought him out anyway and Zigic preferred to do this away from the rest of the team.

He found Riggott standing at a whiteboard with an e-cigarette clamped between his teeth, scanning the jumble of information linked by straight lines which cut across each other. So many potential suspects that Zigic felt envious of the officer in charge, a new name, one he didn't recognise. He'd heard they were bringing someone in to replace DI Hawkes, in remission now but with little prospect of ever being fit enough to return even if he wanted to.

The complexity of the case explained the lack of bodies in CID, only a handful of people at their desks, all in the kind of deep focus which practically hummed in the air with the sound of keyboards rattling and phones ringing on unmanned desks.

One murder and the whole of the department was mobilised. Meanwhile he had four officers to solve five murders. Six now.

'What's this one about?' Zigic asked.

'Drugs,' Riggott said. 'We're having ourselves a right old turf war in Bretton.'

The whole department scrabbling to find who murdered a drug dealer. Zigic knew you weren't supposed to judge the victim, should remain neutral, leave your morality at the front steps, but how was it right that this man warranted more effort than the victims staring out of the boards in Hate Crimes? Three men murdered for nothing but their skin colour, two people killed while they waited to be picked up for work, not so much as a littering fine between them.

And were the press breathing down DI Sawyer's neck? Were they hell.

'Hope you've got something good to tell me, Ziggy,' Riggott said. 'The ACC has been over to the mosque this morning, reassuring the community that we're close to making another arrest.'

'Do they know about the suicide yet?'

'Official release is this afternoon.' He started towards his office. 'Where're you lot on the second attacker?'

'We were making progress.'

'I don't like "were".'

'Tomas Kaminski, he was friends with the man we arrested, had a history of violence against Muslims, links to a far-right group back in Poland.'

'There's that fecking past tense again.' Riggott began hunting for a drink among the opened Sprite cans on his desk; couldn't find a live one. 'What's the problem? Skipped off back to old country, has he?'

'He's dead.'

'When?'

'About four weeks ago. He could still be in the frame for the first murder but that would mean there's more than two of them involved.'

'Meaning you want to chuck Kaminski's murder down here?'

'No.'

Riggott's eyebrows made a quick leap. 'You reckon you know who did him then?'

'I'm beginning to suspect his ex-girlfriend might be responsible. Although I'm not entirely sure why yet.'

'Who is she?'

'Sofia Krasic.'

'Yon woman from the hit-and-run?'

'Yes. We haven't questioned her yet but we have strong reason to believe she was responsible. Some of the details are open to discussion but I think she might have information about the murders and I want to keep this in Hate Crimes so we can maintain close contact with her.'

'Don't want someone else blundering in, pissing off your witness?'

'She's a tough customer.'

'You keep it then,' Riggott said. 'But if it's her, get her charged. You need to start closing some of those cases, Ziggy. Press are turning.'

'I don't care what the press thinks.'

'Course you don't, but the ACC does and he's holding our balls in his big sweaty palms, deciding whether to tickle them or crush them.'

'If the custody suite ran like it's supposed to the press would be covering Lukas's bail hearing today. They'd have had their headlines. I can't be held responsible for someone else's screw-up.' Zigic brought his voice back down. 'We're trying, believe me.'

Riggott showed him an understanding face, made a smoothing gesture with his hand. 'What about the hit-and-run? Kate tells me the boyfriend's off the hook.'

'We're nowhere,' Zigic said, feeling himself slump in the chair, the weight of it all pressing him down. 'Back to the beginning. We need an appeal for witnesses, anyone who saw the car in the days leading up to the attack.'

'I'll have a wee word to Nicola.'

Zigic rubbed his eyes. They felt swollen and gritty, particles of dust or pollen in there, grating every time he blinked. 'It really looked like Gilbert.'

Riggott tucked his e-cigarette away in his shirt pocket. 'Crack on with the Krasic girl, that'll buy you some goodwill.'

Zigic went back up to Hate Crimes, his mind already moving ahead to the interview room, planning the best way to approach Sofia Krasic. She wouldn't make it easy, he knew that much, but she was the only person who could shed any light on Tomas's behaviour and the position she was in now he imagined even she would realise that full cooperation was the wisest course to take.

Wahlia had wheeled a fresh whiteboard over to the far side of the office and was marking it up. Tomas Kaminski's photo was at the top, Sofia and Anthony Gilbert in the suspects column, the first photographs sent in from scenes of crime up there, more for focus than information. Interior and exterior shots, the remains of Tomas's body.

A second team were at Sofia and Jelena's house on Green Street, looking for evidence of the fight Gilbert had described, one which had painted the kitchen with blood. No matter how well Sofia cleaned up there would be traces still, waiting to have an ultraviolet light shone on them.

Parr was supervising, organising door-to-door. Not the best time of day to catch the neighbours at home but they could always hope, and at this point Zigic didn't want any more mistakes being made. Everything that could be done would be done, no matter how pointless it seemed.

Grieves he'd sent to Boxwood Farm, told her to talk to the management, the line hands, anyone who was on the same shifts as Jelena and Sofia, look for quarrels, jealousy, threats uttered with enough power to suggest an eventual follow-up.

They should have done that days ago, not got wedded to the idea of Anthony Gilbert's guilt, not been so willing to push the case aside for one he considered more pressing. Now he was divided between hoping Grieves found something which led to their driver and closed the case and hoping she found nothing so he wouldn't be proved wrong.

He sat down at Ferreira's desk, her computer screen showing the first page of results for the White Brethren search she'd run earlier in the afternoon, everything in Polish, and when he ran the first one through Google Translate it made little more sense.

He went back to the original version, found the language was straightforward enough for him to follow, a reportage piece from a newspaper based in Krakow, some fearless journalist interviewing a multiple murderer in the safety of a prison visiting room, making it sound like he'd stepped into the cage of a hungry lion. The piece was long on description, short on fact, and Zigic got the impression the journalist wasn't entirely unbiased, detected a strain of admiration for this twenty-two-year-old thug who'd murdered four migrant workers in the city, all North African, hacking each of them to death with a machete before the police caught up with him.

Several of the other results covered the same crime, a dozen more were about a Polish death metal band who'd named their debut album *White Brethren*, coincidentally or out of solidarity, he wasn't sure. The fascist group didn't have their own site and that surprised him. The Internet seemed to be one of the few elements of progress the far right actively embraced.

'Have we got anything on Tomas's cause of death yet?' Zigic asked.

Wahlia turned away from the board, tapped the back of his head with the marker pen. 'Early thinking is blunt force trauma. Pretty major, stove his skull right in.'

'Sofia's a lot smaller than he was.'

'Maybe she got him while he was sitting down.'

Zigic could imagine that, her coming at him from behind, while he wasn't expecting it. A man his size, with his propensity for violence, you would have to hit him once, hard, not give him a chance to get up and retaliate.

Ferreira came into the office, handed him a folder.

'Gilbert's statement.'

It was short and matter-of-fact and Zigic read it through twice, setting the sequence of events in his mind, the parts played by Gilbert and Sofia not quite as he would have expected. Her behaviour over the last few days made sense now, but he wanted to hear it from her own lips, to test her version for the ring of truth.

44

Sofia fixed Zigic with a hard, accusatory stare as he entered the interview room, didn't shift her gaze as he took his seat and waited for Ferreira to perform the formalities.

She looked exhausted for all her rage, dark eyes heavy-lidded and bruised by sleeplessness. Sitting slumped with her arms wrapped around her body, taking shallow breaths through her mouth as if her ribs were troubling her.

Next to her the duty solicitor, Mr Kelley, sipped his tea, wetting his stiff grey moustache, which was a shade darker than the sparse, too long hair he wore swept straight back from his forehead. His expression was blank in a practised fashion, saying he'd seen everything, heard everything, a thousand times before, and nothing that happened in here would surprise him.

'Miss Krasic is in a very delicate state, Inspector,' he said, wiping his moustache dry between his thumb and fingertips. 'I'd appreciate you bearing that in mind.'

'This shouldn't take too long,' Zigic said, not breaking eye contact with her. 'Not if Sofia cooperates.'

'I have told you everything I know.' Her accent was more pronounced, her voice softer. 'I do not know where Tomas is.'

'We're not looking for Tomas any more,' Zigic said, and a little of the tension dropped from her face. 'We found him a couple of hours ago.'

Sofia gasped, her hand going to her side a moment later. 'Where is he?'

'Where you left him. In that derelict cottage near Maxey.'

Her head dropped. 'Anthony told you?'

'It doesn't matter to him any more,' Zigic said. 'Jelena's gone, there's nobody left to protect.'

Except himself and Sofia, and Gilbert didn't care about either of their fates now. It was the one moment of emotion in his account, the last thing he said – 'I've got nothing left to live for.'

'He told you I am innocent?' she asked.

'You're not innocent, Sofia. Not by a long way.'

'But you know I did not kill Tomas?'

'You covered up his death.'

'It was an accident. He fell and hit his head, there was nothing any of us could do to stop it. He was drunk.'

'Gilbert has admitted pushing him,' Zigic said. 'Tomas was getting aggressive with Jelena. He'd been acting out of line with her for months, hadn't he?'

Sofia nodded. 'He was not the man I thought he was. I told him not to touch her but he would not listen to me. He said he was being friendly.'

'And you let that go on for months?' Zigic asked. 'You hated her going out with Gilbert but you put up with Tomas harassing her?'

Sofia looked away from him, her cheeks burning. 'He was only like that when he was drunk.'

Zigic watched her posture close up, the shame she felt growing in her chest, deepening the spots of colour on her face.

'Why didn't you call an ambulance?'

'Jelena wanted to,' she said. 'But we explained to her that it was not a good idea. Nobody would believe it was an accident. We had been shouting, the neighbours, they would tell you this. Anthony said we would all go to prison.'

'The doctors might have saved him.'

'No. He was dead.' Her voice was firm but Zigic wasn't sure she meant the words. A single blow to the back of the head, a man with Tomas's build, there was a good chance he hadn't died straight away. Might even have still been alive when they left him in that tumbledown old cottage. 'Anthony said he knew a place we could take the body.'

It was the same story Gilbert had told, going into the kitchen to find Tomas pinning Jelena to the counter, his hand inside her jumper while she tried to wriggle out of his grip, not the first time he'd made a grab for her and they were past the point of pretending it was a joke. Tomas laughed though and backed away with his hands up, unconcerned by Gilbert's shouting, which brought Sofia into the kitchen and divided his attention long enough for Gilbert to shove him, throwing both hands at his chest. He was much the smaller man but Tomas was drunk and off balance and the next thing they knew he was slumped on the floor in a pool of blood, his skull fractured as he hit the sharp edge of the worktop.

They waited until dark and carried Tomas's body out to his car, wrapped in the duvet from the bed he shared with Sofia, no thought for the DNA on it, how easily they would be traced if he was ever found.

'Is this why you attacked Gilbert in hospital?' Zigic asked. 'You wanted to stop him leading us to Tomas and what you'd done?'

'I did not attack him,' Sofia said wearily, clinging to her innocence. 'How many times must I say this? I only went to talk to him.'

'To make sure he wouldn't tell us about Tomas?'

'To ask him if he killed Jelena.'

'I don't believe you.'

Her palm slapped the table. 'Why would he tell you? He killed Tomas, not me. He should have said nothing.'

'But he did. Because he wants us to catch whoever killed Jelena,' Zigic said, matching her angry tone. 'You let us waste our time pursuing Tomas when you knew he couldn't have been responsible, all to save your skin. The man who did this might be out of the country now because you were too selfish and scared to tell the truth.'

Sofia bit her lip, tears forming.

'Anthony loved her enough to come clean,' Zigic said, leaving the rest of the sentence unspoken, letting her think the implications through. This man who she hated, who she'd pushed away from her sister and, in all likelihood, planned to murder, loved Jelena more than she did.

She wept for a minute, wiping the tears away with the cuff of her sweatshirt before they could reach her jaw.

'You're lucky Anthony's taken responsibility,' Zigic said. 'He could have put this on you if he wanted to. But you're not in the clear. You'll be charged as an accessory and for preventing the legal burial of Tomas's body. You've also perverted the course of justice. These are serious charges. I think you know that.'

'I was scared.'

'I've no doubt you were, but that isn't a defence.' Zigic knitted his fingers together. 'You need our help and we need yours. Now, the night before Tomas died a man was murdered a few streets away from your house. We discussed this earlier.'

She nodded hesitantly.

'You told us you didn't remember Tomas coming home that night. And you claimed you couldn't remember where you and Jelena were.' He paused, checking that she was following him. 'But I think you were lying because you didn't want us to pursue the matter.'

Ferreira's mobile bleated into the silence and Sofia watched her stand and excuse herself from the interview room, the sound of her voice blocked off by the door closing.

'Where were you that night?' Zigic asked.

Sofia took a deep breath and winced at the pain it sent through her chest. 'We were at home.'

'What about Tomas?'

'He said he was at work but he wasn't I think. He had blood on his clothes when he came home. He said there was a fight at the club. Two men . . . it was not strange. It happened many times before.' She frowned. 'People are not happy until they have hurt someone.'

'I thought Tomas worked at Boxwood.'

'He was a doorman also. Only some nights. Fridays and Saturdays, when it is busy.'

'But this was a Sunday.'

'Yes. He did not work on Sundays. Never. That is why I think he was lying.'

'What did he do with the clothes?'

'He threw them away.'

'The ones we found at the house?'

She shook her head. 'I told you, there was an accident at the farm. These were other clothes. He put them in the rubbish bin. It was collected the next morning.'

They were long gone then. Into landfill or the incinerator, any useful traces beyond their reach.

'How did he seem to you?' Zigic asked. 'Was he acting strangely?'

She considered it for a moment, lips pursed, eyes fixed on the table. 'When he comes home from work he is tired. Angry. He does not like the job but the pay is very good. He was not like that that night.'

'What was he like?'

'Big,' she said, drawing herself up in the seat, perhaps subconsciously mimicking him. 'I do not know how to say it. Like he had won something.'

The interview-room door opened and Ferreira gestured for him to join her in the corridor, her expression halfway between shock and triumph.

'Two twenty-six. Inspector Zigic leaving the interview room.'

He closed the door behind him.

'We've got a match for the DNA on Ali Manouf's body,' she said. 'It was Pyotr Dymek. I'd asked Jenkins to run him through the system before we'd ID'd him and it's just come back. Dymek killed Manouf.'

Zigic sat down on the radiator, the metal cold, the ridges sharp, thinking of Dymek at the bus stop talking to Sofia, pushing her out of the way as the car came towards them. Saving her because he knew her? Dymek heading home to Łódź, his rucksack stuffed with cash. Running away from something? From the crime he'd committed and the DNA he'd left behind?

'So, Tomas murders Didi? And Dymek murders Manouf –'

'And our mute Lukas kills Asif Khalid,' Ferreira said. 'But we're still a man short, aren't we?'

The pieces were fitting together. This was a gang thing, a racial thing – not exactly how they'd expected it to turn out but the motivation was the same. Three perpetrators dead, a hit-and-run, a maybe-accident and a suicide. The universe meted out its own punishment sometimes, Zigic thought.

He stood up, the threads of this case within his grasp finally.

'OK, these men are a unit, right? A cell. So we have to assume they got together somehow.'

'They're all Polish,' Ferreira said. 'It might have happened back home.'

'I'll deal with that side of things when I'm done with Sofia. You and Bobby gather everything we've got on Tomas and Dymek.' He stopped with his hand on the door. 'And call Parr and tell him we need a thorough search of the house now. If Tomas came home covered in blood he must have washed up afterwards. And we need his phone.'

'On it.'

He shoved through the door, harder than he meant to, sending it slamming into the wall with a bang which made Mr Kelley jump in his seat. Sofia didn't react. A childhood spent in a war zone would do that to you, he imagined, cauterise your nerves.

'Two twenty-nine. Inspector Zigic returning to the interview room.'

He sat down, on the edge of his seat, wanting to get this finished quickly. After weeks of stalling and dead ends they had movement and he knew from bitter experience that momentum had to be harnessed immediately and not let slip.

'Alright, Sofia, I need you to tell me about Pyotr Dymek. He was a friend of Tomas's, right?'

'Yes, from work. Why does this matter? Pyotr is dead.'

'He knew him from working at the clubs?'

'Yes.'

'Do you know who their boss was?' Zigic asked. 'Was it an agency?'

'Yes. I don't know what agency though.' She shifted in her seat, perplexed by the sudden shift in questioning. 'Pyotr is dead. The nurse told me this.'

'How well did you know him?'

She shrugged. 'He came to see Tomas sometimes when we are out. If we are in a bar maybe he would have a drink with us.'

'Why didn't you tell us you knew him sooner?'

'We were not friends. Tomas knew him.'

'What was he doing at the collection that morning, Sofia? We know he was heading back to Łódź, there was no reason for him to be there.'

She closed her eyes for a couple of seconds, chin dropping. 'He was looking for Tomas. He said he needed to speak to him. It was very important. He did not understand why Tomas was not answering his phone.'

'Where *is* Tomas's phone?'

'I threw it in one of the bins at work,' she said.

Another piece of evidence lost.

Zigic pushed the annoyance away, drew her back to the point. 'What was so urgent he needed to talk to Tomas about?'

'I did not ask. I wanted him to go away and stop asking me questions. But he kept talking. "Has Tomas gone home? When did you see him last? Is he sick?" He was desperate. Scared, I think.'

'What was he scared of?'

'I do not know.'

'What did you tell him about Tomas?'

'That he was visiting his mother. Pyotr did not believe me. He wanted me to give him her phone number.' Her chin rippled and she wrapped her arms around her body again. 'And then it happened.'

The white Volvo accelerated up Lincoln Road and Jelena turned away from the headlights speeding towards her. She looked at Sofia as the car mounted the pavement and drove straight at her, tossing her up in the air like she was weightless, landing on its roof as Dymek shoved Sofia away to safety. It was the last, maybe the only, good thing he had done in his life.

45

Shotton looked at the schedule in front of him on the table, eight appointments, twenty minutes each, names of the people he was meeting and a brief precis of their grievances. It was the usual stuff, bin collections and traffic-calming measures, planning issues and operations at City Hospital which hadn't gone as they expected. The grinding day-to-day business of the constituency.

Most MPs didn't bother with their surgeries; the ones in the safest seats would strike out to the provinces once a month or so and make a token appearance, all the while checking their Twitter accounts and sorting out dinner reservations for when they could escape back to London.

He didn't have the luxury of disinterest.

Which meant turning up at school halls and community centres, like this one in Woodston, three or four times a month, reminding his constituents who he was and that he would be there for them no matter how petty or unworkable or downright insane their complaints were. All the glossy flyers and endorsements in the world couldn't convert floating voters as effectively as simple face-to-face interactions and the good word of mouth which came from them.

He was dreading today's though.

Talal Raziq, one of their city councillors, was due to sit in with him as usual, but he hadn't arrived. An uncharacteristic laxity which could only be down to the riot on Friday night and the murder of the young man on Cromwell Road. It was Talal's neighbourhood, likely he knew the young man's family, and he'd clearly realised showing up here would damage his standing within the community.

Shotton couldn't blame him. It was just good politics to publicly distance yourself from toxic friends. Privately was another matter.

He took his mobile out and tried Talal again.

No answer.

The office door opened and his next appointment came in, a plain, heavy woman with twin boys in a pushchair she struggled to negotiate in the room's narrow dimensions. Shotton got up to help her, moving one of the plastic chairs aside.

'We really should move to a more child-friendly location,' he said, giving her a warm smile which she ducked her eyes from. 'How old are these fine young gents then?'

'They'll be three next month. Oscar and Madox.'

'I've got a Madox too,' he said. 'Are you an admirer of his poetry?'

She smiled at that. 'I named him after the painter.'

Shotton gestured for her to sit down and listened while she detailed her problems with a local care home's treatment of her grandmother, all the while wondering how a woman who'd named her son after an artist had arrived at a point where she was wearing cheap, washed-out clothes and an aura of beaten-down poverty. She was in tears by the end of the conversation and he handed her a tissue, promised he would look into the matter, reassuring her that a letter was often all it took to straighten these things out.

The next two appointments came and went and no sign of Talal. He wouldn't call him again. This needed to be discussed in person.

Talal was their 'silver bullet' – as Marshall liked to say – a third-generation Pakistani businessman, devout, highly respected. As long as he campaigned under the EPP banner nobody could say they were a racist party. He commanded a significant voting block too, which was of greater concern. Up to 5 per cent of the turnout hung on his word.

Shotton went out of the cramped office and into the main hall, where a long folding table was set up ready for the after-school club. Christian was sitting drinking tea at the far end with the woman who managed the centre, listening as she talked about the break-in they'd had on Sunday morning. She cornered him every week to bend his ear and he took it with the forbearance only an ex-copper could muster.

He stood up as Shotton approached.

'Could I have a word, sir?' He placed his cup and saucer on the table. 'Excuse me, ma'am.'

'A private word?'

'Yes, sir.'

They went out into the car park, where his previous visitor was still sitting in her car, furiously scribbling away at a notepad propped up on the steering wheel. The woman was a professional complainer, from what Shotton could make out, always opposing some planning issue or other. Retired too early and bored to death now, nothing better to do with her time than mount campaigns against the most innocuous developments. She was currently trying to stop a house three streets away from her own being converted into flats.

He'd pointed out that the city was in desperate need of one-bed properties for youngsters trying to set up home and she'd stormed out of the office.

'I've had a call from my contact,' Christian said.

That drew Shotton's attention back. 'Good news?'

'I think so, sir. They've identified one of the murderers,' he said, squinting against the afternoon sun. 'The first death I think. We only talked for a couple of minutes. They've got a name though.'

Shotton braced himself, sure that the name Christian's contact had given would be Poulter's or one of his men.

'Who is it?'

'Some foreign bloke. He's dead now though.'

He wanted to laugh. The relief so overwhelming that he only just managed to stop himself. Not Poulter's men. Not any of the others either. His money had been well spent and his reputation would remain intact.

'Are they sure about this?'

Christian nodded. 'Definitely, sir. Polish I think. But it's not just

306

the one man. There was a gang of them. A neo-Nazi group by the sounds of it.'

Shotton's relief faded slightly. It wasn't the ideal outcome but still far better than he would have expected.

'Thank you for your help on this, Christian.' He took his wallet from his back pocket and slipped a couple of fifties out.

'That's not necessary, sir.'

'Don't offend me,' Shotton said. 'Treat your children to a day out or something.'

Christian didn't look at him as he took the money, acting like it was a bribe rather than a bonus, but he'd get used to it, Shotton thought. There was always something useful a police contact could provide and he had a feeling Christian would prove to be a discreet intermediary.

A battered Transit van pulled into the car park as they headed for the main doors and Shotton hung back to meet the man. Another regular. One of the army of leafleters who'd helped him get elected, a painter and decorator who'd volunteered to plaster up their posters and, when it was necessary, blank out any inconvenient bits of graffiti which popped up around the city.

'Colin, how are you, mate?'

A firm handshake, a clap on the back.

'Can't complain, Mr Shotton.' He smiled. 'Well, I *am* going to complain or else I wouldn't be here.'

Shotton laughed. 'Come on in then. Let's see if Mrs Lamb can find us both a cuppa.'

She brought them tea and biscuits in the office while Colin talked about his daughter, away at university in Wales, studying media. Shotton managed to offer enough to keep him chatting, but he was thinking about what Christian had said, how best to play the situation from here.

Once Talal knew the truth he'd come round. One fire put out.

But there was more political capital to be made.

When the news broke he would be able to carefully and skilfully

307

turn the debate to his own ends. If anything highlighted the danger of unchecked immigration from Europe it was this. Neo-Nazi murderers, racially motivated crimes, in a city as small as Peterborough. If it was happening here it could happen anywhere.

This was a gift he wouldn't waste.

Once he was alone Shotton called Talal's office. The receptionist took his name and there was a pause as she passed the message along. He half expected Talal not to accept his call but eventually he answered.

'No, Richard. Whatever you want, no.'

'We need to talk about what happened.'

'"What happened"?' Talal snapped. 'Your thugs murdering a boy for sport? Asif was a good man, I know his father from years back, they are a good family.'

'The ENL did not kill Asif.'

'I've spoken to the men who were there. They say there were hundreds of ENL, the police couldn't control them.'

'Listen to me,' Shotton said. 'I have it on very good authority that the police are about to release the name of the man responsible and he isn't even English. He's a Pole.'

Silence from Talal. The sound of his breath whistling through his nose as he considered the new information, weighing up the balance.

'This doesn't hurt you, my friend. Just consider it for a moment, your supporters – your community – they don't like this unfettered immigration, do they?'

'We're being made to feel like foreigners in our own country,' Talal said. 'All because the Poles are white, they think they have more right to be here than us. Families who have lived in Peterborough for four generations.'

Shotton could feel him softening, knew that he was close to recapturing the man's valuable support.

'This is the problem with immigration,' he said. 'We share a history, your people have roots here, but the Poles don't. And when the news is released later this afternoon that Asif was killed by one of them all of your problems will go away.'

Through the office door he heard his final appointment arrive, a loud man already voicing his displeasure.

'We have to stand together, Talal. We've done too much good work to let it be undone by a handful of extremists.'

'It was not a handful. It was hundreds.'

'That's a gross exaggeration.'

'It's what the people think,' Talal said. 'They've been coming to me, saying "Why are you associated with these animals?" They think I'm betraying them. My own wife calls me your lapdog.'

'Please, Talal –' Shotton stood, knowing now that he'd miscalculated. He should have gone to the office, talked to him face-to-face, man-to-man. He'd underestimated how much the riot had cost Talal within his community. 'Listen, this helps us, you have to appreciate that.'

'How does it help? To have a young man murdered in the street and your people want to see more blood. They do not even have respect for the dead.' Talal cleared his throat, but the emotion was still there when he spoke, a mixture of anger and regret. 'I cannot be a part of this any more. I will send you my official letter of resignation.'

The phone went dead in Shotton's ear.

For a moment he was frozen, staring at the display as it switched to black, then his foot shot out and he kicked the flimsy plastic chair across the office, sending it crashing into a filing cabinet, the sound drowning out his curses.

Christian burst into the office, shoulders squared for violence.

'It's fine,' Shotton said, smoothing a hand over his tie, forcing a smile. 'Just a text about the cricket score.'

He righted the chair and slowly sat down.

'Send the next one in, would you?'

The man was small and bald and very angry but Shotton wasn't listening. The words washed over him while he ran the numbers in his head, the losses represented by Talal's defection, the gains accrued by his recent media presence. Damage done versus opportunities remaining.

Now was not the time to dwell on the negative.

The riot would be forgotten but the murder would linger in the city's collective memory bank and if he was very lucky the trial might just coincide with the week of the general election. Racial disharmony meant votes for the English Patriot Party, this he knew for a fact.

The fight was far from lost.

46

Grey Shield Security was based in an unprepossessing breeze-block unit on an industrial estate in Orton Southgate, surrounded by plastic window manufacturers and Internet start-ups which had moved beyond the spare bedroom but not much further, party suppliers and a hot-tub showroom. Nobody was very busy at half past three on a Monday afternoon, with the sky already darkening and rain in the air, along with the sweet, yeasty aroma from the bagel factory nearby.

It was a discreet location though, looked like a place you'd go for run-of-the-mill burglar alarms and CCTV cameras with short ranges, designed for spying on prowlers and monitoring expensive cars parked on downmarket streets.

The website told a different story. Sleek and no-nonsense, it offered an array of services from security teams for commercial concerns to personal bodyguards and something called 'complete defence solutions'.

Zigic wasn't sure what that entailed but it sounded sinister.

The company boasted that it recruited personnel from the military and the police, only the most reliable men and women, highly trained and above reproach. No mention of the ex-cons on their books, the men like Tomas – and Zigic guessed he wouldn't be the only oversight – who'd learned their craft on the wrong side of the law.

He pulled into a space in front of the unit, next to a hunter-green Range Rover with tinted windows, so chunky it might have been armour-plated, and climbed out of the car. The office door opened with a light buzz, letting him into an anonymous reception area, the glass-and-chrome desk unmanned, the modernist black leather chairs empty. There was a single white orchid in a pot on the windowsill, filling the room with a rotten-flesh smell.

As Zigic closed the door a middle-aged man in a modishly tailored suit came to meet him, hand already outstretched.

'Detective Inspector is it now?' he said, smiling with too many teeth on show.

Zigic shook his hand. 'DCI Broad.'

'It's been a long time since anyone called me that.'

Five years, Zigic thought, then realised it must be longer. Ten since Broad took early retirement from the force, barely forty-five then, and nobody could quite understand why he left, no obvious cloud hanging over him, his prospects of promotion good enough to carry him to Chief Superintendant if that was what he wanted. He claimed it was for his health and looking at him now Zigic saw the change had done him good. He had the lean build of a runner, a tanned complexion and a thick head of hair.

'Well, let's go through. See if we can't help you out in your hour of need.'

Zigic followed him into an open-plan office, clinical-looking with its polished concrete floors and aluminium lights, the company logo in laser-cut steel bolted to the smoke-grey wall. There were four desks, well spaced within glass partitions, designed to give their customers a semblance of privacy. Only one was occupied right then, likely the woman Ferreira had spoken to on the phone.

Broad was going to handle this personally though.

His office was at the back of the space, these glass walls frosted, thicker, the same chrome-and-leather scheme but everything subtly better. They took their seats on either side of his desk, where stacks of brochures and client folders were arranged with military precision.

'So, Tomas Kaminski. What can I tell you?'

'I need his full records,' Zigic said.

'That's not a problem.' Broad reached for his keyboard and typed while he spoke. 'Which is he then? Victim or suspect?'

'Both,' Zigic said. 'Had you had any trouble with him?'

'Not that I can see here.' Broad tapped the keyboard, scrolling, face set in concentration too fixed for the simple task. 'We had him on as a doorman. I don't deal with that side of things though.'

'Maybe I should speak to whoever does?'

'Michael's away on holiday. Honeymoon, I should say. He'll be back next week, but I imagine there are time constraints involved.' A printer began to hum under his desk, the paper tray racking brashly. 'Is this to do with the hit-and-run on Lincoln Road? I saw your press conference, Ziggy – this thing's got people's blood up.'

'We're not sure exactly how Kaminski's involved yet.'

Was this natural curiosity? he wondered. Broad might have left the police but he still thought like a detective, wanted to find the pattern, slot the pieces he knew into it and see how they fitted. Or was it something else? Concern for his company's image prompting him to ferret out details he had no right to, preparing to shape a suitable narrative for when the news became public.

'There are two other men working for you. Pyotr Dymek and –' Zigic reached into his pocket for the mugshot taken a few hours before Lukas hanged himself. 'This man, we're not sure of his surname but we think he's Lukas something.'

Broad took the photograph and studied it for a moment, shook his head. 'He looks a right piece of work.'

'He's in police custody,' Zigic said. 'But he isn't talking.'

'The dead don't very often.' Broad smiled, eyes sharp above his rimless reading glasses. 'I still have friends at Thorpe Wood, Ziggy. And they're just as loose-lipped as they've always been.'

'Then you'll know we're under pressure.'

'Bob said as much.'

Funny, Zigic didn't remember Broad and Riggott being such good mates when they were in CID together. What he remembered was two DIs both trying to climb the same ladder at the same time and being less than sportsmanlike about it. With Riggott the barbs were strictly professional. Broad took a more personal pleasure in knifing his perceived competition.

'You'll appreciate why we need to find out some background on him then.'

'Always best to clean your mess up quick.' Broad's fingers skipped across the keyboard. 'Here we go . . . Lukas Wrabowski. Another doorman. I'll print this lot off for you too, shall I?'

'Thanks. And whatever you have on Pyotr Dymek.'

Broad nodded, transferred his attention to the computer again for a few seconds, a hint of annoyance creeping in around his eyes, corners of his mouth turning down.

'This hasn't got anything to do with that hit-and-run, has it?'

'You know I can't discuss an ongoing case.'

'Look, Ziggy, I might be a civilian now but I spent twenty years sitting where you're sitting and I'm not about to start running my mouth off.' He settled back in his chair, elbow on the arm, his hand curled into a fist which gave away the anger he was trying to keep out of his voice. 'It's those murders, isn't it? Three now, right? You think one of my employees is responsible?'

'It's a possibility. We're still trying to work out exactly who did what.'

Broad snorted, fist clenching and opening again. 'Ten years I've spent building this company. We've got a spotless record – we've worked damn hard to earn our good standing – and it'll completely go to shit the second this gets out.'

Never mind the three men who'd been murdered.

Innocent men, stamped to death, left in the street while their killers disappeared into the night, went home to shower the blood off and climb into their beds, get up the next morning and pull on the Grey Shield uniforms they had no place wearing. If Broad did his job properly, if he brought his well-honed detective's mind into play and took the time to notice the kind of men he was employing, his reputation wouldn't be under threat now.

Ten years was long enough off the force to blur your morals apparently, and even though Broad still carried the air of a copper his brain ticked just the same as any other businessman's. Self-preservation first, second and third.

That was what Zigic needed to appeal to.

'I'll do my very best to keep your company out of this,' he said. 'There's no reason at all why you have to be mentioned, but three of our suspects have worked for you and there's a high probability the fourth one does too.'

'Christ, another one?' Broad looked queasy, eyes rolling towards the ceiling, as if he expected it to physically fall in on him. 'What the hell kind of fuck-up have you made, Ziggy?'

There was the Broad he knew and hated.

'My fuck-up? What about yours? Did you take the time to check Tomas Kaminski's criminal record before you employed him? Six years in prison for murder. Links to a neo-Nazi gang. We're not talking about a few youthful indiscretions here, Alan. Kaminski was a hardened criminal.'

The colour was rising through Broad's winter tan, the crêpey skin around his mean blue eyes crimping.

'Or maybe I'm being unfair to you. As I recall you were a very conscientious detective.' Zigic nodded to himself. 'I imagine you're just as careful now. More careful even, considering that reputation is everything in this business. So I wouldn't be at all surprised if you did check Kaminski out and you just didn't care what he'd done.'

'Look –'

'He was a tough guy, right? Perfect for security work. And who cares if he cut up a couple of Turks back in the old country? No one's going to find out.' Zigic leaned across Broad's desk, his elbow knocking over a photograph in a chrome frame. 'Except I've got a press conference due in a little over an hour and, fuck-up that I am, I don't have much progress to report. Now, what can I possibly say that will distract the press from my inability to make an arrest?'

Broad's fingers closed around the arm of his chair.

'Maybe they'd like to come down here and watch us execute a search warrant for your files. What do you think?'

'You're an ungrateful cunt,' Broad snarled. 'That's what I fucking think.'

Zigic spread his hands wide, smiled. 'I learned from the master.'

47

'We were so close,' Ferreira said, as she pulled up in front of the house on Oxford Road.

They'd already been to the address Broad had for Lukas Wrabowski, walked down the side of the red-brick semi and into the overgrown back garden, heading for the converted outbuilding where Pyotr Dymek lived. Three days ago, mere hours before Asif Khalid was murdered, his killer within touching distance, and they didn't even know he existed.

Zigic looked up at the first-floor windows, curtains drawn, no signs of life.

'He was probably in there watching us.'

'It didn't scare him though, did it?' Ferreira said. 'His mate's dead and we're at his door and he still goes out that night and kicks someone to death. What does that tell you?'

'That whoever was pulling the strings is arrogant.'

They got out of the car, two uniforms joining them. At this time of the afternoon the house would probably be empty, its other occupants still at work, but they didn't want to take any chances. Dymek and Wrabowski were linked and the possibility that the fourth man they were looking for lived in the house too couldn't be discounted.

Zigic had the keys they'd recovered from Wrabowski's belongings when he was arrested, the only thing on him.

He waited until the uniforms were in the back garden before he knocked, gave it half a minute, gripping the keys tight, metal teeth biting his fingers. Behind him Ferreira shifted her feet on the gravel.

'They're out,' she said. 'Let's just do this.'

He unlocked the front door and they stepped into a gloomy hallway, faintly damp-smelling and tinged with stale cigarette smoke. Nothing was lying around but it was a shared house and you guarded your possessions in places like this, especially when you didn't know or trust your housemates.

At the far end of the hall a door stood open onto the kitchen, another door to the right led into a communal sitting room done out with an old-fashioned Dralon suite and a teak coffee table littered with beer cans and takeaway cartons. Among them sat a copy of the local Polish-language newspaper, the latest edition judging by the photograph of Asif Khalid dominating the front page.

The third door was locked; a bedroom, but Wrabowski's key didn't fit.

Ferreira lingered for a moment, ear pressed to the cheap plywood, satisfying herself that the room really was unoccupied.

Upstairs they tried the doors until finally the key turned on a bedroom at the back of the house.

'I was expecting paraphernalia,' Ferreira said and Zigic wasn't sure if she was joking or not, but he shared the sentiment.

The room was no different to any other of the kind he'd seen. A pine single bed and a flimsy wardrobe, an armchair too bulky for the room and a portable television on a desk. The only thing which struck him as unusual was how tight the sheets had been stretched across the mattress, reminding him of an army barracks.

Ferreira pulled on a pair of latex gloves before she opened the wardrobe – nothing but carefully folded clothes inside, and Wrabowski's Grey Shield uniform hanging up above a pair of black boots polished to a high shine. The same type he wore when he killed Asif Khalid.

'He thought he was a soldier,' she said.

'Tomas told Sofia he was an army medic.'

'My money's on that being pure fantasy.'

Zigic checked the desk drawers, lifted the cushions on the burgundy floral armchair, found nothing but dust and a few biscuit crumbs, which told him Wrabowski wasn't all that precise in his cleaning habits.

'He must have a mobile.'

'Mattress,' Ferreira said.

They took one end each and flipped it up against the wall, exposing the narrow slats and the matt-black body of a laptop lying across them.

'Even better.'

Zigic went to the window while she bagged up, seeing the uniforms milling about on the grey-slabbed patio, attention directed across the back fence towards the neighbouring garden, where Dymek's lady friend from Łódź was taking her washing in, wearing hot pants and a vest despite the single-digit temperature.

'We should talk to her,' he said.

Ferreira came over to the window. 'Men confide in whores, right?'

'It's what I hear.'

She smiled. 'Anyone else, I wouldn't have let that go so easily.'

They left the uniforms stationed across the road, with a good eyeline to the front door but not close enough to spook Wrabowski's housemates when they arrived home from work. They would be brought in to give statements, alibis requested and checked before they were released.

Zigic thought of the man he'd spoken to the first time they were there. Tall and rangy, a physique made for scrapping, but light enough to bolt from the scene of a crime without too much trouble.

The problem was they still had no idea if that was the kind of man they were looking for. Until CCTV yielded some clues or a witness came forward they were guessing.

Ferreira took the lead with the neighbour – Marinka.

She kept them in the hallway, stood near the staircase with one foot on top of the other, nervously twisting her hand on the newel post, short red fingernails and a ring around her thumb. The house smelled of air-freshener and used sheets, a faint odour of heavily spiced aftershave from her last client.

'This is about Pyotr?' she asked, her accent thick, voice deeper than her slight frame suggested.

'When did you last see him?' Ferreira asked.

'The day before he was killed. He came here and said he was going home for a few days.'

'Do your clients usually tell you when they'll be away?'

Marinka took no offence at the question. 'Pyotr was my friend also.'

'How did he seem to you?'

She considered it for a moment, looking at her hand as she gripped the wooden acorn which topped the post, raking her thumb-nail down its ridges. 'He was not like himself. He was usually a happy man. Always joking.'

'Maybe he didn't want to go home,' Ferreira said gently.

'No. He was scared.' She closed her eyes, frowned. 'He said that if a man came here looking for him I should say I did not know where he was.'

'What man?' Zigic asked.

'I did not ask. I thought he had some debt he was running away from.'

'And did he come?'

She nodded. 'The day Pyotr died. It was very early. I heard banging and I got up to see what it was. There was a man at my front door. I thought he would break in.'

'Did you answer it?' Zigic asked, praying that she had.

'No. It was still dark outside. I would not open the door to him but I came down and he must have seen me. He shouted at me through the letter box.' She nodded towards it, the slot caged, some junk mail sitting there. 'He said he needed to speak to Pyotr, it was an emergency. Pyotr's wife was dying.'

'But you didn't believe that?'

'I know when I am being lied to,' she said. 'I told him I did not know where Pyotr was and if he did not leave I would call the police.'

'How did he know to come to you?' Ferreira asked.

Marinka shrugged. 'Men like to talk about the women they fuck.'

'Can you tell us anything about this man?' Zigic asked, hearing the desperation creeping into his voice. 'Please, Marinka, this is very important.'

She shrank back slightly, pressed her body against the staircase, and when she spoke she looked down at her feet. 'I did not see his face.'

'Was he Polish?'

'Yes.'

Zigic took out a photograph of Lukas Wrabowski. 'Could this be the man?'

'He is my neighbour,' she said, sounding perplexed. 'Why do you have his photograph?'

'Is it possible this was the man who came here?' Zigic asked.

'No. I know Lukas's voice. It was not him.'

They spent another few minutes trying to draw something further out of her but she had shut down, scared by the possibility that whoever killed Dymek was still out there, perhaps. Wary of exposing herself to his wrath. Zigic gave her a card and she tucked it into the back pocket of her denim shorts, saw them out with a hollow promise to call if she remembered anything else.

A few fine spots of rain hit Zigic's face as the door closed at their backs. He saw Moore and Hale parked across the road, the engine of their car running, heating the interior, the wipers swiping lazily over the lightly spotted windscreen.

'What do you make of that?' Ferreira asked.

'He's cleaning up a loose end,' Zigic said, pausing in the gateway, thinking of the shovel in the Volvo's boot, the only new thing in there. Bought for a specific and immediate purpose. 'Dymek spat on Manouf's body, he left evidence behind that could get them all arrested.'

'So he had to die?'

'It would explain why he was running home.'

'The Volvo was bought the morning after Manouf was murdered,' Ferreira said. 'He could have gone after Dymek straight away.'

'Maybe he couldn't find him. He came looking here . . .'

'No sign of Dymek. So he drives off down Lincoln Road and sees him standing at the bus stop talking to Sofia. Loses it, accelerates, and runs him over.' She glanced up at the neighbouring house. 'Lukas would have known whether he was home or not. Why not just ask him?'

'Would you want the rest of the gang to know how expendable they were off the back of one mistake?' Zigic said. 'Not exactly good for morale, is it?'

'It's a messy way to get rid of Dymek.'

'You're assuming he was thinking rationally at the time.'

As they headed for the car Zigic looked along the street and stopped when he saw one of Lukas's housemates coming the other way, the man he'd spoken to a few days earlier, Adrian Mazur. He stopped as well, froze for a second, staring straight at Zigic.

Then dropped the carrier bag he was holding and ran.

Zigic started after him, hearing Ferreira shouting at Moore and Hale, the patrol car's engine roaring to life.

Mazur was moving fast. His feet slapped the pavement, a red rucksack banging against his back. A car door opened into his path. He tried to swerve but it clipped him, forcing him to slow for a few seconds, allowing Zigic to draw closer. No more than ten yards between them. Zigic could see that he was hurt. His gait was uneven, his face flushed as he turned back to look across his shoulder.

Always a mistake.

Zigic sped up. Eight yards between them.

Six.

Mazur rounded the corner onto Lincoln Road, scattering a group of women coming the other way. Zigic sprinted past them, in the man's slipstream now, closing in along the empty space he was cutting up the middle of the pavement.

There was a pedestrian crossing ahead. Vehicles idling at the red light. Engine noise drowned out by the sound of a siren as the patrol car came out of a side street. It was driving the wrong way up the empty road, aiming for Mazur as he stuck a hand out, grabbed the post and swung round onto the crossing.

Zigic overshot by a few feet and by the time he righted himself the lights were on amber, horns sounding as Mazur stepped out in front of a car, slipping the rucksack off his back.

In the other lane a pickup truck shifted gears noisily and pulled away and Zigic swore as Mazur pitched his rucksack onto its flatbed, the driver ignorant of what had happened, accelerating off to his next job.

Mazur turned round, facing Zigic now, breathing heavily as he put his hands out to his sides, his face a picture of relief.

PC Hale bundled into him from the side, wrenched his hands behind his back and cuffed him, getting no resistance. Whatever he was worried about them finding in that backpack was gone and he let himself be placed in the patrol car without a fight.

48

All they got from Adrian Mazur was his wallet, which contained nothing but the usual; thirty pounds in cash, a debit card close to expiration, and his photo ID for Grey Shield Security.

Everything came back to that place.

The files ex-DCI Broad had been so reluctant to part with were now being sifted through by Wahlia and Grieves, time sheets and shift rotations examined, staff records searched for Polish employees who had worked with the other members of the gang.

So far they'd established that Tomas Kaminski and Pyotr Dymek had started at the company within a week of each other. Maybe not a significant point, but Zigic knew that it was common for people to suggest friends, vouch for them. Lukas Wrabowski was a more recent employee, six months in the job and they could find no trace of him in England before that. He'd called Inspector Strug in Poznań and drawn a blank, got the distinct impression that his Polish counterpart was becoming impatient with the interruptions to his day.

Not that it mattered any more. By committing suicide Lukas Wrabowski had put himself beyond questioning and justice, but his laptop was with the techies now and that might yet yield the secrets he'd asphyxiated himself to avoid giving up.

'OK,' Wahlia said, pushing back from his screen. 'We've got Mazur on doorman duty with Tomas six weeks ago, only a couple of nights, but his main job's as a security guard at the shopping centre.'

'Day or night?' Zigic asked.

'Day,' Wahlia said. 'So he's free to go out murdering of an evening.'

'Why wasn't he at work today then?'

'Grey Shield's only an employment agency like all the others. They call them when they want them. Don't let them get too comfortable in one place by the look of this either.' Wahlia took off his heavy-framed glasses and rubbed his eyes. 'That's common with retail security though, stops them getting too friendly with the careerist shoplifters.'

'And it's playing havoc with fathoming out who wasn't working when the murders took place?' Zigic guessed.

Wahlia nodded. 'It's slow going. We could do with an extra pair of eyes on this.'

'Parr should be back in an hour or so,' Zigic said, checking his watch.

He'd sent him to oversee the search of the house on Oxford Road, sure they'd found everything it was going to yield already but there was always a slim chance that Mazur had left something incriminating behind.

'What we do know,' Wahlia said, slipping his glasses back on, 'is that Mr Mazur's doorman shifts stopped materialising because he has some impulse control issues. He broke a bloke's jaw throwing him out of a club.'

'Was any action taken?'

'He was put on a written warning according to his file, but it didn't go any further.'

Another dent in the highly polished facade of Grey Shield Security, Zigic thought. He swivelled in Ferreira's chair to look at the whiteboards lined up along the wall, the three murders and the hit-and-run, Tomas's still maybe accidental death, no board for Lukas's suicide. Seven deaths, a terrible knot of misery they'd been trying to unpick for weeks, no idea that the crimes might be linked, and now he could see the slim filament tying them all together.

One man, faceless, wearing a Grey Shield uniform.

Ferreira came into the office and shooed him out of her chair, plugged a USB drive into the tower under her desk before she sat down.

'Contents of Dymek's mobile,' she said. 'Nothing spectacular, a lot of messages going back and forth between him and Tomas, a few to Lukas. We've got another number, which could be our mystery man.'

'Shout it out,' Wahlia said and she gave him it.

'The messages are in Polish, so . . .'

Zigic looked at the text file on her screen, the grey bar on the left showing just how much there was to go through.

'It can wait,' he said. 'Let's talk to Mr Mazur.'

Adrian Mazur had requested a solicitor the second he stepped into the station's reception area, the action of an old hand, at odds with his lack of a criminal record. At the time it sparked a small moment of hope in Zigic's chest; you only wanted a solicitor because you were going to talk. And if he was prepared to do that, the right combination of threats and coaxing might get them to the truth.

That wasn't how it was going though.

Mazur was evasive, withdrawn, sitting at the table in Interview Room 2 with his eyes lowered, hands tucked into the pockets of his hoodie, the shiny fabric drawn tight across the points of his knuckles. Five minutes in and he'd spoken less than a dozen words – 'yes' and 'no' answers – ignored some questions altogether.

Zigic asked his last one a second time.

'Why did you run, Mr Mazur?'

The young man cleared his throat, glanced at his solicitor, who wasn't paying any attention to him.

'I don't know.'

'You didn't run away last time we spoke,' Zigic said. 'In fact you were very helpful. So why run today?'

He remained silent.

'Something to do with the contents of your backpack maybe?'

Mazur shifted in his seat and Zigic could see the tremors shaking up through his body as his legs twitched under the table. The instinct to bolt still strong in him.

'What was in there that you didn't want us to see?'

'Nothing.'

Zigic sighed and opened the file he'd brought in with him, started laying out the photographs he'd laid out so many times during the last few days; Didi and Ali Manouf and Asif Khalid. Photos of them alive sitting above the ones of them dead, lurid, glossy shots, saturated with colour; dark skin, white bone and so much blood.

Mazur refused to look at them, kept his eyes locked firmly on Zigic.

'Why are you showing me this?'

'Your friend Pyotr killed this man.' Zigic pointed at Ali Manouf's photograph but Mazur didn't follow the gesture. 'And your friend Lukas killed this one – look at him.'

Mazur's eyes cut quickly to the photo and away again.

'They are not my friends,' he said quietly. 'We are neighbours. That is all.'

'You share a house.'

'Because we work for the same people. They find us room when we sign on with them.' He stared at Zigic, said again, 'They are not my friends.'

'Can you tell me where you were on Thursday morning between five thirty and six?' Ferreira asked.

'At home. I am always at home then.'

'What about on Saturday February first, between eleven thirty and midnight?'

Mazur shook his head. 'I don't know, how would I remember that?'

'Twelve thirty and one a.m. on Monday March twenty-fourth?'

'I can't remember.' No force to his words.

'Friday night. Between ten thirty and eleven?'

'No.' Mazur shouted, slamming both palms down on the table. 'Why are you asking me this?'

'Because three men have been murdered,' Zigic said. 'And your friends were responsible. But they weren't acting alone.'

'I told you, they are not my friends.'

'No, they were your foot soldiers.'

Mazur's face froze, eyes wide, mouth open.

'But they weren't good soldiers,' Zigic went on, his voice low. 'At least, Pyotr Dymek wasn't. He screwed up and you had to get rid of him before he incriminated you. So you killed him.'

'No.'

'Three murderers working with you. Two of them living with you.'

Mazur shook his head. 'No, this is crazy. You are mad.'

'Innocent people don't run.'

Mazur was breathing heavily now, colour rising in his gaunt face, and under the table his leg was jiggling, nervousness threatening to spread through his entire body and turn into a fit. Zigic could see the fear behind his eyes and it surprised him, after the cool and stoic way Lukas Wrabowski dealt with this selfsame situation. He'd acted like a leader, defiant till the end.

Mazur didn't seem like a man who could command respect.

Fifteen minutes of questioning and he was close to the edge.

Zigic brought one last photograph out of the folder and laid it on top of the others – Jelena Krasic, young and pretty and smiling like she thought she would live forever.

'You're a real hard man, Adrian, driving that massive car through her. You must have seen her face as you did it. She was looking right at you.'

Mazur's hands shot out and he swept the photographs off the table. They settled slowly, face up, one of them floating all the way to the door.

'She was twenty-four,' Zigic said. 'She was about to get engaged. A nice girl. And you ploughed through her in that big white tank of a car without a second thought. You just wanted to take Pyotr out and you didn't care who else died.'

'I cannot drive,' Mazur said wearily. 'You look. See if I have a driver's licence.'

They already knew he didn't.

'That means nothing.'

328

Mazur turned to Ferreira, making the same mistake that so many suspects did, thinking a female officer would be more sympathetic.

'Please, I did not kill anyone.'

'Then help us,' she said. 'You lived among these murderers – who's the fourth member of the gang if it isn't you?'

'I don't know.'

His shoulders sagged and his chin dropped onto his chest, the strip light bouncing off his shaved head. For a minute he closed his eyes and Zigic imagined him furiously digging around for a name to throw at them, someone else from work, another Pole with a bad attitude who would look a more promising suspect.

'Last week,' Mazur said slowly, 'a man came looking for Pyotr. It was dark still and he woke me up banging on Pyotr's door. I thought it was somebody trying to break in.'

'What day was this?' Ferreira said.

'The day Pyotr died.'

'Why didn't you tell us this when we spoke to you at the house?'

'I thought it was an accident. Why would you care if some man was looking for him?' Mazur glanced between them, checking their reactions, and obviously he didn't think they were buying it because he kept talking, speeding up, becoming more animated. 'I went downstairs into the kitchen. I could see him from the window. He was very angry, banging on the door. Pyotr was not there though. He was next door with his *kurwa*.'

'Did you recognise him?' Ferreira asked.

'No. It was dark. I could not see his face,' Mazur said. 'But when I went back to bed I saw a large white car parked outside the house. He was the man who killed those poor people.'

49

'He really expects us to buy that bullshit,' Ferreira said.

She opened a can of Pepsi and swore as it fizzed over her hand.

'It chimes with what the neighbour told us,' Zigic pointed out.

'Of course it does, because he knows he went for her first.'

Zigic thought of Mazur's expression as he laid the photographs of the dead men out in front of him, no pleasure in his eyes, just revulsion and shock. Tough emotions to fake. He ran though, senselessly, and they wouldn't have an explanation for it until his rucksack was recovered.

'Where are we with the bag?' he asked.

'I spoke to the office,' Grieves said. 'They've got it off the truck and I've sent a car to collect it but it'll take them a couple of hours to get there and back. The company's based in Grantham and it's rush hour now – you know what the A1's like this time of night.'

Not night, Zigic thought, looking away through the east-facing windows, but very nearly. The sky was almost fully dark, a pink glow smeared above the dual carriageway, people heading home already. But not from this office.

There was reams of paperwork to go through and more coming in all the time, as Wahlia identified potential suspects from Grey Shield Security's records, men who'd worked directly with the murderers, ones with criminal records, a handful with clean histories who he'd highlighted purely because of their shift patterns, available on the nights of all three murders and the morning of the hit-and-run.

The last group was their focus, opportunity more important than any other factor right now.

Adrian Mazur was among them, writ bold at the top of the

suspects column, three more Polish names below his, one struck out already – a man who'd spent last Wednesday night in a cell downstairs, sleeping off the previous evening's antics. There was a single English name at the bottom of the list and as Zigic stood looking over the board he realised it was familiar.

'Christian Palmer,' he said. 'What about him?'

Grieves twisted in her seat. 'He's not Polish.'

'But he's got a nasty temper, hasn't he?' Ferreira said.

Grieves turned back to her work quickly, a flush rising at her throat. She mumbled a reply Zigic didn't catch, but he saw the look of disgust on Ferreira's face, a flicker of contemptuous humour around her mouth.

'It's the same bloke, isn't it, Bobby? Ex-PC Chris Palmer?'

'Yeah.'

'Our man might not be Polish,' Ferreira said, eyes boring into the back of Grieves's head. 'These neo-Nazi groups are pretty inclusive as long as you're not brown.' She rapped her fingertips on the desk. 'What do you think, Deb? You know him better than the rest of us. You think he got a taste for it?'

Zigic started for his office. 'A word, Mel.'

She followed him in and closed the door. 'I guess this is a private conversation.'

He paced around behind his desk, only the lamp there burning, throwing a cone of light across the scattered paperwork, leaving the corners of the room in darkness.

'What the hell was that about?'

Ferreira folded her arms. 'Maybe you should ask Grieves.'

'I'm asking you.'

She let out an extravagant sigh, taking a couple of steps closer to the desk. 'Do you know why Palmer's not a copper any more?'

'I barely know who he is,' Zigic said.

'Palmer and Grieves were partners, back in uniform. The same time I was down there. And there was a death in the cells – this kid – he was pulled in for a bit of green, scared to death, and he started

331

mouthing off about needing to leave. Palmer went in there and threw his weight at him. All sixteen stone of it.' She tossed her hair out of her eyes. 'The kid had an epileptic fit. He was dead in a minute.'

Zigic recalled some vague stirring of gossip, not the details, and now she'd filled them in he still couldn't remember Palmer. There were so many of them in uniform, big men, all attitude and mouth. The bottom of the food chain so they exercised their scant power wherever they could and frequently overdid it. But the people they targeted were in no position to complain.

'What's this got to do with Grieves?'

'She helped cover it up,' Ferreira said. 'And, funnily enough, I don't fucking like it.'

Zigic sat down, rocked back in his chair. 'Were you going to mention this any time soon?'

'What's the difference now?'

Through the closed door he could hear Wahlia's voice going, talking on the phone, saw Grieves walk out past his desk, head down.

'Does Riggott know?'

'Probably not.' Ferreira perched on the edge of the chair opposite him. 'I can't prove any of this. I only know because she asked me what to do about it. Then ignored my advice.' She shook her head. 'It was years ago now. There's nothing to say.'

'But you don't think she's reliable?'

'No, she's totally reliable. She'll do whatever you tell her.'

'That's not what I meant and you know it.'

Ferreira placed her hands on the edge of the desk, leaned into the lamplight. Her face was serious now, all trace of emotion gone. 'Look, we're getting close. But we need her here to sift through all that shit coming in.'

Telling him exactly what he was thinking, acting like the rational one. She was regretting speaking up already, he realised. That barb she'd been dying to fire at Grieves for a week had found its mark and done its work and she felt how hollow the victory was.

332

'Let's keep this between us for now,' he said, reaching for the phone, ringing on his desk. 'What have you got for me?'

'We're into the laptop, sir. I think you'll want to see this.'

They went upstairs to the technical department, a series of small offices crammed with equipment and storage rooms where countless laptops and desktops and mobile devices containing every imaginable horror were waiting to be cracked. They had a massive backlog and a chronic staffing problem due to the fact that the police paid a pittance for the skill set required in comparison to other industries.

Ethan was standing in the corridor waiting for them, one hand hooked around the back of his neck, a strained expression on his face. He'd been at the station less than a year, came straight from university, but the job was telling on him already. Every murder and assault he'd witnessed wiping a little of the youthful innocence away, the effect compounded by hours spent in windowless rooms, using caffeine and sugar to maintain the necessary state of perpetual attention.

'That was quick,' Ferreira said.

'There wasn't much in the way of security,' he said. 'The laptop was, like, five years old or something, totally archaic.'

They followed him into his office, a cramped space which smelled of plastic and singed wires, despite the immaculately kept work-station. Lukas Wrabowski's laptop sat open in front of an ancient leather swivel chair, ripped and patched with electrical tape. Ethan shoved the chair away with his leg and tilted the lid back so they could see it properly.

The screen was filled by a video player. A man dressed all in black, his face obscured by a balaclava with a mesh section over his eyes. He stood in front of a blank off-white wall, with a swastika flag hung high up, the shot framed carefully to show its whole, cutting the man off at the waist.

Ethan hit a button to start the video and the man's voice started up, speaking Polish in a deep and booming tone, pitched to sell his message.

'What's he saying?' Ferreira asked.

Zigic gestured for her to wait, trying to pick out familiar words, but the man's vocabulary was odd, complex-sounding, and after the initial introduction it became difficult to follow. As it played on, the man becoming more impassioned, his voice rising, Zigic heard a theme developing within the words he did understand – blood, fire, nation, pride.

'Start it again please.'

Ethan hit a button and once again the man settled his bulk, tucked his gloved hands behind his back, and began to speak.

'Brothers, the time for talk is over,' Zigic said, translating a few beats behind. 'There is a disease in our land and it lives in the blood of our neighbours and our co-workers, they will tell you they do not have this disease but we see this lie in their actions, in the . . .'

Zigic tailed off and the man's voice took over, angry and incomprehensible, his body seeming to grow as he neared the end of his speech, a long, rattling section where he barely took a breath and then, with a sudden snap, he raised his right arm in a Nazi salute.

'Is it Wrabowski?' Ferreira asked. 'It looks too tall.'

'I don't think it's him,' Zigic said. 'This man wants a platform, he wants to convert and indoctrinate. Wrabowski would have talked to us if this was how his mind worked.' He turned to Ethan. 'Where did this footage come from?'

'I found it in his Internet history. He's a member of a closed group – *Bialy Braterstwo*.'

'White Brethren,' Zigic said. The group Tomas Kaminski got involved with while he was in prison. 'When was this posted?'

'Three days ago.'

'Just before Asif Khalid was murdered,' Ferreira said.

'Where's this online group based?'

'It's in Polish, but that doesn't mean anything.' Ethan pushed his hand back through his hair. 'I can dig about but I'm going to need help and it's going to take a while.'

'Get whoever you need,' Zigic said. 'And do it fast.'

334

'OK.' Ethan nodded. 'It's not the only one of this guy. At least, I think it's the same man, the flag's there, he looks the same build.'

'Show us another one.'

He leaned over and tapped the keyboard, opening another page which showed the off-white room, the swastika hanging lower and tighter stretched in this shot, the man visible to the thigh. When Ethan played it the dialogue was different but spouting the same message.

After a few seconds Zigic told him to stop it.

'Run copies of these and send them down to us – I want a translator to look at them.'

'Yes, sir.'

'We need to know when they were posted, when they were recorded if possible. All of them.'

'Of course.'

Ferreira had her phone out. 'What's the web address?'

'Hold on.' Ethan took a notepad out of a drawer and printed a long address, some numbers underneath. 'This one's his user details, you'll need them to get into the group.'

Zigic thanked him and turned to leave.

'Don't you want to see the rest of it?' Ethan asked.

'The rest of what?'

'The murders.'

50

Zigic drove without thinking, everything on automatic, accelerating along the unlit parkway. Its uneven surface vibrated up through the chassis, up into the steering wheel he was gripping tight, his arms stiff with tension, his shoulders squared with it.

He could feel the muscles under his skull clenched, told himself to breathe. It was nothing he hadn't already watched half a dozen times, an unfortunate young man kicked to death in a quiet street while people slept in the houses around him. Or pretended to sleep, too scared or ambivalent to go out and see what the screaming was about.

It was different this time though.

The CCTV footage of Didi's murder was low-quality, the camera ten yards away, set high and angled down. Only now did he realise how those factors had combined to soften the attack, created a merciful sense of distance. Impossible as it would have seemed twenty minutes ago he now knew that was the 15 certificate.

The version on Lukas Wrabowski's laptop had been filmed on a camera phone – a good-quality one Ethan had told them as he'd turned away from the screen, eight megapixels, capable of night shooting.

And the hand that held it steady had been only a few steps away, close enough to capture the effect of every single boot strike and the terrible change in expression on Didi's face before it was stamped into a gut-wrenching oblivion.

There were others too. Not just Ali Manouf and Asif Khalid.

The site contained a dozen more videos, more dead men, killed with knives and iron bars, their bodies lying in unidentified cobbled streets, unmistakably European but not here. As he'd watched them, with Ethan looking away from the screen and Ferreira asking questions he couldn't answer, Zigic had realised those murders had probably gone unpunished.

This was not just their problem any more.

He turned off the parkway and slowed as he approached a roundabout, heading into Old Fletton, thinking how peaceful the houses looked. How was it possible that a city like this had been harbouring a violent, racist gang with roots which went back to a prison cell in Poland?

Did it originate with Tomas Kaminski?

They couldn't ask him now. Couldn't question any of them. Unless they found the fourth man in the gang this might never stop, because why would it? That hate didn't go away, it grew and festered and the filmed evidence of it was broadcast to the select few with access to the White Brethren site to be laughed at and admired and inspire more senseless murder.

They needed Adrian Mazur to be their man. Safely celled right now, trying to come up with his alibis. Because if it wasn't him they had nothing and the person responsible could be anywhere, fleeing across Europe if he was cautious or if he was arrogant, and Zigic prayed he was that arrogant, patrolling the silent corridors of some office building in his Grey Shield Security uniform.

At the mouth of Church Street he slowed, caught behind a Tesco van, as the driver searched for an address, which he finally found, pulling onto the kerb and allowing Zigic to pass.

The Polish Ex-Servicemen's Club was at the bottom of the road, a fine old Victorian building which had sprouted several less attractive extensions. Over the years its original members were joined by political refugees who came over during the fifties, then the more recent arrivals during the late nineties who flocked to it as a reminder of home and a way to contact people who would help them get established.

It was waning now though. The older generation were dying off and the younger ones found there were enough Poles in the city to render it pointless. New England had plenty of bars and cafes they could use and when Zigic went inside he realised there was little here to tempt them.

It looked like any small-town bar back in Poland. Grubby white walls and wood panelling stained with decades of cigarette smoke, flags and football club banners hanging here and there, wonky tables and vinyl chairs, heavy velvet curtains drawn against the night and the draughts which leaked in around the sash windows, a concession to the few customers already in. Old men, bowed by a lifetime of heavy lifting in the now defunct brickyards.

There was no flat-screen television, no music playing, and what conversation there was carried on at a low pitch, despite the evident heat in it, gestures stabbed across the tables. They'd been having the same arguments for years, Zigic imagined, and still hadn't righted the world.

The woman behind the bar put down her magazine as he approached.

'What can I get you, love?'

'Just a Coke, thanks.' He scanned the faces looking back at him as she opened a bottle, didn't see the man he wanted. 'Is Jurek in yet?'

She nodded towards a table in the corner, a newspaper and a half-drunk pint there. 'He's in the Gents.'

'I better have a whiskey as well then.'

Zigic paid her and carried the drinks over to the table, sat down with eyes still on him. Unfamiliar faces were rare in here and someone looking for Jurek was bound to arouse interest. He was well known in the community, the owner/editor of the local Polish-language newspaper, a man who knew everyone worth knowing and the secrets they wouldn't like exposing. Back in Warsaw he'd been an investigative reporter, but that was twenty years ago and he'd learned the cost of journalistic integrity the hard way.

'I was wondering when I would see you,' Jurek said, clapping

338

Zigic on the shoulder. He lowered himself carefully into the chair, winced as he did it. Old wounds, badly healed, but Zigic knew he wouldn't thank him for asking about them. 'So, which is it, the car accident or the murders?'

'Straight to business?'

'We want to see our dead avenged, Inspector.' Zigic hesitated a moment too long for Jurek's liking and his face darkened. 'You can rely on my discretion if that is what you are wondering.'

'It's not you I'm worried about.'

Jurek grunted agreement and nodded towards the back door. 'I need a cigarette.'

Zigic followed him out past the toilets and the closed door of a disused function room, noticing just how badly the old man moved now, how much effort it took him to force down the bar on the fire door which took them into the car park that wrapped around the side of the building.

There was a hint of frost in the air, wind rising and sending a spray of rubbish swirling across the cracked and patched tarmac. The flyover droned nearby but still the neighbouring churchyard seemed to exude its own deep and permanent silence.

Jurek lit a cigarette, his back turned against the wind. 'I heard on the radio you arrested a Polish man for that boy's murder. He killed himself in your cells they said, this Wrabowski.'

Zigic didn't even realise they'd announced it. Everything was running out of his control.

'He hanged himself, yes.'

'And what if it wasn't him?'

'It was, we had ample forensic evidence.' Zigic punched his hands into his pockets. 'He was a member of a neo-Nazi group, the White Brethren – do you know anything about them?'

Jurek exhaled, blowing the smoke away from Zigic.

'They were very active in the bigger cities in Poland during the eighties and nineties. Anti-Semitic attacks mainly, desecrating graves and memorials. There wasn't much more than that left for them to destroy.' He frowned, flicked the ash off his cigarette. 'By the late nineties they began to fracture, many left the country – to look for work I imagine – and the ones who stayed behind took exception to the influx of migrants from Africa and the Middle East. There were some murders but the police were not interested.'

'I thought they were a prison gang,' Zigic said.

'Later, yes. But it was drug dealing that led them there, not murder.' Jurek took another deep draw on his cigarette. 'They stepped into territory which was protected so the police rounded them up and they were put in prison. I am out of touch now, of course, but the last I heard they were finished.'

Zigic thought of the videos he'd seen; blood on cobblestones, lit by ornate street lights.

'They're not finished, Jurek, believe me.'

A motorbike's engine sawed through the quiet, moving slowly along the narrow residential road, then retreated, heading into the housing estate that ran down to the River Nene.

'They're operating over here now,' Zigic said. 'Wrabowski and two of his friends. They're all dead, but the ringleader's still out there and we need to find him. Have you heard anything about this? Gossip, whispers, anything.'

Jurek flicked his spent butt away. 'There are tensions, for sure.'

'With who?'

'My countrymen are fiercely patriotic, you must understand that.'

'But they're in England now.'

'Yes, and they have their streets here and they regard them as home.' Jurek's face twisted, like he was struggling to find the right words, an odd predicament for a man of his profession, Zigic thought. 'Damn you for making me say this . . .'

Zigic waited and when Jurek spoke the words tumbled out.

'The Poles hate the Asians and the Asians hate the Poles. It is a culture clash. Islam and Catholicism. If you are a believer there can be no peace. Not when you live so close together. The Asians disapprove of our bars moving into their streets, they rent us over-priced, badly maintained housing and then hate that we are their neighbours. The young boys especially. There are fights so often and nobody calls the police.'

'Wrabowski wasn't a boy,' Zigic said, anger creeping into his voice. 'Do you want to see this turn into an all-out race war?'

'Our community cannot be held responsible for the actions of these extremists.'

'If you shield them you will be.'

'Who is shielding them?' Jurek asked incredulously. 'You should know better than that, Inspector. Groups like this do not operate in the open. These men do not flaunt the scalps they have taken. They are a terrorist cell.'

He was right, Zigic realised. The closed website and the hate speech – they were mimicking the behaviour of jihadists.

In the distance the motorbike's engine rumbled, growing louder as it returned from the warren of quiet closes and cul-de-sacs.

'I am sorry I cannot help you more,' Jurek said, reaching out to shake Zigic's hand, discussion over. 'I hope you find him.'

The motorbike rounded the corner at the bottom of the hill, slowing until it stopped outside the Polish Club. The man riding pillion jumped off and darted across the road, something in his hand which flared into life a split second before he threw it. Street light glinted on the bottle as it sailed through the air, the flame just a blur.

Glass smashed and Zigic was running, fast but not fast enough to catch the man, who climbed back onto the bike, chased by a fireball which blew out the Polish Club's front window. The driver gunned the engine and they were gone.

'Call the fire brigade,' Zigic shouted, pulling the hood of his parka up as he rushed through the front door.

The hallway was already filling with smoke and he collided with the barmaid as she burst through a door marked 'Staff Only', leading an old man by the hand, his face covered in blood, a shard of glass sticking out of his cheek.

341

She shoved Zigic in the chest. 'For fuck's sake get out of here.'

'How many of them are still in there?'

'None. I told them to go through the back.' There was blood on her hands and soaking the front of her jumper. 'The whole room went up.'

There was a crack and the building shuddered around them, followed by a sound like it was breaking open. She grabbed him by the arm, forced him towards the door with a strength she didn't look capable of, trailing the old man who dropped to his knees the second they were into the open air.

Outside Jurek stood slack-jawed, looking at the smoke pouring out of the ruptured window, the flames lighting the one above it where the fire had punched through the ceiling.

Zigic rushed round the back, found the rest of the men in the car park, one of them screaming on the ground as two of his friends used their jackets to try and beat out the flames covering his back. He writhed and bucked and tried to crawl away from them, scraping his scorched skin against the tarmac and crying out curses and prayers.

Another man stood nearby, still holding his empty glass, wiry grey hair singed on one side, his face livid. He looked frozen with shock but when Zigic touched his arm he flinched, dropping the glass.

'Is there anyone left in there?'

'What?'

'Is there anyone inside?'

'No.' The man looked at his friend, now still on the ground. 'Is he dead?'

Across the road residents were coming out of their houses, phones in their hands, filming the rising smoke and the desiccated bushes in front of the broken window as they caught light. Nobody came forward to help, nobody drew close enough to be in danger, they simply stood, silently, and watched the building burn through the screens of their smartphones.

DAY SIX

51

The next morning Zigic saw the amateur footage on the BBC News Channel, stood in the kitchen watching it as he waited for the toaster to pop, thinking how minor it looked, so little to see, just a tattered curtain touched by flames snapping through the broken window and an almost cosy-looking light in the window above it. Not serious enough for anyone to have died.

The man he'd seen cursing and screaming in the car park had been loaded into the back of an ambulance, alive but only just, while his friends looked on, clutching the jackets they had used to beat down the flames, the smell of smoke and burnt flesh on the fabric.

Zigic didn't want to think about how close he'd come to being in there too.

The newsreader's voice cut across the muffled din of sirens as the first patrol cars could be seen arriving.

'Police and community leaders in Peterborough have again appealed for calm after the Polish Ex-Servicemen's Club was firebombed in the city yesterday evening. The attack is believed to have been carried out as retaliation for the murder of local man Asif Khalid. Mr Khalid's killer, Lukas Wrabowski, a member of the city's Polish community, took his own life in police custody on Sunday.'

There was no containing this now.

Ironically Riggott had taken control of the investigation. It was exactly the kind of incident Hate Crimes had been established to deal with but with so much for them still to do he'd decided it was best handled in CID.

That was what he said anyway.

Zigic knew it was nothing to do with easing the pressure on

them. It was pressure from above which was worrying Riggott. The Chief Constable and the mayor and all their shadowy cronies, they needed to be seen to be doing their utmost to quell the rising tensions in the city, which meant applying rank and diverting manpower. Uniforms on the street and increased patrols, high-profile policing.

Stefan and Milan ran into the kitchen and Zigic changed the channel quickly, finding cartoons but they were too busy squabbling to notice. He poured their juice and got their cereals, answering the tirade of questions they threw at him, mostly dog-related since the people next door had just brought home a rescue, some sad-looking mongrel with visible ribs and half its fur missing. The boys saw none of that, only the big brown eyes and the neediness which drew the dog through a gap in the fence when they were out playing in the garden at the weekend.

He was going to cave in to them. They all knew that. It was just a matter of time.

'Ask your mother,' he said when Anna came down, then escaped upstairs to change.

They were still pestering her when he returned ten minutes later, showered and dressed for work. She scowled at him as he grabbed his jacket and his keys, told him he'd be cleaning up after it when he kissed her.

The radio came on as he started the car but he turned it off again, in no mood to listen to whatever the local news was reporting. Whatever they were saying it made no difference, the job in front of him hadn't changed overnight, despite the firebombing.

Today's task remained the same: find their missing ringleader.

Ferreira pulled into the station behind him, tucked her car into the next space. They'd finished late yesterday evening, pushing ten when he ordered her and Wahlia out of the office, convinced that a good night's sleep was more likely to yield progress than another worn-out hour in front of their computers.

'So, last night was pretty rough down Lincoln Road,' she said, going up the steps ahead of him and opening the door. 'Three Polish places had their windows put in.'

'We never should have released Wrabowski's name. Not until we had another arrest.'

'It would have only delayed the inevitable.'

'This isn't an inevitable reaction,' he said.

'No, just the expected one.'

They went through reception, up the glass-walled stairwell, past CID which was already fully manned and buzzing with activity. A double murder and now this new spate of damage overnight, the situation was escalating and they needed a swift, hard response. Even that might not be enough, he thought.

Ferreira dumped her bag and booted up her computer, then went to start a pot of coffee, while Zigic checked his messages – one from Ethan timed at 4.36 a.m., a rundown of his initial findings.

The White Brethren site was well shielded, as they feared, its true location obscured by a proxy server. Getting hold of the owner wasn't impossible, but it would take time and resources and ultimately wouldn't bring them any closer to the man they wanted. Ethan had pulled some information from the video footage of the murders though, much of it already known to them, the time and date of filming adding nothing new, the make of the phone a useless footnote.

The hate-speech videos were filmed on a camera, eight of them in the last four months, the most recent batch uploaded a day before each of the murders, but with no way to trace their origin that information was also useless. If the man speaking was responsible it might mean something. If not, they were simply incitement.

There was another message, flagged as urgent by Kate Jenkins, Adrian Mazur's name on the subject line. Zigic took a deep breath before he opened it, then clicked the mouse.

He swore at the screen.

'What?' Ferreira called.

'Mazur's blood type doesn't match the deposits on the airbag.'

She swore back at him.

Another suspect ruled out. Another dead end.

He went out into the main office, telling himself they would break this today because he knew they had to.

Ferreira was looking at something on her mobile.

'Alex just messaged me,' she said. 'Apparently we've set alarms off accessing the White Brethren site.'

'Don't suppose he offered to help?'

'He's coming up today. They're getting very jumpy about this turning into a domestic terrorism story, I guess. Or they've fucked up their brief and we're going to take the fall for it.'

Zigic poured a cup of coffee. 'Maybe he wants to take the reins.'

'Would you care if he did?'

'I just want to catch this bastard.' He handed over her coffee, poured another for himself. 'If Alex knows something useful we need to talk to him.'

'I don't think we get a choice.' Ferreira smiled. 'Unless we catch him this morning.'

Zigic went to the murder board. Two names outstanding; today's work would be tracking them down and bringing them in, taking swabs, getting alibis, checking them out. He was beyond the point of optimism now. Even the tentative kind. Too many dead ends already gone down. Too many suspects through the interview rooms.

'What happened to Adrian Mazur's rucksack?' he asked.

'I'll go and check.'

He sipped his coffee and thought of the look on Mazur's face as he saw them outside his house, the intensity of his panic, then the relief as he stood being handcuffed, certain that whatever incriminating material the bag contained was beyond their reach.

The search of the house had yielded nothing but today they would go back and try to match the room in the videos to one there, a long shot but worth it, Zigic thought.

He eyed Christian Palmer's name at the bottom of the list of 'persons of interest'. Not a viable suspect but he knew these men, had shared long shifts with them, and in situations like that people tended to talk. He might be an ex-policeman but his instinct should still be working and it was possible he'd gleaned something which could point them in the right direction.

'Got it.' Ferreira held up a grubby red rucksack by one of its straps.

She emptied the bag across an unused desk, pulled out a half-full bottle of mineral water and a creased T-shirt that smelled of washing powder, then at the very bottom, tucked into a corner they found what they were looking for.

'No wonder he ran,' Ferreira said, weighing the bag of pills in the palm of her hand, small bright pink things each stamped with a star. 'There must be, what, two hundred in here?'

'Enough to put him inside, anyway.'

They had Adrian Mazur brought back up from his cell. He looked like he hadn't slept, heavy-eyed and stubbled, his lips cracked.

'Where is my lawyer?' he asked, standing in the middle of the interview room.

'We can call him if you want,' Ferreira said. 'But you'll have to go back down until he arrives and that will probably be another three or four hours.'

He rubbed his arm, glanced at the door, blocked off by a guard. 'I should not talk to you without him.'

'We know why you ran, Adrian.' She showed him the bag of pills. 'And frankly I don't blame you. These are going to get you into a lot of trouble.'

'They are not mine.'

'They were in your bag.'

'I did not have a bag.'

'There are cameras on top of those traffic lights,' Zigic said. 'We can prove you threw your rucksack and these pills away when we were after you.'

Ferreira moved closer to Mazur; soft steps, gentle voice. 'You need us to help you. And we will, but only if you help us.'

He looked between the two of them, wanting some sign from Zigic, verification. He nodded and gestured towards the table.

Mazur's shoulders slumped but he trudged over and sat down.

Ferreira set the tapes up, leaving the bag of pills on the table in front of her, a reminder to Mazur of what was at stake, and his eyes kept drifting towards them, mouth a straight line, chastising himself or cursing them. Maybe realising now that if he hadn't run, if he'd just spoken to them there on the street, answered their questions like a concerned citizen, none of this would be happening.

'OK, Adrian –'

'I did not kill anyone,' he said quickly. 'I swear to God I didn't.'

'We know that.'

Relief washed over Mazur's face and he huffed out a wobbly breath.

'What we need from you now is information,' Zigic said. 'We have three murdered men – innocent men, Adrian – and two of their killers lived at the same house as you. The man who came looking for Pyotr Dymek on Thursday morning is involved in this. Do you understand?'

Mazur nodded.

'He was friends with Pyotr and Lukas. So it stands to reason he might have come to the house before. Socially.' Zigic watched him give another hesitant nod. 'You know who I'm talking about, don't you?'

'I only saw him once,' Mazur said. 'He came home with Lukas and they went up to his room. They were up there for an hour. I heard them talking. They were laughing a lot. I think they were drunk. Lukas was drunk very often.'

'When was this?'

'A few weeks ago.'

'Did you get a good look at his face?' Ferreira asked.

'I opened the door for them. Lukas did not have his key.'

'Can you describe him?'

Mazur's face contorted as he trawled his memory. At least Zigic

350

hoped that was what he was doing, rather than trying to decide on a description which would satisfy them.

'He was the same height as me. He had blond hair. Short blond hair. Like this.' He mimicked spikes, flicking his fingers over his skull. 'He did not look strange.'

'Does he work at Grey Shield?'

'Yes, sir. They came home from work together. He was wearing our uniform.'

'So you do know him,' Ferreira said.

'No, I have not seen him at work.'

Ferreira shifted forward in her seat. 'We need a name.'

'I would tell you if I knew it. But I have only worked there for a month. I do not know the man's name.'

Zigic rapped his knuckle against the table. 'Alright, that's a good start. What we're going to do now, Adrian, is get you to look at some photographs and see if we can find this man.'

'I will try,' Mazur said gravely. 'I want to help you.'

52

Ferreira paced around the close confines of the interview room while Mazur studied the photographs she'd brought him, the official identifications of every Polish employee on Grey Shield Security's books. Forty-two of them, more than anyone was expecting, but she guessed they were built for the job as a race, big men, no-nonsense.

Looking at Mazur now, long-limbed and lean-muscled, she couldn't imagine many people wanting to square up to him.

He put another sheet of paper aside, moved onto the next, discarded that one quickly. Over his shoulder she saw a beetle-browed man with thick black hair peppered grey, nothing like the description he'd given, but the man's name was in the suspects column upstairs, targeted for arrest today, and she wondered once again if Mazur was selling them a line.

The clock on the opposite wall ticked past the half-hour and she stretched where she stood, feeling a pent-up energy rolling through her body. She wanted to be haring across town now, running down the suspects they'd identified, those two men who'd shared shifts with the murderers, whose time sheets showed they were free Thursday morning to drive through the Krasic sisters like they didn't even exist, aiming for Pyotr Dymek.

But Zigic had sent Grieves and Parr out to grab them. Orders from above that when Alex arrived within the next couple of hours there was to be a full 'council of war', which meant she and Zigic were to stay put, prepare to make a report which would be taken back to the Domestic Terrorism Unit.

She wondered what Alex's aim was.

If they were monitoring the White Brethren's website then the group was obviously a known quantity, which raised the awkward question of why they hadn't done anything about it. Hate speeches, footage of multiple murders, three of them right here, open cases; how much more did the service need before they'd step in and act?

Was it another watch brief? Like the one Alex had for Richard Shotton? Sitting back and letting things develop seemed immoral to her, smacked of power playing rather than policing.

Alex wasn't police though, she reminded herself.

His whole purpose in contacting her at the weekend had been containment. They'd had a few drinks, fucked for old times' sake, but he'd made his message clear – don't step on toes, don't expose his inside man.

Did he even care whether they caught this murderer?

At the table Mazur paused for a moment to take a drink from the can of Coke she'd brought him, the bubbles fizzing in it were absurdly loud in the small grey room.

She glanced at the clock again, two interminable minutes gone.

The translator had arrived at nine, a young woman with a Polish name and a cut-glass English accent which Ferreira couldn't tie to a particular city. Wahlia showed her up to the technical department, came back down smiling like he stood a chance.

'No,' Mazur said finally. 'He is not here.'

Ferreira moved round the table. 'Look again.'

'I have looked twice. He is none of these men.'

'These are all the Poles working at Grey Shield.' She jabbed her finger at the pile of photographs in front of him. 'He's in here somewhere.'

Mazur just shook his head. 'Maybe he is not Polish.'

Ferreira rolled her eyes. 'You said he was.'

'No. He spoke Polish but many people do. I speak some Russian but I am not Russian. They teach us it in school.'

She grabbed the sheets of paper. 'Right. Let's try something else.'

Upstairs Wahlia was alone in Hate Crimes, standing in front of the board like it had mesmerised him, a cup of coffee steaming gently in his hand.

'Great, you're not doing anything,' Ferreira said. 'I need photographs of every Eastern European man Grey Shield have on staff.'

'No joy?'

'No. Mazur's decided the bloke might not be Polish now.'

Wahlia dragged himself away from the board and returned to his desk, cleared a spot for his cup among the time sheets and the mobile phone records, the space more cluttered than it had been half an hour ago. Files being pulled in readiness for the arrival of their suspects.

'Any word from the field?'

'They're on the way back in,' Wahlia said. 'One down, one to go.'

Ferreira took out her tobacco as he started gathering the information she needed, snapped the last black paper out of its packet.

'They're wasting their time,' she said. 'If it's the bloke we want Mazur would have picked him out. He was right there in the pile with the rest of them.'

'Assuming he actually wants to pick him out.'

'Yeah, I've been thinking that too.' She sealed the rollie then realised she didn't want it. 'For all we know, Mazur's another recruit.'

'He was living with them . . .'

'Tough to ignore what's going on when your housemates are coming home covered in blood and bits of brain.'

'People see what they want to,' Wahlia said.

He was right. Not just civilians and witnesses. They'd done the same thing. Seen a spurned lover with a record of harassment and decided he was the most likely perpetrator of the hit-and-run. Seen three Muslim men kicked to death and decided the ENL had started delivering on their bile-flecked rhetoric. And in both cases they'd been wrong.

The phone on Zigic's desk started to ring and Ferreira went through to answer it, finding his desk covered in Polish police reports, the computer screen showing a page about the White Brethren. Cramming for their meeting later.

'DI Zigic's phone.'

'Hello, who is this?' the translator asked, voice clipped and icy.

'DS Ferreira. What's the problem?'

'Oh. There's something rather strange about these videos. I think it would be best if you were both to see them.'

Ferreira called Zigic's mobile as she went out through the office, got him as he was coming up from CID, and they met in the stairwell, both still holding their phones to their ears.

'Riggott?' she asked.

'They've caught the boys who firebombed the Polish Club.'

'That was easy.'

'The family frogmarched the kid who was driving down here first thing. They're saying he was led astray by his mate.' Zigic held the door open for her. 'He's named his friend and Riggott's having him brought in now. They're only seventeen, the pair of them.'

'Old enough to know what they were doing,' Ferreira said.

'They'll end up in a young offenders' institute for a couple of years, then back out to live the rest of their miserable lives.' He frowned. 'God knows what kind of shit they'll get into when they're grown men.'

It wasn't like Zigic to be so venomous, but he'd been there when it happened, only luck preventing him from winding up in the intensive care unit, and she knew it would take a while for him to shake that off.

They went to the office at the end of the hall where the translator was working. Her suit jacket hung over the back of her chair, a cup of tea and a packet of vending-machine biscuits untouched on the desk. She'd brought a slim, silver laptop with her and was transcribing the speeches onto it as they played on a separate flat-screen monitor.

A video was paused as they entered and she was standing waiting for them, her hand in a tight fist in front of her mouth.

'Joanna, what have you got for us?'

'I haven't finished the translations yet,' she said, gesturing towards her laptop, a few paragraphs of type abandoned mid-sentence. 'I thought this was too important to wait.'

'What is it?' Zigic asked.

'This man, I don't think he's Polish.'

She looked at them as if she expected to be shot down.

'That chimes with what Mazur just told me,' Ferreira said. 'The man he saw at the house wasn't among the Polish employees, and now he's saying he thinks the guy might be bilingual.'

Zigic appeared unconvinced and Ferreira knew how unlikely it sounded.

'So what is he, if he's not Polish?'

'At first I thought he'd just been over here for a few years and had picked up a slight Fen accent.' Joanna reached for the mouse which controlled the main screen. 'It's quite common. But then I noticed he was using some odd dialect words. From the Zakopane region. And the accent there is . . . peculiar, I suppose you'd say. The equivalent here would be a Liverpool accent, something strong and idiosyncratic. Not easy to train yourself out of.'

'We know the region he's from then,' Ferreira said, wondering why the woman thought it was such a big deal.

'No, that's the thing. He doesn't have a trace of that accent.'

Joanna started the footage running and Ferreira heard a Polish voice like any other, strained to pick out a Fen inflection, but couldn't. Next to her Zigic leaned on the back of the chair, face drawn in concentration until he finally shook his head.

'What are you telling us?'

She stopped the video. 'In my opinion Polish isn't this man's first language. He's learned it from somebody who originated in the Zakopane region, hence the presence of dialect in his vocabulary, and given these factors and his unmistakable Fen accent, I think he's English.'

53

'How the fuck did we miss this?' Ferreira said.

Zigic grabbed the armrest as she stamped on the accelerator and shot past a line of cars, punching her horn when a white van moved to enter the lane ahead of her, forcing the driver to swerve back into line. He gestured out of the open window as they passed, his anger lost in their wake.

'We should have checked him out more thoroughly,' she said. 'Christ, I knew Palmer was a piece of shit, but this?'

Zigic hadn't believed it to begin with. Not when Ferreira suggested it in the translator's office. Not when she showed him Palmer's service file, 'Huruk' in the space for his mother's maiden name. He couldn't conceive of a third-generation Polish ex-copper, even one with Palmer's dubious reputation, being capable of leading a neo-Nazi gang into a series of brutal murders, filming it and disseminating it, making those fire-and-brimstone hate speeches.

They'd taken Palmer's photograph to Mazur, tucked among the employee IDs of ten other men, and waited for him to make his decision; he fastened on him instantly.

Palmer was the man who'd come to the house with Lukas Wrabowski and spent the evening getting drunk in his room, he was the man who had almost smashed the front door down looking for Pyotr Dymek on the morning of the hit-and-run.

And now, according to Grey Shield's records, he was working a personal security detail for Richard Shotton. Something Ferreira had barely stopped talking about since they left the station.

'He must know.'

'I really doubt that, Mel.'

'You don't think it's all part of the same thing?'

'According to your friend at the unit Shotton was paying the ENL off to keep them in line. I'd say it's pretty unlikely he'd do that then endorse multiple murder, don't you?'

She gave a non-committal murmur.

'He's a politician.'

'Not for much longer.' She smiled humourlessly. 'Once this hits the press he'll be dead in the water.'

'It's hardly going to look good for us either, is it?'

'Palmer's been out for years.'

'He's still an ex-cop.'

She slowed at the roundabout, then accelerated suddenly, the Golf's GTI engine growling as she cut in front of an ambulance coming at speed from their right, sirens going, lights blazing, temporarily separating them from the patrol car which had trailed them all the way from Thorpe Wood.

It caught up fast, was on Ferreira's bumper as she was forced to stop at the edge of Thornhaugh village, traffic-calming measures narrowing the road.

'Do you think there are others?' Ferreira asked.

'In the gang?'

'In the station.'

'I hope not,' Zigic said, thinking of the bad press this was going to cause, how much harder it would make their job. It was already near impossible to get people to trust them in the city's immigrant communities. 'We have to assume Palmer's an anomaly.'

'Long time since you've been in uniform.'

'I know what they're like,' he said. 'They mouth off, they hate everyone, but this thing goes way beyond knee-jerk bigotry.'

'He learned it somewhere.'

They passed through the centre of the village, a nicer location than they were used to finding suspects in; stone and thatched cottages, horses in well-kept paddocks lined with long runs of new-built stable blocks where a few women were out for a morning ride. It was another world, impossibly remote from the dingy side streets where Palmer's victims had died so violently.

Manor Farm was half a mile outside the village, set in gently rising countryside, grassland on two sides and behind it a stretch of sparse woodland, where a cluster of vehicles were parked up, their owners disturbing the air with volleys of shotgun fire. It was an impressively wide Georgian pile of a place, until you rounded the curve in the lane and saw that it was less than thirty feet through, the dressed stone frontage giving way to red bricks on the gable walls.

Ferreira turned into the driveway, a rough track patched with rubble here and there.

'He's not concerned with security, is he?' she said, as they approached a set of high metal gates which stood open, letting them drive right up to the front door.

Evidently it hadn't been a working farm for a long time. No machinery and no old outbuildings to house it, only a former cowshed recently converted into office space, with skylights cut into the slate and a long glazed wall looking across the gravel driveway.

A young man in heavy glasses and shirtsleeves rushed out of the office to meet them, casting a worried glance at the patrol car blocking the gate.

'Is there some kind of problem?'

'We're looking for Christian Palmer,' Ferreira said.

'He isn't here.'

Zigic nodded towards the Range Rover parked nearby. 'Mr Shotton's in though?'

'I'll deal with this, Marshall,' Shotton said, appearing at the doorway.

'They're looking for Christian,' Marshall said. 'I told them he's not here.'

'Isn't he?'

'No, he called in sick first thing this morning.'

Shotton turned to Zigic. 'What's this about?'

'We need to speak to Christian, as a matter of urgency. We believe he has vital information pertaining to our current investigation.'

'And which investigation would that be?'

'Christian's part of a paramilitary neo-Nazi group,' Ferreira said. 'Or maybe you knew that much already.'

Shotton smiled stupidly, his disbelief genuine, Zigic thought, but the man was a politician, adept at hiding his true thoughts. He kept his eyes on Ferreira for a few seconds longer, as if she might shrug and laugh and say it was just a joke.

Shotton desperately needed it to be and when the reaction he wanted didn't come he touched a nervous hand to his temple, brushed back his hair to try and hide the tremble.

'I don't know what you're talking about.' Looking at Zigic now. 'You must be mistaken. Christian is an ex-police constable. He came with impeccable credentials. I really can't believe he'd be involved with something like that. Neo-Nazis? He isn't the type.'

'The White Brethren,' Ferreira said, enjoying torturing him a bit too much. 'They're a pan-European terror group and Christian Palmer, your trusted bodyguard, is a very active member. More than a member, he's one of their spiritual leaders.' As she spoke the colour was rising in Shotton's cheeks. 'If you want to make a stand right now and defend him, by all means go ahead, but don't expect it to end here.'

'I have no intention of defending him,' Shotton said, nerves giving way to anger. 'And quite frankly I don't care for your attitude, Sergeant.'

Zigic put out a placating hand. 'We need to search your premises, Mr Shotton. We'd appreciate your cooperation.'

Marshall cleared his throat. 'Surely it couldn't –'

'Alright,' Shotton barked. 'Look wherever you want, but Christian isn't here. And the idea that I would shield him is frankly preposterous.' He stabbed a finger in Zigic's direction. 'If I see any insinuation that the party was involved with this, you'll be hearing from my lawyers and your Chief Constable.'

360

He stalked back into the office, shoulders squared with tension, and a moment later he appeared in one of the long windows, his phone pressed to his ear, watching with a grim expression as Ferreira led the uniforms into his HQ.

Zigic headed for the main house, gravel crunching underfoot, the sound of shotguns reverberating across the open fields, already feeling that this was a waste of time. Palmer's car wasn't here and he doubted Shotton or his assistant would cover for the man. He looked in the deep sash windows as he circled the house, saw rooms stuffed with too much old-fashioned furniture, a kitchen with a few herbs dying on the windowsill and a cat asleep near the range.

His mobile rang as he completed his circuit of the house – Wahlia.

'Grieves has just called in from Palmer's place –'

'Is he there?'

'No. His wife said he went out to work as usual this morning – she's got no idea what he was up to by the sounds of it. She's collapsed, totally lost it.'

'We need to know if there's anywhere else Palmer might have gone,' Zigic said. 'Family, friends, anything.'

'Mother's dead – no other family – and she reckons his only friends are a couple of Polish guys he knows through work. But they're not close apparently.'

Zigic sighed. 'Well, they won't be much help to him now.'

'Grieves found the room where he was filming the speeches though,' Wahlia said. 'It's full of World War II memorabilia, uniforms, flags, God knows what else.'

'What does Mrs Palmer think to that?'

'He's a history buff.'

Could she be that ignorant of her husband's actions? Zigic wondered. It wasn't an unusual interest but it was far from normal.

'Alright. Look, if there's anything else –'

'I'll call.'

Zigic slipped his phone away, thinking of Palmer leaving home this morning, kissing his wife, getting in the car, giving her no clue where he was going. What had stopped him coming into work? It was clearly planned – he'd called in sick.

But why now?

He'd been living a double life for months, maybe years, and was now going about his business with two deaths on his conscience, assuming he had one, three more murders he'd instigated and directed. He clearly wasn't scared of being caught. He should have stopped after killing Dymek. All loose ends tied up. But he hadn't stopped. The next day he'd led Lukas Wrabowski down Cromwell Road and watched him kick another young man to death.

Then he'd gone home, just as usual, and Monday morning he'd come to work.

What had changed since yesterday to make him drop off the radar?

There was only one explanation.

Zigic reached in through the open window of Ferreira's car and punched the horn, bringing her out a couple of seconds later.

'Come on,' he said, moving round to the passenger door. 'I think I know where Palmer is.'

54

The blown-out window of the Polish Ex-Servicemen's Club had been boarded over since last night, but the building bore traces of the fire, smoke stains fanned out across the brickwork, shreds of singed fabric snagged in the branches on the bushes in front of it. The main door was locked and sealed over with police tape which fluttered in the light breeze.

They'd parked along the street, not wanting to give Palmer advance warning of their arrival; Zigic and Ferreira leading, four uniforms with them, everyone in stab-proof vests just in case he'd armed himself. If he was hiding out it was for a reason and Zigic didn't think he'd let himself be brought in without a fight.

The yard at the back of the building was covered with a sheet of water, bits of debris from an overturned bin floating on the rippled surface, crisp packets and fag ends and soggy receipts. They splashed through it, six pairs of feet making more noise than he would have liked, moving towards a service door standing slightly ajar.

Zigic pushed it open and led them into a narrow corridor, less water on the floor there, but the smell of smoke was thick in the air, and up ahead he picked out the door to the main bar, saw the paintwork bubbled from the intense heat which had blasted it, the brass handle blackened.

Above them the building creaked and cracked, but he didn't have time to worry about structural integrity.

He directed two men upstairs to the second floor, another pair to the first and winced at how much noise they made as they went, boot heels thumping like a stampede.

'We stay together,' he told Ferreira.

She nodded, eyes wide in the gloom, holding her baton down by her side, fist tight around it.

They moved quickly through the ground-floor rooms; started with the burnt-out shell of the main bar, the furniture still sitting as he remembered it, but charred now, and brittle-looking, then into the lounge, which was perfectly untouched, curtains drawn, stools turned upside down on tables and a couple of fruit machines standing ominously unlit in the corner.

Overhead, doors were opening and closing, floorboards complaining.

They checked the kitchen and the storage cupboards, nothing much in them, the toilets and the long, bare function room at the back of the building, where the sprung floor amplified their footsteps. It was cold and still, a thick layer of dust on the plastic chairs stacked along one wall, felt like it hadn't been used for years.

'He's not here,' Ferreira said, voice barely above a whisper.

Zigic thought he caught a whiff of sweat on the air, but turned and followed her out again, pausing at a door marked 'Staff Only'.

'Must be the cellar.' The door opened with a hard shove, a smell of damp and spilled beer rising from the darkness, a caustic hit of cleaning products. 'Give me your torch.'

He took it from her and switched it on, aimed the beam down the worn stone steps, the light catching on crates of bottled drinks and aluminium beer barrels.

For a few seconds he just listened, holding his breath, straining to pick out some noise beyond his own hammering heartbeat. He could feel Ferreira at his back, hear her breathing, shallow and fast.

'There's nowhere to go, Palmer.'

His voice echoed dully into the cellar, answered by a dragging sound, something lightweight being slowly moved, followed by a strange tinkling, like pieces of broken glass showering the tiled floor.

'The only way out of here is if you come peacefully.'

He swept the torch beam across the floor, wanting to identify Palmer's position before they went down. The stairway was narrow though and the cellar extended for several yards on either side of it, plenty of space for Palmer to hunker down and wait for them, pick the perfect moment to strike.

'We only want to talk to you.'

'Do you think I'm an idiot?' Palmer said, voice low and distant. He sounded calm. Unnaturally so. 'You know what I've done.'

'Why don't you come up here and we can talk about it properly?'

No answer. The sound of shuffling feet, muttering.

Ferreira gave him a questioning look, gestured towards the stairs, impatience drawing her closer to the top step, making her fingers flex around the baton's moulded grip.

'You come up or we come down,' Zigic said. 'Either way we're taking you in.'

'I'm armed.'

'He's lying,' Ferreira whispered. 'We can take him.'

Zigic shook his head. 'Call armed response and get the others. Send them round the back in case he tries to go through the service hatch.'

Reluctantly she retreated, shouting to the uniforms who were still uselessly searching the upper floors. There was no point being quiet about it now. Palmer needed to appreciate the gravity of the situation, realise he was caught and accept it.

'Why here, Christian?'

'You should ask the scumbags who did it.'

'We've got them,' Zigic said. 'They won't get away with it.'

'Yeah? And what's going to happen to them? They'll serve a couple of years inside, no big deal, is it? What about Marek? That man worked like a dog for forty years, finally gets to retire and some Paki bastard near kills him.'

The club's back door opened and closed again, the uniforms moving into position. He needed to stall Palmer, keep him talking.

'How do you know Marek?'

'From here.'

'Did your mum bring you?' Zigic asked. 'She was Polish, right?'

Palmer laughed, a humourless snort. 'That's a worthless tactic, trying to establish a connection with me, earn my trust. You can't negotiate with me. Soldiers don't answer to the authority of the police. We're outside it. Above it.'

There was the voice from the hate speeches, the same rhythm and fervour.

'You're not a soldier,' Zigic said. 'There's no war.'

'Yes, there is, you just choose not to see it. You're blind to what's happening in this country, but it's coming. They want to take over. And if it's left to people like you they'll win. We'll be reduced to a medieval existence under sharia law.'

'Is that what all this shit's about?'

'Somebody needs to make a stand,' Palmer said, his voice rising up from the cellar, booming. 'You should know that better than anyone. Look what they did to your people.'

'I'm English.'

'You might have been born here but you're not English. You're a Serb, so don't pretend you don't understand what I'm saying. They did it in your country and they'll do it here if we let them. Women and children burned alive in churches, old men murdered in the street.'

Zigic leaned against the door frame, fighting the urge to go down there and drag Palmer back up with him.

'And who won? Not your people. The Islamists started it and your people were bombed.'

'That was a war,' Zigic said. 'You're a murderer. Nothing more.'

'We are on the same side.'

Palmer's footsteps echoed across the tiled floor but still he didn't move into the light, and Zigic imagined him wild-eyed and puffed up, swelling into his role.

'We're on the same side but you can't accept it,' Palmer said, exasperated. 'You've been brainwashed, along with the rest of them, by the lies of politicians and the media, who want us to believe everyone is the same and culture means nothing any more. They want to take away our national pride but they can't. It's in our blood. We're different. We're better.'

'So that gives you the right to murder anyone who disagrees? They were innocent,' Zigic said, his own voice rising. 'You weren't taking out extremists, you killed ordinary, innocent people. You're not a soldier, you're a terrorist.'

'One man's terrorist is another man's freedom fighter.'

Ferreira came back through the warren of narrow corridors, moving at speed, baton gone.

'Armed response is on the way,' she said, speaking close to his ear, too low for Palmer to hear. 'ETA five minutes.'

He needed to keep Palmer talking, keep him down there, contained in the cellar, but he was sick of the sound of his voice and with every passing second he felt a tug towards the stairs, a growing desire to rush down and haul him out of his rathole.

Palmer could be armed, but he doubted it. The attacks he'd perpetrated were carried out with feet and fists and there was nothing to suggest he had a gun except his own blurted claim which was designed to keep them in place and buy him time.

'I'm sorry for the girl at the bus stop,' Palmer said, sounding deflated. 'I wish it didn't have to be that way but all wars entail collateral damage.'

'You chose to do that,' Ferreira snapped. 'You could have got Dymek alone if you'd wanted to.'

'He was running. He would have exposed us.'

She started to reply and Zigic stopped her, sensing the change in Palmer's mood, the reflective tone. If they stopped talking now he would stew down there for a few minutes, replaying his failure, allowing the armed response team to draw closer.

Ferreira checked her watch, mouthed 'three' at him.

'Dymek wasn't a soldier,' Palmer said finally. 'He was a thug. He didn't appreciate what we were trying to achieve.'

'Not like Lukas?'

'No,' Palmer said. 'No, Lukas was a true warrior. He wouldn't talk, would he? No matter how hard you pushed him.'

'How do you know that?' Ferreira asked, straightening from the wall.

'I've still got friends at the station.'

'Grieves?'

'Lots of friends at the station,' Palmer said, voice trailing away, feet pacing, slow, deliberate steps and something crunching under them. He stopped. 'I'm glad you're here, Mel.'

'So am I,' she said. 'I'm just sorry you weren't arrested and locked up years ago when you killed that boy in the cells.'

'That was a happy accident. One more drug dealer off the streets.'

Ferreira glared into the dimness of the cellar. 'How do you think you'll get on in prison, Christian? All those Muslims, all those black guys. You think they'll be gentle with you?'

'I'm not going to prison.'

Sirens hollered in the distance, getting closer and louder.

'If you think you're going to take the easy way out like Lukas did you better think again.' Ferreira took another step towards the cellar door. 'You'll be on suicide watch, checked every fifteen minutes. You'll be stripped naked so you can't hang yourself. Nothing is going to keep you from serving your time.'

Palmer laughed, a ragged, maniacal edge to it. 'You won't even get me in a holding cell.'

'Armed response are coming. They might shoot you in the leg,' she said. 'But they'll take you alive. You're going to suffer, Christian. For years. You'll spend the rest of your life being some Muslim gangster's bitch.'

He wouldn't, Zigic thought. He'd be placed in protective custody, too much of a target for anything else. The prison authorities would protect him, lock him up with the sex offenders and all the other coppers who'd moved across to the wrong side of the law. He wouldn't suffer like he deserved to.

The sirens stopped and voices shouted outside.

'You won't get me out of this cellar,' Palmer said, coming to the bottom of the stairs, into the torch's piercing beam. There was something in his hand, not the gun they were expecting. A small black cylinder with wires running out of it. Palmer smiled, 'Not in one piece anyway.'

Zigic dropped the torch as Ferreira slammed into him and he felt the heat before he heard the detonation, then the whole building quaked and he was deaf, hitting the floor hard, Ferreira landing heavily on top of him, her forearm striking his face, the pain coming from all directions at once; dull through his body and sharp at his leg, his eardrums shot, vision swimming, his whole head scrambled.

He saw Ferreira screaming but couldn't hear her.

She crawled away from him, away from the cellar, through the thin sheet of water on the floor, blood trailing behind her, turning it pink.

Zigic struggled to his feet, felt his left leg give way and dropped to his knee, another bolt of pain shooting up through the bone. Forced himself up again, taking his weight on the other leg, bracing himself against the wall where small, hard pieces of stainless steel were embedded in the plasterwork.

'Mel.' He formed the word but all he could hear was a high, stinging buzz in his ears.

She'd stopped moving, lay face down in the water.

He inched towards her, saw the blood darkening her jeans, dozens of holes ripped through the thin denim, the fabric shredded across the back of her calves, her flesh punctured by panel pins and stubby tacks blackened in the blast.

A chemical smell rose from her body as he crouched over her and the action sent him sprawling again. He looked down at his own leg, a single nail driven deep into his thigh.

He reached out and turned her face from the water. Her eyes were closed and for a long and terrible moment he thought she was dead, but then he felt her breath across the back of his hand and he slumped where he sat, awkwardly pinned against the wall, shouting for help.

55

At the station a doctor pulled the nail out of Zigic's leg, swabbed it with antiseptic and bandaged the wound, saying something which was probably meant to be reassuring but the ringing in his ears was still too loud for him to properly make it out. Dr Harrow smiled sadly and stuck his finger up in front of Zigic's face, wanting him to follow it. Checked his ears and wrote down 'perforated eardrums' on a notepad, as if he hadn't already realised, then gave him a packet of painkillers and told him to go home, exaggerating the shape of the words for him.

There was nothing for him to do now, so he took Harrow's advice and went home, driving slowly, concentrating on keeping the car exactly in the centre of the lane as his ears buzzed and his sense of equilibrium came and went.

The house was empty and he was grateful for the quiet, couldn't have faced Anna's concern right then, the questions he wouldn't be able to hear her ask. Last night was bad enough, returning late with the smell of petrol and smoke on his clothes, having to lie to her about how close he'd come to being burned alive. He'd told her he arrived after the fact but he could see she didn't believe him, only pretended to because it was easier.

If she knew about this – no, *when* she knew about this, because there was no hiding the bandaging around his thigh and no escaping the news this evening, the photograph of Ferreira they would run with because the press liked to focus on officers injured in the line of duty, especially female ones. Once Anna knew, he would have no peace.

She'd said it before, last year when he was shot. 'Detective inspectors aren't supposed to be on the front line.' Throwing it at him like an accusation, as if he'd wilfully put himself in danger, like an adrenalin junkie or a man with nothing to live for.

Zigic stripped in the kitchen and shoved his clothes into a bin bag, knotted it and left it by the back door, then went upstairs to run a bath, dimly perceiving the rush of the water. He couldn't wash his hair because of the damage to his ears, so he stood at the bathroom sink and carefully combed out every nauseating scrap of skin and flesh, rinsing the comb's plastic teeth under the tap, watching the last traces of Christian Palmer run away down the plughole.

As he lay in the bath he thought of the forensics team now poring over the crime scene. He hadn't looked in the cellar before he left, more concerned about seeing Ferreira into the ambulance, but he knew the photographs would be waiting in his office when he returned to the station. Flat, precise images which couldn't capture the heat and the smell and the sudden, plummeting sensation as he realised what Palmer was about to do.

Riggott had arrived at the Polish Club a few minutes after the ambulance left, took charge with swift efficiency, dismissing the armed response team who'd arrived too late, calling for the bomb disposal unit who would have to secure the scene, check for booby traps and any lingering chemical hazards before the police work could begin.

Not that there was much to take charge of. Reports would be written and forms filled, then stowed away in records, the crimes Palmer and his gang carried out reduced to an official statement of sympathy and the hollow finality of 'the investigation is now closed and no further suspects are being sought'.

It was no kind of justice for the victims or their families.

He closed his eyes and replayed the case from the beginning, testing his management of it, the course they'd taken and the mistakes they'd made, trying to identify the ways this could have been prevented.

When he opened his eyes again the water was cold and the sun had moved around the side of the house, plunging the bathroom into a chill gloom. His watch, propped up between the taps, showed him that it was almost four o'clock.

He dressed, sitting on the bed to pull on his jeans, still unsteady on his feet, and went downstairs to check his phone for messages. Three calls from Riggott followed by a text message sent a few minutes earlier, calling him back to the station; a car was on the way.

Zigic waited on the pavement, pulled up the hood of his parka to block out the fine breeze which knifed his perforated eardrum. The buzzing was less intense now and he found he could hear the engine noise on the Castor Road nearby, the plaintive whine of next door's dog wanting to be let back in.

The patrol car arrived within a minute and he climbed into the back, no small talk with the PC behind the wheel and he wondered if it was out of consideration for his condition or because of Palmer's death. He still had friends at the station after all.

There was a reception committee outside Thorpe Wood, camera crews humping their gear in for the imminent press conference and reporters hanging around smoking and speculating. A few of them turned as he passed, fired questions at him he didn't answer. He hoped this wasn't what he'd been brought back for.

Grieves was coming out as he went in and they both stopped dead, toe to toe. She couldn't meet his eye, moved to step around him without looking up.

'Sorry, sir.'

Zigic blocked her off. 'You were feeding information to Palmer.'

'I didn't know he was behind all of this.'

'What did you think he was interested for?'

'We were friends, he asked what was going on. He was always asking about work. He missed it.' Zigic moved closer, straining to hear her and she retreated again, caught between him and the reception desk. She stammered, 'I would never have told him if I knew what he was doing.'

The desk sergeant was watching them across the top of his newspaper and Grieves looked to him for help, got a shrug in response. She was toxic now, sharing Palmer's taint, and she would find out how quickly her fellow officers turned once that happened.

'Do you really think I was helping him?'

'You helped him before,' Zigic snapped. 'If you'd had the spine to tell the truth when he killed that young lad he might not have got the chance to do any of this.' He poked a finger in her face, making her flinch. 'This is on you, Grieves, and I'm going to make damn sure Riggott knows it.'

'This isn't fair.'

'Fair? Go to the hospital and tell Mel what's fair.'

Grieves shouldered past him at that and bolted for the door, down the steps and into the car park, and Zigic watched her all the way, thinking that if there was any justice she would never walk back into the station as a police officer.

But he knew the outcome wouldn't be so drastic. An official reprimand, an extensive carpeting in Riggott's office and then a few uncomfortable months before she was transferred to another station.

Plenty of coppers had done worse than her and survived it.

Wahlia met him on the other side of the door and walked with him to the lifts.

'Hospital called,' he said, speaking loudly. 'Mel's out of surgery.'

'How is she?'

'Sedated.'

A detective sergeant from CID strode past them, paused to shake Zigic's hand and said something he didn't hear, his mouth barely moving. No obvious expression on his face to judge by.

Zigic felt like they'd screwed up. Failed to catch Palmer in time, failed to contain him, and now Ferreira was lying unconscious in a hospital bed, God knows what damage done.

It could have been worse, he told himself, if Palmer had got into the city centre with a nail bomb this would be a major incident, dozens dead or injured, more even, but he felt no better for the knowledge.

'What does Riggott want?' he asked, sure that he was shouting.

'The guy from Domestic Terrorism's here,' Wahlia said. 'For debriefing.'

They went up to one of the infrequently used meeting rooms which had been done out for guests with a tray of tea and coffee, bottles of mineral water and biscuits, but it wasn't exactly inviting, despite the late-afternoon sun streaming in through the south-facing windows. The light was cold and harsh, showing up the shoddy padded chairs and the dust across the conference table.

Riggott was already in there, seated with his back to the window, Nicola Gilraye next to him, both of them looking to the man at the head of the table who rose as Zigic entered the room.

'You must be Dushan – I've heard a lot about you.' They shook hands. 'I'm Alex.'

He was about Ferreira's age but looked much older, serious and capable in his sober grey suit, carried an unmistakable aura of influence around him.

'Sorry to have dragged you in,' he said. 'But I need to know we're all on the same page and this is your case.'

Zigic sat down opposite Riggott, noticed the strain around his eyes, an uncharacteristic slouch in his posture.

'So, where are we at?' Alex asked.

Zigic brought him up to speed on the morning's developments, precising the run-up to it, knowing it didn't reflect well on them.

When he finished Alex paused for a moment and Zigic thought he was going to ask after Ferreira, but he didn't.

'Do we know what set Palmer off?'

'We think the attack on the Polish Club provoked this today,' Zigic said. 'But there's no way to know for certain. Whatever it was, it started with the White Brethren. Someone there must have been pulling his strings, helping him with the bomb-making.'

Alex frowned. 'Let's not get ahead of ourselves. This is a gang thing. There's nothing to suggest we're dealing with a terrorist organisation.'

374

'Except for the fact that they were being monitored by your Domestic Terrorism Unit?'

Riggott lurched forward, spine stiffening. 'You knew they had a presence here and you didn't tell us?'

'They weren't considered a credible threat.'

'Well, they look pretty fucking credible from where I'm sitting.' Riggott threw himself back in the chair. 'How many other cells are there? D'you know that at least?'

'This isn't helpful.'

'If he was part of a wider, UK-based organisation we need to know about it.' Riggott threw his hands up. 'What're you going to do if this shite spreads?'

'It won't.'

'You fancy laying your job on that?'

'We're moving off-topic.' Alex reached across the table for a bottle of sparkling water, poured it into a glass. 'As far as we can ascertain this gang is operating independently from the central organisation in Poland and there's nothing to suggest this is anything other than an isolated incident, inspired by actions abroad, but with no concrete links to the power structure over there.'

It was a meaningless string of words, a politician's answer.

'Palmer's been posting to the White Brethren site,' Zigic said. 'That's a concrete link as far as we're concerned.'

Alex sipped his water, placed the glass down carefully in front of him. 'Granted, it appears that there may be a degree of communication and possibly encouragement, but that doesn't make this a concerted or organised campaign.'

'And that's the whole point of small, independent but ideologically allied cells, isn't it?' Zigic said. 'If you unearth one, the others remain safe. However many of them there are.'

'The existence of other cells isn't your concern. You are dealing with a *gang* of thugs with far-right sympathies.'

There was a moment of silence as they considered the implications, nothing any of them could say to that. Alex might be outside their own hierarchy but he still had rank over them, and if he needed to pull it in order to make sure his message was accepted, Zigic had no doubt that he would.

'So we're clear,' Riggott said slowly, steepling his fingers on the tabletop. 'You've tear-arsed up here to "advise" us not to frame these crimes as acts of domestic terrorism.'

'They don't constitute terrorist acts.'

'Don't you tell me about terrorism, son,' Riggott snarled, giving Alex the full benefit of his West Belfast rasp. 'I see a man making bombs in the cellar of a fired-out pub that's fucking terrorism. We'll toe the line for you – we don't have a choice – but don't sit there and come that bollocks with me.'

Alex folded his fist into his palm like he was thinking about throwing it at Riggott's face. 'What do you imagine will happen if this becomes a domestic extremism story? You've already seen the effects of rising tensions between the Polish community and the local Muslims.'

Zigic thought of the shops on Lincoln Road which had been vandalised last night, windows smashed, interiors wrecked. A Polish cafe and the grocer's next door, owned by the same family, respectable, hard-working people with no links to the criminals whose actions had brought this down upon them. Further along a hairdresser's had been trashed, its mirrors shattered, chairs thrown out onto the pavement; a Lithuanian business but the distinction hadn't mattered at the time.

'Do you want these retaliations to escalate?' Alex asked. 'What starts here could spread right across the country. Every Polish person in every town and city in Britain will come under suspicion of being a closet neo-Nazi. You know how pernicious that can be, neighbour against neighbour, nobody feeling safe to walk the streets. Then the vigilantes step in with their baseball bats . . .'

Riggott said nothing, face set hard against the truth of it.

'This could easily erupt into full-scale race riots.'

Riggott rose from his chair, buttoned his suit jacket and smoothed

376

his tie. He gestured towards Gilraye, who had sat silent through the entire meeting.

'Speak to Nicola, she's head of lying to the press.'

'Actually –' Alex reached into his pocket, brought out a folded sheet of A4. 'I came prepared.'

He slid it across the table towards Zigic, gave him a pointed look.

'I'm not doing this,' Zigic said.

He stood up and walked away before anyone could stop him and if they were arguing he couldn't hear them, didn't care how it would look when the lead officer didn't face the press, didn't care if Domestic Terrorism put a black mark next to his name. They had blood on their hands and he'd be damned if he was going to take responsibility for their public cleansing.

He signed out a pool car, the station steps cleared now, everyone in the Media Room waiting for the story of the ex-copper with the right-wing sympathies and the Polish mother who'd blown himself to pieces this morning. Zigic was sure that however Alex chose to spin it, the story would hang together perfectly.

Later he would have to tell Sofia Krasic why her sister was dead, that despite their assumptions it was nothing personal, just a callous act by a man trying to protect his liberty. Her bail hearing had been scheduled for this morning and he realised he had no idea where she was, remanded into custody as a flight risk or returned to the house where she'd colluded in covering up her boyfriend's murder.

But right then it was just another task he couldn't face.

He stopped at the petrol station near the hospital, bought tobacco and papers and a disposable lighter, knowing Ferreira would be cranky from nicotine withdrawal when she came round.

A nurse in A&E escorted him up to the fourth-floor ward where she was recovering in a private room with the curtains drawn and that chemical smell filling the air, snagged in her hair and soaked into her skin. She was lying on her front, partially covered with a blanket, legs bare, face turned towards the far wall, away from the light glowing next to her bed.

'Don't try to wake her,' the nurse said. 'She needs to rest.'

Zigic closed the door behind him and went round the bed, placed the makings of her cigarettes on the side table.

He tried not to look at her legs but after a few minutes sitting in the visitor's chair he found his eyes straying towards them. Dozens of bruises dotted her skin from heel to thigh, a wound at the centre of each one, stitched up and shining with antiseptic under transparent dressings. Some of the wounds were small, where the nails had gone in straight, but he knew those were the ones which had done the most damage, driven deep into muscle and sinew and cartilage. The shallow ones would distress her most though, he thought, the long, raking gash across her left calf, another just above the back of her knee.

The stitches were small and neat but the scars would always be there.

Looking at her face, clenched with stress even through the sedation, he cursed himself for letting her get so close to the door, for being slow to process Palmer's actions and too stunned to push her out of the way before she pushed him.

None of this should have happened.

He rearranged the blanket, drawing it down across her legs.

She didn't stir.

He sat for a while, replaying the moment in his mind, the split second which passed between seeing and acting stretched out impossibly. Could he have closed the cellar door? Should he have taken Palmer's threat more seriously? Pulled back and waited for the armed response team to arrive rather than trying to reason with him?

A nurse came in and checked on Ferreira, asked him if he wanted something to drink.

He didn't.

She turned on the television set high in the corner of the room before she left, the sound down too low for him to hear even though the buzzing in his ears was beginning to subside, some house-hunting programme. Anna was probably watching it in the kitchen, daydreaming of high ceilings and original features and three spare bedrooms.

Zigic found the remote control and changed the channel to the BBC News, catching the tail end of the press conference, Riggott doing the talking, his posture ramrod-straight and defiant. He finished with a curt nod, stood up and left the Media Room without the usual invitation for questions.

A breaking-news banner flashed up on the screen and they cut away from the empty table to pre-recorded footage of Richard Shotton at some local event, the silver fox in full-on charm mode – *English Patriot Party leader steps down over bodyguard's neo-Nazi links.*

Zigic laughed, turning to Ferreira automatically, forgetting that she was in no position to respond. Her eyes were still closed, the dark spots of her irises darting back and forth behind her lids, dreaming or remembering or some horrific conflation of the two.

There was nothing he could do for her and no point in him being there, but he couldn't leave.

Not yet.

Acknowledgements

A massive thank you to my wonderful editor Alison Hennessey; no writer could ask for a more dedicated and positive influence. If you've enjoyed this book it's down to her editing as much as my writing. It's been a real pleasure working with the whole team at Harvill Secker, an ingenious and energetic lot who've graciously smoothed my path into the professional writer life. Bethan, Áine, Louise and Vicki, thank you ladies.

Thanks also to my agent, Stan, for doing what he does how only he can.

I owe major thanks to all the bloggers and reviewers whose kind words and generosity made the experience of releasing a book into the world so much less daunting. Special mention to the folks at Crimesquad and Crime Fiction Lover – drinks when I see you! Drinks too for Luca Veste, Howard Linskey and Nick Quantrill, for providing moral support and patient ears when called upon, for Col Bury who put me straight on the awkward details of police procedure, and Kyle MacRae who patiently explained how to set up a pan-European terrorist forum. Any mistakes are of course my own.

Lastly to my family – I couldn't have done this without your support and constant encouragement, those vital chats and long lunches and much needed days away from the laptop. You're the best.